Overdue

A. A. REYNOLDS

Overdue

Book 1 of The Archivist

Production copyright FurPlanet Productions © 2025

Text Copyright © A. A. Reynolds 2025

Cover Artwork © Shapeless Ink 2025

The Korps Universe © Karen King 2024, and used with permission

Published by FurPlanet Productions
Dallas, Texas
www.FurPlanet.com

Print ISBN 978-1-61450-659-1
Electronic ISBN 978-1-61450-660-7

Table of Contents

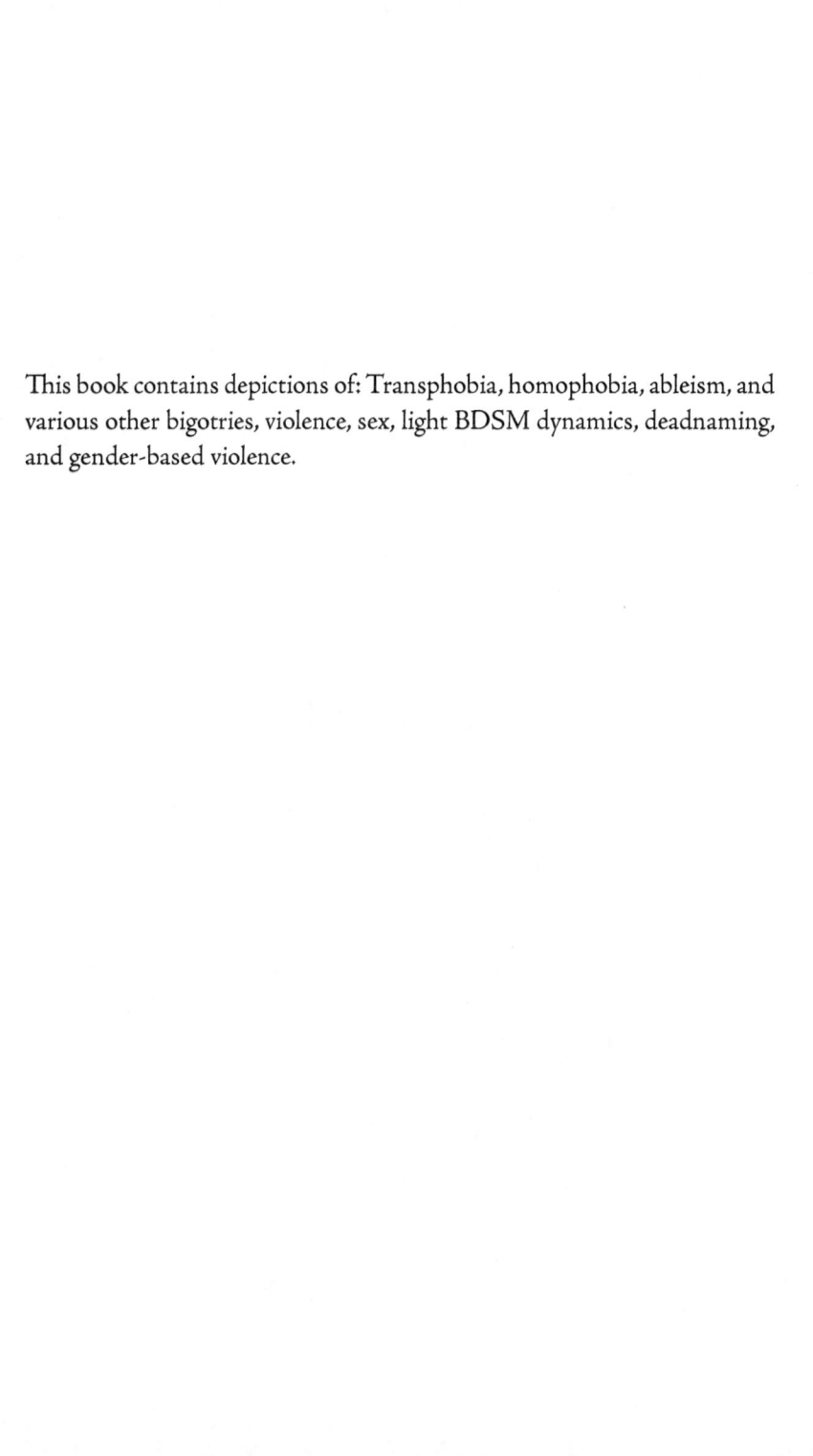

This book contains depictions of: Transphobia, homophobia, ableism, and various other bigotries, violence, sex, light BDSM dynamics, deadnaming, and gender-based violence.

To the wonderful folks that make up the MFBC… you are all family, and I can't thank you enough for this. To Grace, especially, your tireless work and commitment to shining this book to its brightest finish will never not be appreciated. Thank you to The Darkest Oceans System for your collective tireless enthusiasm for the original draft. And finally, thank you to my husband for your support and encouragement. This book would not be possible without any of you.

To the scared version of me from seventeen years ago… you'll get through it.

FOREWORD

BY KAREN KING

Nearly seven thousand years ago, an event shook the world. An arrival of something ancient: the merging of humanity with the world of the beast, the eruption of superpowers, and the proliferation of the supernatural. In modern day, this world appears much like our own, but for the pantheon of species that occupy it, and for the extensive presence of superheroes and supervillains alike. While many states have their own super-powered forces, a vast variety of independent actors exist.

Among the most prominent independent supervillain groups is an organization known as the Korps. As far as most are aware, the Korps is an organization dedicated to world domination, led (in theory) by the shadowy Overlord, a being who has repeatedly shown up since the beginning of recorded history to try and wrap their vicious claws around the neck of the planet.

The truth, of course, is significantly more complex.

Led by high-value superpowered beings, the Korps sees itself as less of a state and more of a governance method, seeking to disintegrate repressive state-based hierarchies, and install systems of governance much more capable at effectively distributing resources to those in need. It sees state actors – "Heroes," police, paramilitaries – mete punishment out on innocents and go unpunished in turn, and knows, for all the cartoonish pretensions of the supering world, that this is the true evil, and it cannot go unchallenged.

Operating a number of satellite companies, most under-the-radar, the Korps is extremely well-equipped technologically and medically, allowing its members to essentially build the body they need from scratch, and permitting this capacity at scale. The Korps knows that inherently top-down monocultures become stagnant without personal expression, which it encourages in its members – a reality at odds with the widespread public perception that its members are simply brainwashed.

A notable tool at their disposal are the RCGs, or Rose-Coloured Glasses, a high-capacity HUD, communications tool, and computer-brain interface, so powerful they can be used directly as a VR headset. They can function as an assistive device or therapy tool – but the nature of the technology means they have the power to more directly alter one's thoughts. Alternately viewed with relief, mistrust, or fear by varying parts of the supering world, it is known that wherever they are worn, the Korps is not far behind.

Having emerged in the wake of the Second World War, the Korps has gradually spread its influence, eventually emerging more into the public consciousness in the 1990s, and with increased visibility, and increased emphasis on immediate action, comes more entanglements...

The Korps began as a big pile of superhero and supervillain tropes that I'd built up a love of through various types of media, like the James Bond movies. While I originally just threw it together as an action playset of stock characters, over time, it began to morph into something very different. Using pop culture's stock antagonists to take swings at the injustices unfolding around me began to carry more and more emotional weight.

In an era when information became more and more readily available, we were able, at any time of day, to pull out our phones and view some kind of great injustice unfolding, live in front of the world – to see police forces with the budgets and supplies of small national armies crushing peaceful protestors, to watch the deceptions of nations exposed constantly and slip by unpunished, to see the suffering of those in need on our feeds 24/7...

It became increasingly clear to me, and to many, that the status quo is not a state of normalcy, but something imposed by force. Equally, to many, the concept of rallying the villains — those who challenged the status quo — and giving us a context in which we can, in some sense, strike back against it all... It struck a chord among those of my generation. In a world where fighting back seems so hard, an entity like the Korps is something compelling.

I am now sitting here writing the foreword to an actual, published work about it, and my mind is reeling. Giving the Korps as a set of narrative tools to the wider community feels like it's uncorked a flood – a need to right wrongs, a need to highlight injustices, a need to tell intimately personal stories, stories of love, stories of redemption, rushing out onto countless pages from countless perspectives.

All I have ever wanted to do is to help give people a community, and the tools they need to create, and to build the stories they need, and it is an honour and a privilege to introduce this one to you – one of love, one of *breaking free*, one of deep wounds beginning to heal…

– Karen King

CHAPTER 1

"THE BURDEN OF KNOWLEDGE IS PAID IN BLOOD."

The crushingly tall voice echoed through the bleak, featureless landscape. The words seemed dispassionate, almost matter of fact, but the voice itself had a cadence that made it seem like English wasn't the speaker's first language. The words rippled through the ground of the unfamiliar dreamscape like waves on a lake, levelling the few distinguishable features of the terrain into perfect flatness.

Lexi felt her body drift and fracture, diverging apart, as if she were light passing through a prism. All at once her senses were split, experiencing her surroundings in isolation, and struggling — *flailing* — to communicate with each other. The Highland cow had several reflections that seemingly managed to occupy the same space as her body but were simultaneously disjointed and disconnected. Frantically, she checked herself over. She had two horns, same as always, lightly curved and pleasingly androgynous. They were not too thick to be clocked instantly as male, yet neither too angled to be immediately assumed female. A crown of thick auburn hair in a stylish undercut (only slightly darker than her tawny coat) sat between them. The rest of her body was… also there. Thick fur, split hooves, a ropey tail, and an average build, with little in the way of discernibly gendered features. Despite all that, she still felt *separated* into disparate instances of herself.

The Highland looked over one shoulder, then the other, then up; there was nothingness in every direction. Her dreams weren't usually like this. Even in her all-too-common nightmares, she never felt herself… *echo* like this.

"*THE BURDEN,*" spoke the voice again; compared to the previous statement, it was nearly a whisper, despite retaining all of the same forceful intensity.

Finally, frustrated, Lexi demanded an answer from the void. "Who are you? Where am I?"

The ground beneath her hooves shook with a deafening roar, cracking in neat parallel lines that ran infinitely into the distance, in all directions. A fragmented section of ground to Lexi's left was the first to rise skyward, rocketing upwards in an endless stack of books and paper; the same thing happened to her right, a few seconds later. More endless pillars of tomes rose from nothingness and reached so far into the sky their tops vanished.

All was quiet for a moment, the stacks of higgledy-piggledy shelves and brimming bookcases settling with faint, warm creaks. A few stray pages rained down weightlessly — like feathers on a light breeze — but among them all, one page stood out.

It was yellowish in colour, drifting downwards faster than the others, and with a curious tab on one edge. Only as the manilla landed face down on the floor did the bovine realise the sheet was actually a folder; the creased edge was bleached more than the rest of the paper stock, and frayed slightly with loose pulp fibres, betraying the object's well-worn nature. Lexi picked it up from the floor where it landed, and with hoof-nailed fingers cautiously turned it over. There, on the front of the tab, a single word was crisply typewritten:

CONTINUUM

The word felt so wrong and so *familiar* at the same time. Lexi searched her memories, but nothing came to the forefront of her mind. Nothing, that was, beyond a strange unease. Something inside her, something stronger than mere curiosity, itched to see what the folder contained. The compelling force drew her to the odd warmth and weight of the folder, and she delicately opened it.

The contents were just as understated as the folder itself: a single scrap of paper, with just five words haphazardly scrawled on it in a mess of thick black ink:

The Voice is a friend.

The Highland had an answer to one of her questions, at least, but she wasn't sure from *who*. The diction, the handwriting — neither seemed to match the words she'd heard. The message was written too hastily and too warmly to have originated with the voice's owner.

Suddenly, Lexi became very aware of the utter *quiet*. She couldn't even hear her heartbeat anymore.

The cow looked around, convinced that only a moment before there had been *something* to hear in the void, some background noise, like faint wind or the idle static of lightly fluttering pages. When her gaze returned downwards again, the folder and its baffling contents had vanished from her hands.

"What do you want?" When she spoke again, Lexi was quietly relieved she could at least hear her own words.

There was a long pause, and then the voice returned. "TO REMIND YOU."

A faint, warm light grew in the distance and the towering spires of books seemed to part and bend out of the way, giving the Highland a better view of its source. The light grew brighter and more blinding as it neared — racing towards her with a painful strobing flicker to hues of red and blue — until, at last, a siren pierced the silence. In an instant, Lexi was standing in the rain, on a cold, dark, *familiar* night.

The hospital's inpatient entrance was before her, just how she remembered it… except for being almost *fuzzy* around the edges, like parts of it were being seen through frosted glass or a thick fog. She stepped under the sea-green steel awning that welcomed patients and visitors, and the automatic doors slid open with a rubbery squeak. A lone nurse worked at the inpatient desk, busily tapping away at a keyboard, as shadowy half-remembered figures walked with purpose from nowhere to nowhere else.

The nurse seemed to speak up, but the cow could register no discernible speech in the white noise she heard. Before Lexi could ask her to repeat what she'd said, the environment flashed and changed, and she suddenly stood in the intensive care ward. She'd been in a lot of them. Never as a patient, but frequently enough as a visitor that she recognised this specific space, and the one instance when she'd witnessed it. She looked to her right, knowing already what she would see.

Her mother was laid up in the hospital bed, her face tired and vacant — sleeping, but not restfully. Her body was covered just barely by a hospital gown, and wires ran from multiple shaved patches on her chest, arms, and torso. The ECG beside her quietly beeped out a notice that the older bovine was still alive, but barely. She wasn't intubated, but an IV bag hung from a stand, silently feeding her fluids.

Lexi closed her eyes, trying to blink away tears that didn't seem to want to come in the first place. She took a step past the privacy curtain that obscured the other half of the room, knowing what she would see there too.

There, sitting on the floor, was her younger self, wearing a shirt a few years too big for her — a hand-me-down from her half-sister that she'd gotten in a care package one Christmas. The young cow was only five years old, and her eyes were fixed on the tiny boxy TV mounted in the corner of the room, near to the ceiling. It was muted, but that didn't matter to the impressionable calf. What *mattered* were the pictures of a national Hero, small enough on the screen that he seemed approachable and less imposing than other adults. He was her *friend* — or, at least, she wished he was.

Howard Bride, the superhero Greenbelt, was a member of the UK's Home Counties Heroes. He was neither the most prolific in his Heroism nor the most powerful, but he had the advantages of the best PR and a face made for television. With a new political era dawning at the end of the 90s, he quickly became the poster child of a forward-looking, globalised Britain, ripe with reform to old systems that were *definitely* going to work better for everyone.

The badger on the screen pulled an exaggerated action pose for the camera and laughed silently through the television's static-laced reception. He never took himself too seriously, back then, something Lexi and the public alike appreciated… but that had started to change as the years went by.

"D-do you think I could b-be like him, Mum? He helps people and… nature, like you always say we should," the small cow said, still sitting cross-legged on the floor.

Her unconscious mother in the hospital bed remained silent. Illness had ravaged her body time and time again, but she never did lose her sense of right and wrong. She was stubborn in the face of debilitating medical bad luck, and in the few truly lucid moments she'd had — free from the haze of her medicated state — she imparted on the young Highland the importance of *believing* in something.

The two of them had been out foraging for wild mushrooms together, trespassing on private land (a concept for which the once-punk older bovine held a deep disdain) earlier that day, before her symptoms flared up, and they had to cut the hike short. Her breath was ragged by the time they got back to their bungalow, and searing pain was clearly visible on her face. She'd collapsed in the hallway. Unable to take another step, she'd told Lexi to call for an ambulance for her and to tell them the address, just like they'd practised.

Lexi shivered, realising that she couldn't remember exactly how many times something similar had happened before this *specific* memory, only that she'd... had to be strong, for her mum, more often than any child probably should have. Strong *and* helpful, like the Hero on TV.

"...I w-want to be like him," the young Highland on the floor whispered to herself, her eyes glued to the screen.

The door to the side room swung open slowly, and in stepped a Labrador, his muzzle grey with age, but the rest of his coat still a sleek shiny black. "Hi Michael! Are you still doing okay in here? You haven't come out to ask for anything, so I just wanted to check. Do you need a drink at all?"

The small cow looked over her shoulder and peered around the curtain, not wanting to pry her eyes from the tiny TV. "Hi, Dr Gold. I'm okay..."

Dr Gold closed the door behind him, looking up at the screen. "Oh! Oh dear; I'm sorry, Michael, I don't think there are any cartoons on at this time of night. I could see if there's some books in the children's wing, if you'd like?"

The child thought for a moment, looking up at the screen, and the flickering image of her personal Hero. He was grinning and saying something she couldn't hear to the Border Collie interviewer. "D-do you have any books with G-Greenbelt?"

"The Hero? You like him, huh?" Dr Gold crouched down beside the young cow and watched the TV with her for a second.

"Yeah. He... he likes to help people... and he says we should look after each other, and he likes nature. Like Mum does..."

19

The canine looked back to the older bovine defiantly clinging to life in spite of her body. "Mmm. You know, I think I saw one of his comic books in a waiting room, recently. I'll go and see if one of the nurses can go fetch that for you."

The cow didn't react. She still stared at the screen, even as the interview with her Hero faded into a brief station identification, followed by the start of a terrible soap opera.

Dr. Gold stood up again and headed to the door, stopping just short of leaving. "We got a call from your dad. He said he's not able to pick you up until Monday, and your grandparents didn't answer the phone. I'll, uh... I'll get some blankets for you, so you can sleep next to your mum, okay? Then we'll try and get hold of your grandparents again, see if they can't pick you up."

The young cow's expression remained the same, quietly forlorn, but she replied in the way that her mother had taught her was polite. "Okay... th-thank you, Dr. Gold."

Lexi watched the memory play out as the Labrador left the room, a sadness visible in his eyes; just like that, it faded away to nothing, leaving the cow standing again amid the towering stacks of books, crushed. A pained, ragged breath rattled from Lexi's nose as she struggled to hold back tears, wishing desperately to just sink into the ground, and for it to be soft and warm and forgiving.

The moment she moved, the pillars gave way and melted to nothing. The sky above grew speckled with points of bright light, and soon the stars flared into being, turning the inky void to a pleasantly warm purple. Her body rocked with sadness all the same, though, and catching her breath past the lump in her throat she cried out.

"Why remind me? I don't... I don't want to remember this!" She receded into the embrace of the floor, very suddenly as soft and forgiving as she had wished it, despite still resembling slab-like obsidian tiles. "It hurts so much! Why are you showing me this?"

"YOU MUST REMEMBER WHAT HOPE FEELS LIKE. YOU MUST KILL YOUR HOPELESSNESS, OR IT WILL KILL YOU. THE BURDEN OF KNOWLEDGE IS PAID IN BLOOD — AND THERE IS YET MORE TO SPILL."

The words didn't make *sense*. Hope was a distant memory that the cow had given up as unattainable. All that was left in her life was rolling with the waves of Fate, taking the punches as they came with whatever resilience she could muster.

Trembling, breathing laboured, Lexi found herself unable to close her eyes. As she laid still on the unreal floor, an inky void ate at the edges of her vision until it was all-encompassing, and the cloying silence was gradually replaced with the deafening whine of aircraft engines—

September 29, 2019

"—Sir? Sir, are you okay? You're bleeding!"

The koala's gentle nudging finally shook Lexi awake. It took a second or two to get her bearings and recover from the strangely surreal dream that had just passed. The in-flight entertainment display — textured plastic edges worn and grimy with age — was what came into focus first. It displayed a tiny icon of a plane slowly approaching a large site labelled YYZ — Toronto-Pearson International Airport.

Toronto. I'm over Toronto right now. Something about bleeding?

The Highland looked to her left, where the wide-eyed, grey-furred holidaymaker sat, offering a napkin with an expression of well-meaning concern on her face. Lexi's sleepy haze continued to fade, and with the returning sensations came the feeling of something warm dripping down over her lip. "Sorry… you said I'm bleeding?"

"Your nose! Must be the cabin pressure, right? My second cousin is married to a buffalo, and he gets the exact same thing on flights," the koala spouted cheerfully, overbearingly shoving a napkin into the cow's open hand.

"Oh… that. Thanks, yeah; cabin pressure," Lexi replied. She held the cheap, scratchy napkin to her nose, strenuously channelling as much effort as she could into her best impression of someone who was Awake and Put Together. She didn't 'get nosebleeds', really, but the sudden start of one wouldn't be the *first* strange thing her body had done in the past few months. Lexi excused herself, heading for the bathroom after unbuckling her seatbelt and folding away the tray table from her economy-section aisle seat. "Sorry, thanks for the tissue. I should go get this cleaned up before we land."

She hurried down the aisle, bloody kraft-brown paper stuck to her nose with one hand, the other fishing in her pocket to check her phone was still there — the only reliable connection to *anyone* she would have, once she landed. It was, thankfully, exactly where she expected.

Lexi shut the bathroom door behind her and fiddled with the lock, double-checking it was secured before daring to peer in the tiny mirror. She pulled the tissue away and dabbed the last few drops of blood dry, stuffing the offending nostril with a small wad of toilet paper. That, at least, felt better than the napkin, and she gazed again at her reflection to verify whether she looked reasonably presentable.

"Presentable" would have been a definite improvement. Instead, the twenty-six-year-old bovine looked *remorselessly* tired, with heavy bags under her eyes, dark enough to be visible through burnt-orange fur. She'd tried her best before departing to clean herself up, but there was only so much that could be buffed out in a day. Between her horns was the same side-shave she'd always dreamt about having, but it was much messier after an eight-hour flight. Though she'd wanted to, she hadn't had the guts to grow it out in the UK — she was technically out of the closet, but still trying hard not to be *too* obvious in a country that sullenly frowned upon visible nonconformity.

Maybe now, now that I'm starting over.

Somewhere too in her reflection was something *bigger*, longing to come out. Grey-market HRT had done *some* work, but there was still a long way to go. Lexi doubted that her body would ever truly be hers, the way she wanted it to be, but she was at least on the road to something more comfortable.

The bovine swept her fringe back with an exhausted sigh and thought back to her strange dream... even if it was unpleasant, and brought back things she didn't want to remember. The past, for one. Her parents. Leaving Mum behind, to try and find a better life. Greenbelt, and the disappointment *he* had turned out to be. Despite all that, it didn't feel like a nightmare, somehow; it felt more like a confrontation.

CHAPTER 1

Whatever, she thought. It was probably just the stress of uprooting her life. Perfectly understandable, really.

The body she inhabited for the duration of the dream was... comfortable, though. It still didn't *quite* feel right, but it was better than what she was used to in the waking world. Closer, maybe, to what she wanted, in spite of what she'd had hammered into her.

Dr Endicott had been emphatically clear all those years ago that there was a *right* way to be trans, and being AMAB meant Lexi had to *look* and *behave* a certain way, and most specifically to like and want certain *very* girly things. The doctor had very thoroughly impressed upon the cow the importance of *passing,* fitting a stereotype. Even after being refused access to transition care for supposedly not putting "enough effort" into her performance, and discovering nonbinary identities, she still struggled to reconcile her own wants and desires with what doctors at large seemed to want *for* her. She still longed to be *acceptable.* To whom, she didn't know — society, maybe? That would never happen in Britain, though. That was part of the reason she was on the plane.

Her new home would be a place that actually recognised her gender identity in law. Citizenship and the legal protections it offered were still a few years out of reach, and Canada was by no means perfect... but at least things didn't seem to be moving backwards there. Or, at least, not moving backwards as fast as the eager reactionaries back home had accomplished. Until she could claim citizenship, though, Lexi would avoid rocking the boat, stomaching what it took to stay settled and out of trouble. *Then,* maybe, she could relax a bit.

She'd been a theatre kid in high school, so putting on a convincing act came naturally — at least, when she was fully awake. In the cramped confines of the bathroom, she still looked like death warmed over. Beyond that, even, as if death were nuked in a microwave for just a *few* minutes too long.

A fateful *bing* sound filled the space, telling Lexi to return to her seat. They'd be landing soon. She shuffled back to her seat and buckled in, the holiday-making koala giving her a gentle smile as the plane descended towards the airport.

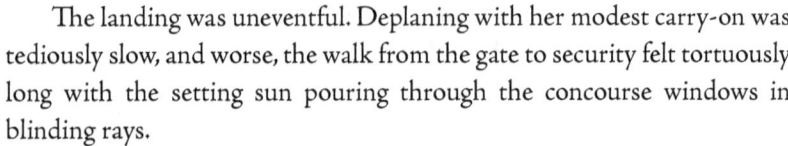

The landing was uneventful. Deplaning with her modest carry-on was tediously slow, and worse, the walk from the gate to security felt tortuously long with the setting sun pouring through the concourse windows in blinding rays.

Lexi tapped into the airport's wi-fi the first moment she could. The usual public network sign-in prompt came up, along with a boilerplate list of disclaimers and terms of service. Except... not quite boilerplate. Just above the "I Agree" button, one particular disclaimer stood out: *"Thorntech Rose-Coloured Glasses devices (RCGs), cannot connect to our wireless network. If you wish to access the network with RCGs, please report to security for screening."*

It seemed *very* specific and *extremely* excessive. Everyone was aware, of course, of the rumours that Thorntech supplied (or were somehow linked to) the Korps with their iconic headgear. The sinister supervillain organisation was classically represented in the media as black-and-magenta-clad criminal sex maniacs who seemed to haunt polite society from the shadows. But even in the stuffy and uptight UK, Lexi had never before seen such a naked attempt to scrutinise their use in black and white terms-of-service restrictions. Maybe the villains were a bigger problem in North America than she'd imagined?

They're just smart glasses, though, Lexi thought, faintly baffled. Heroes and villains alike had always had a thing for quirky accessories and strange costumes, and no one had ever conclusively *proved* that Korps devices were Thorntech. Who was to say that the company wasn't deliberately making a controversial design choice for free marketing, or that the Korps hadn't somehow managed to reverse-engineer the bleeding-edge tech before it was widely available to consumers? Or even that the villains weren't augmented to the nines, and that the sleek visors they wore were just part of the *drip?*

Lexi sighed and ticked the last box as she entered border control, joining the line to the electronic customs declaration kiosks. It didn't take long for her phone to buzz with a notification.

Hey hun.

Waiting for you in arrivals with a coffee crisp and a bag of all-dressed chips. Got to get you started on the Canadiana diet.

You won't miss me, I'm the 8-foot tower of hunk. ^.=.~

Drac was already there, and judging by the timestamp on the message, he'd been in the arrivals hall since before the plane had even landed. Lexi chuckled to herself. *Fashionably early goofball.*

The pair of them had known each other for years, and had started dating without even realising it, in that very not-neurotypical "Wow, I love talking to you every day, and we have so much in common, anyway, I hope you find someone" way. Not a day went by that they didn't excitedly infodump, chat about deep topics long into the night, or even just checked in to make sure the other was doing all right if they'd been quiet. After months of such exchanges, they eventually, awkwardly, figured out they were in a relationship, though they'd never met in person. When Lexi's personal situation had gotten increasingly worse — a slew of shit service economy jobs that kept ending in redundancy, the UK's regressive attitudes on trans rights, and political instability — Drac had been the one to suggest outright leaving the country, for an extended vacation together.

Quietly, the both of them knew she wouldn't be going back. There were plans in place to pool all the money they had together, to apply for a work permit and extend her stay. It would set them back a lot, but there wasn't anything for her in the UK anymore. The two relatives she still spoke to weren't going anywhere, of course, but even they seemed to encourage her to seek better options elsewhere.

Her pitiful life savings seemed a small price to pay for a chance at a new start, she concluded, as she dutifully checked off the line of the kiosk screen declaring that she was importing no foreign fruits.

Good job prospects back home had evaporated, now that her recently achieved university degree in environmental engineering was functionally useless. The government had shelved nearly all climate-related projects, and as good of a science communicator as she had become, no one in the UK's incestuous press circuit was ever going to hire a confused queer with a *passionate* disdain for political inaction. She got out while she could, and if things didn't work out in Canada, well… she didn't want to think about it. She'd happily work whatever job she could find, though, if it meant a shot at some kind of stability.

Eventually the inspection line shuffled forward towards a row of booths, and soon enough, Lexi was standing in front of one herself.

The tired-looking marmot in a black-and-grey uniform behind the plexiglass screen spoke up. "Passport and declaration, please." His voice was friendly, if a little muted by the professionalism of someone who'd obviously been doing exactly this one job for many hours straight.

Lexi slipped her passport and the flimsy kiosk receipt through the slot in the plexiglass window and waited.

He asked the question, not making eye contact. "Name?"

The cow felt a knife twist somewhere in her gut. Her chosen name wasn't on her passport yet. It was *technically* legally recognised, but she hadn't managed to change everything over to it yet. The people she cared about — and one or two institutional organisations besides — knew her as Lexi. "Michael Hayes."

The words tasted bitter on Lexi's tongue, but the marmot seemed content with the answer and moved on to his next question "And your reason for visiting Canada?"

"Visiting my boyfriend," she replied with much less hesitancy.

The marmot's gaze drifted from the passport and onto the cow's face for the briefest of moments with a professional indifference. "And the duration of your stay?"

"Six months," Lexi offered. That was the plan if things didn't work out, anyway. As long as legally permissible, assuming she couldn't get an extension or a work permit.

The officer folded the slip of declaration paper into the passport and returned it without so much as a stamp for her to look at. "Welcome to Canada; enjoy your visit," he recited briskly.

She took the papers and stuffed them in her pocket, walking through the narrow passage between the booths with a strange underwhelming feeling — and then, suddenly, *elation*. She'd *made* it. There were still hurdles to jump, and bridges to cross, but this was it. She was going to be seeing her boyfriend any minute now. She was going to be able to let the stress melt off her, even just for a short while; she could *unwind*.

The cow raced towards the arrivals hall as quickly as she could at something that *looked* like a walking pace, a beaming smile spread across her muzzle. She checked her phone and frantically tapped out a message to Drac that she was through border control. Their reply came back a few seconds later, directing her to where they stood at Arrivals Door C.

Lexi stopped walking and started half-running, and as soon as she saw the impossible-to-miss rack of horns peeking above the rest of the crowd, she sprinted directly into her boyfriend for a hug she didn't want to end. The gold-scaled dragon eagerly wrapped his arms around her, his tail steadying the carry-on luggage that threatened to topple over behind the bovine.

So happy just to be in each other's company, at long last, neither of them said anything intelligible for a while.

"You look even cuter in person," the dragon smirked. He held up a single fry and used it to point across the table at Lexi before munching on it.

The drive to the nearest burger place had been short, but as the sun started to set, the day had begun to feel very, very long. Lexi snorted at her boyfriend's remark and was quickly reminded of the nosebleed she'd gotten just before landing when she started to smell iron. The cow grabbed a fresh napkin and held it to her nose, sighing and looking back with tired eyes at the stocky drake. "I'm just the *picture* of beauty right now, I'm sure."

"Damn right you are," they grinned, raising both horn-studded brows in a playful leer.

A smile crept across the bovine's face. "It's so nice to just... be *physically together*. Like, one big, difficult part is out of the way, you know, and now..."

"Now, it's just the rest of our lives," Drac replied with a warm grin, stealing an onion ring from Lexi's combo with the very tip of a talon. "Oh, did you text your mom to say you landed safe yet?"

"Oh! Yeah, I did. Morrigan, too. I told Mum I'd call her tomorrow when I'm a bit more rested and we're settled back at your place."

The dragon gave a slow nod and sipped on their root beer, casually looking out of the window and into the parking lot, checking that the huge truck that just pulled in hadn't damaged his reliable little hatchback. "Yeah, that's probably for the best. You could use *at least* a day to decompress. That was a lot of travel. I take it that the CBSA didn't give you any trouble?"

The cow took another french fry, dipped it in ketchup and crunched it down with a quiet, relieved sigh. "No, thankfully. I don't know what I got so worked up about, honestly, thinking they were going to confiscate my HRT meds because I didn't have a script for them…"

The dragon nodded, affectionate understanding on his face. "That's anxiety for you."

"Yeah, yeah. You're right. I mean, there was this thing in the wi-fi terms of service at the airport, they almost seemed more worried about RCGs than—"

The dragon interrupted with an exaggerated mime to keep quiet, clearing his throat to emphasise the delicacy of the topic. "Well, yeah… they're, uh. You know…"

"*Villain-affiliated?*" Lexi offered with an airy, performatively dramatic whisper.

Drac huffed through a smile. "Sorry. Force of habit; spend enough time working in tech, and you might get a little paranoid about ambient data harvesting too."

There was a quiet, almost awkward moment. The dragon just didn't want to get into trouble, she knew; they'd been averse to conflict for a long while. *It must come with the territory of being so big and physically imposing,* the cow supposed, trying not to swoon over her partner too much as a result of the thought.

Drac broke the silence as he scrunched up the wrapper to his now eaten sandwich and tossed it in the paper bag between the two of them. "Oh, right, I meant to ask. Did you get your mail forwarding set up? For all the important stuff? Wait, did I ask already? Sorry; the last couple weeks have just been so hectic, with… well, prepping everything on my end for you coming over."

Lexi gave an appreciative nod, "Yeah, I did. Still no word from the university as to when my diploma will get sent out, though. Wish they'd have just let us do a graduation ceremony like every other place, but apparently, they'd lined up a Hero guest speaker who took umbrage with the syllabus. The student union threatened to boycott the graduation if he was there… the whole thing was such a mess."

"Greenbelt?" Drac asked, with a finger pointed at the cow over their root beer.

"Greenbelt." Lexi confirmed with a roll of her eyes. "Apparently no one told the faculty that one of the courses that would be graduating this year contained a case study on political corruption around climate justice and greenwashing, and *he* was one of the examples. The whole university staff imploded over *that* fuckup." She tutted and scrunched up her face in months of bottled-up frustration. "That careerist piece of shit, though... a finger in every pie, and money in his pocket from both Labour and the Tories to just do *nothing* and repeat nice soundbites. He used to be this big hopeful figure, doing PSAs about recycling and the new energy infrastructure of tomorrow, right? But we can't have nice things, and he was bought and paid for before I even got into high school, so... whatever, I guess."

There was a moment of quiet as Lexi slumped back into her seat, staring out of the window. The hazy orange glow of sunset was fading into an array of rich pinks and purples over the distant Toronto skyline. "I thought I'd be changing the world by going into Environmental Engineering, but no... the truth just gets buried, and anyone who you think might be on your side gets bought, one way or another. That whole degree was such a waste of time," she seethed. "Sorry, sorry for the venting, I just... I wanted someone to *believe* in, for all those years. Never meet your heroes and all that, right?"

The dragon leaned in across the table, his wings unfurling just enough to make use of the newly-freed-up space behind him. "Hey, you've got *yourself* to believe in now. You're a strong person, even if you don't see it. Dropping everything to travel halfway across the world to meet a stranger? That takes some courage!"

"You're not a stranger!" Lexi protested. "We've been talking for years!"

"Sure! But I'm a big spooky dragon from a faraway laaaand!" Drac wiggled their fingers at head height, in their best impression of some monster or other. "And, you know... there are people out there who really have a strong sense of justice? Or at least they *seem* to, I guess. It's been in the news the last couple weeks that someone leaked a whole bunch of dirt about a corrupt development company in Mississauga."

Lexi quietly tried to remember the maps of the area that she and the dragon had pored over during a hyperfixation on mapping hypothetical transit lines, some years ago. "That's... just outside Toronto proper, right? Like, not far from here?"

"Right here, actually! The airport is technically in Mississauga, and Toronto starts a couple of blocks over that way," he pointed with an over-the-shoulder talon. "Anyway, it turns out someone did some snooping and uncovered a bunch of supply chain nonsense that looks like it's going to land a few deserving folks in jail. It went straight to the press with some documentation and evidence. Real thorough stuff too, look." Drac slid his phone over the table. There, on the screen, was a news article he'd pulled from his recent browsing history.

Lexi scrolled down, tapping on one of the pictures halfway down the article. It appeared to be of a typewritten document with a numbered list of evidentiary files sent to the newspaper, like a table of damning contents. Above the list was a short blurb about what the snooper had found and how it might be useful to be made public, all of it in tersely polite prose.

Something stood out about the photo of the document, though. Among all the letters hammered into the paper by the typewriter were just two appearances of the letter X, and both had a slight, but consistently observable imperfection. The letter sat higher on the line than the surrounding ones, and the inked impression was slightly fainter. It was only noticeable in contrast by how otherwise *perfect* the rest of the text was.

With a start, Lexi realised she'd been fixating intently at the screen longer than was probably normal. The cow pulled herself away from the screen with a calm sigh. "Huh. I guess there really are folks out there that put in the work, still. Did they have any clue who the tipoff was from?"

Drac pulled the phone back across the table and very quietly explained, "Mhmm; 'The Dark Dossier'. He's with the Korps, and the pundits think he's been around a long while, too. Some kind of... specialised telepath that can put ideas in your head with writing, or something like that, anyway."

Suddenly, her boyfriend's hesitancy to talk too loudly about RCGs in public made more sense; it wasn't strictly taboo but admitting that *maybe the villains do some good* was a bridge too far. It was something she would desperately need to start internalising and carrying over to real-world conversations. Saying the wrong thing online might be mostly harmless or passed off as a joke, but in the flesh — where other people could hear — consequences could be more serious.

"So..."

"Yeah. I mean, look, they do bad things, but once in a while something like this happens, and it's... kinda hard not to feel satisfied that *someone* who deserved it got what was coming to them," they mumbled, carefully avoiding any direct praise. "Anyway," Drac hastily added, "We should hit the road, now that rush hour has died down again; hopefully we won't get stuck outside Milton." The drake rose from his seat and dutifully collected the scraps from the table to toss in the trash on the way out.

Lexi threw her hoodie on — one of the few items of clothing she had packed for the purpose of boymoding — and followed behind, waiting until they were both in the car again before continuing her thought. "Do you ever think that... maybe some villains aren't as bad as the media says?" She asked the question with quiet hesitancy. The dragon was silent, and suddenly she feared she'd misjudged the situation. Or maybe she shouldn't have been quite as blunt. She'd *kind* of expected there to be quiet after a question like that, but it was still strange to see them glance at her the way they did.

Draculion started the car and carefully backed out of the spot, navigating back onto the 401 West. It wasn't until the two reached the highway before he finally replied, muffled by the muted din of evening traffic. "Listen... I think that with us both being queer, our experiences, our *generation's* experiences..." He cut himself off, clearly composing his words before speaking. "The Korps, well — it's not exactly black and white, right? Not like the law-and-order politicians like to see it. *Especially* when there's some kind of outgroup caught in the crossfire as collateral damage. Like, you do a *little* bit of part-time activism with a tenant union, or protest police shooting innocent people, and all of a sudden, you're in their firing line; God forbid wanting better climate policy, or housing built for people to actually live in, or even just a little less pointless suffering in this world. And all they do is wring their hands and say they *can't*, so sorry, the police and Heroes need bigger budgets; and anyway, it's impossible to get anything done with people like us *agitating* all the time... Honey, we aren't on the same level as *any* kind of supervillain, but we're certainly treated like we're in bed with them."

The answer was diplomatic, but as they focused on the road ahead, Lexi could see there was a faint hint of unease on the dragon's face. They were right; they both had some background in activism, either sporadic or organised. Drac had helped manage small-time demonstrations, Lexi had attended marches, and they'd both dealt with varying levels of flack for it. The cow wondered if being publicly dispassionate and keeping her head down would get easier with time. She cared, a lot, but being quiet seemed the safer option. Better to let that hope that she could change the world die for good if she wanted to survive, she frustratedly reminded herself.

Drac broke the tension by flexing his hand out over the steering wheel, taking on an overly theatrical tone. "As for the insidious Dark Dossier, with the little spree he seems to have been on recently — as reported on by our *stalwart* and extremely *unbiased* news media — he's probably pinning more targets up on the wall of his secret lair, fiendishly plotting the downfall of the world, one landlord and private company at a time!"

The rest of the drive was punctuated with laughter at just how *ridiculous* the situation was. Neither of them wanted to directly acknowledge the reality they'd just skirted around: they might not be proper *villains*, but they were dangerously close to being someone's idea of acceptable collateral.

It was better to just keep quiet, really.

Chapter 2

Deep beneath Toronto, in a subterranean base that the Korps called home, Maxwell thoughtfully tacked another sticky note onto the whiteboard at the back of the directorate's office. He mused for a moment on his recent handiwork. Carefully written names and locations adorned the sides of the freestanding surface, flanking a paper map of the East Coast pockmarked with pinholes from previous uses. Each note pointed to a location on the map, and below it all, was a single name written in marker, underlined and circled.

"Who *are* you, Rob Slotis?" the wolf murmured. His voice was low and gravelly, with the barest hint of a native French accent softened by decades of speaking English.

He took a moment to consciously check the time on his RCGs' display — already two in the morning. Exhausted, Maxwell heaved a slow breath through his nose in frustration, before finally deciding to retire to his heavily worn desk chair. He removed his magenta visor, set it on the desk, and closed his eyes in attempted concentration for a moment.

The office around him was draped with reminders of his hard-earned tenure. Every item in the room, more or less, was rich with its own significance and value, its own *story*. That only made the dead ends on the whiteboard all the more annoying.

The richly lacquered wooden coat tree by the door, for instance, had been lifted from the offices of a financial institution during an operation in the late eighties. The coffee table in the office's crash area was the former property of a Winnipeg land developer, and the cork-inlay coasters on top of it were stolen as part of a kompromat raid on a Westmount mansion. Lifting his head and peering to the ceiling, Maxwell caught a glance of the white half-mask that had defined his early career, placed as if to stare down at him from the highest shelf. Every tool and artifact and furnishing reminded Maxwell of how much he loved his job.

The typewriter on his desk, too, was storied. It still sported its original duck-egg blue finish but otherwise showed its age; some of the keys had been re-tooled and re-finished, though one particularly-sticky arm nonetheless remained half-depressed at all times. One of the rubber feet had been replaced too, and the paper label on the side of the chassis was heavily worn and yellowed with age. The decades had left its once-proud declaration — PROPERTY OF HIS MAJESTY'S GOVERNMENT — only barely legible.

For all of his trophies and keepsakes, however, Maxwell himself was probably the oldest and most storied artifact in the room. The grey wolf was nearing his ninetieth year, but age hadn't managed to slow him down; he'd simply refused to let it. His only concession on that front had been withdrawing from the more *intense* kind of field operations in the early 2000s, though he never quite stopped being an active menace. Desk investigations could, after all, be just as dangerous to the status quo... so long as the person behind the desk knew what they were doing.

That wasn't to say the tall lupine never went topside, of course. He still found excuses to do some light breaking-and-entering here and there, to say nothing of occasional blackmail, and even some subtle espionage. It kept him *sharp*. More importantly, it kept the gnawing withdrawal symptoms of his powers at bay... and made sure, too, that the name Dark Dossier wasn't easily forgotten, despite the prime of his villain career trailing far behind him.

Rob Slotis, though, wasn't giving up his secrets easily — a fact that rubbed Maxwell's fur entirely the wrong way. Korps intel had nothing on the target, apart from what little Maxwell himself had managed to uncover; most of that had been purely accidental, at that.

The first time the name appeared had been two weeks prior, on a light off-the-books operation Maxwell had carried out himself. He'd broken into a warehouse where he suspected he might find some incriminating evidence against an arms dealer and was proven correct. However, among the other documents he'd rifled through in search of his quarry were a whole *series* of shipping manifests, their descriptions left notably blank other than the words "Unknown heavy machinery/sensitive equipment".

That wasn't compliant with Canadian customs import paperwork, he knew. In any event, the goods had apparently been expedited out of the location in a tremendous rush — at least, if judging by the scribblings in the margins — though no new destination was listed. Next to the consignment number was a contact reference, and the only part that had been filled was a name. *That* name. *Rob Slotis.* Something about the manifest had piqued Maxwell's curiosity, furiously pinging the part of his brain that inferred something was *off*, so he took it with him.

Days later, during another of the wolf's evening extracurriculars, the name appeared again — that time, in the records of a military contractor's business ledger: thousands of dollars made payable without comment. No indication of what the work entailed, how long it took, or even when it was carried out. But there, clear as day: there was the same name. There wasn't a shred of identifying documentation to be found. The payment appeared to have been cash in hand, something *itself* that raised questions. It wasn't as if there was any shortage of ways to surreptitiously obscure accounts payable, or the original sources of shady fund transfers. This felt decidedly, obstinately old-school.

A week after that, another instance of the name appeared, while Maxwell was again running an on-a-whim job to keep himself occupied. He could swear it was *following* him. Whoever this person was, Maxwell had become fixated with finding them and digging up all of their secrets. Something… something was surely going on and not knowing *what* itched at the inside of his skull. For better or worse, this was his new white whale: a name that just seemed to keep cropping up, and *nothing else*, only deepening the wolf's conundrum. It troubled him. The thought of failing to solve the mystery reminded him of Operation Felt.

No, Maxwell shuddered to himself, as the rising fear of failure made its way through his spine. Whatever this was, it would *not* be a repeat of Operation Felt. He ran a paw through the well-groomed undercoat of his neck scruff, heaved a nasally sigh, and frustratedly donned his RCGs for a status update on the Division's non-Slotis affairs.

All current preservation work was going well, he found approvingly. No materials checked out by agents were late for return, and Philip, the division's chief engineer, had already filed his usual nightly report hours before. Maxwell took a moment to look over the report; everything looked good on the containment front, and there was minimal activity coming from Vault F, with the exception of a single spike in psychic activity earlier in the day. *The vault turning over in its slumber,* the wolf reasoned; odd, but not alarming.

It was at that moment that a familiar voice drew his attention to the office door.

"Still haven't decided to get some sleep yet, I see, André."

Maxwell — or to those that knew him beyond the adopted codename, André — swivelled his chair to face the voice's owner. "No, Liam, you know me better than that."

The brown bear standing in the doorway sleepily rubbed at the back of his neck and sipped his cup of vile coffee. Even from behind his desk, Maxwell's sensitive snout assessed it as strong enough to remove paint. Liam's softer middle had peeked out from under a well-worn comfy T-shirt as he'd raised an arm, trawling his claws around the side of his jaw to scratch at his chin thoughtfully. "I checked in again with Recon and Intel. Still nothing. This Slotis guy never *physically* met with the developer in Mississauga; it's all just phone calls. We managed to triangulate the position of the caller, but any security footage from those locations at the time of the call were conveniently missing. Not wiped or deleted; the field team might at least have been able to recover something, if that was the case. I mean *non-existent.* It's like the whole security system — the hardened, hard-wired, on-site part too — was just remotely *turned off* at the time. Hell of a way to cover your tracks."

The wolf graced his jaw with a few claw tips in agonising contemplation. "So, either coincidence, or Slotis wants to play it *extremely* safe by destroying all the evidence, and he has the means of ensuring that."

Liam sleepily trudged to his own desk chair, sitting in the deep groove his ass had worn over many late nights doing this exact kind of puzzling out with his co-director, mentor, and partner. "Sure seems that way. Paper trails are usually where people get sloppy, but not this guy. André... whoever this is that you've discovered, they don't want to be known."

A defiant grin slowly crept its way across Maxwell's pale muzzle. "My dear, I believe I must have missed the part where that was meant to stop us."

The air cracked with laughter. Both of the men knew they wouldn't be dissuaded by something as trivial as someone trying to remain hidden. The unknown was a challenge to them, and they prided themselves — and the division they ran together — on never backing down from such a challenge.

Liam steadied his mug of coffee and wound down with a deep gut chuckle, staring at the ceiling through his own set of RCGs and recalling the division's *unofficial* motto aloud. "We have what you need, and we know what you have."

The Korps Archives & Records Division — KARD for short, and often euphemistically still just referred to as 'Records', its long-ago name at founding — had been around for a very long time. It'd had its ups and downs, its rough starts, and teething problems, but it had never lost sight of the mission: KARD's long-term goals were to collect, maintain, preserve, and disseminate *any and all* information that would be of use to the wider Korps. A library, yes, but *villainous*, at least as far as the Hero world would be concerned.

The wolf looked fondly out of the floor-to-ceiling windows on the door side of the office. The glass walls overlooked the division's main atrium — a space that had started as little more than a glorified storage area stuffed with filing cabinets and desks decades prior. In the present day, though, what could be seen from the co-directors' office represented only a small fraction of KARD's collections. Dozens of bodies, synthetic and organic, busied themselves among the stacks across six floors, two wings, and multiple internal departments. At the centre of the main atrium (suspended between the deep balconies of the second through sixth levels, and casting an imposing shadow on the lowest floor) hung the central archival vaults. Five of the archive chamber's walls were glass, allowing the casual observer to see the vast collections inside, and watch as KARD archivists and librarians carefully attended to them.

That was where the *real* meat of the Division's collections was. Information too delicate, sensitive, or dangerous to be freely accessible to Korps agents *or* civilians, without accompaniment or suitable oversight. It had been the result of back-breaking effort and fierce dedication, and Maxwell's mind drifted back to those humble beginnings…

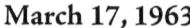

March 17, 1963

The Dark Dossier looked at his watch. It was nearly midnight, which meant that Evans should still be awake for another twenty minutes — at least, based on the intelligence the wolf had been gathering over the past several months. A solid *year* of training had been building to this moment. Everything before had been slowly chipping away at crumbling mortar; now the wolf waited patiently, staring intently at the last intact brick.

A single dewdrop dripped from the leafy canopy above the eager supervillain-in-training, where he'd been uncomfortably taking up a position for several hours. It landed on the cheek of his near-featureless white half-mask and quickly ran off its surface. The weather in the UK was just as miserable as the canine cared to remember: cold, and *wet*. Regardless, he didn't let it distract him. He checked over his toolbelt and satchel one last time, feeling for the things that he would need. It was all still there, waiting to be used.

In the near distance, the kitchen light of the quaint farmhouse vanished. That left only a warm, solitary glow emanating from the living room window, a short sprint from Maxwell's position. That was the signal that his target — one Mr. Thomas Evans — was finally retiring for the night. He pushed himself out from the ornate hedgerow, and bolted towards the farmhouse's far side, where he'd already scouted out an easily opened window.

The wolf braced himself against the cold brick of the pantry's external wall and took a breath. With a swift, practised motion, he pulled a small steel prybar and shim from his belt and had the window open within seconds. He'd pre-oiled the hinges days earlier on a previous recon, which paid off with deathly silence. Maxwell heaved himself up and through the portal, closing the window behind him; only the very most skilled of operators would have picked up even a *hint* that he'd been stalking the house for hours.

The Dark Dossier hesitated, still, as light crept in from under the pantry door. He waited prudently until the light clicked off, followed soon thereafter by the sound of footsteps wearily climbing a set of stairs that creaked with fatigue.

The canine knew there was a revolver upstairs in the man's bedside table, and another in the drawer of the writing desk in the living room. He had to catch Evans between the two spaces, or risk losing the upper hand. Combat training had softened his fear of firearms somewhat, but he didn't want the risk of wrestling a gun out of his target's hands if he didn't have to. Peering around, Maxwell's eyes scanned the shelves of the pantry, seizing upon perhaps a dozen items that would make perfectly good improvised weapons, before landing on the wine rack. Grabbing the heaviest and most expensive-looking bottle — a 1945 Château Mouton Rothschild, per the faded label, V-for-Victory emblem and all — he put his plan into action. He kicked the pantry door open, took two steps out, aimed, and hurled the bottle through the air from its neck like it was some cumbersome throwing blade.

It connected forcefully, and the retired lion slumped into a crumpled heap on the staircase. Surprisingly, the bottle didn't smash; in fact, it survived the concussive throw better than the pile of feline did and was stopped from rolling down the stairs by getting caught in the crook of the lion's arm.

Maxwell picked up the Bordeaux, wiping away smeared blood on its base with the lining of his dark overcoat, before carefully sitting it on a shelf just inside the pantry. "I'll be back for you later," he murmured to himself. "A little something for Chester, for the trouble. As for you…" The wolf turned back to the crumpled mess of his former boss' body and straightened himself out, adjusting his flat cap before getting on with the task of dragging the lion to the kitchen.

The veteran officer of the crown was heavy, but Maxwell had *much* more practice in fireman-lifting limp bodies than even a few years prior. He slumped Evans into one of the wooden chairs at the kitchen table and produced a bundle of high-quality rope from his satchel. Inside of a minute, the lion had his wrists securely bound behind the chair's back, and his ankles tied to its legs. The wolf double-checked his work; he didn't want any room for error. Not this time. Not like there had been with Marcus.

Maxwell set his satchel on the worn wooden table before calmly making himself at home, rummaging through the cupboards for a glass, and pouring himself some water. He didn't get to enjoy the crisp refreshment for longer than a brief sip, before the stirring retiree fastened to the chair began to slur and sputter out demands.

"Who are you? Do you have *any damned idea* who I am! I'll have you fucking *hanged* for this!"

Maxwell ignored the impotent rage, comfortable in the knowledge that the most immediate police force and capes were far too busy to interfere — dealing, as they were, with a little distraction he and his getaway pilot had gone through pains to set up earlier in the night. Without a word, he walked back to the kitchen table and methodically started pulling out the images he would need from his satchel and arranging them into a pristine stack. With a soft breath and a flourish of his overcoat, he pulled out another chair to sit and began staring his target down.

"Why, of *course* I know who you are, Tommy. You're rather the point of why I'm here at all."

The wolf brought the grisly photos down to his lap, out of the other man's line of sight, and started shuffling through them to find his ideal starting point.

The lion, for his part, went silent, huffing through his proud nose and emanating sheer *contempt*. Everything about him carried the weight of his past: broad shoulders, framing a very slight hunch in his back from decades of desk work, and a middle only slightly softened by fat. A neatly groomed and maintained mane, dye less, showing off the fantastic silvers and greys without shame. His scowl seemed chiselled into his face, and even appearing bloodied, in a bathrobe, and wearing a single forlorn slipper didn't make the expression any less intense.

Maxwell adjusted his own wiry figure, bathing delightfully in the defanged visage of the man that had made his life a living hell for years. He doffed his cap and mask and set them quietly on the table, before sweeping back his hair and cooly staring down the feline. "Do you recognise me? It's been a few years, no?"

"Of course I do."

"Then you know what this is."

"You consider this a fitting revenge, I imagine. It was you that got Marcus, wasn't it? I heard about that a few weeks ago. Beaten to death in his garage, body savaged and found in the trunk of his favourite car. So, now you're here, to... what? Finish the job?" Evans remained exceptionally composed for someone tied to a chair — no doubt instilled by decades of experience in military intelligence, Maxwell supposed. Marcus shared that experience too, but he had been decidedly *less* cool when the wolf stood over him. Maybe he'd recognised the murderous glint in Maxwell's eye for what it was.

"Something like that," Maxwell offered mildly.

The lion straightened his back as best he could manage, "Tch... you think this'll bring Alcott back? You think your little *vigilante* spree over in the States will make up for your mistakes? You're nothing, André. Just think; if you'd have toughed it out, you could have been a chief officer with the SIS by now. You must be what, thirty-four? Thirty-six? You could have been so much more. But no, that was never for you, was it? Not since that old fairy of a doctor put ideas in your head about *justice*. So, what are you now, then? A lonely Red sympathiser who keeps himself hidden from anyone who might care enough to love him? We all know what happens to people *you* care about, don't we, André."

The words were cold and bitter, taking a low grip around the wolf's heart. Even after all this time, put on the spot, Evans still knew how to provoke him. Maxwell bit down on the inside of his cheek until he started to taste the iron in his blood and took a breath. These old tricks of berating and talking down to him wouldn't work. Not anymore.

"You know, Evans, you did teach me one thing. Not directly, mind, but as a function of knowing you. The most dangerous thing in the world isn't a bomb, or a gun, or any superpower. It's information — *secret* information."

Evans didn't move, holding a fixed glare. "What do you want?"

Maxwell took in a sharp breath and delivered a line he'd been waiting to. "Simple. I want to destroy your legacy, Tommy. I want everyone to know what you did. What the *Ministry* did, in the name of Queen and Country."

He let the air sit quiet for a moment before leaning in and holding up one of the photos. It was a hasty development, clearly taken from a concealed camera, the sort with which he knew that Evans was very personally familiar. But it was still clear in what it showed — a document. A document with Evans' signature on it. A document which had been marked with three different stamps, each appearing more recent than the last: TOP SECRET. ARCHIVED. TO BE DESTROYED.

Maxwell took in a breath and focused his mind, peering deeply into the lion's consciousness as he unleashed his powers. He'd never personally experienced being on the receiving end of an unconstrained transference — a small quirk of his possessing an apparently-rare form of telepathy — but he'd heard testimony. Words from former colleagues turned victims, medical and official reports. Apparently, it stung, ached, even *burned*, like someone was reaching into your skull with an object both sharp and dull at the same time. One subject had described it so memorably that the words had never left his mind since — like watching a film reel of their experiences catch and melt in a projector that was running too hot and feeling it the whole time.

Evans winced and threw his head to the side with a pained yowl. "You little... fucking... *upstart!* Aghh! H-how did y—"

Maxwell launched himself from his chair, one paw wrapping around the lion's jaw and wrenching his head back to face him. All the anger that he'd felt crawling under his fur at Evan's earlier attempt at manipulation, all the *rage* he had over their shared history, was channelled into the swift movement. "How did I manage that? Your psi-blockers should have prevented it, *no?* You're required by our former employers to take them, and you were *always* an upstanding officer, weren't you Evans?"

The wolf watched as fear visibly gripped the lion.

"I have been staking you out for two weeks. The residence time of your state-mandated ramparzidole hydrochloride tablets is just three days, but you've gotten sloppy, Tommy. I replaced them with sugar pills eight days ago, and you never even noticed — just like with all those fellows you used to bring to my little prison cell of a room. You're all mine, now."

Evans' gaze flitted left and right almost imperceptibly, as he began to shake.

The wolf held up the next photo from the stack, decidedly more graphic. It had not been taken from the same camera that had snapped the shot of the confidential file; no, this image was one taken from directly inside that file, one of many. The print was black and white, but the sheer amount of blood was clearly distinguishable as a stark, shiny pitch-black.

"Look at them, Tommy. Look at the things you did. I know you never had the stomach for it, but *I* had to see all of it, so god damn you, *look at them!*"

Evans held his eyes tightly shut, shakily drawing breath in and out through his nose. Sight wasn't necessary to the process, but Maxwell's mental fingers probed deep inside the lion's head and forcefully tucked the image away in his memory regardless. Judging by the man's pained, writhing whine, he'd been successful a second time.

Maxwell pulled another photo from his lap. He grimaced briefly as he refreshed his own memory of the familiar horrors it contained, before transferring it forcefully into the retired senior agent's mind.

"I will make sure these are the *only* things you remember."

Another image was cast into the lion's mind, burning away some other past events in its wake; childhood memories and recollections of happily married life, the jokes shared with colleagues, the stress of late nights, a perfectly made supper, lines from a song — all rendered the mnemonic equivalent of smouldering ash, for all Maxwell cared. What *mattered* was that they were replaced with the bitter, cold, unyielding records of the souls that Evans had allowed — *encouraged* — to be tormented. Image after image was pushed into Evans' head, until the stack was spent and cast across the floor in a disordered mess.

"Do you remember that one clerk that you kept in those damned archives with me, early on? Pine marten, maybe forty or fifty, I imagine. Humphrey, that was his name. Do you remember how the pills you fed me to keep me *docile* made my imprinting all the more potent? Dangerously unfocused? How *sick* they made me? *What happened to Humphrey,* Mr. Evans?"

Maxwell didn't wait for an answer. His vice-like grip around the lion's jaw began to waver; concentrating his powers so hard — at least, without any kind of chemical enhancement — quickly led to a deep, drained fatigue. "Allow me to refresh your memory... I was carrying a box with a burn order on it. I tripped and fell and scattered at his feet the unredacted material — experiments, torture, *research* into the limits of the superpowered body. The *atrocities* your government committed. I didn't wake up for three days after I had accidentally burned that entire box into poor Humphrey's mind, and you told me you had him *committed.* Because he became a threat to the country's security, of course; all that endless babbling about all the things he knew, because I... because *you* wanted to keep me as the service's damned *pet.* And you had to find some way to control me, so you made *use* of that accident, and engineered it into a tool. *That's* what I'm going to do to you, Tommy," the wolf said coldly. "From quietly honoured national treasure for those SIS sycophants, to a blubbering national disgrace that they'll have no choice but to silence for good."

Maxwell finally let go of the prideful lion's trembling jaw and sunk backwards towards the floor, exhausted and panting for breath. His skull ached in ways he hadn't felt since that day he last saw Humphrey lucid. He collapsed against the table leg and grit his teeth through the discomfort of overextending himself, content that his former employer wasn't going anywhere. Even if Evans could, it'd end badly for him.

After taking a moment to compose himself, letting the pain slowly subside, he stood unsteadily and grunted as he reached into his satchel once more.

"I'll give you the generosity of choice, though. I might seek revenge, but I'm a fair man. Fairer than you ever were, I dare say; fairer than you rightly deserve."

The husk of a man gazed at Maxwell listlessly from his bindings, no doubt preoccupied by the horrors of the work he had spent his life obscuring but seemed to display just enough cognition to understand the wolf's words. Maxwell pulled a bundle of rope from the bag, already tightly fashioned into a noose, which he cast over one of the kitchen's high ceiling beams and clambered atop the table to fix in place. Upon returning to the ground, he calmly re-donned his mask and hat.

"Funny that you mentioned hanging. Finish the job, and maybe none of this gets out. You won't have to live out your remaining years in some *institution* with the horrors you made… or, as I did for so long, perpetually worried that you'll be finished off by a shadow down a hallway."

The canine collected the photos strewn about the floor and carefully bundled them back into his satchel. He cut the former intelligence officer free from his bindings and cleaned away those stray lengths of rope too. "They won't investigate too hard when they find you, you know. Just another loose end they won't need to tie up. Suicide is convenient for them like that," he sniffed. "Secrets go to the grave, Tommy; that's what you always used to say, wasn't it? That's why you were so incensed by me escaping. You should have killed me when you had the chance."

He put the satchel on over his shoulder and fastened his overcoat, taking a moment to breathe in the air one last time, as a petty criminal turned vigilante. Killing Marcus had been messy business, but he'd had to do that for himself. Evans was wrong; this wasn't just revenge. This was something more. Maxwell would leave this quiet farmhouse a supervillain with a body count.

He'd felt strange about killing Marcus. Rage and passion had boiled over in the moment. It almost scared him that he was capable of that… that *overkill*. Conversely, this was just professional wetwork, albeit with a few extra flourishes.

The lion in the chair seemed so much smaller than he had all those years ago, especially as he stood. He seemed meek and broken, understanding what he needed to do to protect his own future, peering up at the twisted kindness the noose offered. He solemnly stood on the chair, and with a whimper, pulled the loop of rope past his face and behind his well-groomed mane.

Maxwell left the same way he came in. He only got as far as the pantry when he heard the sound of wood clattering against the kitchen's cold flagstone floor, and then the momentary choking of his old master. The wolf picked up the bottle of claret that had come in handy earlier in the night and tucked it into his satchel, before climbing out of the pantry window.

The Dark Dossier trudged through the night for a mile and change until he came to the narrow clearing where Chester had expertly set down the helicopter. The hyena leaned against the bare aluminium frame of the Alouette's tail boom and took a soft drag on his cigarette, the warm orange glow just barely illuminating his muzzle in the dark. "I take it our business here is *concluded*, then? Mister Evans took the ultimatum?" The American's motor-mouthed Southern drawl was always a welcome sound, obscured slightly by the light whistling of the wind though it was.

Maxwell came to a stop and gave an affirmative nod, slipping his mask off to tuck it safely away into his bag. "He did. It… it didn't take much convincing in the end. Part of me was preparing for Plan B, but it went smoothly enough. Although," he sighed, "I tired myself out a bit faster than I had hoped."

Chester stepped forward on one prosthetic and let his still flesh and blood leg do the balancing at the rear. "Ahh, now, you *see?* And *here* you were worrying about yer first big operation. You're a natural, Maxie boy." He paused, taking the moment to toss his cigarette on the ground, snuffing it underfoot with one of his garish Cuban-heeled boots. "Glad to have been a part of this with ya'. It is *not* often that a humble pilot like yours truly ends up being an op partner for something *this* big. I surely hope that changes, if you don't mind me saying; there are a whole *mess* of folks back in the states who need their keisters kicked in, and, well... I got one foot with no feeling, so the other is aching for an extra workout, if you catch my drift. Anyway! You did good work tonight, I reckon."

"Thank you, Chester. I wanted you here with me on this; it's nice to have a familiar face." Maxwell slipped his paw into his satchel and clasped his fingers around the wine bottle's neck. "I managed to leave with a gift for you, too... as a thank you. For everything."

Chester blinked and scrunched his nose up just a little as if about to sneeze. "Ah... a claret? Well, that is *awful* kind of you..."

It dawned on Maxwell he hadn't even taken the bottle out of his bag to reveal it yet. His heart sank just a little, as he realised he'd accidentally transferred something on someone *again* — and after such a successful operation, too. He'd hoped those days were long behind him now; he'd trained so hard to carefully control his powers, to get away from the failures of his past self, the mistakes and accidents, the hurt he had caused with no intent... the wolf felt his fingers let go of the glass. Maxwell pulled his hand back to his chest as he felt the flutter of anxiety. "Oh... Chester, I am so sorry, I... I did not mean to—"

The pilot cut him off with a long drawn-out sigh and a single finger held up to silence him. "Ah, ah, ah... we are *square*, Maxie. There is *no* deadline on self-*improvement*... fer which I am *personally* rather grateful." For a brief moment, the hyena went quiet, and his eyes drifted to the scrubby brown grass. "Now, *you* have done real good moving on from where we found you, some years ago, and there's no harm in a little *accident*, all right now? You didn't replace anything important, I *assure* you; I still know how to fly this bird here," Chester said, with a cheery gesture to the helicopter. "I bet you just weren't concentrating too hard, and it slipped out, on account of what you had to do to Mister Evans back there. We all make mistakes, pal; no sense in beating ourselves up forever about 'em."

Maxwell quietly nodded and felt his body begin to slowly untense, starting at the shoulders and working its way down, until he felt almost weightless. "Thank you… you're right. I'm sorry I—"

"It's *quite* all right. Now, tell me you didn't go and get yourself *so* tired *out* you forgot to pick up a memento of yer own?"

Maxwell silently turned back towards the way he had come, the farmhouse only a distant silhouette on the night sky. The incalculable secrets he had managed to fish out of the less-well protected archives of the SIS — or at least, the scant few photos of them — weighed heavily in his satchel.

"Not yet. I think we still have one more stop to make tonight."

Chester raised his muzzle and zipped up the worn leather flight jacket he always wore. "Yessir. Let's go make some history, kid."

The pair climbed into the helicopter. Chester went through his usual, well-practised preflight checklist with unwavering *excitement* in his voice, and within a moment, he had the rotors spun up.

The light aircraft crested over the treeline and began climbing high enough to safely tack east. "Well, Maxie boy, how goes it?"

Maxwell took one last glance back to the farmhouse from the air and sighed with relief. He could *feel* the accumulated fear and spite he'd held in his chest slowly melt into the vast night sky. "Tomorrow morning, the front page of State Affairs will be covering just a handful of the countless crimes the late Mr. Thomas Evans committed and covered up, all in the name of domestic security. *Operation Felt.* I wish I'd saved more from the archives while I could, but… well, there's some things that are… *were*… that is, I mean–"

Chester cut him off again "One step at a time, one *step* at a *time*. You're already primed to upset a whole heap 'a the right folks with this stunt. Sometimes you have just *got* to let momentum do its thing. That paper will list the Dark Dossier as a source tomorrow, and folks'll start chatterin'. If MI6 can be targeted, well then, what makes their secrets any safer? You are a real, *genuine* supervillain now, Maxwell, and don't it just feel *good*?"

The Dark Dossier felt the warmth of a satisfied smile cross his muzzle. He bared his teeth through the helicopter's bubble window. As the world passed by, it felt small enough to hold in his paws. "Yes… it does."

September 30, 2019

Maxwell grazed his thumbpad over the cheek of the mask in his paws and smiled with quiet satisfaction. "That was back when KARD was just Records, of course. Boxes and boxes of material waiting to be organised and filed away. More came in every day than we knew what to do with; soon, expansion was inevitable."

The bear slowly rose from his chair, walking to the windows that looked out onto the vast hexagonal main atrium of the Division as it stood in the present day, quietly contemplating how much it had changed even in his own shorter time with the Korps. "Mhmm… no slowing you down, though, is there, puppy?" Liam could practically feel the heat from the wolf's cheeks, even at a distance. After so many years, the bear hadn't lost his ability to charm the older man.

"Here I am, old enough to be your father, but you always know *just* how to make me feel energetic," the wolf cooed.

The bear smirked over his shoulder and tucked one heavy paw into his pant pocket. "Thanks; it's the coffee I make. You've always liked it, the mild stuff, anyhow; I remember our first date—"

Maxwell interrupted with a single crooked brow. "Date? Is that what we're calling it now?"

Liam tilted his head back with a toothy grin and closed eyes, one finger pointing outwardly from the handle of his coffee mug. "Don't interrupt me, puppy."

"Mm. Pardon me, sir," the grey-muzzled puppy lilted playfully.

"And yes, what else would you call it? I'd never had a guy willing to put six others in the hospital for me, and the flowers were very nice too. We went back to my apartment after that, remember? I made coffee, patched up your knuckles, and we worked out what to do next. I never looked back once you brought me here."

There was a quiet moment of reflection for the both of them, as the night hours of the division quietly passed. Things had come so far in both of their premierships as co-directors of KARD. Maxwell had overseen the early years and its rapid expansion through the 60s and 70s; back at Sandy Hill, and the lost Long Branch site. He'd wanted to do more, to go back to the SIS and finish the job, expose absolutely *everything* they'd been hiding... but there had simply never been enough time or resources to pull another stunt quite like that, much to his dismay. For his part, since the mid-80s, Liam had been the enthusiastic muscle behind much of the Division's field work. While Maxwell was busy working in the shadows and subtly compromising targets, the bear kicked down doors and ransacked private offices to get the dirt they were after.

The two complemented each other in so many ways, it was hard to envision a task they couldn't overcome, dismantling obstacles bit by bit and rebuilding the spoils to their own ends. And yet... there was that *name*, the one so frustrating to the wolf. *Rob Slotis.* Its owner and his motives remained a vexing mystery.

Liam turned from the window and set his empty coffee mug down on top of one of those very spoils — the battered remains of an old filing cabinet. He fondly remembered using it as a makeshift shield in a showdown with a *Superté* Hero who'd tried (and failed) to stop him getting away from a raid in a Trois-Rivières industrial park, back in 2003. "We've done incredible work, and I'm happy to be part of it. For tonight, though... André, *please* get some rest. The world will still be here tomorrow, and we'll still both be as stubborn as ever."

Maxwell returned the mask to its place on the high shelf behind his desk, nodding wearily. After a moment, he walked to the door just beside his beloved co-director and gently placed a paw on the bear's shoulder. "Thank you, for keeping an eye on me. You and our dear little, blue-scaled assistant, you both keep this old wolf sane."

Liam gave the wolf's back a gentle pat. "Of course. If anything comes up while you're sleeping, you know UI and I will keep you informed. Speaking of being kept in the loop, actually... ROSE?"

A warm voice drifted across the office from various directional speakers hidden in the walls, and in nooks of the various shelves. The AI it belonged to was capable of pinging back and forth across multiple instances over the RCG network, interfacing directly with the minds of those that wore the pink visors without a need for verbal communication; despite that, the two men tended to default to talking aloud to her. It felt more *natural*, the bear considered.

[Yes, Liam?]

"Can you make sure KARD's finest here actually makes it back to his quarters tonight, and doesn't fall asleep in one of the reading rooms? Nurse O will have *words*, if she finds out he's been sleeping in chairs again."

[Of course,] ROSE replied, a faint sound of familiar cheer in her voice.

Maxwell snickered, but he couldn't hide just how tired he really was; the wolf's eyes betrayed a bone-deep exhaustion. "I'm not made of glass, dear."

"No, but I can see right through that suave exterior, and you need some rest," replied the bear, voice low and quiet as he leaned in for a sweet kiss. "Sleep well, André."

"Until tomorrow, my dear."

Chapter 3

October 16, 2019

The spire-like stacks of books were different, this time.

Instead of disorganised piles that would surely drive a librarian mad, they filled rows of neat, uniform wooden shelves, which on closer inspection featured scarcely visible joinery; it looked almost as if they had been hewn perfectly from the trunks of impossibly tall trees. The ground, too, was different. No longer a vast flat expanse, it instead appeared with the soft swells and hollows of a forest floor — that was, if constructed not of organic matter, but instead a patchwork of undulating marble. Starlight twinkled above the dream forest of knowledge, casting a gentle glow down through an unseen canopy of papers.

Among the changes to her dreamscape, after several moments, Lexi noticed a decided absence of... *something*. The voice wasn't there; or, if it was, it was staying quiet. *Playing dumb*, even. The only sounds to be heard were the clapping echoes of her hoofsteps against the ground. The cow decided to pluck a book from one of the narrow cases, and flick through it. It was her dream, after all, she reasoned; couldn't she do what she wanted?

As it turned out, she couldn't. The pages were full of jumbled symbols and sentences that seemed to drift from one form to another, despite her best efforts to parse the contents. Lexi might have been aware she was dreaming, she realised, but perhaps wasn't quite as lucid in her mind as she'd thought. As she leafed through the volume, the sound of the pages flicking against each other carried off into the distance, at least making for a comforting white noise. As she closed the book and put it back, the spine and cover *rippled*, changing size and colour, flitting between identities in defiance of her desire for it to all make sense.

"Well… I guess I'll just keep looking for something else, then," she murmured. It occurred to her that, for whatever reason, she felt content to know that the book didn't *want* to be read.

The cow walked on deeper into the shifting surroundings of the printed forest. After some time, she noticed that the spires were getting wider — more and more resembling correctly-proportioned bookcases that might exist in the real world, though they all still rose so high she couldn't see the tops. Their arrangement gently shifted too, eventually converging into a neat grid of orderly rows and aisles. She had just reached the fourth case along a new row, when she noticed her own body start to feel… different.

She was heavier, and slower, somehow. If it wasn't for the fact that she could readily examine the bookcases and their contents around her, she no doubt would have had a difficulty realising she'd gotten taller, too. It wasn't just a few inches, either; where moments before her head might have come to the fifth shelf of a case, now she was at eye level with the seventh. The books were smaller compared to her hand, too, and—

—*Was* it her hand? It looked like hers, but the colouration was less vibrant. The auburn brindle of her fur appeared dulled, and her hoof-nailed fingers were heavy with lines and scars that she didn't recognise. It must have been her hand, she reasoned; she could control it, and she felt things through it. The sensation managed to seem both familiar and strange at the same time.

Her confused gaze drifted to the cuff of the sleeve she appeared to be wearing. It was a dark, almost-black soft fabric; in the low light, it was difficult to tell, but she thought she could see traces of a rich purple. It wasn't *just* a sleeve, either. She examined the heavy robe — almost *ceremonial*, she wasn't sure why that word came to mind — adorning her strangely tall and stocky body. The garment was snugly fitted around her apparently ample chest and hung the rest of the way down her body, fastened by a heavy belt around her middle.

In trying to get a better look at the belt, the Highland's hair fell in front of her eyes — the same way it always did, if she didn't keep it styled to one side. It too was different, a sleek, silvery grey that instantly reminded Lexi of the colour her mother's hair had gone by her mid-fifties.

Am I older? Why am I old now?

It was a strange thing to think, but stranger still was the fact that it didn't really seem to bother the cow. At least, not in the way she imagined it should? She didn't feel as if she'd blinked and lost years without realising it; no, she felt content. *Accomplished*, even, like she'd done so many more things than she could even remember.

In the waking world, there had been a lot of times when she couldn't imagine being older, even a little bit. The thought wasn't unpleasant; it was just impossible to picture. She remembered the last year of high school, where one of the last assignments her tutor had given the class was to write where they all saw themselves in the future; in two years, in five, and in ten. Two years had been easy for Lexi — she'd be finishing college — but after that, she didn't know. The age of twenty had seemed incomprehensible to her but she had eventually reached it. The years kept coming after that, too, but getting older still seemed unlikely to her. Not undesirable; *unlikely*.

A reflective melancholy sank through the bovine's body and grounded her more firmly in the dream world, complete with the minor aches and pains that her brain had apparently seen fit to furnish her aged frame with. Lexi turned her hand over in front of her face, looking again at the small scars and marks of age. "It's not so bad," she caught herself saying. Her voice was low, warm and husky, to her pleasant realisation. "Don't sound too bad, either."

A different voice called out behind the cow — one apparently full of the anxious nerves that she'd misplaced, by the sound of it. "Hello?"

Time stood still. When Lexi turned her head, her upper body dragged with it, lagging behind slightly. She once again felt herself scatter into a spectrum of *moments*, all just slightly out of sync with one another; in the jittering intersection, her breathing grew shallow and impossibly loud until it blared into a relentless static. The bookcases about her flashed out of existence, as the entire dreamscape shifted and blinked in and out like a bad screen input. Finally, everything went blank… with the exception of those oddly twinkling stars, high above.

There was nothing, and Lexi was suddenly very *alone* in the nothing. The white noise faded away to the sound of early fall winds whipping through bare branches.

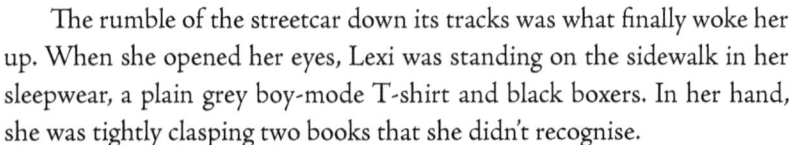

The rumble of the streetcar down its tracks was what finally woke her up. When she opened her eyes, Lexi was standing on the sidewalk in her sleepwear, a plain grey boy-mode T-shirt and black boxers. In her hand, she was tightly clasping two books that she didn't recognise.

Her head tried its best to make sense of the situation. The last thing the cow could remember was getting into bed, and here she was standing outside, bare-hoofed and starting to shake with an uneasy anxiety as a knot tied itself in her guts. It was dark out, and the light from the passing carriages of the light rail train briefly illuminated the street sign nearby. The Highland knew the street name, and the shape of the building it was next to; over the past few weeks, she'd grown at least somewhat familiar with the local area… but knowing where she was didn't comfort her much, considering she had no idea how she'd gotten there.

Drac's condo was a block away, but getting into the building would be hard without the spare key fob that her boyfriend had given her. What if she was trapped out on the street all morning? What if something happened to her on the way home? This had to be a dream, still; it *had* to be. Without wanting to think about it anymore, she started pacing as quickly as she could through the crisp early morning air, eyes fixed on the corner she'd need to turn in order to get back to the midrise she'd been calling home for the last handful of weeks.

The first leaves of fall blew across the asphalt with a light breeze, briefly making the bovine twitch nervously before she remembered that, yes, it *was* normal to hear sounds other than the thumping beat of her own heart. Lexi turned the corner, grateful there wasn't anyone else awake out on the streets and began shifting her pace into a frantic sprint for the door. She tried to ignore the feeling of grit between her split hooves with every step.

Everything will be okay, everything will be okay, you can just wait in the vestibule until someone leaves for work; no need to buzz the apartment and wake Drac up in a panic. Or I can wait until the cleaner arrives. You've seen her a few times, she'll let you in! You can just say you heard a noise and went to investigate but got locked out because you were sleepy and forgot your fob!

Lexi scrambled to keep her thoughts as calm as possible, but nothing could quite prepare her for what she saw as she got into the condo's small vestibule. The internal door that granted access to the lobby had been propped open with a shoe — one of *her* shoes. She stared at the unsettling sight for a long, hard second. Only when she went to push the door open with one hand, and pick the footwear up, did she remember she was still holding the two books that had apparently materialised in her sleep.

Both looked used, their perfect-bound spines showing the careless creases of more than one read. One seemed to be a reference guide for foraging — specifically, Ontario mushrooms and wild plants. The other looked a lot more technical and appeared to be some sort of introductory textbook to amateur radio operation. The cover for the foraging guide looked familiar, and with another brief moment, Lexi realised where the two books had come from. She'd walked past a few little free libraries in the neighbourhood a few days ago — the kind that the locals had set up, on a take-one leave-one honour system — and remembered the brightly-coloured illustrated toadstool on the spine of the field guide. She didn't recognise the other one, but that mattered less, compared to the fact her shoe was propping the door open.

Lexi took a deep breath and considered the situation logically. If she'd been sleepwalking, she probably wouldn't have had the good sense to intentionally prop the door like that, nor the courtesy to avoid disturbing Drac or anyone else. On the other hand, she thought, maybe this was all pure coincidence? What if she *had* been sleepwalking, put her shoes on, and happened to lose one in the doorway by sheer unconscious accident? The other might be in a hedge, for all she knew. The cow stacked both books in one hand, nudged the door open with a hip, and picked up the scuffed red and white canvas shoe, before making her way in a daze to the elevator.

She got out on her floor and quietly made her way back to their apartment. She tried the handle as silently as she could manage, and found it unlocked; when she cautiously pushed inwards, the only sound to be heard was that of her dragon boyfriend's faint snoring. The cow closed the door silently behind her and looked down at the shoe rack. Her other shoe was still there, undisturbed. She made them a pair again, and for a moment, was at a loss about what to do with the books. The kitchen counter was as clear as any other surface and would have to do.

Lexi slinked into the bathroom and flicked the light on. She splashed a little water from the faucet on her face, thinking that maybe it would help ground her... but it only succeeded in making her face wet. It did at least give her something else to focus on as she grabbed her towel and patted her fur dry, and that in itself gave her a moment to finally breathe.

The dream came back to the forefront of her mind, but something about the recollection seemed off. She could feel a clawing itch behind her eyes as she tried to remember where the voice that said Hello had come from, or what its owner looked like, but she couldn't focus; there was too much *static* in her head getting in the way, like trying to identify a figure on the TV through terribly bad signal. Maybe there was a shape there, or maybe there wasn't. Maybe it was simple pattern recognition, and she was just imagining forms in an abstract mass of visual noise. It *was* only a dream, she told herself — but once again, that mattered less, compared to the fact of her sleepwalking. The bovine flicked the light off again and slowly made her way through the darkness to the bedroom, crawling back into bed.

Drac stirred slightly and rolled over. It rocked the entire bed frame; he was clearly too tall for its modest dimensions, but also too comfortably frugal to replace it with something bigger. "Mhmm... s'up, honey... Were you in the bathroom?"

Lexi tucked herself in and petted the dragon's flank, nestling under one of their wings before she sighed, trying to blink away the residual anxiety. "Yeah. Bathroom. Go back to sleep, honey."

Drac's voice rumbled out over his toast from across the small kitchen's island unit. "You look tired as hell. Did you not sleep at all last night?"

Lexi sleepily rolled a spoonful of porridge about in her maw and swallowed, taking a moment to pour just a little more maple syrup into the bowl in front of her. "I did! Sort of."

Drac raised a horn-studded brow with their familiar, honest concern. "It's been weeks, honey. I really hope you start getting some actual, restful sleep soon…"

The cow spooned another heap of porridge into her mouth and sighed through her nose just a little, speaking with her mouth full and her head even fuller. "Promise you won't get mad?" She paused, just long enough to swallow. "I must have been sleepwalking last night. It started with a weird dream about being in a strange place… my body changing a bit too, I think? I don't remember too much. Then there was this *voice*, and I turned around to see who was there. That was when I woke up."

Drac breathed in with his whole chest, and nodded along slowly, easily slipping the remaining slice of toast into his maw whole. "Was that when *I* woke up? I remember you going to the bathroom…"

"No, I… I mean, I left the building. I don't know how far I went, exactly, but at the very least down the street," the bovine replied, sheepishly looking down the length of the narrow condo to their unit door.

Drac's scales seemed to shift in a noticeable shock, pinning back more tightly against their cheeks and jawline as they paced around the island unit. "Holy shit, really? How did — are you okay? You didn't get hurt or anything, did you?" Their digits, claws included, carefully patted down the cow's arms as they checked her over for any signs of injury.

"No, no, I'm fine." Lexi's voice slunk into a dismissiveness that felt all too familiar, and realising it, she bit the inside of her cheek as a light personal punishment for falling into old habits. "I think I just took a couple of books from one of the free little libraries down the street? I had them in my hands when the LRT going past woke me up." It wasn't quite full disclosure of how fully *shaken* the cow had been in the moment, but it at least moved the conversation towards that direction.

Heavy arms that betrayed the dragon's strength wrapped oh-so-delicately around the bovine. He pulled her against his chest in a loving embrace that left his chin resting neatly between the bases of her angular horns. "Jesus! You could have been hit by the fucking train! I didn't realise you'd left the building at all." Drac pulled himself back from the hug, hands resting firmly on Lexi's shoulders as a question perched on his tongue. "… Wait, how did you get back in, then?"

"Despite being asleep, apparently I had the faculties to prop the door open," Lexi said with bemusement, faintly impressed with herself.

The dragon rubbed burly thumbs across the front of their cow's shoulders and let their tense frame sink down with a sigh that trailed into a smirk. "Too smart *and* nimble for your own good. Christ, I'm just glad you're okay."

"Well, guess that just means I need to be restrained overnight, huh, big guy?" She deflected, *almost* expertly — old emotional habits died hard, and if there was one thing she knew, it was that a well-timed sex joke could remove all tension.

"*Hah!*" the dragon snorted out. Drac placed a soft kiss on Lexi's cheek, offering her a smile. "Okay, how about we go to the Shoppers or somewhere today, and pick up some sleeping pills? Make sure you get a real good rest tonight. We can even make a trip of it."

Lexi turned back to the bowl to finish her porridge, getting a glob with a bit more syrup in it than she was expecting; she had to quickly swallow, lest the sweetness overpower a palate which reliably demanded all food walk the fine line between sweet and savoury. "Mmm. Yeah, that sounds like a good idea... I think I could do with a distraction."

"Okay, why don't we go to that new strip mall with the fancy grocery store on Hook Street? A real domestic little treat — maybe get you out of the house long enough to stop dwelling on what's going on in the UK. I was working remote today, anyway, so it's not like I can't bump off an hour now and work it later," Drac offered.

Since she'd arrived in Canada, there hadn't been a day that Lexi didn't scroll through feeds of the news back home with quiet despair. Moves by her government to upend what few legal protections for trans people there were, attacks on the poor and barely functional welfare state... and the whole time, craven austerity apologists insisting that another few years of tightening the national belt was just what the country needed to get back on its feet.

She didn't know why she kept looking. Perhaps she hoped that there would be a change some day, something that she could root for and cheer on, even from the outside. Deep down, though, she knew the wish was futile. The UK was a country in the desperate grip of sneering elites who had almost utterly convinced the public that things were *meant* to be miserable. No country had both quite as much institutional rot and the endless capacity to excuse it as the UK, she thought wearily.

A bitter feeling of guilt at *escaping* — the simple fact of not being there to suffer, alongside everyone else — came riding up Lexi's throat, and sat with a weighty presence until she could swallow it down again. Her mother and sister had made peace with the fact the country would never improve, but Lexi still felt bad, leaving for greener pastures. Maybe... maybe, when things were more settled and stable, if she could get a job, she could invite them both over to Canada. She could try to sell them on leaving that miserable island behind, too.

She remembered to smile and obscure the feelings, though. "Oh, I love mundane domesticity! Let me grab a hoodie first? It was kind of cold outside this morning." She rinsed out her bowl and made her way to the walk-in closet via the bedroom, knowing that Drac intended to leave right that moment. His quirks were numerous and lovable, and needing to act on a thought as soon as it happened was just one of them. The cow had always admired her boyfriend's ability to just put down tracks and start *doing* something without the herculean effort it often took her.

The closet was tiny, and tightly packed with the couple's few lifelong possessions. She rummaged through her suitcase as neatly as she could, pulling her hoodie out from the bottom, quietly ashamed that she still hadn't found the energy to fully unpack her tiny luggage. It wasn't as if she hadn't had the time to do it, just that there were so many other things that enticed her attention, healthily or not. *Later*, she thought; that could be another useful distraction, maybe.

Lexi zipped the hoodie up and paced back to her boyfriend, who was already in his shoes and waiting by the unit's door — exactly as she expected him to be.

"Up next, boy, do we have a treat for you folks — that's right, we're talking to local super, the *Silver Bullet*, about his recent triumph over the Duke Street bike theft ring. Join us after these messages for that exclusive interview!" The car radio's reception was clear, although a mean autumn wind whipping down the length of King Street muffled the audio a little.

"A super who broke up a crime ring of bike thieves? That almost sounds quaint," Lexi huffed sardonically. "Isn't that more the kind of thing that police would handle?"

The dragon in the driver's seat came to a stop behind a growing queue of cars at the light ahead and let out a sigh heavy with familiarity. "I mean, Silver Bullet is PHL, an Ontario's Heroes second-stringer; he may as well be police. He's got a history of excessive force, assault, and harassment, so I wouldn't be too surprised if 'crime ring' is just code for 'loosely affiliated homeless folks' who were just trying to make some money to get by."

Lexi looked over with a distinct lack of surprise. She tutted to herself as the car started to move through the intersection, wishing deeply for the world to not be a disappointing mess for just a *single* second. She felt equal parts quietly thankful she wasn't the one facing off against a superpowered cop, and guilty that she was lucky enough to not be. She'd never been in trouble with the police, in fact, but the thought of even being *questioned* terrified her. That was the point, she had supposed for years; scared straight, and all that. She was all too aware that having done nothing wrong might not stop a cop with a chip on their shoulder from *finding* something to get pissy about. "Figures. Let me guess, no news coverage of his past bullshit? Or has it all just been memory-holed?"

"Memory-holed," Drac confirmed matter-of-factly as he made the turn onto Hook Street and pulled into the uncrowded strip mall. "He's not exactly a media favourite, but no one's calling him out on anything, either."

As much as Lexi wanted to, there didn't seem much point in saying anything; these situations only ever led to her silently seething, getting more and more mad. *Of course*, no one in the local press was holding a local Hero to account for his past crimes; he probably had the entire police department backing him up, and if he didn't, any dissenters would no doubt be quietly dealt with.

As she stepped out of the parked car, the strip mall was quiet, and only a handful of souls dared brave the autumnal winds to explore it. Most of the horseshoe-shaped new development's storefronts still lacked tenants; there was a lone shawarma place at one end, and a BBQ joint a few doors down from it. Next to that was an off-brand dollar store, and then the chain grocery store. A little further down the row, though, was something else: the Hook Book Nook. The small storefront was dim, but visible through the windows seemed to be a cluttered state of frozen move-in and setup.

Something in her itched. Lexi felt her body being pulled towards the store. Drac had already started making their way towards the market, and she *had* been following them… right up until she caught sight of the bookstore. Her feet carried her across the small grass verge that separated one strip of parking spots from another; the bovine was only faintly aware of what she was doing, and that her mind should be elsewhere at that moment yet couldn't stop herself. She stepped up onto the sidewalk, feeling her hands reach out in front of her without any mental input. Her reflection in the store window came into view, and with it, a vacant expression on her muzzle she hardly recognised. She looked driven — but by what, she didn't know.

Past her reflection and through the glass, Lexi could see shelves upon shelves of old books, stacked tall and deep into the unit. Some must have been library discards or charity donations, judging by the condition of their covers. Others appeared new, or at least well-cared for. Boxes and plastic totes were strewn across the floor, some filled with still more stock. She wanted to be *in there*; she wanted to be able to search through the collection.

Her trance took her to the door, and her hands reached to try the push-bar handle, but it was locked. Something inside her screamed that she had to get *inside*, and through a descending fog of conflicting senses, Lexi couldn't disagree with the internal demand. Maybe she could find another way in if she went around—

A hand of gold scales and hard talons came down firmly on her shoulder, pushing her weight through her arm into the door, and making it clack inside its metal frame. "Lexi, honey, what are you *doing*? Are you okay?"

The Highland felt her soul tightly compact back into her body, like someone stuffing clothes into a too-small suitcase, and sitting on it to force the zipper shut. She shuddered with unease, as her spatial awareness adjusted, too. All too slowly, she managed to force out a few words. "Yeah? I'm—"

"What's going on?" Drac insisted, stroking the cow's arm to comfort her.

Lexi felt the muddled coldness of processing fill her mind. *Deflect. Nothing can be wrong. Don't burden him.* She swallowed and gave a faint half-smile. Theatre kid she might have been, she never had much practice playing a ditz. "Oh, sorry! I sort of zoned out. Must still be tired, I guess. Hah, didn't even realise the place wasn't open yet!"

She very carefully neglected to mention the part where she'd *dissociated entirely*, and had been watching her actions helplessly, a passenger in her own body. The tug from deep in her chest towards something in the unopened store persisted, like a magnetic attraction, but she had at least regained control of her faculties. She could work with that; she'd have to.

Drac pulled her into a hug. "Let's get inside and out of the wind. I figure tonight we'll just watch a movie and have some pizza, maybe. Just chill, and focus on keeping you away from anything stressful, okay?"

The hug helped with her anxiety a little, but the cow still felt the faint tell-tale burn in the corner of her eyes, the one that warned tears would be on their way very soon if she didn't bottle them up. She steeled herself, and moved a hand up to clasp the dragon's, trying her best to reassure them that she felt fine. "That sounds good."

The pair walked back across the parking lot and into the grocery store in silence together, with the dragon leading the way through the aisles as they methodically filled a basket with essentials (and a few treats). It wasn't until they reached the pharmacy to look for sleeping pills that Drac slowly reopened the conversation.

"I was thinking… maybe things just feel a little bit in limbo right now, you know? You're still waiting for your diploma to turn up, you've got one foot back in the UK keeping up with your mom and your sister, we don't know what's going to happen with visa extension stuff. It must be pretty paralysing."

He's right, Lexi pondered. She existed in an awkward half-world, where she knew what she was working towards, but couldn't yet do anything about it. She was playing the waiting game, and she'd never been good at it — not because she was impatient, but because she needed to be *doing something* to not let the intrusive thoughts win. There wasn't much that consistently kept her occupied and distracted, and all the while, the stress of the various *unknowns* made her skull itch. She would run out of her HRT in another couple of months, the paperwork to apply for a work permit would need to be filed soon too, and though she and the dragon had priced it all out ahead of time, *what if?*

What if she couldn't get a job quickly enough, to make back the money they'd be spending on an immigration lawyer? What if the work permit application was rejected? She'd have to go back to the UK, as a semi-out trans person. She might even have to go back in the closet, to make getting a job easier. Or... or what if she couldn't get hormones, here in Canada? She'd been obtaining hers back home through barely-legal means to begin with, so it wasn't as if she could just hand over a prescription history, if she was asked. What if—

"—What if we went somewhere this weekend? Did some touristy stuff to keep you occupied? We could maybe hang around Toronto for a couple days. Get a hotel, try some fun food places, that kind of thing?" Drac finished their sentence, neatly cutting through the white noise of Lexi's inner monologue while dropping a store-brand pack of sleep aids into the basket.

Don't be a burden, don't be a burden, don't be a burden. That's a two-hour trip each way! The thought rattled around her head, until she could think of a way to excuse herself from the offer. "That sounds nice, but that's a lot of driving. I know you hate the 401, so I wouldn't want to put you through that. Plus, I mean... hotels can't be cheap in the city, right?"

He nodded an acknowledgement and gave a mild shrug in response. "Well, sure, but it would be nice, right? That's really all that matters."

Lexi damned Drac's cool dismissal. How they could be so relaxed about sacrificing time and energy on her like that was still alien. Somehow she felt undeserving, but the proverbial 'So what?' was hard to argue with. She was being outwitted into taking time for herself. Beyond that, though — and an easier pill for the Highland to swallow — was that there were two people in this relationship. If Drac wanted to get away as well, she wasn't about to protest. This could be for *them,* and that made accepting the offer much less guilt-inducing. "Okay! Saturday, then?"

The pair rounded the corner to the self-checkouts, but on the way, Lexi's eye was caught by a headline peeking out from a newspaper rack. "X MARKS THE ROT," proclaimed the tabloid, adding "Veteran Villain leaves careless clue in recent document dump." She recognised the photo that accompanied the annoying alliteration as the same one Drac had shown her weeks ago. It was a closeup of the mistyped Xs on the document list, a feature that had, apparently, since become front page-worthy. The Highland scanned a few lines from the body of text as she walked by but nothing new or interesting jumped out at her. The quoted experts had come to the same conclusion as she'd suspected — just an artefact of a typewriter in need of some love. Sure, not many people still used typewriters, but it wasn't as if the Ontario Provincial Police were going to go door to door checking the stuck keys on each one.

Must be a slow news day, Lexi shrugged to herself. She joined her boyfriend at the checkouts and paid up.

The drive back to the condo was filled with idle chatter about the things they could do on a short-notice weekend break, but they didn't get much further than deciding on one or two restaurants they'd like to try. Neither really were the touristy type, after all.

Lexi was the first to spot the brown envelope leaning against their unit's door as she stepped off the condo building's elevator. Even at a distance down the hall, she recognised the red of her home country's first-class stamps.

"Oh, is that…" Drac garbled, his mouth busy finishing off the last bites of a sandwich they picked up at the grocery store's deli.

The cow gave a nod, and bent down to pick it up, tucking it between her chest and the grocery bag she carried. Once inside, Lexi ensured the groceries got put away, first, in an attempt to seem less full of anticipation than she actually was. *Years* had built to receiving this one bit of paper. Even if she didn't think she'd get much use out of it in Canada, it was at least one less loose end to tie up; the degree had led to some depressing realisations, and the work to get through it had embittered her tremendously, but it was still an *achievement*. It was something her mom and her sister would say they were proud of her for getting, it was almost something she could be proud of too.

She already knew her results; she'd found those out back in August. The diploma, however — the physical *thing* — mattered in a different way. It was proof that she had, and could, dedicate herself so thoroughly to something.

With the last of the groceries away, and Drac smiling to themself, Lexi returned to the envelope that she had laid on the kitchen counter.

"It's funny," she said, "it feels lighter than I expected it to. Something so small, but it's six years of hard work."

Drac only nodded enthusiastically. She knew the novelty had long since worn off for him since he'd received his own, but he was excited that Lexi was excited.

The cow turned the envelope over in her hands and stopped. She hadn't noticed it at first, but the name that it was addressed to was wrong. It was her deadname. She'd only told a handful of people about her new name, of course, but among those in the know should have been her university's records department. She'd even had to send in a formal declaration that she was now going by Lexi.

Discomfort welled in her heart, but she did a good job of hiding it. Maybe she'd just never bothered to correct the name on the postal address she had logged with the university? That sort of oversight happened all the time, she reminded herself. Over a decade past her parents' divorce and the closing of all their joint accounts, Mom was still getting letters from the bank addressed to "Mr. & Mrs. Hayes."

Lexi opened the envelope and pulled out the diploma. It was beige, with the university's emblem embossed in the top corner, official seals present along the bottom, and a signature that the Highland could barely make out. It was just how she imagined it. Except —

This certificate is awarded to MICHAEL R. HAYES in recognition of their successful completion of a BSc in ENVIRONMENTAL ENGINEERING with Distinction on JULY 10TH, 2019, it read.

There was more text below that, but Lexi didn't bother reading it. The name was wrong *on the diploma*, too.

"I did everything they asked…" she said, her voice quiet, and broken. "I sent off the declaration, and answered questions about my gender, and proved it was me and… and they *still* put the wrong name on it. They told me that this would be correct. They *told* me!"

Drac stepped in by her side and said nothing. They offered a comforting hug with one arm, but Lexi stood immovably fixed on the paper in her hands.

Her chest began to burn with a deep rage that spilled out into her arms, causing them to tense. She fought against the urge to just crumple up the damn thing. "I... I have a piece of paper that belongs to me... in a name I don't... I don't *want!*"

Lexi picked the envelope up without a further word, slipped the diploma back inside it, and laid it address-side up on the counter. The cow walked out from under her boyfriend's wing and arm, grabbed a marker from its place amid the collection of pens on Drac's desk, and came back to the envelope.

She crossed out her deadname with a single stroke in thick black ink — and then again, and again, and *again*. The tip of the marker squeaked across the shiny printed label's surface with the force put to it, transferring her anger as calmly and as pointedly as she could. Tears welled in her eyes, rolling off her soft cheeks. Her nostrils flared through laboured huffs of *hate*, and finally she threw herself over the envelope, scrawling and scratching her feelings in huge messy letters, over and over, until the cheap plastic of the marker's body shattered in her clenched fist:

HE'S DEAD. I KILLED HIM.

Lexi permitted herself a saddened, lowing wail — just one — before tucking the anger back inside, where it belonged. She looked at her handiwork and heaved a long, frustrated breath through her snout. The bovine stared at the reminder of her home country's pervasively casual *contempt* for trans people, disinclined to offer even the most basic respect even when jumping through the hoops put in their path.

The diploma was nothing, really. It didn't even matter. She wasn't likely to get a job in the industry, and even if she did, she knew she'd never be happy with it; so many in the environmental circuit had to contend with perpetually depressing news of their field yet were pressured to be all smiles by their institutions and minders.

No, none of it mattered. Not the diploma, not what her country thought of her, and especially not her old name. It had belonged to a frightened man that she didn't recognise anymore. A man whom she'd *buried*. She might have been frightened of the many unknowns in her life, but she wasn't *scared* of herself, like he had been. Even if she kept a few aspects of herself hidden in an attempt to make things easier — simple pragmatism — it wasn't the same. It couldn't be.

Finally, sniffling and breath catching in her throat, Lexi let herself sink into her boyfriend's arms for a good, long *proper* cry.

Chapter 4

December 25, 1960

Maxwell's hand grasped at the bitterly cold steel railing running up the apartment building's stairs. The elevator — visible through its mesh cage in the centre of the stairwell — had been out of service for weeks, and he felt exhausted, cold, and *weak*. Climbing the full flight upwards was the last thing he'd wanted, but he considered that his next squat might be more forgiving. His time in this building, in this city, was probably coming to an end one way or another; it would be better if he moved on, sooner rather than later.

The wolf silently stared down the hallway at the next landing, trying to gauge whether he was on the right floor. He'd lost count of how many storeys he'd climbed in his sleep-deprived state and squinted at a patch of exposed brickwork on the left wall as he staggered forward. This was definitely the right floor; he'd recognise that particular sign of neglect anywhere. He could have simply read the number on the wall, but reading was something he tried to avoid wherever possible. He didn't want to risk another sleepwalking accident that would transfer his current address into someone's mind. It was far safer to just avoid engaging with written information altogether. It didn't stop him sleepwalking, of course; that was what the sleeping pills and pilfered alcohol were for. If anything, depriving himself of reading made the itch worse, but he told himself it was better than walking around as a loaded weapon.

Somehow, he found his way to the apartment door, and fumbled with the key in the lock, his body swaying slightly. Finally inside, Maxwell shut the door behind him. He slid the deadbolt across, then the chain lock he'd installed himself, and finally turned the latch to lock the door from the inside.

As far as any other resident of the building was concerned, Maxwell was just a quiet new neighbour. In reality, his apartment had previously been condemned, the owner found dead months ago after an unfortunate accident, and the key to the door had mysteriously gone missing during the police investigation. The wolf had nothing to do with the death, but he had been keeping as low a public profile as he possibly could for years; he certainly wasn't above living in a dead man's apartment. At least, until someone else (next of kin or otherwise) tried to gain entry.

There wasn't any proper furniture to speak of inside, just a few overturned milk crates as stools, a single folding steel chair that Maxwell had fished out from a dumpster, and a makeshift bedroll. The kitchenette's tiny, ancient hotplate and electric kettle were barely functional, but it didn't matter; the wolf barely ate, anyway.

Maxwell's head started to swirl. The empty stomach he'd been nursing for the last two days was starting to catch up to him, or maybe it was just the alcohol. It didn't really matter. Either way, it just made passing out easier. The wolf didn't strip out of his jacket; it was far too cold for that, even with the heat in the apartment still working, albeit about as poorly as the gurgling, ever-dripping faucets did.

He pulled back the salvaged quilt on top of the bedroll and removed the white Halloween half-mask from his sleeping arrangements. It had been a few weeks since he'd last struck as a vigilante. The wolf had been dubbed "The Dark Dossier" by some newspaper a while ago, and though Maxwell couldn't bring himself to use the moniker personally, the police and press had no such hesitancy. He could simply change the costume, of course... but it would be a lie to say there wasn't a faint thrill to being recognised. Being *notorious*.

Maxwell put the mask down and slid himself under the thin quilt. It would be another few weeks before he could muster up the strength to carry out another masked hit on some well-deserving target. Maybe the owner of the machine parts plant a few blocks away who'd recently laid off a bunch of workers, he mused. The papers were already accusing the wolf of six shades of communism for what he did to that factory owner in Chicago; another, similar stunt would hardly make him any *more* infamous.

Besides, no one knew who the Dark Dossier was. He was just a figure in a long coat and a cheap mask, carrying out acts of espionage and blackmail. He pocketed enough lifted funds along the way to mostly tide himself over, but his actions also improved things for others in *some* small way. A contemporary Robin Hood he was not; he just needed to survive. Still, it was hard not to be choosy about who he targeted.

The apartment was deafeningly silent for a long while. Hunkering down in the chill night, Maxwell waited for sleep to take him.

He soon slipped into his usual restless nightmares of the night he lost his father, the smell of gunpowder and the sound of angry yells from rough men who wanted their heads rocking his sleep. His father refused to give up, protecting the boy to the end. The events played out as they always did, being bundled out of the window by the older wolf, noticing how his old man was bleeding, and then hearing those final words.

I love you, now run.

Maxwell jolted upright, launching himself backwards against the corner like a scared pup. He never could sleep well, and it was usually the memory of gunshots in the dream that hurled him awake. He scanned the room in an instinctual panic. Normally there would be nothing but his anxiety in the room with him, but—

A dark figure stood several feet away in the shadowy corner of the room, far from the dim city lights trickling in through the window — short, lithe, clad in something sleek and black with their face covered. The only prominent feature was the curled horns, betraying the goat's pedigree.

Maxwell felt his heart race and his breathing fail. He silently prayed that this was all just another nightmare, because if it *wasn't*, then someone had finally found him. CIA, SIS, it didn't matter anymore. Whoever they were, they'd entered silently; hell, they might have been in the apartment before he even got home. They were probably going to kill him, there and then — and if they *weren't*, they'd take him in just to beat every goddamn secret out of him first. His past had finally caught up to him.

And then the figure spoke, in clear, perfect French, with just the hint of a rural accent: "Tu as *toujours* eu le sommeil léger, André."

Playing dumb, perhaps too dumb, Maxwell replied in plain English. His own accent was muted, something the SIS had beaten into him; the result resembled some strange blend of British Received Pronunciation and casual American English, with only a few notable lilts. "How do you know my name?"

The figure tilted its head curiously and crossed its arms to match. "Well now, I'm glad you still understand your native tongue, even if you don't speak it anymore." The voice was... soft. Gentle, even. Its owner almost sounded playful, and a little parental, but there was a distinctly gravelly *bitterness* to it too.

Still nervous, the wolf pushed his back to the wall to steady himself, kicking off the floor with what little strength he could muster. He had to get upright, had to get ready to *defend* himself — not that he suspected it would be of much use. He was physically very much a wreck. "Who are you? Who sent you? I know you're here to finish me, so why the games!"

A black-booted hoof stepped into the shallow light coming in through the window, and the figure pulled down the scarf obscuring its dark face. "You are safe. I'm not here to hurt you. I'm someone who has been looking for you for a very, *very* long time. And I am so relieved to have finally found you."

The voice started to sound familiar, but Maxwell refused to believe what his ears were hearing. He could disbelieve his eyes plenty — especially with his usual self-medication in mind — but he'd never before experienced auditory hallucinations. "... Petit?"

"*Oui.*"

"H-how can you be here? They told me you—"

The goat formerly known to Maxwell as 'Little' gave a soft, slow affirmative nod, the sparkle of a sympathetic tear forming in the corner of his eye. "They told you I was dead. That makes an unfortunate amount of sense. I vanished off nearly every radar after the war — and not by accident, either. But it really is me, André."

Maxwell didn't even wait for the invitation. He threw himself forward to pull the man into a tight embrace and began to sob uncontrollably. He buried his face into the short goat's neck, and his paws threatened to never let go.

Little returned the hug, his gloved hands mournfully shrinking away after brushing over the wolf's malnourished, bony rib cage. "I am here, my boy, I am here. It's okay. Everything is going to be just fine. I'm only sorry it took so long."

The pair stood there in each other's arms for what felt like hours, until finally the wolf could bear to pry himself away, mostly in disbelief. "H-how did you find me?"

"My partner and I have been staking out your apartment for a week now, but we've been following your trail as the Dark Dossier for a while. Truthfully, I first tried to catch up to you in Boston but... well..." the goat offered, drying his eyes with the back of a sleeve.

Boston was a long time ago, and the wolf didn't care to remember any of what had happened there. He couldn't stop himself from asking, nonetheless. "You were in Boston?"

"Regrettably, not soon enough, but yes. We never got to you in time, and you kept a very low profile for a while... but now is as good a time as any to give you this. Happy Christmas, I suppose." Little produced a small strip of yellowed paper from one of the many pouches around his belt. The object was folded neatly into a square and speckled with age.

Maxwell recognised the one torn edge and felt his heart flutter in disbelief. He reached out, claw tips pinching together to delicately, reverently take the small scrap and unfold it. It was a letterhead, torn from the document it once introduced, adorned with neat markings that betrayed the small government office it belonged to. Below the header, just above the tear line, was a single sentence punched hard into the paper by a typist with urgency: RIEN QUE POUR VOS YEUX — *for your eyes only*.

Across from the typed words was something the wolf didn't remember — neat cursive, a firm and simple statement. *Family does not give up.*

"I have been waiting to give that back to you for some years now. I never gave up looking for you, or trying to find a way to make contact, though there were a few years I had to go underground," the goat revealed. Something in one of his belt pockets made a faint beeping sound, and he quickly pulled a palm-sized black something from one of the other pouches, extending its antenna. Little held the device close to his mouth and spoke clearly: "Call received, Chester. Go ahead."

The voice on the other side of the line washed through with a soft drawl that carried an urgency to it. "Well, I *do* not mean to alarm you, but I just picked up some police chatter; it *appears* as though our presence here coulda been noticed. We should make a move here, quite soon, I reckon."

The goat cursed under his breath, confirming over his comms device that he'd heard and understood the frustrating news before holstering it again. "I don't mean to hurry this along, boy, but I need an answer now. I have been part of a larger organisation for some time. Like the resistance, but… different. I wasn't so much recruited, as I was in the right place at the right time. I'm a *villain*, André, and if you want, we can protect you and take you in. Shelter, food, family – that's why I came here. Not just to say hello, but to offer you a home. If you want, there's a seat in the helicopter on the roof for you, but I need that answer now."

There was no hesitation in Maxwell's voice. "I want to go with you." If Little had come for him, after *everything* he must have gone through… there wasn't a chance in hell Maxwell could turn the offer down.

A familiar smile crossed the goat's muzzle, and pinched at his cheeks. "Good. Let's get you home, then."

Maxwell stuffed the letterhead into his jacket pocket and picked up his mask, racing to the door with only a slight stumble, unfastening the various locks. Once the pair were out in the hall, Little led the way; the goat took Maxwell by the hand, guiding him up the stairs to the roof. There — as promised — was a helicopter, painted a sleek black with a neat magenta stripe down one side.

Little made sure the wolf got seated first, then introduced his partner from the cockpit. "André, this is Swashplate, but you can call him Chester. Chester already knows all about you; he's been my partner for this whole operation, and a good pilot."

The hyena in the ratty bomber jacket calmly kept his muzzle perfectly forward, not taking his eyes off his instruments for a second. "Pleased to meet'cha face to face, son, as it were. Now, I understand you had a little to eat but a *whole* dang lot to drink, so… there's a puke bag under the seat, there. You *use* that, if need be, all right? We are gonna be moving *real* quick for a bit."

Before Maxwell could ask exactly what constituted 'quick', Chester demonstrated first-hand, as the helicopter took off and leaned into the frigid night air. The wolf thankfully managed to keep the contents of his stomach in place, but the motions of the helicopter weren't the only factor making it challenging. A nervousness had started to creep into his body, as he gave his situation a second thought. He realised that although he knew the goat fondly, he hadn't seen him in years. Moreover, if an organisation had a *helicopter*, and the means to spy on him, they were serious about their villainy. He felt foolish for forsaking his usual prudence, but then, he was still at least a *little* drunk. Tentatively, he turned to Little and tried to speak, but the whir of the engine made communicating impossible.

As the goat saw the wolf try to talk over the noise, he held up a single finger, using the other hand to pull down a headset from an overhead strap — the same kind both he and the hyena pilot were already wearing, Maxwell realised. He waited intentionally until the headset was on and secure before speaking over the crackly internal comms system.

"Who are you with?"

"Korps, if you've heard of them," the goat replied, holding his hand over the wolf's reassuringly. "They're based out of Canada. When I joined, there were already a few familiar faces working on their intelligence efforts. People we knew only by codenames, back during the occupation. They recruited a lot of people like me and Chester."

Maxwell had heard of the Korps, but only insofar as they were apparently an organised group — not that they would have counted among their members anyone that he might recognise. "Resistance? Socialists? Spies?"

Chester chimed in over the headset from up front, his smirk audible even amidst the static. "Gay! But, well, it turns *out* there's an awful lot of overlap between intelligence operatives and gay communists — in that they always seem to end up *over* a *lap*, if ya' ask them politely."

The goat stifled a snort with a gentle eye roll. "You don't have to be, of course. A lot of queers have to be quiet about it out in the world, but it happens there's a lot of us, and we have a common cause. You know as well as I do that information is a powerful tool. I think when you see the collection we've started to build… you'll feel at home. I'm one of the heads of the Records team — it's a combination position. Sorting, analysing, and storing intelligence for use by the wider organisation. It's a busy job; there's always more to do than we can keep on top of these days, so I'd be glad for the extra hands. You don't have to be out in the field if you don't want to. I'd understand if you didn't. Either way, there'll be an adjustment period, I'm sure. But I'll be there with you."

For the first time in years, the wolf didn't feel insecure in himself. Whatever the future held, it would be far more bearable than the life he had on the run, just barely scraping by. He was already a wanted man; organised villainy might just be his best hope at building something of a *life* in the shadow of his past.

Anything — *anything* — was better than running forever.

October 17, 2019

His long sigh made the edges of the letterhead flutter. Maxwell didn't take it out of its protective frame very often anymore. Only occasionally, when he needed a more potent reminder of what kept him going. Turning the paper over in his paws to feel along the worn creases, the wolf contemplated what Little — given name Léon — would have done about someone like Rob Slotis.

Maxwell had stumbled across another new breadcrumb with *that damned name* on it, while on one of his extracurriculars the previous week. This time it gave away something more concerning than the mysterious figure's seemingly-unlimited resources – a hint of what they might be doing with them. It had been a sticky note tucked away in the desk drawer of a wealthy man's personal library of rare reels of film and other eclectic media: *Reference — R. Slotis.*

He had practically turned the collection upside-down when he'd found it, seeking even the barest shred of more information. For one, what could his mystery man even have *wanted* with a monied but otherwise small-time collector? The name was everywhere, taunting the wolf.

Ulhauriear's gentle plodding into the directorate office pulled Maxwell out of his focus. The kobold had been the directorate's dutiful assistant for some time, ever there to help in any way she was able. The old wolf's recent absorption in the Slotis affair had left him little capacity for his day-to-day administrative duties, and she had dutifully picked up the slack. Not that the diminutive blue-scaled draconid betrayed any sign of struggling under the workload, of course; she took every task in stride, and carried it all out with the fervour it demanded.

Ul gently placed the stack of papers she was carrying on Liam's vacant desk and turned to catch Maxwell's glance. She raised a single hand in an uncertain gesture, until appearing to notice the slip of paper he held. "Oh... it's been a while since you've taken that out, hasn't it."

Maxwell gave a single, near-motionless nod of acknowledgement, and stared back at the faded words on the paper. He heaved a deep sigh, and slipped the letterhead back into its frame, carefully *feeling* the weight of the glass and steel before setting it down on his desk. "I needed a reminder. Just to feel it. To remember not to give up."

Tracking Slotis had already grown in scope beyond KARD itself, and sprawled outward into the in-trays of various other teams and divisions. Any intel on the mysterious name attached was flagged — with various other stakeholders but also ROSE as a counter-check — to be forwarded immediately to Maxwell, but so far, he had been the only agent who'd found anything.

The assistant to KARD's directors crooned softly and made her way to Maxwell's side, offering her hands to his paw, gracefully holding it between her own. "You will find what you need to find. You always do! But, please, Director, be gentler on yourself? You're very important to all of us."

The two shared a moment then, looking into each other's eyes before the canine drifted his attention back to the frame on the desk. "You're right, dear. Of course you are. I apologise if I've seemed somewhat... *consumed*, recently."

Before the kobold could reply, her stubby snout suddenly whipped about to the office window, gazing across the atrium to the large, suspended chamber of the secure vaults. A second later, a priority alert came through Maxwell's RCGs. It was Phillip, KARD's chief engineer, calling for the directors (*and* their assistant) to immediately attend Vault F — though Liam would be unable to assist, having departed KDS two days prior for one of the Korps' stateside sites, training new KARD recruits.

Without hesitation, both wolf and kobold hurried their way to the gantry that granted entrance to the secure vaults, two storeys above the atrium floor. Phillip met them enroute; the chubby, boiler-suited skunk hurriedly blurted out the situation. "No containment breach, but the resonance of Vault F's bridge field shifted just outside of nominal levels. That's new! I've never seen it do anything like this before, not even in historical data! This kind of field manipulation shouldn't be *possible* with the containment system's current power consumption!"

[Vault F squirmed and got close to breaking some of the bridge cables,] ROSE helpfully summarised.

Vaults A through E were physically present in reality, confined to the usual three spatial dimensions; they were simply particularly secure storage for KARD's restricted or volatile materials. Vault F however... Vault F was more complicated. Vault F was the reason the division needed a dimensional field theorist like Phillip.

When the trio arrived at the vault entry bulkhead, everything *stopped*; the sensor displays around the portal showed level returning to normal. Maxwell squinted. If anything, the background measurements Phillip would usually be poring over seemed quieter than ever.

"S-systems normal," the skunk forced out as he tapped away at the largest control panel. "I... I don't know what happened, it just... It was like it tried to *move*, but now it's still again. All quiet," he murmured, almost in disbelief.

Ulhauriear stepped her way towards the bulkhead and pressed the flat of her palm against the cold steel, closing her eyes and quietly chanting.

Magic and science, Phillip and Ul agreed, were just two aspects of the measurable universe. The pair had their tensions in years past, under Maxwell's directorship, but the skunk had come to admit he had seen more than could possibly be explained with his expertise in dimensional field manipulation alone. Likewise, Ul had been impressed by the skunk's unique mastery of numbers and abstracted mechanics. Together, the pair made for formidable custodians of Vault F, but their respective worlds didn't usually communicate well... or at all. There were some notable exceptions, but generally, magic stuck to magic, and science stuck to science.

"It does not seem troubled, but it feels *evasive* to my asking," Ul rattled out, her face as perplexed as Phillip's.

Maxwell stepped between them and firmly placed his own paw to the bulkhead, concentrating. He felt some strange reverberation in his soul seeming just *slightly* out of place. "She's... she *was* restless. Perhaps I should go in, and ask more directly..."

Knowledge of Vault F was restricted, access to it even more so. Even among the personnel permitted to enter the secure vaults that *weren't* kept behind several tons of steel and anchored in place with cross-dimensional tethers. Obtaining clearance involved both the magical and the scientific: a battery of physical tests, exposure trials, and rituals with fluids of questionable origin, painstakingly developed by the division over the years. If a subject failed any part of the process, it was deemed too risky to permit them access.

All of the trio gathered outside the vault were cleared, but standard operating procedure was that only *one* high-clearance individual would be permitted access at a time, unless the situation was drastic — and absolutely never more than one of the *directorate*. While personally frustrated about it, Liam had never passed the access rites, though not for lack of trying. Whatever the reason for Vault F rejecting the bear, it put Maxwell in the position of not only being one of the most experienced with traversing it, but the only member of the directorate *able* to do so.

Ul looked up at the old wolf hesitantly. "I think that would be a good idea," she offered.

Philip gave an affirmative nod to the directors' small assistant and added: "If you do, we should probably be sure to use the recovery harness… just to be safe."

Maxwell's expression hardened, immediately just as fixated on solving the new riddle as the mystery of Rob Slotis. He thoughtfully tapped his claws at the steel and slowly withdrew half a metre or so. With a deep breath, he fell into the coolly professional demeanour garnered from decades of experience, wasting little time in removing his cozy sweater vest. "Agreed. Notify Liam and the archival leads. If I find anything out of the ordinary, I will attempt to bring it back for them. I'm sure she wouldn't get restless over *nothing.*"

Phillip set about conducting the opening of the bulkhead, beyond which was a small airlock-like preparation room. Several lockers lined one wall, with the opposite side of the room being the home to a series of powerful hydraulic winches, each fitted with a huge spool of personnel recovery-grade tether, and a bench securely bolted to the floor between. The cables ran to a feeder device on the ceiling in numbered channels. At the far end of the room was another bulkhead, much smaller in size, looking more like a reinforced fire door than the huge slab of steel that Philip had pivoted open on its massive hinges.

Maxwell handed his sweater vest off to his dutiful assistant, and stepped through the threshold, opening one of the lockers and quickly donning his harness suit over his usual Korps-casual attire. The suit was large, loose and flexible, like a heavy rubber diving suit, complete with a steel ring around the neck for attaching a full-cover helmet. The torso was built around a reinforced five-point harness, fully adjustable to the wearer. Much as the Korps's usual design aesthetic leaned into black and magenta, research had deemed that bright safety orange and functional greys remained the most sensible options for KARD's highly specific expedition equipment.

"Standard procedure, Director?" The skunk asked as he interfaced with the screen beside the bulkhead.

Maxwell gave a firm nod. "Yes. Two hours' submersion, maximum." He adjusted his RCGs, pushing them up the bridge of his muzzle, before finally donning the facemask that came as part of the suit. It was a wide-visored item, hugging the edge of his jawline and wrapping securely under his chin.

The kobold signalled that she would be monitoring the vault from outside and doing her best to ritually ensure safe passage for the wolf. "Be safe, Director."

"Of course, my dear."

With that, the exterior bulkhead closed shut with a deep pneumatic hiss, and the canine tended to attaching the tether to his harness. While the preparation room cycled to open the interior bulkhead into the vault, Maxwell checked in with ROSE, while he was still able; once he crossed the threshold into Vault F, his RCGs would lose connection to the network.

"Madame, I will speak to you again in two hours. Until then I will rely on your closed systems for support if I need to, though I will ever miss your personality."

[Of course. It appears likely any cause for distress would be located between Sectors 8-Alpha and 11-Alpha. This is however based on limited information, much of which is proxy data only, and we of course lack any sensor readings at all in the unmapped regions. You'll have to use your judgement.]

The confirmation was helpful, but unsurprising. For decades, actually getting an overview of what was going on inside Vault F at any given time had proved impossible. The more of the interior KARD's cautious expeditions mapped, the less it seemed to make sense as a space. Maxwell considered that to be the point of the entity, such as it was, and had come to respect F for its patience.

"Thank you, ROSE. Please set a timer for me, before I lose signal."

[Confirmed. Be safe, Director.]

A countdown appeared in the top right of Maxwell's visor, taking up only a small portion of his field of view, and gently reminding him of the need for urgency. It wasn't that more than two hours inside the vault would be dangerous, exactly — but those past expeditions had observed exponentially increasing, disconcerting *strangeness* the longer they had remained inside. One poor soul had been lost for a full *day* back in the late 70s, the wolf recalled and needed a week to recover fully. All of that was classified, even among general KARD personnel.

Heavy steel clamps unlocked, and the internal bulkhead door slid to the side on a guided track. Maxwell stepped forward and out onto the utilitarian catwalk that vanished off into the strange teal void. Sound was different in this in-between space. To his mind, it carried the same way that a clap on a snowy day did (or rather, didn't); muffled, muted, compressed, and localised right back to its point of origin. On either side of the catwalk's railings, the distance seemed to stretch on forever in all directions, with only faint shadows at his back hinting at the industrial form of KARD's vault containment wall.

The space was impossibly large, and never failed to impress the wolf, even after decades as its chief custodian. Were the interior aligned with its exterior infrastructure, he should have been walking somewhere between stacks 49 and 56 in the division's west wing right now, but Vault F had never cared for spatial congruency. Philip favoured describing the in-between space as a pocket dimension of sorts, a bridge from one place to another. But no one could quite describe what (or *where*) the 'other place' actually *was*, or why every observer perceived it differently.

An unassuming wooden office door with a frosted glass window built into it marked the end of the catwalk, and the start of Vault F proper. The letters on the glass seemed to jumble themselves and drift in and out of the wolf's perception, an imperfect but well-meaning simulacrum of a space with which Maxwell was deeply familiar. He reached for the handle and pulled.

It even *creaked* in the same way as the SIS Records Office door.

Inside, the unmistakable warm mustiness of countless bound tomes and battered manila files filled the air, saturating everything. Maxwell stepped in, and the door creaked closed behind him, phasing through the tether attaching his suit to the prep room. Corridors of endless cream-enamelled steel shelves stretched out in imposing blocks, starting to meander off course and into strange patterns in the distance. The ceiling was low, and it wasn't really a ceiling. It was another steel catwalk, above which was another, and another, and so on, forever — all granting access to more of the same shelves upon shelves of knowledge that the vault contained.

[T-01:52:14.03,] read the timer on his visor's HUD. The canine made tracks forward, keeping his hands out from his sides a little, feeling the strange soupy atmosphere for any anomalies that might suggest the direction of the disturbance. As he did, a deep echoing rumble roared out from some distant location, whining and cooing like an unimaginably large animal.

It was reassuring, in a way, to hear the vault make a noise like that. It didn't use words often, not distinguishable ones, anyway. But the sounds were a sign it was at least present, and aware that Maxwell was inside it. Curiously, moreover, they didn't seem to indicate distress; if anything, the noises sounded inquisitive.

"Ah, so you *are* with us… what seems to be the matter, my dear Fate?" the wolf cooed back with a gentle tone. He didn't like entering the vault under more *medical* conditions. There was good reason to, of course, but getting to know the entity and space it took the form of had caused him to grow a certain intimate attachment over the years. Vault F had a *personality*, but it was still largely unknown, and to be treated with a cautious respect.

Still walking forward, Maxwell let the enigmatic tug of strangeness wash around his parted fingers. It pulled him towards a corridor on the left, and then one on the right, forward some more, and then deeper still into the stacks. The vault clacked, *flexed*, and sheepishly drew a breath that seemed to flutter every loose page and sheet of paper on the shelves.

Maxwell felt the pull draw him further, round several more corners, and past shelves he didn't fully recognise. Books seemed to change colour, size, and shape whenever he blinked, and some faded from reality all together. Other books were entirely out of place, bearing reference numbers on their spines sharply dissonant with the shelves' classifications. Still more were lined with titles so long, and made of such incomprehensible characters, that the words themselves floated off the surface of the book cloth and hung in the air. That was when the wolf's gaze flitted across the chronometer in the corner of his visor's display, and sickly unease gripped his stomach.

[T-00:03:45.06]

Time had jumped, and he hadn't even felt it. Something was wrong. *Incredibly* wrong. The shelves around him started to dissolve into a black featureless void.

Maxwell's breathing quickened, fogging up the mask and obscuring his vision just enough to make the slow creep of panic worse. He turned, reaching an arm back for the tether to give it a firm yank; it would alert Philip, Ul, or anyone else monitoring the preparation room that he needed help. But the tether wasn't there. His *harness* wasn't there. His *suit* wasn't there!

Nothingness swallowed the wolf whole; all he could hear was the pounding, relentless rush of blood circulating through the capillaries in his ears. Then, suddenly, with a flash, he was in another familiar-looking room, where the stifling heat of a muggy London summer pervaded his senses. Drab walls sank to dishevelled and scuffed baseboards, themselves framing heavily worn wooden floors. They must have been well-looked-after, once, Maxwell had always thought. It was his workspace from his days in the SIS, a room he hadn't seen for decades, even in his worst dreams… complete with *almost* everything he remembered. The canine felt his throat dry out.

The room was nearly a perfect replica. Nearly. The *desk* was wrong. In his memory, it was always far more cluttered with national secrets and transference request orders. In the Vault's iteration of the space, there was just a single manila folder laying neatly on the desk's scratched wooden surface. His eyes widened. "What in the Overlord's name…"

Maxwell's limbs moved, automatically, approaching the item for a better view. The tab on the top edge of the folder read 'CONTINUUM'.

He didn't recognise the folder, or the name, nor could he work out why the vault would be showing it to him in a recreation of *this* room, of all places. It was a decidedly uncomfortable reminder of the things he had done at the command of his former handlers.

Curiosity filled him, however, and he reached for the folder. It felt empty — *inconsequential,* even — until he settled the spine in one paw and let the fold spill open. Impossible amounts of paper filled the inside, seeming to double in weight with every passing moment, not even giving the elderly wolf a chance to blink. The words on those pages shifted and blurred into a mass of writhing ink, and before he could drop the folder out of sheer overstimulation, the world was black once more in all directions.

When Maxwell opened his eyes again, he was somewhere else in the vault. It looked different — wood, instead of enamel and steel, and weathered with what appeared to be centuries of age. It smelled different, too; the scent was richer. *Earthy.*

He went to check the timer on his HUD, but his gaze caught nothing; all at once he realized that his RCGs were gone, too. His body felt strangely light and hazy, as if he wasn't really present at all. The wolf's focus was interrupted by the sound of heavy fabric ruffling against itself, around the corner of the nearest stack.

Taking a cautious step forward, Maxwell hesitantly reached a paw out to steady himself on the end of the bookcase. From there, he caught a glimpse of something. The figure that stood half down the aisle was tall, much taller than he was himself; more than that he couldn't make out, his vision twisting and blurring. Faintly, he managed a cautious hail. "Hello?"

The figure turned and it spoke in quiet disbelief, body going loose and head tilting. "…Mon papa loup?"

October 19, 2019

Slowly, ever-so-slowly, the wolf opened his eyes and was met with the warm off-white glow of a bedside lamp – the kind that was a standard fixture in every Korps Medical facility he'd ever seen. He stretched his hand out, struggling somewhat against firmly tucked-in sheets, and exhaled with great, exhausted effort.

"Ah. Director Maxwell, you're awake. Please do remain in bed so that I might complete my scans. I'm well informed of your reluctance to relax, even on instruction." The voice was synthetic and politely snarky, distinctly that of an O-Unit.

The vulpine drone moved to the edge of the bed, coming into the wolf's view from his horizontal position, all four sleek white limbs working at once to check various aspects of his condition. Where Nurse O's mouth would be on any flesh-and-blood fox was a waveform, delicately dancing to her words and punctuating them with brassy emphasis, as if her bedside manner didn't already.

"You are in quite good health, all things considered."

His hand instinctively rubbed at his throat, sore in a way he recognized from unpleasant memories as the aftereffects of emergency intubation. Even as he wrestled with the last memories he had, he still found himself asking the obvious question. "All things considered?"

The synthetic nurse finished her checks and stood upright. "You were officially missing for two days. Extraction from your last known location — classified above this unit's access level — was met with failure. However, you appeared again of your own accord earlier this morning, and routine checks were carried out as part of your recovery. You appear to be in good condition, though deeply in need of rest. I must inform you that you are not to return to your post at KARD for at least two days."

Nothing about the statements made sense, but the old dog knew better than to question the judgement of Nurse O, no matter which of her was relaying the order for medical leave. He tried his best not to be dismissive, still reeling from the several revelations presented to him. "Are Liam or UI available to speak to? I imagine... I imagine they are cleared to discuss the specifics of what happened."

Nurse O raised her chin in a single motion and stopped at a perfect angle before chiming back with her reply. "Of course. Both are waiting to see you, and I am satisfied you can receive visitors, but one last thing, if I may." She didn't wait for permission to continue. "You are stubborn, Maxwell, and resilient too; regrettably, there are no known treatments for those two comorbidities. Please try not to do *whatever* you did, again, before your next scheduled checkup. Speaking of which—" The synth produced a hypodermic needle on a servo, from a shifting panel on one breakaway palm armature, and steadied the wolf's arm with her other three hands. The process made quick and painless work of injecting its contents. "A simple nanite booster to aid in recovery. It should tide you over until your next full physical."

With the bedside snark neatly completed as part of her routine, the O-Unit made her way dutifully to exit the room, passing through in perfect synchronisation with the pneumatics that slid the door into the wall. The burly figure of a bear holding a small bouquet of flowers entered the room soon after, followed closely by the hurried scampering of the directorate's dutiful assistant.

Maxwell sleepily commanded the bed raise just a little with a hand gesture over one of the side bar's sensors, gratefully smiling to see his two close confidants, but still internally shaken and unsure of everything that had led to him waking up in the Medical sector.

Liam spoke before the wolf had the chance to, leaning into his words with a heavy, relieved sigh. "Glad to see you awake, dear. The nurses said your vitals are all good, but... for the Overlord's sake, André!" There was an almost desperate look of pain in the bear's eyes as he put his hand on top of Maxwell's. "You had us all worried as hell. What happened in there?"

The wolf rolled his head forward, keeping that grateful but uneasy smile as his kobold assistant made herself comfortable at the foot of the bed. "I... I don't know how I was gone for two days. I can't explain that." Maxwell paused, thinking back to some of his earliest excursions into Vault F and the problems he'd encountered there. The strangeness of the place persisted, but he'd personally never experienced something like this before. Well-cared-for canine teeth clenched together through a stern look of concentration as he did his best to recount his recollection. "She seemed normal at first; nothing too out of the ordinary. Then I felt drawn deeper, and the materials around me started to lose their coherence... I checked my timer, then, and... I'd almost reached my submersion limit. It had felt like minutes, and when I reached to pull on the tether, it wasn't there. The entire harness suit was gone, and I have no memory of taking it off. After that, I can't be sure that the rest wasn't a hallucination. What time did the preparation room report the tether had been detached? Was the suit recovered?"

The room went quiet for a moment, and Liam hung his head a little, rubbing anxiously at the back of his broad neck. "André... the tether feed and winch was ripped from the prep room wall about ninety minutes into the submersion. The entire assembly was destroyed — pulled onto the catwalk and, near as we can tell, sucked clear into the void between the containment wall and the Vault. Philip's team is still working on a sturdier replacement. We thought we'd *lost you*, because as far as we knew, you were still attached to the tether. You really didn't feel a thing?"

Maxwell's eyes met the bear's for a long moment, "I didn't. The suit just wasn't there. She didn't hurt me, but she didn't want me to go, either. I think she thought... I think she *needed me* to see something there."

Quiet as she may have been until then, the kobold at the foot of the bed filled her chest and rattled out her own offering on the events. "It does seem that way. The nurses told us you are in good health, Director, but... w-what was it that you saw?"

"My old office... cell... whatever you'd call it, the space where I worked back when I was on the SIS leash. There was a file on the desk, not one I remember, and when I opened it... it felt like whole worlds poured out in my hands." Maxwell went quiet again as he tried to articulate his thoughts, realising how the next part would sound, and feeling puzzled that after a *lifetime* of seeing and doing the kinds of things he had, this incident had felt so exceptional. "And then... I saw someone."

Liam's expression dropped from attentive listening to a gape of disbelief. He finally let a word fall out of his slackened jaw. "*Who?*"

"I don't know," Maxwell replied, bereft of any meaningful answer, concentrate as he might. There were reports of many *things* seen in Vault F, but no one had ever observed a *someone*. "They were taller than me, by a foot or more..."

"Threatening? Did it... *they* hurt you? I always knew that damned place must be dangerous if it never let me in..." Liam accused.

"No, no, they seemed... gentle. Surprised to see me; like they knew me, but I didn't recognise them."

As he spoke, the wolf felt a question burn in his mind. Was he just losing it? Chasing a shadow of a name that no one seemed to know, seeing it appear time and time again in the indulgent little ops he carried out just to keep his skills sharp, stumbling and losing track of time in Vault F, seeing... *imagining*... a person in an impossible location? He was getting on in years, admittedly; though he tried desperately not to slow down, was regularly given bills of good health at his checkups, and even occasionally took a dip in a nano-fluid tank to help repair anything that needed it, he suddenly felt significantly more fragile, and commensurately less sure of his abilities. The thought that he didn't know what had happened to him scared the wolf more than he wanted to admit.

Maxwell found himself asking a question to which he desperately needed the answer, but wasn't sure it would help clear the anxiety. "How did I... how was I found?"

The bear exhaled and rubbed at the ruff of his neck again, casting a glance to the kobold, and then back to his co-director and partner. "You just *appeared* in the prep room, about six hours ago. ROSE detected vital signs in there and alerted everyone with clearance. Philip's crew was already doing some systems monitoring outside the bulkhead, so they got to you first. They opened the door, and apparently, you were just laying on the floor like you'd decided to take a nap in everything you walked in there with... except your RCGs. Which of course means—"

"—No record of what they might have recorded, to compare... against..." finished Maxwell. "Hence asking what I remember."

"*Mmhmm*," Liam hastily confirmed. "Listen, André. Whatever you saw, it doesn't matter if we can't explain it right now. What matters is how we deal with it, and that you're okay. I already had access Vault F limited for now; Command got a bit spooked at a senior agent going missing, *understandably*, and on O's advice, ordered you take some leave for a few days to clear your head and recuperate. Just a couple of days off, while Phillip's team runs deeper tests on the Vault, seeing if anything strange comes up. The Boss *themself* even suggested that maybe you and I take some time together, and step back from everything. I mean, in much more purple prose than that, you know, like they do."

Maxwell's muzzle twitched in anxiety at the idea. KARD had been *his* baby for a very long while, even when the division's prime responsibilities were shared between himself and Liam, even back in the 60s when he was *technically* reporting to Léon. "The *Overlord*? Really?"

"Mhmm. He said you deserve a break — an enforced one, if need be."

Rich grey eyes cast their gaze to the sapphire Kobold still sat at the end of the bed, not having taken her eyes off him. "And what of our dear assistant? What do you think?"

The fins that lined the rear of Ulhauriear's gentle jaw and met with her cheeks flicked to attention, accompanied by a deep blue blush, growing under her scales. "I-I agree, of course, Director. Arrangements have been made that the division will be well looked after, by myself and some of the team heads, while you and Director Liam are away. We'll all look forward to your return, but… well… it's like your letterhead – family don't give up! The division will carry your work on while you're gone. We won't rest!"

Maxwell didn't really have a choice, he supposed. Though he was happy to entrust the division's day-to-day to the kobold and the collection of senior researchers he'd seen grow up and into their responsibilities as team heads, he couldn't pretend he liked being taken out of commission like this. The Overlord — well, Command, but really, the Overlord specifically — knew more about Vault F than even he did, more than they would ever let on. If *they* were insisting he take time off, it was probably sound advice. The wolf forced as much of a comforted smile as he could manage, under the circumstances, before replying. "Well… I know KARD will be in good hands, so what did you have in mind?"

"I figured we could go topside, pay Martin a visit at Dropp's, and spend some time between there and my place," Liam replied, finally putting the bouquet of flowers down on the small side table.

Dropp's was a home-away-from-home for the wolf, though he'd be hard pressed to remember the last time he'd actually stayed there. The small bookstore acted as a front business, happily selling a well-curated selection of books to the discerning patron, but in years past it had been a dead-drop location for lifted materials and sensitive intelligence. The mail-rail line that ran from the store's deep basement to a sub-level of KARD's western wing was still there, but had seen little use in the past two decades, largely superseded by bleeding-edge Korps tech. *It would be nice to see the place again*, André thought. He halfway expected a neurologically linked digital reply to cross his synapses, warning him of any construction, street events, and even local weather phenomena around the front site, but no such reply came, reminding him he still lacked his RCGs.

"That does sound refreshing. D-do you suppose we could stop by a supply depot to pick up a replacement visor?"

"Absolutely. I'd have already done it, but... well, it's been a busy day," the bear offered. "Plus, I'm sure ROSE will help take your report of the anomaly — you know, while everything is still fresh in mind. Philip, Ul, and I have already filed ours. Oh... and I suppose it wouldn't hurt to get changed into something more appropriate, either."

The wolf looked over the rim of his non-existent glasses, staring down at his partner with a disapprovingly (but still much needed) *knowing* smile. "I imagine there's no discouraging you from your wardrobe of disguises?"

Liam grinned, nearly flashing all of his pearly-white daggers. "Nope."

CHAPTER 5

October 19, 2019

Neither of them said anything on the drive into Toronto, with the exception of the odd muttered expletive from the dragon when someone cut him off.

Neither of the pair really wanted to talk about the diploma incident. The brown envelope it had arrived in, now covered in Lexi's furious scrawls, was stowed away at the bottom of a drawer with all the ceremony it deserved. The few days since then had been marked with ups and downs in the cow's overall mood, and though the drive was frankly *terrifying* compared to what she was used to back in the UK, she looked forward to the city. The radio had at least filled some of the dead air, but the moment a news segment came on, once again talking about Hero-centric happenings, Drac abruptly switched the radio off without explanation.

Despite being excited, Lexi had felt quietly muddled with guilt for the entire journey. The idea of driving for two hours, just for a weekend break, was not a familiar one to the bovine. Her mother — who couldn't drive and simultaneously had numerous mobility issues — always instilled in her that being driven *anywhere* was an immeasurable gift, for which she must always be thankful. Further, if the driving wasn't enough, the fact that the drake had been so tender with her (despite her inability to do anything but be what she *assumed* was a burden) was also a strange new experience.

As hard as she tried, however, Lexi couldn't help but get lost in that uncomfortably familiar spiral as they entered the city proper via the Gardiner Expressway. Despite years of long-distance dating, and Drac's pronouncements and reassurance, she wasn't used to someone simply... *taking care of her* like this. It felt wrong, in the way that indulging in luxury goods felt wrong. That money could be better used elsewhere; cheap no-name alternatives, or just plain going without, had always more than sufficed.

The cow's mental health wasn't instant coffee or tinned beans, though. Lexi knew instinctively that she had to look after herself, had to *decompress* properly, but it was all easier said than done. She knew that sense of being undeserving was certainly some kind of trauma response, but she still wasn't sure how to deal with it in any practical way.

When she resurfaced from her spiral of light dissociation, Drac was already looking for a spot to park in the hotel's multi-level garage. Lexi internally shook her brain, trying to get it to focus on her surroundings instead of spinning in place like a flywheel. Once they'd mercifully found a spot on the fifth level, Lexi climbed out of the car and followed the dragon closely at his side, taking in the smells of the city air and trying to decide if she enjoyed them.

The hotel itself was right on the lakeside and apparently functioned as a convention centre throughout the year. Judging by the relatively light foot traffic flowing through the hotel's common areas, though, nothing particularly special was currently going on.

A dark-haired bat greeted them both at the check-in desk and took a few details, noting that Drac was apparently a sufficiently privileged member of the hotel's loyalty program for the pair to get free breakfast every morning. It wasn't until they made their way to the elevators, keycards in hand, that the bovine side-eyed the dragon and asked about it. "You come here so often you have a membership?"

Drac smirked, shifting the rucksack (carrying a full weekend's worth of clothes) higher up on his shoulder as they thumbed the elevator call button. "Nope; I've stayed here maybe three or four times, total. My old job sent me here for a conference. A *mandatory* conference," they grimaced. "They set me up with some business elite status card, so that my food was covered for the stay. I left the company eventually, and a year later I'm here meeting friends for something, see the card in my wallet still, and figure I'd try it. Turns out they opened it in my name, not under the corporate account, and never cancelled the membership."

Lexi felt herself smile. "Scandalous! And here I thought you wouldn't so much as steal a stapler." There was at least some comfort in knowing that breakfast would be paid for by some faceless company, and not her boyfriend; he was already doing so much. *Maybe,* she thought, *maybe that means we can do something I don't have to feel guilty over.* She pulled out her phone and began signing in to the hotel wi-fi. Just like the airport, there was a disclaimer about RCGs. They weren't permitted to be worn around the hotel's public spaces or the convention centre, for nebulous 'security reasons', but apparently their use in rooms was fine? *I guess you can be villain-coded in private, just not where good honest people can see you.* It seemed to be simply policy, with no force of law behind it, but it once again stuck out to the cow all the same.

Once she was online, she started scrolling through a list of small local attractions, but most of them had a price attached. Once again feeling in the pit of her stomach not wanting to be any kind of *burden,* financial or otherwise, Lexi refined her search terms down even further. The free and cheap attractions seemed like they'd be either too busy, or sensory hell. She added yet more qualifiers to her search and eventually hit upon a list of 'quiet Toronto gems' on the kind of listicle that seemed designed precisely for her demographic: age 25-40, and not particularly touristy, sporty, or interested in loud venues.

The elevator door opened onto an unassuming hall, with plain walls and a carpet in the hotel chain's signature colours. Drac marched on to their assigned room, opening the door and sighing softly as he dropped his rucksack by one of the side tables. "I'm gonna take a shower, sweetie. Got to get the stink of mild highway anxiety off me."

"All right, honey, go shower. Thanks again for driving us here," the cow responded, the show of gratitude coming nearly as naturally as breathing.

Lexi sat herself down on the edge of the bed and began scrolling through the list of Toronto's lesser-known places of interest. There were a couple of quaint indie coffee shops, a handful of small public parks, and a tiny niche museum to some eclectic piece of the city's history, but one entry stood out among the others: D.E. Dropp & Sons Books.

Apparently, the location in Cabbagetown had once been a bindery, but had since become a bookstore featuring lots of queer literature, as well as serving as a venue for community workshops. According to the store's entry on the website list, it had kept the long-dead men's names on the storefront for the sake of local character, and its red-brick Victorian exterior looked as if it hadn't changed since the day the place was built... with the exception of the Progress Pride flag hanging proudly in the second-floor bay window. The site described it as the perfect retreat for bibliophiles, with friendly and welcoming staff who had been operating the store faithfully for decades. In short, it looked *exactly* like her kind of place.

Cabbagetown wasn't too far away from the hotel, either — about twenty minutes by streetcar, based on Lexi's maps app. "Streetcars *and* queer culture," she muttered to herself wistfully. Although the room was on the twenty-sixth floor of a soulless chain hotel, and looked out onto a dense glass cityscape, there was something undeniably charming about Toronto already.

Drac stepped out from the bathroom at that moment, a towel wrapped around their broad middle, and a fresher, more relaxed look on their face, communicated by a blissfully goofy grin and half-lidded eyes. "Ohhh, that's better," they murmured contentedly, before gazing over to the cow. "What'cha looking at, sweetie?"

Lexi did her *best* not to just blurt out "You," but the direction of her gaze betrayed her regardless. "I was looking up some places we could visit while we're here, a few little out-of-the-way-type things."

"Uh-huh?" The dragon intoned, raising an eyebrow as he stepped back into the bathroom to finish drying off. "Anything stand out?"

For a moment, the bovine felt the need to *not be a burden* creeping into her gut once more, but she managed to quell it. It was just a bookstore — a friendly-looking queer one, at that — and it was only a short trip out from the hotel! It was hard to admit to herself, but Lexi actually wanted something, and for once, she felt like she could ask for it. "Yeah, actually. There's this really cute-looking bookstore…"

Drac poked their gold-scaled head out of the bathroom door, horns nearly scraping the lintel as they did so. "Say no more! We'll get something to eat first, and you can nerd out about books on the way."

"Sounds good to me!"

The veggie shawarma had hit the spot, though if the cow was honest, it was a little *too* hot for her fairly limited palate. Drac had known exactly what he was going to order, before he even got through the door. Apparently he'd frequented the place once or twice while he was staying in the hotel on his prior employer's dime. Either way, the pair were sated by the time they caught the streetcar, and most food was good food to Lexi, so a full belly was almost always a happy one.

The two got off at their stop and navigated the streets of Cabbagetown — Drac with more decided *purpose* in their stride than Lexi, who became preoccupied taking in her surroundings, and admiring the neighbourhood's architectural charm. It wasn't too long before they'd reached the bookstore, though, and Lexi's attention was finally focused on admiring the single building rather than the entire street.

'Quaint' really might have been the only word for it. The exterior was weathered red brick, with yellow-accented features and an understated, pleasantly simple carved bargeboard painted in a striking black. Just like the photo on the website, the pride flag she'd spotted hung proudly in one of the second-floor windows. Her partner, meanwhile, stood at the foot of the short staircase leading to the door and gestured upwards with both arms and a slight bow, in the most exaggerated, gentlemanly pose he could manage.

The black door was *heavy*. As Lexi pushed it, she couldn't help but be a little surprised that it was built so sturdily; she'd traversed industrial fire doors that opened with less effort. After a second or so, a hydraulic arm above the door helped with the task of opening it the rest of the way, something for which the cow was thankful. The entryway opened out into an airy room, walls lined from floor to ceiling with sturdy wooden bookcases, all of them full. The carpet was a rich magenta, with tiny black flecks making up a dotted grid, tiling its way around the stacks. Each stood alone, like wide obelisks.

Nestled away to one side of the large room was a staircase, itself also somehow lined with purposefully carved bookcases. As Lexi's eyes followed its steps to the upper floor, the ceiling caught her attention; it was covered in ornate plaster work, showing slight signs of its age, but nothing of neglect. The store was beautiful in a very specific way, in so many words. It was almost hard to believe it had been any kind of industrial workshop in the past.

A gentle breeze rushed by the pair as the door closed behind them, carrying with it the unmistakable scents of vintage paper and polished wood, both gently bleached by sunlight through the wide front windows over decades.

"Good afternoon, folks," cooed an older, friendly voice from somewhere unseen deeper in the store.

What the cow had assumed was some decorative wood panelling was actually the front counter, which looked as though it had been ripped from the study of a stately home. The owner of the voice stepped around a structural pillar at one end of the desk, almost ominously, revealing himself as a tall, pale brown ferret. The man placed a bundle of assorted books down gently at the checkout and adjusted his stylish pink-hued tortoise-shell glasses. He re-rolled the sleeves of his crisp dark shirt to his elbows and gave the new arrivals a polite nod, before he started casually inspecting some books on a nearby shelf.

Drac wasted little time, and began browsing the shelves on the near wall, not looking at anything in particular. For her part, Lexi wandered closer to the desk, not knowing where to start. She could only gawp as she peered across the literary panorama and turned to the shop clerk. "This place is *amazing*," she murmured.

The ferret gave her a warm smile as he looked around the quiet space for a moment, taking it all in and nodding again — in agreement, rather than acknowledgement. "Well, I certainly think it is! I'm Martin, by the way; I run most things around here. Just holler if you need anything?"

A long moment passed, the silence stretching out for what felt like minutes (but was, she realized, probably mere seconds) until the cow *finally* realised that the sweetly studious-looking ferret was gently, subtly asking for her name. The understated politeness of complete strangers was yet another thing she'd need to get used to in Canada, it seemed. "Oh, uh… Lexi, right, sorry!"

Martin made his way back over to the desk to shuffle through the stack of books he'd left there, fanning a paw to dismiss the unnecessary apology; the reassuring smile never left his face. "Lovely to meet you, Lexi. Can I ask what your pronouns are?"

The Highland's brain stopped for just a moment to consider the question. She'd really never been in queer-centric spaces, in her day-today life. Or at all, really? There was that one LGBT club in college, but even that was overshadowed by its tenuous existence; the room it was hosted in belonged to an uptight media studies lecturer, who insisted on conspicuously grading papers while the club was in session. Was this what *good* queer-positive spaces were like? The ferret — Martin, he'd said — was so thoughtful and considerate, she felt stunned at the apparent *normality* of what he'd said. Was that normal? Had she missed out on that much, for so long? "Oh. Uh, she/her, I *guess*, I mean... yeah. She/her. Sorry! Sorry. Just... not used to people asking."

The ferret left the books alone for a moment and walked down the length of the desk to grab what looked like a card and a stamp, swiftly thumping the rubber down a handful of times on the little slip of white card. He held it out to the cow, one elbow casually resting on the corner of the woodwork. "Well, Lexi, welcome. If those pronouns ever change, you just let me know. In the meantime, your first book with us here is free! Who knows, maybe you'll find something here that helps with settling into queer spaces."

Lexi reached out for the little card. It had the store's name neatly printed across the top in black, which she realised was boldly underlined in the same rich magenta that accented nearly all the signage in the store, once noticing it. Below, there were ten lined spaces with pink dots stamped inside each, filling the loyalty card. She smiled, feeling a little silly at how overwhelming (in a positive way!) she had found the simple act of just walking into a bookstore. She couldn't begrudge the ferret calling her out as inexperienced. She was, after all. Still, the acknowledgement itself put her at a little ease, like she was being *seen*. "Thank you, that's so kind!"

The older ferret went back to shuffling the books, apparently trying to correctly order them. Eventually satisfied, he scooped the stack back into his arms and wandered over to one of the shelves, near a comfy-looking reading nook. "Think nothing of it. Now, is there anything I can help you find?"

Lexi searched her mind for anything in particular that she might actually want to look for. The cow hadn't really planned on doing more than browsing, just taking in the atmosphere, but it would feel dismissive of Martin's kind gesture to say that she was 'just looking'. An old fascination from years past, leapt to the front of her mouth, practically blurting the words out before she even realised what she'd said. "Do you have any books on monsters? Like… myths and legends, monster and cryptid horror, that kind of thing?"

Martin raised a brow and flicked an ear at the inquiry. He tucked the last of his little stack into the shelf and adjusted his glasses again, then clapped his paws and rubbed them together enthusiastically, like he'd just been *waiting* for someone to ask for his help. "Well, if it's *classic* spooky you want, we have Lovecraft, Shelley, Poe, and Stoker, just to name a few. But if you want something more contemporary that features mysteries, beasts, and tales of the strange," he said with a dramatic, stage-actorly flair, "then we also have a little collection over here!"

The cow eagerly followed along, tail swatting side to side behind her in excitement as the lanky ferret proudly marched towards a small section off in the corner. An understated sign plate above it read *POPULAR HORROR*.

Right next to the selection was a half-curtained-off door with a neatly-handwritten note pinned to the magenta drapery: *18+ ADULT SECTION — PLEASE SHOW I.D. TO MANAGEMENT FOR ENTRY.* Lexi was keenly interested. She'd always felt more comfortable with erotica than traditional porn; it could feel more intimate, but in ways that meant she didn't have to think about her body very much. It was rare, though, she ever found something that met her tastes *exactly*.

The ferret pulled down a few personal recommendations from the popular horror shelves, including, Lexi noticed, a few entries in the apparently rare *Terato Falls* series. Lexi looked again at the curtain to the adult section, wondering silently just what she might find inside, and after a moment Martin caught the cow's eyes wandering. "Oh, if you want to go in there, that's fine! I'll just need to see some ID first."

Lexi's cheeks immediately began to burn, and part of her mind yelled at her to deny her interest. She could just say she was looking around, or that she liked the colour of the curtain, or that she was struck by how politely the sign was written, or—

No. She was not going to be scared. This was a place she could be *herself.* She thought back to how she'd always hated talking about anything sexual, even among people her own age. Years of hiding herself had meant suppressing any kind of honesty or openness about it. But sex *wasn't* a taboo subject, and she shouldn't live like it was only something to be talked about between her and her partner. Martin worked in (owned?) a queer-friendly bookstore with an adults-only section. He definitely didn't seem like the type to judge her. Hell, he had even just initiated a discussion about it; he *wasn't* going to judge her. She reached into her pocket and slipped her UK-issued provisional driver's licence out from its slot in her phone case, handing it out to Martin with renewed (but still-measured) confidence. "Sure thing! Uh, it was issued in the UK, I hope that's fine."

Martin took the card and briefly scanned it with his eyes, handing it back face down with another friendly smile. "That all looks good... for the record, the undercut really suits you!" He pulled back the curtain, more fully revealing a door which looked to be just as heavy and sturdy as the one at the store's main entrance.

Tucking the ID neatly back into her pocket, Lexi remembered a little late that it was three years old; it still had an old pre-transition photo of her, not to mention her deadname. She appreciated that Martin hadn't so much as raised an eyebrow at either. *I love this place*, she thought, as she opened the door and stepped through the threshold.

The adult section proved much the same as the rest of the bookstore, separated by a door though it was, the cow wasn't sure what she had expected. If anything, at least, the casually explicit nature of the materials on display put her at greater ease. The shelves and cases were still organised into easy-to-parse categories, and in the middle of the room was a small table stacked with a few highlighted books — more personal recommendations from the staff, as well as a few fliers for queer-friendly adults-only events around the city.

It didn't take Lexi long to find a section that fully enamoured her, all of it unrepentantly capital-Q Queer, with some strikingly vibrant covers. Her heartbeat swelled, thrumming a pleasantly comforted rhythm as she scanned the titles, almost in awe. The cow pulled out an interesting looking book, the cover of which was a dangerous pink, clashing with hard angled shapes in bright yellow. The synopsis explained that it was the work of someone finding their true selves through sexual exploration, and practising radical self-love in a world that seemed so determined to tell xem it was wrong to do so.

Xem. The neopronoun felt enticing on her tongue as she mouthed out the blurb in a hushed whisper. Lexi was aware of neopronouns, but only insofar as they existed, and some people used them. Never had one stood out to her so much as being beautifully, poetically *authentic* as the one emblazoned on the book in her hands. There was something aggressively attractive about the genderfucked bunny on the front cover, too; xe was clad in latex and harness strapping, xer shiny black figure contrasting astoundingly with the bright tones of the background, yet still somehow seeming perfectly in place there. The cow tucked the copy of *Fuck the Binary* under their arm, and drew an excited breath, looking around with a delighted, giddy smile at the rest of the room.

"I wonder if they have any erotic fantasy..."

Lights passed by overhead and fans whirred, making sure the tunnel was kept cool and dry. The miniature engine car of the narrow-gauge mail-rail train came to a gently pre-programmed stop, at the wide but completely empty station deep beneath Toronto's premier covert Korps front-slash-bookstore.

Maxwell and Liam quietly rose from their narrow bench seat in one of the tiny carriages and stepped out onto the smooth concrete. It was decorated with countless worn markings and zone delineations from much-busier years past, when D. E. Dropp functioned as a dead drop for collected materials to be funnelled directly to KARD's receiving bays.

"Home away from home," the wolf announced. Maxwell led the way to the wide freight elevator at the far end of the platform. He calmly tapped the worn old call button panel before turning back to look down the length of the station. He let memories drift into his consciousness, recalling when the tunnels before him were a hive of activity, ferrying new materials and works into the rapidly expanding new division, under his personal direction.

The elevator doors opened with a gentle squeak. The warm magenta insignia of their division – a stylised winged file folder with a thickly-stamped helix in the centre – was painted across the back wall of the elevator, slightly scratched from many years of material carts bumping against it.

Liam walked in alongside his co-director and rested against the handrail along the left side of the elevator. Maxwell could actually hear him clearly, with the trundling metallic rattle of the train no longer drowning out all other sounds. "So, any thoughts on how you might want to spend your time over the weekend?"

The wolf held a soft smile, trying not to dwell too hard on the reason he was being mandated time off. "Well, I really should spend some time catching up with Martin. Beyond that, though… perhaps the three of us could enjoy a little date night?"

ROSE spoke through the canine's mind via his brand-new pair of RCGs. His personal settings, preferences, and much of his casual communication with the AI had been backed up and instantly restored through the network, allowing the face-mounted assistant to pick up her familiarity directly where she'd left off. [*Not letting a major Vault incident slow you down, I see.*]

"*Of course not, my two favourite boys deserve some attention,*" Maxwell thought, in a reply tinged with regret. It had been far too long, honestly, since he'd made time to unwind. "*I really have been too caught up in my work to just… enjoy things.*"

Liam pushed out his chest as the elevator rose, and gave a deeply breathy, but muted chuckle. "I'd like that. I'm sure Martin would, too. It's been far too long, honestly, and as nice as it is to see you occupied, your mind whirring away at solving problems… we all do love you for other reasons, André."

The elevator opened up to a flat wooden panel that made up the back of a bookcase. It slowly swung on heavy hydraulic servos, and the unassuming basement of Dropp & Sons was revealed to the disguised elevator shaft. It was a plain affair, about as inconspicuous as a basement could possibly be — a few shelves here and there, some boxes stacked high with old signage and banners, and one or two chairs that hadn't been needed for any functions in weeks, or perhaps months. The pair stepped out amid a reflective silence, and the bookcase gently swung closed again behind them, once more hiding the elevator from prying eyes.

The staircase up to the first floor was just as plain as the rest of the basement, but for the dual wall sconce at the top of the stairs. The light fixture was a subtle signal; if both lights were on, everything was clear. If only the left was on, there were customers about; and if both were off, it wasn't safe to enter the store still wearing anything that could be earmarked as obvious tells that the site was one of the Korps's many Toronto-area front operations. The signal system had been long superseded by ROSE's ability to check on the building remotely, but there was no harm to maintaining the comfortably traditional redundancy.

Only the left bulb was lit, and ROSE helpfully prompted the wolf and bear that there were presently two customers in the store — one in the adult area, and one browsing the shelves around the political philosophy section. Liam spoke up first, gently providing the wolf with a prompt. "So, you thought the boiler was leaking, and I decided to take a look at it, handyman that I am?"

Maxwell smirked and reached for the door handle. "Is that your cover story, or is that your roleplay idea, *mon ours?*"

"No reason it can't be both," the bear shrugged with a sly smirk.

The basement door creaked open by Maxwell's paw, just a few feet from a tall golden dragon, who was too distracted with scanning a back cover blurb to notice the older duo exit. The wolf walked out first, expertly and smoothly carrying on a fake conversation with the bear a few steps behind. "Do you think it's something we'll need to get repaired?"

Liam always relished the opportunity to play a character, the wolf knew; though he was far more of a brawler than an actor, his physicality and swagger lent themselves to a certain kind of role. He clasped his huge paws together, and hummed for a moment, trailing into workman-like sucking at his rear teeth. "Welp… it's not urgent, at least. That tape should hold for a month or two, and we can just empty the bucket, if need be."

The dragon appeared, like any other customer, to be completely disinterested in the pair's small talk. Martin, however, was just as enamoured with the act — or, at least, with the performers. The ferret called out playfully, acting out his own customary part of the charade with a flamboyantly airy squeak to his voice. "There you both are! You've both been down there so long I wondered if you'd gotten lost. Here I was, about to send out a search party."

Maxwell made his way to the desk, taking note of the ferret's coded line, and trotted out an excuse that would (if they were listening) surely trigger no suspicions among the customers. "My dear, I'm not so young, and the stairs aren't as forgiving as they once were."

With a close nod and gentle lean towards the old wolf, Martin replied quietly, in less coded language. "I hear that hasn't stopped you getting into trouble. Please do take care, dear; you're far too precious." The ferret punctuated the end of the sentence with a gentle kiss to the canine's cheek.

There wasn't really so much *need* for the old-fashioned cloak-and-dagger games anymore. While the store still functioned as a dead drop, it worked much more usefully as a dissemination centre for propaganda, and *occasionally* as a safehouse with a direct link to KDS, their subterranean headquarters beneath the former RCAF Station Downsview.

The heavy-set bear joined the pair around the checkout, making eyes towards the twinkish older ferret, breaking the act quietly. "Hey, tall, cute, and bookish; Maxwell is taking it easy this weekend. How are things up here?"

"Can't complain. It's been a slow day, though; only two customers so far, and you walked by one, coming in from the basement." Martin nodded ever-so-softly toward the dragon's back, across the other side of the store.

Liam glanced towards the adult section's door with a faint nod of acknowledgement. "Is the other one still in there?"

"Mmhmm. It's her first time, I think," the ferret replied, leaning on his elbows behind the desk as queerly as possible.

The bear raised a brow with an annoyingly infectious smile. "Wow, first time in a bookstore? Kids these days, I tell you…"

Martin rolled his eyes and cast a mock-disapproving glance to the wolf, who also seemed to be wincing from the bear's dad joke. "No, sweetie, she's British; I don't think she's ever been to a *queer* bookstore before. She has that kind of… sweet, innocent awkwardness to her, you know?"

"Oh, *first time!* Why didn't you say so? I'll go check how she's doing," Liam smirked.

"If you insist. Really, though, don't go terrifying the poor dear, now!" Martin added with a flourish, turning back to the grey wolf with a knowing grin.

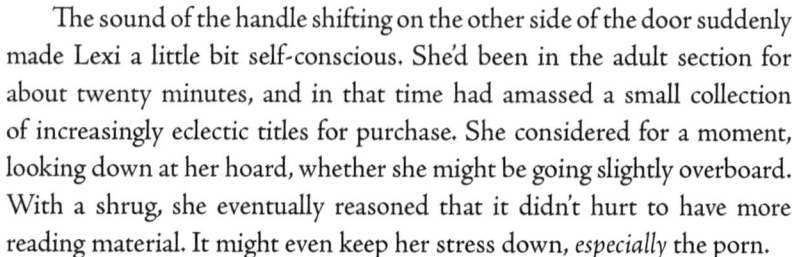

The sound of the handle shifting on the other side of the door suddenly made Lexi a little bit self-conscious. She'd been in the adult section for about twenty minutes, and in that time had amassed a small collection of increasingly eclectic titles for purchase. She considered for a moment, looking down at her hoard, whether she might be going slightly overboard. With a shrug, she eventually reasoned that it didn't hurt to have more reading material. It might even keep her stress down, *especially* the porn.

Her mind cleared again with the thought. Though the very particular collection of books highlighted a certain fascination, she didn't need to be scared; whoever was coming through the door was an adult, and unlikely to be judgemental. And if they were, well, she could own it. The Highland took a breath and tried to not look flustered as the door swung open, revealing... a bear wearing beige cargo shorts, a red graphic tee with a *terrible* joke about fishing on it, and a baseball cap that looked as if it had seen its fair share of lost bar fights.

"Hey there! I'm Liam, Martin's assistant. I was just checking in to see if there's anything you need help wi—" The bear interrupted himself, as he caught sight of the small stack of books in the cow's possession. "Ah! Seems like you've got a heavy load already there, huh?"

She realised, then, what *else* the bear was wearing: a sleek jellybean-shaped visor with a slightly luminous pink hue. *Rose-Coloured Glasses*, she thought, *out in the wild*. She wasn't sure she'd ever seen a set in person, but now that she was thinking about it, it did make sense that they would come in handy for managing the inventory of a rambling independent bookstore. The cow delicately tucked her undercut behind an ear after balancing her finds in arm and smiled awkwardly. "Hi, uh, yeah — I think I'm about ready to pay, actually."

The older ursine gave a warm smile and backed out of the door, holding it open; he was tall and burly enough that his cap grazed the lintel, just a little. "Well, sure! Come right on through, and I'll ring you up."

Drac appeared from around a corner, holding a modest single book in their hands as they caught up with their girlfriend. "I see you found a few things..."

Lexi grabbed a couple of Martin's earlier recommendations from the popular horror section and added them to her pile, even though she hadn't taken much notice of what they were – it was *mostly* to obscure some of the more scandalous titles in her pile. She took the stack to the desk and neatly put them down with a twinge of embarrassment. "Mhmm, I did!"

As the bear lumbered towards the desk and began to ring up the small stash of books, Lexi could feel the room practically heat up around her, as her eyes drifted across the titles making their way into the delightfully decorated paper bag. *Play it cool! No one's going to say anything. Liam seems nice, and Martin was very polite. Everyone here is chill.*

The thoughts got harder to believe wholeheartedly as the bear waved a barcode scanner over each book, and their titles appeared on the small customer-facing screen of the register: *Fuck the Binary, Monsters XXX, Terato Falls: Junkyard Dog, How to Summon a Boyfriend,* and more. The cow grimaced nervously, not realising she had picked up so *many*; she momentarily became worried about the price of everything, until the negligible total on the register eased her nerves.

The bear's paw came down on the last book in the pile. The cover was a stylish photograph of two hands elegantly tied behind their owner's back with vibrant red rope, and a simple title making no secret of the contents: *Rope Play 101.*

Liam had, until that point, displayed fairly professional disinterest in the contents of the cow's purchase, but the cover of the bondage how-to guide seemed to catch his attention. A considered and tiny smile of approval crept across his face as he handled it, scanning it and holding a thumb on the bottom edge, almost threatening to open the book. "You know, I always wondered about this kind of thing; I should really see about getting myself a copy. And hey, since you're getting so much here, this one's on the house."

The cow's eyes darted frantically from the book to Liam, to the floor, to Drac, with an intense and growing anxiety. She screamed internally. *Oh god oh fuck oh god oh fuck oh god, what do I say? Just… just calm down. It's a generous offer; he's not judging you.* "Oh," Lexi finally managed to verbalise with a squeak. "Um… that's really kind of you. Here, Martin gave me a little card good for one freebie, I guess that's what you meant?" As she spoke, she fumbled in her pocket for the filled loyalty card.

"Mhmm, sure is! I'll just take that, and—"

As he reached out for the card, the book fell open, and a few of its pages brushed the back of the cow's hand. Liam scrunched his face as if holding back a sneeze, flicking an ear and then his head.

There was a long, uncomfortable moment of silence. Lexi's mind raced. *Oh god, is he shocked? Did he see a word in there he didn't like? Maybe he saw a picture of something and was just surprised? Oh god, oh god, what if he's about to collapse, or pass out, or*— Her thoughts were suddenly cut short as the bear slowly closed the book and wordlessly put it in the bag.

"That's, uh… $54, please," Liam offered, seemingly a little confused and faintly unsure of his words. Agonisingly determined to get the moment over with, Lexi held up and slammed her debit card down on the payment device, waiting the painstaking second for it to beep in confirmation.

Meanwhile, the ferret had joined the bear behind the desk and had apparently noticed the larger man's bafflement and somehow… *off* body language. "Liam, is everything okay there, sweetie?"

Liam stood stock still before nodding a very uncertain affirmation. "Yeah, I… uh, just felt a little faint for a moment, I think."

"Why don't you go and take a seat in the office for a bit," the ferret suggested with a tilted head, patting the much larger man's arm. Agreeably, Liam slowly nodded and wandered his way to the staircase, fingers reaching up to pinch the bridge of his muzzle.

Martin reassured the cow softly as she watched the bear ascend. "He'll be fine, I'm sure. Probably just dehydrated," he murmured, with a knowing tap to the side of his pointed snout.

[*Liam, your neural activity is through the roof. I'm assisting as best I can, but I need to know what you experienced.*]

The bear tried to concentrate on ROSE's words as best he could, but closing his eyes only revealed more picture-perfect mental images, taken straight from the book that had been in his paws seconds earlier. He hadn't even seen any of the contents, yet all the details were fresh in his mind's eye. He replied silently, thinking his messages through carefully — but his train of thought still wobbled substantially on its tracks, and his replies were short and punchy. *"I don't know. Felt like an involuntary telepathic connection. Imprinting, kind of like what Maxwell can do. Less focused, though. Scattered. All over the place. Disorienting. I think that book I was holding is the only thing that got transferred, but it's hard to tell."*

[Acknowledged. I'm checking your vitals and suppressing some autonomic responses right now. I'm detecting nothing concerning in your immediate surroundings, D.E. Dropp doesn't appear to be under attack, but I have a suspicion about what happened.] The AI in Liam's sleek magenta visor then opened a local-area channel, broadcasting to all nearby RCG devices. *[Liam experienced an intense telepathic event. Condition is stable but disoriented. Potential source of event suspected to be the customer highlighted in your HUDs now.]*

A pinkish box was drawn around the cow, currently putting a book about rope bondage in her bag and waiting for Martin to ring up her boyfriend's single purchase. Maxwell's decades of experience in operations lurched into gear as he mentally communicated across the local channel. *"Received, Madam ROSE. Liam, further details?"*

Liam, from the office upstairs, relayed his thoughts back. *"Felt a lot like one of your transferences, dear, but far less focused. I'm pretty sure I have an encyclopaedic knowledge of wrist and body tie options for both restraint and aesthetics, now."*

Martin quickly joined in the mental conversation as well. *"Copy that. I'm not picking up anything out of the ordinary on my RCGs since Liam moved upstairs."*

"Madam ROSE, what do we know about the suspected source?" Maxwell remained as composed as ever, making his way casually to a shelf near the door, lining himself up for possible interception as ROSE listed every bit of information they had gathered so far.

[Name (preferred): Lexi — Source: offered (conversational; recorded via RCG device, MARTIN, L.)]

[Pronouns: She/Her — Source: offered (conversational; recorded via RCG device, MARTIN, L.)]

[Name (Legal): Michael Hayes — Source: UK Provisional Driver's License.]

[Age: 27 — Source: UK Provisional Driver's License.]

[Current Address: Basingstoke, UK. — Source: UK Provisional Driver's License.]

[Known affiliations: None.]

[Cross-referencing with UK watchlists... completed. No responsive records located.]

[Known powers: Searching UK Powered Persons Register... completed. No responsive records located.]

[Summary: Lexi Hayes is not currently known to the Korps and is not registered with UK authorities despite demonstrating signs of telepathic activity. Debriefing Liam suggests an unrealised and untrained power set similar to your own transference abilities, André. Approach with caution. As with your own historic incidents, it may be stress-sensitive.]

That was all the confirmation the wolf needed. He had never met someone else with his particularly specialised power, anyone that could potentially imprint information like he could; if she *was* like him, he couldn't let her go through what he did. The situation had quickly become immensely personal, but Maxwell still tempered his eagerness. He needed to investigate further before he made any decisive moves.

The old dog stepped in front of the door, blocking the path for the bovine and her apparent draconic partner. "Ah, thank you so, so much for visiting us today! It's always nice to see new faces." He turned on the charm, doing his best not to seem intense. "Before you go, might I ask what kinds of things take your interest to have such a heavy haul, there?" He pointed to the bag, feigning curiosity.

"Oh..." the cow replied, hesitantly reaching into the bag, spending a moment fishing for an example apparently at the bottom. "F-fantasy stuff... and some... some gender stuff. A little bit of everything, I guess," she offered sheepishly, holding out the copy of *Fuck the Binary*.

Maxwell wasted no time in placing his grasp on the book, tilting it up towards him to get a better look. He waited, and he braced his mind for it. Then, it *happened*.

Strings of text drawn from the back-cover synopsis, along with several page excerpts and one or two of the photos suddenly planted themselves squarely in the wolf's conscious mind. He could recall the information in utter clarity, as if he'd just read it himself. The longer he focused on the book in physical space, the more information from its pages bled into his mind across the telepathic link the cow was — apparently unintentionally? — holding open. That was enough proof for him. This bovine was clearly the same kind of rare telepath that he was, even if she didn't realise it.

Maxwell retracted his paw, remembering to smile approvingly. "Let me go and get a bookmark for this, for you. Can't lose your place in something so important." He paced to the register and, comfortably out of sight of his target, asked Martin with a raised brow for a *new* bookmark. The wolf rushed himself back, holding out the clean black strip of faux leather, laced and detailed with a silvery-pink geometric pattern that glinted in the light as he handed it off to the cow. "Here we are! Thank you again for coming in, Lexi, and…" He turned bodily to the large dragon, offering out a hand in a manner he instantly realised as *maybe* too formal.

"Draculion! Nice to have met you," the dragon replied, gently reaching out to shake the offered paw with his much larger hand.

Maxwell stepped back with a soft nod. "Well, I won't keep you both any longer."

"Thank you, really, all of you have been so welcoming," the cow commented, making her way to the door before stopping. "Sorry, I didn't get your name?"

"Ah, of course, my dear. I'm Maxwell."

"Thanks, Maxwell," she said with a slightly manic tone, just before the heavy door shut behind her and the dragon. Everything was silent for a moment, but the secure local comms channel was buzzing with activity.

"*Madam ROSE, lock down the store. Liam, how are you faring?*" Maxwell called over the network.

Liam's response came through first, somewhat more relaxedly sardonic than he had been moments prior. "*I'm doing fine now, though I have a strange compulsion to tie something up… I just might have some ideas for tonight, once we're done debriefing whatever the hell that was?*"

[*Tracking target active. The bookmark is online, André, and its current position is now available in your RCG mapping tools,*] ROSE added.

The wolf sighed, and mused aloud. "Thank you, Madam. She almost *definitely* has a power similar to mine. Liam is right; it's unfocused, and I suspect she isn't aware she's doing it. Perhaps it has only very recently manifested."

Martin nodded, calmly, firmly, and with a faint hint of bemused fatigue. "So much for a quiet weekend. I suppose it's not division work, though, so I *guess* you're technically still being a good boy, André dear. We'll convene upstairs and run a report through to Command. After *that*, though, I insist we find a way to help you relax."

Maxwell nodded, and looked back to the door with a strange feeling in the pit of his stomach. He'd need a way to take his mind off everything, near impossible as that task now seemed.

Lexi crashed on the hotel bed, the bag full of books sprawled out next to her while Drac stripped off their shirt and thumbed through takeout options for dinner on their phone. A single, nagging thought came to the Highland's mind, as she began to unpack and process the day's events:

"...How did that wolf know my name?"

CHAPTER 6

October 20, 2019

Maxwell was the first one out of the office door, soon followed by the bear and ferret. The three had all together spent the past several hours reporting to Command (and Recruitment) about the day's events.

With some arguing, the recruitment committee had given the green light on pursuing the cow. It was decided the small team at Dropp's would take point on the situation, given their close familiarity with the bovine's apparent power set. Her otherwise-unknown quantities, Maxwell insisted, would be a good chance for him to keep his mind sharp while absent from KARD proper. It might only be a few days until he was permitted to return to regular duties, but that (and the battered old typewriter from his KDS office, as delivered by a helpful drone, since he couldn't bear to be without it for any *official* purpose) was all he would need to find everything he could on a target, he knew. It might also make him feel better about not being able to personally chase down any leads on Slotis, the wolf considered privately.

The old canine hadn't stopped thinking about what happened to him inside Vault F. It might have been days prior by the clock, but to him, it still felt like mere hours. Either way, the Gordian knot of a mystery couldn't be unravelled overnight. Indeed, no one had quite managed to ascertain the Vault's intentions on *anything* in the decades since it made itself known to KARD.

A heavy paw firmly clasped his shoulder and shook him from the dwelling thought. "You're still thinking too much. We have the rest of the weekend, and *I* think you need a distraction," the bear commanded, no hint of suggestion in his voice. Liam called back to the lithe ferret behind him. "Martin, sweetie, is the back house kitchen still stocked?"

Martin slunk out of the office, closing the door gently before *very* casually leaning one shoulder against the wall. The ferret eyed all six-and-a-half feet of the wolf and the bear beside him with a bedroom gaze as he spoke. "Mhmm. A drone came by and restocked everything, maybe two nights ago? We have everything we need for a few good meals, and the linens in all the rooms are fresh too."

The "back house" was the name affectionately given to the rear quarters of the bookstore. The walls of the entire building were heavily reinforced — a legacy of the days when the tunnel connection between it and KDS saw much heavier traffic – but the back house was an entirely obscured section, hidden away in the guts of the building. It had originally been a designated fallback point in event of other facilities being compromised, like the long-fallen Long Branch site, but in the present day it had come to operate simply as a safe house; agents in the vicinity could lie low to let things blow over, should a job in Cabbagetown or Regent Park have gone badly. More regularly, though, it was a quiet spot within another already quiet spot, complete with some decidedly more-than-basic amenities.

"Perfect," Liam concluded. "How about we head for the room with the *big* bed, hmm? All three of us." His tone was casual, but still just as persuasive as it always was; if there was going to be a distraction, he'd be the one leading the activities. "Plenty of room to cuddle and unwind once the *action* calms down."

The tone of the bear's voice drifted into a lustful whisper the more he went on. Maxwell was by no means immune to it, even as stressed and consumed by recent events as he was. It didn't matter how many decades had passed since their first time together, he quietly smiled to himself; that damn bear could always get it. The wolf caught his tail starting to faintly wag, right as Martin's hand brushed against his shoulder, followed by a gentle kiss to the back of his neck. "Mmm…"

Liam tamped down his ardour for a moment, first, to ask a necessary question. "Colour check, how are we all feeling?" Consent was always of the highest importance. and his tone showed it.

"Green," came the replies from both Martin and Maxwell in unison.

The bear held a grin, raising a single eyebrow as the trio made their way to the unremarkable door leading to the back house. "And what would you say if I were to suggest recording tonight's session, hmm? Something for the good folks back on base to enjoy at their leisure? It's been a while since we shared something like that."

Maxwell's tail, try as he might to hide it, flicked from side to side with growing eagerness. It wasn't that he strictly got off to the idea of being seen — that had, in fact, always been something of a delicate subject for him — but that he *knew* how much his boys enjoyed it. Holding the reassuring hand of his ursine lover on the dunes of a quiet beach hadn't made his first time crossdressing, all those decades ago, *that* much less nerve-wracking; nonetheless, he'd worn the sundress, and loved it, because Liam loved it all the more. "For you two, anything," he cooed, feeling his anxieties start to slowly melt away.

Within giddy minutes of entering the cosily reinforced rooms, the ambient temperature was already beginning to rise from their combined body heat. With all six of their hands occupied, the wolf was grateful ROSE made sure to adjust the lights for them.

Martin didn't waste time; he always had been an excitably-energetic twink. Resting his paws almost reverently on Maxwell's firm chest, drifting up to the taller man's shoulders, he leaned in for a tender kiss. The ferret slowly tilted his head, permitting his muzzle to open around the larger canine's, a soft needy breath pouring from his nose. The heavy off-white ruff around Maxwell's throat flitted with a deep, lustful rumble, in response. The wolf's hands sank around Martin's waist and slid further back, until claw tips met again in the small of the younger man's back. He picked one delicately under the tail fastener at the top of the ferret's pants, and curled fingers delicately around the beating ropey tail as he deepened the kiss with an open maw. Martin's RCGs began to slide off the bridge of his nose, but the wolf delicately lifted a hand to remove them. He promptly handed them to the bear, who had been watching with a tender (but mischievous) smile.

"Yours too, puppy," Liam added, taking Martin's RCGs in a one broad paw. He used the other to gently slide off Maxwell's own visor and set both aside on the dresser at the foot of the bed.

Maxwell's tail continued to flick from side to side, dragging his hips with each slow change of direction, as if he were dancing on the intimate high. The rocking made shimmying out of his pants all the easier too — certainly helped by the ferret's own wandering paws unbuckling his understated belt, and pulling the dark leather completely free with a single, *very* practised motion.

Soon both of them were bottomless, pants kicked off and dutifully collected by the bear to fold and stack neatly on the dresser. His legs bare, Martin teased at the waistband of his lacy black thong with a single digit; always a bit of a show-off, next to his own preference for simple boxers, the wolf observed in delight.

It wasn't long before Maxwell's own hand came down to help, hooking a finger (and then another) down through the thong's waist strap, and sliding further forward along the decorative hem until his knuckles brushed purposefully against his partner's carefully sculpted pubic fur, eliciting the kind of breathy gasp that drove the canine *wild*. The wolf reoriented his paw, leaving the kiss behind to instead bury his nose in the ferret's slender neck, dragging his teeth there just a little. His fingers explored, two lanky digits lovingly spreading his boy's cunt, leaving a third free to slowly sink between the folds.

Martin's hands clutched at the fabric of the wolf's shirt, desperately trying (and failing) to hold back a ragged moan. "*Ffffuck*, Daddy... *please...*"

"Good boy, remembering your manners. You're so wet, dear..." Maxwell murmured into the ferret's neck, pivoting on his feet to face Liam and the tiny minicam in his RCGs that was recording the entire scene. He was speaking for a future audience, after all, as much as for the sake of the needy boy presently squirming damply against his hand. "Why don't you fill that mouth of yours first? Before I see about giving you what you need."

Maxwell watched as Liam followed, stripped nude and crouched by his side. The bear didn't kneel, he *never* knelt; that was tantamount to submission in Liam's eyes, the wolf knew. Liam's fingers busied themselves with stroking the flanks of his thick, meaty T-dick while his thumb disappeared in the thick forest of his pubic fur and the heavy roll of his underbelly.

Before he could sink into the bed proper, Martin had already pulled down the wolf's underwear. Maxwell spread his thighs, one hand delicately tracing the ferret's feather-fine jawline and dragging a single claw tip along its edge to his chin. He pressed a thumb to those sweet lips expectantly. "Open..."

The boy took the instruction well, like he always did, and opened his maw with the kind of airy open-mouth smile that had proudly caught more loads than he could ever hope to remember. A solitary moan drooled from Martin's maw, as *papa loup* André held down that experienced tongue with a thumb to coyly inspect him.

There were so many things that the ferret's mouth could be called; indeed, there were some very *specific* examples that Martin loved more than anything else. The phrase "Cock Holster" never quite sounded right in Maxwell's metre, but there were alternatives his plaything enjoyed very nearly as much. The wolf gave a soft, passionate snarl as he pulled back his sheath, revealing the slight curve of his throbbing dick, and gazed deeply into the ferret's eyes.

"I think this toy will do," the wolf said with a warm command, his thumb pressing down on and exploring Martin's tongue as he watched for the moment the man beneath him began to melt. "It looks almost as if it were made for me." Just as he expected, a little glint grew in the ferret's eyes and then spilled over into a long, needy moan, complete with a limpness that washed from ears to tail and back again.

"*Pleathhh,*" came the mustelid's response, dripping with want.

"And so polite, too!" Maxwell teased his thumb back out of Martin's mouth, and let the sub do the rest. The ferret's mouth was perfectly hot, his dextrous tongue curling under the wolf's tip and tracing every sensitive spot it had come to know intimately over the years. Another tender grunt left the wolf's mouth as he felt Martin's nose press firmly, *demandingly,* against his crotch, having sunk himself down to take in every inch — all except the wolf's heavy, bulbous knot, still partially hidden as it was by the white-grey fur of his sheath.

Liam got in closer, running a hand through Martin's beautifully maintained hair, only to grab at a bunch of it with a carefully rough grasp, holding the ferret in place while the other hand crept between his thighs from behind to dive two digits knuckle-deep into the boy's dripping cunt. "*Good* boy. So fucking wet down here that we're going to have to call up a service drone to clean the mess you're making of the floor, aren't we?" he teased, voice low and coy. "Maybe when they come up, we'll hold you down on the bed with your legs open. Drones need cool-off time too, and who are you to say no to being such a good *hole,* hmm?"

Gasping, Maxwell felt every inch of the ferret shudder under Liam's grip, the moan that rumbled through Martin's throat only adding to the blissful sensations riding down the wolf's cock. He *would* submit to a drone, of course; that was hardly new. Still, Maxwell knew, it never stopped being hot to the ferret that a voluntarily mind-controlled *tool* of supervillainy personified could be above him like that. Martin looked every part the stylishly-proper queer teacher, and the wolf delighted in how nicely that contrasted with seeing him so thoroughly *used* and *lost* in the praise that came with a session like this.

The wolf was just about ready for something else, however, and gave a soft pat to Martin's cheek to signal it to the ferret.

Liam slowly withdrew his fingers and pulled them to his mouth, making sure the ferret saw him savour the taste, flashing his teeth with a heady growl as he cleaned them off. Much to Maxwell's curiosity, the bear then silently reached for a box under the bed, sliding it out and rummaging through the countless plugs, gags, and straps, one of which he removed and put to one side. After a moment, he seemed to have found what he was looking for — and withdrew a bundle of purple rope, before shoving the toy collection back into its hiding place. "Hey, cutie… how do you feel about me trying out something new on you? I was thinking of a turtle harness, nothing too complicated."

Maxwell wasn't sure what that was, but he was definitely *interested*. A quick glance at Martin's face told the wolf he very much *did* know what it was. That was all the encouragement he needed. Maxwell let the bear help Martin to his feet, watching as the smaller man was turned about on the spot by commanding ursine paws.

"Face your betters, sweetie. André wants to see his toy's delight, I'm sure."

Maxwell let himself lean back gently, idly stroking his dick in one hand while admiring the ferret's body in full before him, giving a confirmatory growl with his full throat. He watched as Liam's paws deftly tied a starting loop and then four knots along the trailing ends, before he draped the starting ropework lovingly around the ferret's neck from behind. "It's all fresh in my mind," he mused, while feeling the lengths of cordage in his paws for its give and tension. The bear passed the two loose ends between Martin's legs and pulled them both taut into the corners of his inner thighs, applying a gentle pressure against the ferret's exposed cunt before bringing the ends up and hooking them through the back of the starting loop. After another moment of drawing the rope through the spaces between the earlier knots, the harness was finished and Maxwell began to appreciate how it got its name. Liam pulled the last few inches of rope snug, playfully growling into Martin's ear. "Good. You look pretty like this; I'll have to try what *else* I learned on you, some time."

The wolf's eyes took in the whole sight, delighting in how the impromptu bondage in Liam's suddenly-expert paws accentuated the mustelid's lithe figure. He liked what he saw, and without a word, called Martin over with only his eyes. The paw at his crotch pulled his sheath down enough to reveal his heavy, swollen, softball-sized knot.

Martin didn't even need to take the first step forward; Liam had already walked around to his side, hooked a finger under one of the more secure knots against his chest, and *pulled* him to the edge of the bed. The bed sheets deformed under his crawl over the wolf, crumpling and bunching up at his knees, mercifully helping support him as his body shook and ached with *need*.

"You *do* look very pretty like that, Martin, my dear," Maxwell cooed. He flashed his teeth again in a commanding smile that — even softened as it was by the heavy crow's feet at the corners of his eyes — was no less imposing. "Now, be a good boy… and *sit*."

As the folds of his slickened cunt parted and he needfully sank around the wolf's cock, Martin pushed himself into a more seated position until he was quiveringly *grinding* Maxwell's fat knot inside himself. Maxwell swam in bliss, trying to remain composed, but his voice wavered through a snatched breath, coaxing an only slightly uncharacteristic curse from his maw.

Maxwell tensed as Martin drew his hips upward again, and with palms flat against the bed, on both sides of the wolf's thick ruff, he let himself slide back down. The air was thick with the scent of fucking already, and the ferret seemed to intentionally drink in deeper breaths to take more of it in.

The ropes against the boy's body were a new sensation, not quite unlike a regular body harness, but the wolf found something more intensely *raw* about the cotton weave. With another downstroke from the ferret, Maxwell realised he could feel the two sections of rope either side of Martin's stuffed hole pressing against the bulb of his knot, and for a moment, he wondered if they'd even let it past.

The supple fine fur of Martin's thighs passed between and surrounded Maxwell's wandering fingers. The canine curled his digits in the crook behind his partner's knees, needing to feel more of the warmth of an excitable bottom doing what came naturally to them. His own need had been swelling, building in rippling waves as the mustelid rode him with steady gentle bounces. And then—

Before he could even register why the bed was moving in the way it was, Liam was on top of the wolf's face. He'd always had an aggressive streak when it came to topping that Maxwell loved, and vision framed as it was by the bear's trunk-like thighs, the wolf let out a pleased groan at the tell tale sight of straps hooking under his partner's ass. The bear had donned a strap, and his gruff command told exactly what he was going to do with it. "Mouth". Dutifully, Martin went about obeying with both hands, something Maxwell could deduce by how the bear's heavy right paw reached down and spread his ass to give another instruction. "That goes for you too, puppy. Put that tongue to good use while I make sure our boy works the both of us".

Maxwell didn't protest. His rolling groan was one of pure overwhelming lust, and he had no desire to wait. Before the bear had even fully taken a seat, the wolf's tongue was pushing forward, exploring the familiar creases of Liam's asshole, heated all the more by his excited breaths. He let a single paw lift from Martin's thigh, using it to spread the ursine more and get his face deeper. When Liam finally did begin to put his weight into sitting, Maxwell's tongue was already hungrily probing the dark flesh and savouring the *taste*. Empire Enhancements had done work on all three of them, and the bear was no exception. There was a deep, rugged earthiness to his musk that distantly reminded Maxwell of the forest, or a cabin; it was lightened by a floral sweetness from the sweat that soaked through and clung to the ursine's rich brown coat, whenever he was worked up.

Maxwell felt Liam lean forward as he helped push the ferret down. "Take your Daddy's knot, bitch," were the words the wolf thought he heard, soft and syrupy from the bear's throat, but heavy with intent. The wolf felt Martin relax and sink around him just a little more, the ferret's whines filling the air and then—

Maxwell shuddered, as his entire knot buried to the hilt in his toy. He could feel the new sensation of soft rope pressing against his sheath as

Martin's body locked down tight and firm around his dick, walls trembling out a massaging rhythm from base to tip. All of the wolf's lower half tensed, enough so that it distracted his tongue from the important work of eating the bear out like ursine ass was his last meal. He couldn't hold it. Maxwell threw his head back, gasping for air in the narrow gap under the ursine's thick, sweaty tail dock, howling with a rasp that came with age.

His breathing steadied after what felt like minutes of a body-rocking climax, so lost in the bleary sensations that the motions of his two partners, reaching their own peaks, became lost in the soupy mess of feelings, sights, and sounds. Maxwell opened his eyes and let loose a long-drawn sigh of exhaustion and completion, the arms of Martin and Liam draped over his tired frame.

The three of them laid there for what felt like hours, bodies occasionally moving and feeling heavy, practically bathing in the smell of sex and each other. Parts of them were sticky and used in ways they were all too exhausted to do anything about, for the moment.

Eventually, Liam grunted softly to himself and rose. He unbuckled the strap and dropped it to the floor with a huff, before getting up and wandering unceremoniously to the adjoining room. The light from the back house's kitchenette poured sleepily through the door, soon followed by the smell of fresh coffee.

The bear's custom post-fucking roast blend was gentle on the palate and specifically selected for low caffeine content. He walked back into the bedroom with his blend loaded into a French press, accompanied by three mismatched mugs on a tray. Martin didn't hesitate to claim his own chunky novelty mug, the one which proudly exclaimed "NO ONE KNOWS THAT I'M A BOTTOM" on its side in pink and maroon text.

None of them said anything memorable, or coherent, as they sat and drank. Maxwell watched as Liam tenderly insisted on removing the ropes from Martin's torso before they left marks, the two older men giggling sleepily as the ferret squirmed at how sensitive his body was in the aftermath. Martin, free of his harness, wrapped himself around the wolf while Liam neatly bundled the rope and tied it off, stowing it back in the box under the bed. The trio made their way to the shower, cleaned each other up, and returned sleepily to bed together.

In the quiet warm darkness of the room between the bear and the ferret, and with a clear head — the kind of clarity that came with the bliss of figuring himself so lucky to experience these kinds of moments, to have love and passion and support and care — Maxwell reflected on recent events. He would have to find that girl, and soon. The things that had happened to him... they didn't have to happen to her, too.

July 8, 1955

"There should be a room under the name Maxwell? I'm with Doctor Alcott and the conference..." The wolf trailed off in his speech, tired and a little unsure of himself as he spoke to the diminutive receptionist. Maxwell was young, but the rigours of travel had beaten him down, even with Alcott's help. He was technically a fugitive, on the run from the SIS — and therefore, functionally, Her Majesty's Government. The long sleepless nights in uncomfortable transport of what was effectively his being smuggled across borders was clearly present on his face.

The receptionist peered up at the boy and checked through the reservation paperwork, keeping one gimlet eye on him the entire time.

He nervously rubbed at the back of his neck, trying to avoid the feline's gaze by taking in the surprisingly ornate lobby. Large cream-painted pillars lined their way to the reception desk before flanking off in both directions. To the right was the bar and dining room (closed, at such a late hour), and to the left looked to be a large banquet hall — no doubt where the conference would be held, and where he would eventually meet with the doctor face-to-face for the first time.

The receptionist caught the wolf's wandering attention with a flat, tired tone. "Room 506. The deposit has already been paid for you. Breakfast is between seven and eight-thirty." There was a pause as she expectantly waited for the canine to take the key she was holding out for him. "Is that a French accent?"

Maxwell simply nodded and took the key to his room delicately.

"Fancy French academic then?" the receptionist offered, almost-but-not-quite accusingly.

"Oh... no, just... a journalist, invited to report on the conference." The cover story was terrible, but Maxwell wasn't the one who had come up with it. He wasn't honestly sure he could have actually come up with something *more* believable, though, despite his years working in close proximity to spies and intelligence assets. The wolf had always been in the background, far away from the *real* action. He hadn't even been given a cover name for this whole affair, but perhaps he didn't need one; Dr. Alcott would know better, wouldn't he? The recently-founded International League of Archivists wasn't exactly on the radar of the major players in the intelligence community, but judging by the lengths Alcott had gone to get ahold of Maxwell, they had to have known things they shouldn't.

The receptionist lifted her chin in apparent acknowledgement, before matter-of-factly adding that the elevators were out of order, and that he would have to take the stairs to his room.

Maxwell picked his modest bag up off the floor — filled with the few belongings and clothes he'd managed to pack — and trudged towards the staircase, key in hand. He quietly wished that the handler who had met him at the harbour would have stuck around long enough to see him to his room. The climb up the stairs might have been the longest he'd been unaccompanied in this whole ordeal, if he'd cared to think about it. Instead, his mind was occupied by the worry that in every shadow and around every corner could be lurking one of Tommy's men.

Anxiety lost to fatigue, though, and Maxwell finally made it to his room, about halfway down the fifth-floor hallway. He was thankful to find it empty, except for the dull but serviceable furniture that distantly reminded him of the lodgings so *kindly* provided to him by the SIS.

Before the wolf could remove his worn jacket to hang it on the back of the lone chair in the room, there was a knock at the door. His heart only stopped beating for a second, though, as a whispered, nasally voice followed shortly after.

"André, it's Alcott... are you decent?"

The canine continued to strip from his jacket, letting it crumple into a pile at the end of the bed before walking by the pokey bathroom to the room's door. He peered through the peephole; sure enough, there was the man he'd only even seen in a handful of grainy newspaper photographs, the man who he had to thank for his current arrangements, his features distorted through a fish-eye lens. Still, Maxwell kept the chain engaged before cautiously opening the door a crack. He stood nervously behind it, out of the badger's line of sight, speaking through the narrow opening. "I, uh… hello, sir. I'm decent, yes."

Something changed in the doctor's aura of hushed excitability in that moment. Even in silence, Maxwell could feel the older man's heart sink as he respectfully kept his distance. "…Oh, my boy. It's — it's safe, I assure you. But if you'd rather not let me in, I understand."

Maxwell winced. He'd not been respected like that in a long time, and the man's soft verbalisations were congruent with the reassuring tones of Alcott's letters. Maxwell fought with himself for a moment, and slid the chain guard back, slowly opening the door more fully. His fur was a little matted, he smelled like a ship's cargo hold, and his eyes would be teary if they weren't so damnably dry and tired; he longed to be *seen*, nonetheless.

Alcott stepped forward towards the threshold of the room, his eyes deep and sympathetic. He was a good foot and a half shorter than Maxwell, and wore a clean pressed shirt, brown suit pants, dully practical shoes, and a tie that was — despite apparent best intentions — still a little on the loose side. The badger slowly lifted out his paws, heaving a weary sigh like a man resigned to expending a great deal of necessary effort in the near future. "I'm just glad you're safe. May I come in?"

The courtesy again stunned the wolf, just a little. It had been so long since he'd had actual agency — since he hadn't just been a *tool* to someone else. Alcott walked in, and Maxwell shut, locked, and bolted the door behind him, out of habit. He watched curiously as the badger picked the crumpled jacket off the floor, shook it out, and neatly folded it on the foot of the bed.

"Are you fed?" Alcott asked, over his shoulder

Maxwell nodded before realising that it was only polite to speak too. "Yes sir. They gave me some food on the boat, just before we got into the harbour."

Alcott sat in the lone chair and cupped his paws together in his lap. "You needn't call me sir, André. I promise. I'm not your boss, nor do you owe me anything. I helped you because it was the right thing to do."

Maxwell quietly sat himself down on the edge of the bed, silently enjoying how soft it was, compared to his usual accommodations.

"I know about Operation Felt, André," Alcott said mournfully.

Maxwell had assumed the badger must have known *something*, or else he wouldn't have been willing to risk so much in helping him. Part of him had been pondering all manner of scenarios. Was the doctor associated in any capacity with the US intelligence services? Or with the communists? Was the ILA a front, or was he just an eccentric, with a lot of strings to pull? Ultimately, it didn't matter; *anything* was better than the SIS, and Alcott, at least, seemed... genuine. Certainly more genuine than Tommy could ever manage to fake.

"What I don't know, however," the doctor continued, voice settling with blunt certainty, "is exactly what they did to you. I have sources, and an imagination, but I didn't have eyes on Operation Felt like you must have. I'm sorry that I haven't been able to speak plainly about it before now, but you understand a need for discretion."

The wolf didn't want to interrupt. Part of him wanted to just let the older man continue, explaining what exactly it was that he knew... but the silence punctuated the air, waiting to be filled. "...Who are you with?"

Alcott took in a sharp breath. "Not the CIA, if that's what you're wondering. Nor the Heroes. Just the ILA and my own conscience."

"But you knew who I was. You knew I *existed*. You knew how to reach me. Someone in the SIS mailroom knew you were trying to reach me; otherwise, I never would have gotten your first letter. That was a risk no one would take, unless they *knew* they weren't going to get caught. You don't just have *sources*, you have people inside British Intelligence," the wolf huffed. Maxwell stared at the floor, letting his words slowly pour out, too tired to stop or hold them back, despite being keenly aware that they were leaning towards the accusatory. "Are... are you a communist?"

There was a deathly silence in the room, quiet enough that the wolf's keen ears could hear the hum of the mains from the wall receptacles.

Alcott leaned forward, cupped paws forming a pyramid and sinking between his knees. "If I said yes, would that change how you feel about being here in this room with me, André?"

The wolf exhaled quietly, feeling the corners of his mouth pinch into the faintest of smiles in near-disbelief at how goddamn *brazen* the older man was. Even as much of a mystery as the badger continued to be, he carried the same confidence that Tommy did but wielded it in a completely different way.... a way Maxwell very much liked. "I suppose not."

"Good lad." Alcott put his paw reassuringly on the wolf's shoulder, giving just a gentle squeeze. "We'll talk more tomorrow after breakfast. We can't change what happened to you, André, but we can make sure it doesn't have to happen again. I promise. Now, you should get some sleep. I'm next door in 508; if you need anything... don't hesitate to knock."

Maxwell followed the badger to the door, thanking him and securing the door with the chain again before returning to the bed, alone. An entirely novel feeling filled him, strange and warm. The room looked (and felt) uncomfortably empty, without the older man sitting in the chair. He ran a paw down his leg to the knee, taking in the sensation of his ill-fitting pants that he hadn't changed out of since yesterday. The wolf wanted to sleep... but not alone, again. Not like so many other nights. Not just stuck with his imagination. He wanted to hold someone, and to be held.

He looked at the door to the room, swallowed dryly, and stood up. There wasn't a comb in his bag, or in the bathroom, but running his fingers through tap water and then through his gunmetal-grey fur was at least enough to make him look somewhat less bedraggled. With that task complete, Maxwell left the room, made his way to the door of 508, sucked in a breath, and softly knocked.

Alcott opened the door. His tie was off, the top two buttons of his shirt undone, and his eyes were so *deep*. The badger leaned coyly against the doorframe with his shoulder, a far cry from the way he had carried himself only a moment ago.

The wolf's heart raced in his chest, thumping so loud that it was almost all he could hear. Pulling himself away from the older man's gaze for just long enough, Maxwell could see the room was a double, and the desk was scattered with papers.

Alcott smelled *beautiful* too, and Maxwell could only kick himself for not noticing sooner. It wasn't the heavy cologne that the boys in the SIS wore. It was richer, deeper, and natural. It stirred things in him, things the canine hadn't been able to articulate as anything other than a primal *need* in his moments alone. He wasn't sure how to tell if Alcott was the same way as he was — the same way that Little had apparently been — but he felt safe enough to ask, and that clearly meant something. He *had* to try.

"Can I... I mean, I would like... uh. You are very attractive, and I don't know how these things are supposed to work, but..." he blurted out.

The badger interrupted the younger man's fervid stammers with a knowing smile. "Only if you want to. First time?"

July 10, 1955

Maxwell's paws trembled. Consciousness slowly trickled back to him, like the blood that seemed to drip from his temple. Even in the dim glow of streetlights, filtered through hazy East Coast fog as they were, the dark crimson was clearly visible, vilely glistening. The rest of the alley was devoid of any other discernible shapes, save the bright white leaves of scattered paper.

The wolf pulled his head away from the damp brickwork, casting his bleary gaze at the scraps being blown gently towards a gutter. The pages were filled with text, he could tell that much from a short distance, but his head was still spinning. With a fumbling grasp, he managed to snap up one of the sheets, but struggled as his vision continued to defy his demands. Only the letterhead of the ILA was discernible.

The world started to pour angrily back into his head, memories of the last few days forming, fragmenting, and reforming like an indecisive jigsaw puzzle.

Conference. ILA. League... archivists. Research... More words on the half-clutched piece of paper resolved into meaning. *Permutations on theoretical babelographic isolations...*

Those words were too painful, too *harsh* for his head to handle. Every time Maxwell's eyes scanned back across them in the gloom, all he seemed to visualise were black flashes of angry, *frightened* screams. He let his focus drop to another section of the crumpled page, where he saw a name: *N. A. Alcott.*

Deep, agonising breaths began to billow through the fog as Maxwell felt more memories come back to him. The hotel's breakfast offering had been *excellent,* compared to his usual malnourished scavenging. There was someone sitting across from him at the table, though; that was a strange experience. Older, friendly, warm… tender.

Maxwell fought with his head, his other hand coming up to finally assess the damage. There was blood soaking through the fur of his fingers, but it seemed thick enough that the wound appeared to be not too deep. Still, there was a sharp pain ringing through his skull.

Alcott. That man is Doctor Alcott, he reasoned. They had spent a night together, the first night he had arrived. It was — it was *everything.* He remembered the euphoria, the nervousness. The laughing, awkward and genuine. His smile, his touch, his—

—The alley didn't make *sense!* Maxwell remembered being in the hotel, he remembered shared moments with Alcott, and he remembered mingling with academics and researchers. (They'd seemed welcoming, if reserved.) He remembered a talk being given, various speakers, a general sense of interest certainly, but hardly excitement. But why was he here, instead? Where *was* he, even? The wolf peered around, vision at last starting to focus normally.

The view at the end of the alleyway told him nothing about his location; no landmarks he recognised, no signs or notable features. His shirt was slightly torn up, speckled with more blood of uncertain origin.

Hotel bar… drinking. There was drinking. Not many people. Just Alcott and a few others. Pain seared through Maxwell's skull. Something was horribly, horribly wrong. He hadn't felt this way since he'd been shot. *Shot. Gun. There was a gun! Who had the gun?*

Pain turned to agony and the wolf threw himself to the embrace of the unforgiving brickwork, pitching a paw to his stomach and failing terribly to hold his guts together. He retched, and heaved, and vomited up almost nothing but bile. A few more retches followed, and then he crumpled to the floor, whimpering for a breath that wasn't tinged with acid.

Every muscle shuddered as more made itself clear to him. *Operation Felt. Questions. Alcott asked… questions…* Maxwell's eyes caught more scraps of paper drifting on the light breeze towards a puddle some feet away. *Research. His research. Alcott explained… something about information permanence… Alexandria Anomaly. Asked what I knew of Ptolemy I… Greek, I think? Why ask? What does that have to do with the SIS?*

The bedraggled canine scrabbled uneasily to his feet and steadied himself against the wall. Maxwell recalled quite *clearly* being confused at the questions. Alcott's room was messy with note paper, but the man himself remained composed and familiar; driven, but not *madly*. The look in his eyes was that of someone approaching a finish line, and then—

—Then they looked concerned.

The clarity of the memories such as they were, stood in stark contrast to the flurry of fractured images Maxwell could piece together of several... subsequent events. Something in him had changed; a flipped switch that came with uncomfortable drowsiness.

Note paper. Research. I... took his research. Hoarded it, gathered everything I could... I didn't even understand it, but I took it.

Maxwell stood vacantly in the alley, watching the remains of his first lover's research sink unceremoniously into a filthy puddle. "He was scared... of me..." The words clung to the walls of his mouth and refused to budge no matter how long the wolf let his jaw hang open.

It was the same as the Vichy government office... a need to collect. Blacking out when it happened...

He remembered the trophy he always kept with him, just then, fumbling for it in his shirt pocket. It had been one of the very few personal belongings he cared to take with him when he fled London... but the folded letterhead was no longer there. The pain in his temple seared again, and with it came another recollection: the recoil of a gun launching the weapon back through his inexperienced hand, and against his head, causing the injury he now nursed.

He had shot Alcott, and he hadn't known what he was doing.

Maxwell recoiled in horror from himself. He couldn't flee. There was no escaping this, no escaping the ineffable *wrongness* of his being. Long-buried nightmares launched into his consciousness, the recollection of another gunshot that caused so much pain and turmoil. He was just like that twisted *bastard*, after all, wasn't he?

His crying half-howls and desperate sobbing echoed around the alley, as he pieced together events from his shattered memories. The explanation didn't matter, though. Not as much as the *facts*. He had started to feel comfortable, *free*, that was it. He'd been drinking. He'd started to slip and fade, struggling against giving into that feral *itch* burning through his mind.

Alcott had reached for his gun he had taped to the underside of the hotel desk. The man hadn't tried to open fire on him; instead, he'd used it as a club. He'd… he'd swung it wrong, though, and Maxwell had reached out to block the blow, his fingers had brushed into the trigger, and then — and then the wolf had shot him.

The reality of what Maxwell had done sank into him like a brick in the ocean, forever spiralling down into a merciless abyss. As he stared blankly at the city lights, he grew faintly aware of the patter of rain on overhead fire escapes, and sirens in the distance. When they began to whistle closer, the wolf *ran*.

The SIS was right. Evans was right. He couldn't control his powers. It would just be better if he stayed away from others. The SIS wouldn't take him back; they'd be more likely to kill him on the spot if he tried, even if he could stomach the thought of returning to his post.

Anger and fear tensed his body. The empty pain at the pit of his stomach turned to fire, as feet started to meet the ground in any direction away from the sirens. Brickwork and garbage cans passed like trees on a running trail, street signs and traffic lights looming overhead as he ran. When the sun started to rise, he was still running, stumbling as he reached the harbour. The waters were cold, but it made cleaning blood from fur a little easier. Clothes stolen from a backyard line made for reasonable attire. Anywhere was better than here and somewhere was better than nowhere.

Don't stop running. Keep going. They can't ever find you.

Papa said to run. He said to run. It was an accident, and he said I love you, now **run**.

A dark hoof met the wet gritty asphalt of the alley. An anonymous source claimed to have heard a wolf howling in pain on the night of the shooting, but police and all other authorities had decided not to bother pursuing the lead. Léon — presently answering to the callsign Typeset — was determined not to let the trail run cold. Traces of blood led the goat to a wind-trap corner in the masonry that had gathered some sodden-looking scraps of paper.

He picked one up, and confirmed it was exactly what he thought: part of Dr. Alcott's research. There was no telling how much had been lost, or even if there were other copies available. A man like Alcott had resisted attempts at communication, and remained relatively secretive; he seemed unlikely to have made duplicates.

Static briefly filled the goat's ears, as his bulky headpiece rang through with a transmission meant for him only. His mission support was in a van, waiting a few blocks over.

"Any sign of the target, Typeset?"

"He was here, but not anymore. I've located the secondary target, though — what's left of it, at least. Command will want to look over this." Though his responses were professional and calm, inside, he was anything but. For years he had wondered what had come of that boy, and now, he feared he was too late. "Is there an update on the hotel scene? What are the agencies saying?"

There was a slight pause as his partner fumbled with the receiver in the van, the sound of folding papers coming through on the goat's earpiece loud and clear. "Last update suggests the official line is going to be rough trade gone wrong. No one seems to be in a hurry to apprehend your boy, though; Alcott's ex-wife was questioned, and didn't seem all that torn up over it. Son couldn't officially be reached for comment, but a source at MIT said he seemed evasive. That's everything."

In the midst of gathering the rest of the research he could find Léon found a familiar page of folded letterhead. He held it out into the sun, hoping to dry it off; sure enough, it was exactly what he had suspected. The goat packed it away safely in his satchel with the rest of the gathered materials and pondered what he'd just heard from his partner in villainy.

"Of course they're not in a hurry. He killed a long-rumoured-lavender academic who was becoming increasingly friendly with the socialists. As far as they're concerned, Maxwell probably tied up some loose ends for them," he murmured bitterly. "I don't think... I don't think that he killed Alcott out of any kind of animosity. He wasn't like that when I knew him. I don't think the SIS could have changed that."

"So, what's the plan?"

"The plan hasn't changed. He's just a scared boy, and I will bring him home."

CHAPTER 7

October 22, 2019

The bookstore at Hook Plaza smelled as musty as it had looked from the outside. Ordinarily that would be an achievement, for a new store in a newly finished unit of a strip mall, but it wasn't all that surprising from the state of the inventory.

Lexi thumbed through the collection, not really looking for anything in particular. Despite the momentary anxiety, she had found herself soothed by the bookstore in Toronto. It made a level of sense, she supposed; in her high school years, she had spent most free periods and lunch breaks hidden away in her school's library — away from the noise of the yard and field, the canteen, or anywhere else, really. The school librarian had allowed her to eat at one of the reading tables, so long as she didn't make a mess, and the young cow had always been thankful for that leniency. When she arrived back in Kitchener and found the Hook Book Nook officially open, Lexi had decided to see if it held the same calming aura. To her relief and tempered delight, it did.

I'll have to see about getting a library card—

Her thought was cut short, in the middle of peering through a monolithic old coffee table book of architectural photography, when she heard a familiar voice. Its owner couldn't have been more than a row over, but he spoke in tones hushed enough that Lexi couldn't quite make out the words. She carefully and quietly closed the book, awkwardly shifting it back up to its display shelf, and tried to surreptitiously make her way to the end of the row. Before she could confirm her suspicions, though, the speaking stopped — and Maxwell rounded the corner into the narrow aisle, apparently surprised to see her.

"Ah! Lexi, was it? What a small world it is."

The Highland looked up at him. Canada was *huge*, and it had a comparatively small population. The chances still seemed slim at best. "Uh. Hi, again? Yeah... very small world. What brings you to Kitchener?" She said, having no conception whatsoever of what the city might offer the old wolf.

"Well, I like to keep my ear to the ground. When you get to my age, you begin to exhaust the collections of even the biggest city's bookstores. Occasionally I travel to see if I can't find something new and interesting."

Lexi supposed that made enough sense. She didn't really know anything about how to run a bookstore, but the gently smiling wolf clearly did. Looking squarely into his face, she then noticed that he wasn't wearing his RCGs.

"And yourself, madame?"

"Oh, just browsing. Not really looking for anything in particular; I haven't even started on any of those books I picked up at your store."

"Oh! I was just about to ask if you had. That book about the binary is very good."

Lexi's ears flicked a little, taking just a second to realise Maxwell was avoiding saying the title out loud. "Oh, have you read it?"

"In a manner of speaking," he said with an almost-imperceptible twitch of one cheek. "How are you finding Canada, by the way?"

"Uh... fine?" The bovine stood there with her mouth open, disarmed and unable to articulate why she felt so. "Yeah. Fine, I guess? Nicer than the UK, at least so far."

Maxwell gave another smile and plucked a small palm-sized book from one of the shelves, still idly making conversation as he flicked to a page, occasionally looking down to the cow. "Are you planning on moving here, or is this just a vacation of sorts?"

"Moving, eventually. There's a lot to figure out. Permits, extensions... medication... you know, that sort of stuff."

The wolf tucked the book back onto the shelf and reached into the pocket of his long jacket, pulling out a simple-looking glossy black card. He held it out silently.

Lexi said nothing, and took it cautiously, suddenly feeling like she was in some kind of spy movie. The older man really did have a *presence* about him; it made her question whether everyone really was this friendly and forward in Canada, or whether she was just obtuse. It couldn't hurt to take the card, in any event.

It was for D. E. Dropp, of course, with the shop's phone number circled in careful red fountain pen. Only when she had it in her hand did Maxwell speak up again. "If you need help getting hold of those things, just give me a call. I'm looking to hire a new clerk to work with Martin, and it wouldn't be the first time we've helped with immigration papers, or getting hold of hormones. Give it some thought? I'd be the one conducting your interview, and you've already made quite the impression, believe me."

A second later, he was gone. Lexi hadn't even managed to get out a thank you, and she spent a few minutes trying to work out if she'd imagined the offer. She couldn't have. The card was in her hand, and Maxwell *definitely* said something about a job. It couldn't be *that* easy, could it?

October 25, 2019

A join in the track shuddered the carriage of the GO train, briefly knocking consciousness back into Lexi; her eyes had glazed over, staring out the window at the passing scenery.

She had mused over the offer Maxwell made with Drac for a day or two, before finally deciding it might be worth any risk. Extra income would, after all, make saving for a future together that much easier — though she still couldn't quite believe she could possibly be *this* lucky. The cow had phoned the store, spoken to the wolf, and agreed to come in for her first shift. She'd been informed it would mostly be filling out paperwork, and shadowing Martin to get a feel for the place.

The train slowed to a faintly chugging halt as it pulled into Union Station. Lexi pulled out her phone and fired off a reassuring check-in message to her boyfriend, who'd still had some reservations about her travelling out to Toronto by herself. She was plenty nervous about it too, but back home, she'd regularly made the trip to central London and spent the day navigating via the tube; London was something like three times the size of Toronto, at that. The York concourse was a mess to navigate, and the Highland begrudgingly noted to herself that some of the platforms only had one track between them, meaning a train could arrive or depart from two platforms at the same time — something that seemed almost heretical to her.

She found her way to Front Street and, after a short walk, reached her next method of transit. She'd extensively researched the TTC and Toronto's streetcar network online, the night before, and hopped on the 503 King, eastbound to Parliament. It was only another moment's walk to the shop, from there.

As she rounded a corner — the same one that she and Drac had made their way around together, only a few days prior — she saw familiar figures of the imposing bear, the lithe ferret, and the towering shape of Maxwell himself standing outside Dropp's, apparently waiting to greet her. As she got nearer, it was clear they had just been talking about something; Liam was wearing an obviously smug grin, and Martin seemed to be flushing, just a little, though it was hard to tell in the morning light.

Liam stepped forward to re-introduce himself, a little sheepishly, considering his commanding presence. "Hello again, and welcome to the Dropp!"

"*The* Dropp?" Lexi asked, with an admittedly still-nervous smile.

Martin gave a nod and looked over his shoulder to the signage above the door. "That's just what we call it. Anyway, it's nice to see you again, Lexi."

The four of them were walking into the store together even before Lexi had the chance to properly start thanking anyone for the offer. Once inside, the bear ambled off. He raised the back of his paw to the air in a faint gesture towards another door, tucked away between two bookcases.

"I'll get some coffee on. Lexi, how do you take yours?"

The cow took a moment to think, before settling on what she hoped was the least burdensome way one might impose upon another person to make a coffee. "Uh, just black is fine! Thank you very much, Liam."

The bear's paw returned a silent thumbs up as he wandered out of sight. The others took to their tasks; Martin busied himself with setting up the register and shuffling through a stack of paper on the desk, while Maxwell began to climb the stairs in the corner, politely ushering Lexi along with him.

"If you come with me, Lexi, we'll get to that paperwork first. It shouldn't take too long."

Lexi followed closely, taking in the view of the store from the brief vantage of the stairs. Out of the corner of her eye, she saw the register down below booting up. Briefly — very, *very* briefly — the cashier-facing interface screen flashed a bright magenta symbol, some loading icon spinning on its axis. When her attention returned to what was in front of her, she realised that Maxwell was already down the hall at the top of the stairs, patiently and elegantly holding open the office door for the cow, just waiting for her to catch up.

She thanked the wolf graciously and stepped into the office, expecting to find some particularly arcane, cluttered cubbyhole, like the concentrated *essence* of the rest of the store. She was... disappointed. While one wall was at least neatly lined with a row of bookcases, each of them was filled mostly with binders and file boxes. The rest of the room was modest; small, even. Smaller than it should have been, when she pondered the dimensions of the ground floor in her mental map.

A quick glance to the solitary window in the room revealed that the external wall was thick; about... two feet thick, if she had to guess. It faced out to a narrow alley between Dropp's and the neighbouring red-brick building. She recalled the book she'd stumbled across in the store back in Kitchener, and how it elegantly relayed the architecture common to different time periods around Toronto. The pleasant watercolour image of a building that looked not-too-dissimilar to Dropp's came back to her, and there was no way she was looking at a double-layer brick wall. The more she thought about it, the more she realised all of the external walls in Dropp's were unusually thick. Even the doors seemed remarkably *heavy*, for wood.

Maxwell let the door close behind him, before wandering over to the understated desk. He sat down in a swivel chair that looked as though it might have been pilfered from a Brutalist university library in the 1970s. "Please, do sit down," he offered, a single paw gesturing to the squat, somewhat dusty wingback chair on the other side of the desk.

The dwelling thought about the unusual walls flitted back into the recesses of Lexi's mind, as she remembered why she was there in the first place. She took a seat and tried not to stare, as the canine rummaged through some drawers on his side of the desk, apparently looking for some of the papers that would need discussing and signing. The old typewriter to the wolf's right was an easy distraction. Lexi couldn't *quite* make out a model from her vantage point across the desk, but she could see the keys. The lower row appeared to have one key that didn't sit right, half-depressed even without being touched, suggesting significant age and constant wear.

Maxwell re-emerged from his hunched position over one of the drawers with a small selection of papers in his hand. "Here we are. If you don't mind, I have a short test I'd like you to take. Nothing taxing; just think of it as an aptitude test, let's say."

Lexi silently nodded along. Her ability to keep a cool exterior was starting to buckle, under a combination of stress and strange feelings she couldn't explain, but she nonetheless tried to put it all out of her head.

She reached for the paper being offered to her across the desk and found it to be a full essay of text, clearly written on the typewriter she had been eyeing. On closer examination, though, the sentences were nonsense; they were just random words, without grammatical structure. Her mind started to tick over, and she began to assume that this would be one of those... "social employability" type tests, where the first word that jumps out at you was imagined to say a lot about your work ethic. But Maxwell soon put that idea out of her mind.

"Oh, don't worry that it doesn't make sense; that's rather the point. What I need you to do is to find three words. Just three words, your choice. Focus on those words in your head without saying them aloud, and hand the paper back when you're done. That's all."

When the cow's eyes lifted from the page, she stared; there was a deep, *different* intensity to Maxwell's gaze, though it was still at least partially masked by a friendly smile. Lexi looked back down at the sheet in front of her, and with some background unease, picked three words from the sheet and focused on them: 'Traversal', 'Historiographer', and 'Purpose'.

She quietly slid the paper back across the desk and meekly nodded, a growing sense of discomfort filling her. The wolf put his paw down gently on the paper and breathed out a soft, almost tired sigh.

With a faint rattle of writing implements, Maxwell pulled a red pen from a small pot to the side of the typewriter and circled three words on the paper: 'Traversal', 'Historiographer', and 'Purpose'. He slid the paper back across the desk. The wolf set the pen down and cupped his paws in front of the pensive look on his muzzle.

"...How did you..."

"You told me," he said, speaking with a soft, slow blink, words muffled only slightly through his cupped paws. "Let me show you what I mean." Maxwell pulled another sheet out of the small pile he'd brought out from the drawer. This one was another mass of words in nonsense sentences. He looked at it for a few, endless seconds, then handed it to the cow, along with the red pen. "Circle the three words that come to mind."

The moment she reached for the paper, three words already danced in her mind with all the clarity of a recently spoken line. If it wasn't for the strange, split-second jolting feeling between her eyes and at the back of her neck, she'd have sworn the words had always been in her head. She wasn't so much thinking about them, as she was remembering them... but remembering from *where*, though?

Her eyes peered down at the sheet, and with no apparent effort, the three words were simply *there*. They were there, exactly where her vision first decided to scan, like she had been subconsciously drawn to them. The wolf hadn't *said* anything, but she knew he had communicated to her somehow; the words weren't in her head without his help. She sheepishly took the pen in one hand.

Maxwell had stood up and turned to face the wall. "Have you circled them?"

"...Yes."

"'Twenty', 'Conference', and 'Brighten.'"

The words he spoke were precisely the ones she had circled; the ones that just *appeared* in her head, somehow, before she'd even gotten a good look at the paper. "How..."

Maxwell slowly returned to his chair and sank down into it with what seemed to be relief. "You and I share a power. It's easiest to think of it as a kind of telepathy, but it's rather specific and limited in its scope — restricted to the transfer of information, so long as it has been written or printed in some physical form. The day you first came here, you accidentally imprinted the entire contents of a book on Liam. You then imprinted the contents of *another* book on me. What you just experienced now was a more focused, disciplined form of the same communication — from yourself to me, and then from me to you."

Lexi sat there, stunned. She tried to find words, but the only thing that came out was a nervous laugh — one that didn't get further than a couple of awkward haws. "No... no. No! I mean, that's not true, that's... no, I'd *know* if I had a superpower!"

"How often are you sleepwalking?"

The stunned silence returned, this time with a thousandfold-more-crushing weight behind it. Lexi couldn't bring herself to say anything, but the silence was apparently more than enough confirmation for the old man.

"It was like that for me, too. Sleepwalking, and waking up with material that wasn't mine. I didn't know where I had gotten it. Just that I had been driven to collect and recover information that took my interest... or that I knew I shouldn't have."

Being fixated on physical media could have been a lucky guess — she made no secret of her bookishness — but how could he possibly know that she had been sleepwalking? Unless... unless he was telling the truth? On the other hand, she'd never even *heard* of a telepath whose abilities worked exclusively on printed material, that was the kind of eclectic, problem-causing shit that—

—The typewriter. The *typewriter*, the one inches away from her, right there on the wolf's *desk*, the one with a single stuck key. Lexi looked down again at the sheet in her hands, frantically scanning for any words containing the letter X. Suddenly, it all made sense — the walls being so thick and the doors so heavy, the strange icon she'd caught out of the corner of her eye, the Thorntech RCGs and the immensely approachable (but still subversive-feeling) collection of queer literature in the store. Every time the letter X appeared on the sheet it was raised slightly above the level of the other letters, and appeared just a *little* fainter on the page... just like in the newspaper photos.

The bovine put the paper down on the desk and stared into the eyes of the career supervillain who was apparently offering her a job, dumbfounded. "You're... you're with the Korps. You're the Dark Dossier, aren't you? This place — I mean, the walls must be reinforced, with how thick they are! How... why am I, I mean... *what do you want with me?*"

Maxwell shrugged, a gently worried expression on his grey muzzle. "This — as I'm sure you've figured out — is not precisely a job interview, Lexi. It's a recruitment offer, but not *just* that, either. There were times in the past when... when I hurt people close to me, because I had not yet learned how to *control* my power. If you could be spared the same pains I went through..." The wolf let the long pause punctuate his explanation, unaware that to the cow, the air was full of a pounding heartbeat. "I am simply offering help."

It took a moment, but Lexi finally managed to articulate a response. To her surprise, an untempered rage had begun to burn in her core and quickly overwhelmed the dark forest her heart had called home. Her hands shook as she stood up and leaned with a notable uncertainty over the desk. "Help? You want to *help* me? It's just stress! That's all it is! Whatever you think you know, you don't know *me*, and I *definitely* don't have any superpowers."

Maxwell shrank back; he clearly hadn't expected anger. "Madame, I—"

"No! No, you will not tell me I am goddamn *broken*, that I'm some kind of ticking time bomb about to *hurt* someone! No! No, *no, no, no, no!*" Images of Drac raced through her mind. They were trying to build a life together, knowing it would be difficult, but even the implication that her sleepwalking might progress into something that hurt her boyfriend added a new, discomforting complication. She couldn't stand the thought. "How do I know this isn't just some... some *trick*? Y-you're a telepath; how do I know you didn't just reach into my skull, and pull out what I was reading? I don't know a lot about you people, but I know the Korps recruits a lot of queer folks. So what, some newly hatched trans person walks in, all excited to discover things, and you tell them whatever they need to hear to pull them in? Well? Is that it! *And how do you know about the sleepwalking!*" Lexi was on the verge of tears as she bellowed furiously over the wolf's desk, the small office starting to feel uncomfortably empty, even more than it already was.

The wolf returned slowly to his chair, resting his paws on his knees as he replied softly. "I understand this is a lot to take in. But it is true. I am more than happy to answer any questions you have, as I am sure there are many. I am sure, too, that it is hard to put trust in people you barely know, especially one claiming to know how you *feel*."

With a series of heaved breaths, the cow let her body untense. The door was right there, after all. Maybe Liam was standing on the other side of it; if Maxwell was the Dark Dossier, he was clearly the muscle of the wolf's henchmen. Maybe even a whole shock force of superpowered henchmen were poised there, ready to capture her if she bolted; she had no way of knowing.

"Four layers of steel plating, concrete, and an anti-flak mesh, by the way," muttered Maxwell in a solicitous tone, body language deferential.

"...What?"

"The walls. They're lined with four layers of steel plating, concrete infill, and an anti-flak mesh on the interior," he recited matter-of-factly once again. "But that couldn't have been the only thing that tipped you off to my *exact* identity — which does, I admit, have me very curious."

Suddenly, the door — and what lay beyond it — didn't matter. The wolf seemed to know a lot about her, and yet he seemed to be asking how she knew who *he* was. He must have known that she'd figure it out, Lexi reasoned; still, she found herself playing along despite the anxiety radiating through her bovine form. "Your typewriter. The X key is sticky, and it doesn't print quite right. The same mistype appeared on the documents from Mississauga you leaked to the media... plus, your age. The Dark Dossier has been around for a long while, as far as I know, so..."

A slight smile began to creep across Maxwell's muzzle as the cow unpacked her deductions. "Very astute."

"Yeah, well... it was just a guess." Lexi wasn't sure whether she was being modest or dismissive, but she *did* decide very quickly that she didn't want to think about the fact that the villain's praise might well have been genuine. "You said I can ask anything?"

Maxwell gave a gentle nod. "Anything," he insisted.

Lexi chewed her half-formed question like cud for a moment, before finally settling on the best way to word it. "What... what does 'help' look like? And if, uh, I don't take it, what happens?" She was still unsure if she believed the old wolf, but she couldn't ignore the possibility that he was right.

"You feel at peace around collections of information." Maxwell said, somewhat flatly, like he was recalling his own experiences. "The itch is gone — or at least muted — when you spend a lot of time in libraries, or with distractions that conveniently have you learning particularly eclectic things. *Catalogable* things. The sleepwalking comes out in stressful situations and only worsens when you can't surround yourself with information. Physical information, I mean — digital information networks never quite met the same need for me, but perhaps that's just a function of my age."

The cow cast her mind back to her time studying at university. Most materials were available digitally, but she still made excuses to find physical copies of nearly every textbook she could. The tangible weight of them felt more real and comforting, somehow, than pixels on a screen. *Ah*, she thought.

"The first step would be to ensure you have constant access to printed material with which you are unfamiliar. Dropp's will hopefully suffice in that for now, and should help keep the sleepwalking at bay," the wolf continued.

"...For now?"

Maxwell gave a slow, purposeful nod. "Eventually, you will seek out new materials. Your telepathic field will adjust to your surroundings, the local informational environment, and you'll desire to collect more over time. The more eclectic or restricted the information, the stronger the compulsion. That is the *second* step — finding safe outlets in which to manage that intense urge to collect."

Lexi felt another immediate and obvious question raise itself. "So... *you* must have access to a much larger collection than just a Cabbagetown bookstore, if that's true. How big is it?"

"Well deduced," Maxwell smiled again. "Bigger than you might imagine, and filled with many things that — well applied — give us considerable leverage. *Ammunition, shall we say.*"

"Blackmail."

"Dirty individuals beget dirty information. The powers-that-be are dishonest, and a secret is the most dangerous weapon one can wield to resist them." Maxwell rested his muzzle on the bridge of his knitted fingers, positing the cow with a challenge. "Do you disagree?"

No, in fact, she realised on reflection; she didn't. She could quite easily think of countless examples that proved the old wolf's point, and then some. The various lies and backhanders that had come to light about her *former* favourite Hero were certainly plausible evidence in the canine's favour. "…No, I guess I don't disagree. But if I don't surround myself with books? What happens then?"

The wolf heaved a disquieted sigh and placed his clasped paws on the desk. "The sleepwalking and compulsions will get worse, I'm afraid. Untrained, and under sufficient stress, you may seriously hurt someone in your pursuits." He heaved a deep, sad sigh, his muzzle tilting towards the window, as if gazing out at the city beyond rather than simply one narrow downtown alley. "You do not have to accept this offer, Lexi. But you are a smart girl, and I can help you. You do not have to commit crimes, nor even wear the glasses. The Korps has… *civilians*, for want of a better term. People who associate themselves with us for a better, more comfortable life. I can very easily have your immigration papers filed and expedited, and your prescriptions filled by a friendly pharmacist. That is the offer. It doesn't have to be any more than working here at Dropp's — and that offer extends to your partner, too. You may tell him as much or as little as makes you comfortable."

"That seems too good to be true," Lexi retorted — but she hadn't quite dismissed the offer out of hand, either.

"It does, doesn't it? But it *is* true. I won't lie to you; there isn't anything to be gained from that. Though the offer is simply for help and safety, I would hope that with time, you warm to the idea of more… *active* work with us." Maxwell's tone waxed serious, and his stare grew firm and assessing, though his brows never shifted from their sympathetic arches.

Lexi felt her apprehension ball up in her throat and struggle to find its place in words. "What. *What.* You want me to become a supervillain?"

"I *want* you to make the decision that is right for you. You can leave if you want; I'll still help you where I can, with your permission — through strictly legal channels only, at that, if you insist — and it doesn't have to be any more than that. But I think you could make an excellent Korps operative, yes." His reply was soft, sedate, and matter-of-fact. The wolf hadn't moved his body once throughout the statement, she realised.

As far as her experiences of job interviews, Lexi felt this one was probably in the top five list of disasters. Top three, maybe. Her prospective employer was a known supervillain, actively encouraging her apparently great potential to become a menace to society… and she was suddenly aware that her recent experiences made a great deal of sense as adult-onset power manifestation, the footnote to the more common experience of those who developed their abilities in adolescence. She was going through (yet *another*) late puberty, of sorts.

The thing that made the situation the *most* complicated, though — the thing that lodged itself so far in Lexi's skull she could swear she could hear the thought reverberating through her horns like a giant internal monologue amplifier — was that, for some reason, *she didn't want to say no*. Eventually, something spilled out of the cow's mouth that loosely resembled a sentence. "You're very... *polite*, for a supervillain."

The wolf broke into a small fit of laughter — not the maniacal cackle she'd half-expected, but a genuine chuckle, accompanied by some words muttered in what the cow thought she recognised as French. He came down from the laugh and heaved a sigh. "Oh, my dear... oh, thank you. Hah, well... Why ever would I be rude?"

"I mean, you know? You're a *supervillain!* I don't really know your whole *career* or anything, but you've probably done a lot of crimes, and here you are offering me a job... with excellent *if probably illegal* benefits and compensation! I know that there's more to the Korps than what the media says. Hell, even some vigilantes get flak that they don't deserve but... I don't know? I guess I assumed villain recruitment would be... seedier and darker, somehow. Not... not set in some twee, queer bookshop, in a nice neighbourhood of Toronto!"

The more Lexi exclaimed, the more she began to quietly realise she *still* wasn't saying no. Maxwell must have picked up on the lack of a definite rejection, because he shifted to another angle: "Lexi, if I may ask, do you think the world is as fair as it could be?"

The question was simple, and she knew her answer confidently. "No. No it isn't."

"And do you think that if you had a chance — if you had the means, the resources, the *support* from allies and comrades — you would choose to make the world a better place?"

Again, she knew her answer. This time, she replied more quietly and with a catching sting in the back of her throat that progressed towards her sinuses. "Th-that's, um. That's... all I ever really wanted to do."

"Would you still take that chance, even if it meant going against the system in which you were raised? Even if those actions were condemned by society, condemned by *laws* made to serve only the comfortable and unafflicted?"

Lexi didn't know her answer immediately. She thought back to Greenbelt, and to the disappointment she'd experienced in discovering how the career Hero was just another in a long line of bought-and-paid-for shills. She thought past the badger, too, about how, through her years of study, she knew there could be no hope without change — and she knew all too viscerally how change was resisted at every turn.

She didn't offer a no; instead, she simply told the truth. "I don't know if I'm ready for that yet."

Maxwell simply gave an understanding, if somewhat sombre nod.

A knock at the door drew the wolf's attention, and in walked Liam with a tall French press full of steaming black coffee, and two mismatched mugs. He set it and the two cups down on the desk with a mild greeting, before taking his leave. The wolf poured out the two cups of coffee, and reclined with one in his paws as the faint patter of a light autumn rain began to drum down the window.

Lexi nursed her coffee, stunned by just how good it was, but still so wrapped up in her own head that she couldn't bring herself to comment on it. She peered at the mug in her hoof-nailed fingers; it bore the slogan "NO ONE KNOWS THAT I'M A BOTTOM" in the sort of font she usually associated with *"Live, Laugh, Love"* and similarly vapid sentiments. She wondered who the mug belonged to. Did queer villains have the same top shortage as the rest of the queer community, too?

About halfway through the cup, and still in relative silence, her phone vibrated in her pocket with a message from Drac. Lexi pulled it out and tapped open the notifications; there was a big heart emoji with a stylised dragon's tail wrapped around it, followed by the text. "Hope you're doing good honey! Love you loads ^.=.^"

The cow heaved a sigh and turned to look at the wolf, who had wandered over to the window to look out at the rain. "I want to work here. I can say that, anyway, but I'm not ready to be a villain. Not... yet, at least. If the offer of a fake job is still on the table... and the help getting meds and residency, and getting a handle on these powers... I'd like to take it."

Maxwell gave a gentle nod. "The position is all yours. As for the paperwork, we have access to some very skilled lawyers, and with your approval, I can have some forms prepared as soon as tonight, on the residency front. As for the medications, we can simply have those sent to your home address, if you like."

Just as Lexi was starting to feel at ease with the situation — the same kind of relief that comes with pulling off a bandage, and realising the wound underneath wasn't so bad after all – there was another polite, but hurried knock, and Liam burst through the door.

"Sorry, André. There's been a development," the bear stated evasively, making eyes squarely at the Highland. "Has she been cleared?"

Maxwell gave a curt nod, apparently impatient for whatever news the bear might have.

"Another division's field ops team turned up some documents at a storage site, and you'll never guess what name came up."

Maxwell's expression dropped. "*No!* Rob Slotis?" The wolf sat his cup down and hurried towards the door. "Where?"

"Thunder Bay, some warehouse for transshipment of medical-grade electronics. His name is on a manifest for parts that there aren't any records of elsewhere — no origin, no destination, like the shipment was a goddamn phantom. But there's something else..." With that ominous statement, Liam briefly cast a glance over Maxwell's shoulder, back to the cow.

"Damn," the wolf muttered, before turning around again to face his new hire. "Lexi, I apologise. I was hoping to spend the rest of the day available to you here, to answer any questions you might have, but... I need to attend to this. Martin will take care of you; if you need anything, just ask, and I'm sure he would be grateful for the company."

Lexi wasn't sure what was happening. All she could discern was that some kind of villainous work was demanding the wolf's attention, and whatever it was seemed to have a firm hold on him. Her mind raced at what it could be... maybe a big investor scam, or some shady PMC stuff. Medical electronics, the bear had said? Maybe it was a smuggling operation...

The cow snapped out of her brief reverie, realising someone was expecting a reply. The Highland just about managed a response, kicking herself slightly for how distracted it seemed. "Oh, uh. Y-Yeah, that's fine."

Truthfully, she didn't really know what else she could say. It wasn't as if she could reasonably protest, or pry for more details on what was going on.

Lexi watched as the two of them strode with purpose out of the office door, and back down the short corridor that led to the staircase. Before she even could get up out of her seat, the bear jogged back and leaned around the doorway with a smile, and an overly energetic salute. "Welcome aboard!" he grinned, before vanishing again.

Lexi didn't wait a second longer. She practically bolted out of her chair, letting curiosity take her, peering round the corner just in time to see the pair start to descend the stairs in a hurried pace.

Distantly, she could hear Maxwell calling to Martin. "Please see that Madame Lexi doesn't miss her train home, dear."

As quietly as she could, the cow raced to the end of the corridor to look down the stairs — just in time to see a door on the far side of the main store area close on a downward staircase. What could be down there, she wondered? On the other hand, it wouldn't do to snoop on the gaggle of supervillains she apparently now worked for—

As if reading her mind, Martin spoke softly from the ground floor. Despite sitting comfortably at the front counter, not even looking in her direction, and otherwise seeming occupied with his nose in a book, he'd noticed her curiosity. "It's rude to eavesdrop, Lexi."

The cow cleared her throat immediately and managed to make even that sound apologetic, softly calling her response down through the banister rails. "Sorry, I... sorry, Martin."

"It's all right, I'm just teasing. Well, mostly. You can come downstairs, you know; no great crimes are going on right now. He looked up from his book into space for a moment. "Well, unless you count the various crimes that are perpetuated *every waking day of our lives* by systems and governments ensuring their own hegemony, by making furious efforts to convince the masses it all works for them, of course."

It took a moment for Lexi to realise what was being said, but then, all at once, it made *sense*. It was a position she shared herself, but she wasn't sure she'd ever been able to word as succinctly as the ferret just had. The stability of the world order, of systems on which she (and everyone she had ever personally met) relied, was a complete myth. *Everything* was fragile, and its resilience was greatly exaggerated. The cow imagined it was a bit like a tower of cards; it could fall any moment, if it weren't for the fact that some people were very invested in stopping the wind from blowing. Finally, as she began to descend the staircase just a bit sheepishly, she found herself replying. "That's… a good way of putting it."

"We're queer, my lovely; that marginalisation makes us prone to feeling the contradictions in our bones. Well… some of us, anyway. There's plenty of queers who've found their niche hidden away in the superstructure of the world, making themselves comfortable amongst those who would do us all harm." The ferret's voice wasn't dispassionate; if anything, it carried the tone of someone who'd had this conversation so many times and *so* passionately, that they could calmly deliver truth bombs like gift-wrapped Christmas presents. Then, as if to temper any impression he might be some sort of ethically-bankrupt 'marketplace of ideas' type, Martin added: "The fact that we know and feel these things isn't enough, of course. Actions speak louder than words, after all."

He gave a smile with that last sentence. It was sunny enough but looking into the man's eyes… Lexi could tell he meant a lot more than simply the bookselling business.

Martin tucked a bookmark into his read to save the page and gently placed it down on the desk. "Did you get to read that *Fuck the Binary* book?"

Lexi found herself shaking her head. It was still in the pile of books at home. She'd actually put off starting that one, compared to the others.

"Ahh, well! I won't spoil it, but I think it's very good. I know the author, too; xe's lovely. An affiliate, yes, if you were wondering." His paws gestured at the shop, the shelves, the building, and everything else around them. "And between you me… *amazing* with xer tongue," he smirked.

Lexi caught herself snorting, and then awkwardly laughing, and then… not-so-awkwardly laughing. She had somehow come to feel comfortable listening to a more-or-less complete stranger talk about a subject that had always made them feel… off. Part of the cow wondered if that was just what it was like, to be immersed in a positive queer environment for a change. "That's a hell of a way to break the ice!"

Martin threw his head back in a single guffaw and folded his arms. "Just trying to set the tone; I know what it's like being the new person on the block. I'm curious, though, if you'll indulge me. You're still young, you're from the UK, and you're at least a *little* bit radically queer… what radicalised you?"

"Greenbelt," Lexi replied, a little surprised at how quickly she could pinpoint the moment she'd lost faith in things she once believed.

"I'm not familiar," Martin offered, raising an eyebrow.

Lexi sucked in a breath and got a little closer to the desk. "He's a UK Hero. His whole thing was promoting a lot of the... outward-looking, neoliberal, *things-can-only-get-better* parts of the New Labour years. The kind of progressive attitude that acts as a cover for a lot of deeply conservative action... or inaction, I suppose." She caught herself before launching into a well-justified tirade about the horrible way in which the British media outlets interacted with government policy, and how so many officials were also contributors to those same outlets. "Anyway... he's part of the reason I went into studying climate change and its socio-political impacts. Then, and *then*, I later went on to find out that he was effectively bought and paid for, by *multiple* industries, to just... greenwash them, basically. He was a real useful mouthpiece for a while. Still an active Hero, too. Now, whenever a climate justice protest starts up, or someone says maybe we should be doing more, he gets quoted by the press as a 'sensible middle ground' type, whose position is that we should all just do nothing. He's not even particularly reprehensible! He's just... getting in the way, and stopping anything from actually getting better, and he *knows* he's doing it."

Martin raised his chin. "*I'd* call that reprehensible."

"He didn't always used to be that way, I don't think. I remember him talking a lot about stuff that today would probably be fairly transgressive, you know? Shit like nationalising services, affordability and living wages... but I guess he opted for a comfortable life selling out."

A loud, dramatic "*Mhmm!*" came from the ferret as he rested his chin on the back of a single paw. "Well, I'm sorry. Realising that you've been lied to is never comfortable. I can tell you that Heroes like him are all too common, unfortunately. It's one of the reasons we push back; they might think they're doing good, but they're just cops with capes. Defending the powerful from their just deserts, or even just *criticism* that makes them a little too upset about the temerity of the 'little people.'"

Lexi silently gave a slow nod and let the conversation ebb before she got any more righteously angry at the situation. It wasn't as if she could *do* anything about it, after all.

The ferret stood up and tucked his chair under the desk. "Did you want another drink? It's getting close to lunch, and we usually lock up for a bit to grab some food."

"Oh, uh… okay. Yeah. Are there any good places to eat near here?"

"Well, the back house's kitchen is pretty fully stocked. Help yourself to anything in there; that's what I usually do. I'll put the kettle on. Feel free to look around, by the way. You work here now, after all," Martin mused. He gave a faint gesture with his hand as he headed off from behind the desk to lock the front door, and then out through the opposite exit, the one that presumably led to the back areas.

"How do you know I agreed to the offer?" Lexi called out with a half-smile.

Martin chuckled back, "We're villains, dear. We've got all *sorts* of plans and plots and schemes. You wouldn't still be in the building if you hadn't said yes."

Alone with her thoughts for a moment, Lexi turned her gaze to the door that Maxwell and Liam had gone through. It clearly led somewhere other than outside. And just *who* was Rob Slotis, and why did he have them both so fervent?

The thought nagged at her. Lexi pulled out her phone and saw the message from Drac still sitting in her notifications tray. She navigated to her browser and typed in Rob Slotis, only to be extremely disappointed when nothing of value turned up. She tried again — adding Thunder Bay to her search terms — but that just narrowed the results down to *less* than nothing. She felt her brain itch in frustration.

Her nostrils flared in an irritated huff that was made all the more complete by the impulse to chew her lip a little, and an instinctive flick of her ropey tail. Lexi quit out of the browser and opened the messaging app to respond to her boyfriend instead.

"Hi honey! Sorry for not getting back to you sooner. Yeah, I think I'm doing good?"

CHAPTER 8

December 24, 1944

Night set in just as early as it had done the evening before, but there was a distinct change of mood inside the Riaillé farmhouse. Almost all of the regular visitors had decided to spend time with their families, or the closest approximation, leaving the little white building feeling emptier than the barren fields that surrounded it. It was still cosy inside, but the bustle of strange people with codenames talking in hushed tones had ebbed. Indeed, activity at the unassuming relay station had been dying down since August, when Paris had been liberated; even this far out into the countryside, the resistance moved onto fresh hunting grounds, their work not yet complete.

Maxwell ("Young Maxwell" to some, still, although he was pleased the adjective had become less common in recent months) practically danced through the kitchen, the smell of baked apples lightly filling the one heated room of the building. Little was busy scrubbing down the stove with one hand, while his other swirled a glass of looted whisky. His brother, Big, sat at the roughly hewn farmhouse table with a midnight-black feline who had been one of the few constant faces in the station.

Kitty — the only name by which the teenage wolf knew the cat — wore loose pants and a threadbare, mended men's shirt. André wasn't exactly sure what she did for the resistance. She was maybe 19, not much older than he, but she seemed technically skilled; just a few weeks prior, she'd managed to fix the fritzed-out radio with a pair of pliers, a hairpin, and a reel of liberated jeweller's wire.

That was just the nature of things. Everyone's real names were kept secret, and nothing they did was discussed, if it could be at all avoided. Everyone except Maxwell, that was; he was known by his given name to a few, while most everyone else just referred to him as the boy or called him by his father's name. A scant few others knew what he could *do*, too.

Being among those who did, Little had entrusted the wolf with keeping some stolen documents and items safe under the mattress of his bed. It made Maxwell feel important, and moreover, helped distract him from the bitter reality of the war.

André continued his misstepped lone waltz up to the side of Kitty's chair, and *almost* elegantly presented his paw. He'd enjoyed her quiet company over the months, when Little wasn't fussing and Big wasn't needing help with something, anyway.

Big, the eponymously larger and quieter of the two goats, crooked a single brow as he took notice of the puppy love and smiled. Silently, he reached for the radio set that occupied most of the table and dialled up the volume, letting the crackly signal come through just a little louder.

Kitty looked up from the collection of papers that held her focus. Most of them were technical diagrams of vehicles, at a glance. Her studious green eyes glinted softly in the dim lamp light as she rolled them, barely hiding the playful grin crossing her face as she took the young wolf's offered hand.

The two negotiated a dance in the cramped quarters, neither of them actually knowing where to put their feet. She smelled like engine oil, and her dark fur could well have concealed smudges of grease from her work. Maxwell, too, was far from clean; his pants had flecks of dried mud around the cuffs, and he smelled much like the hay he'd been moving earlier that day.

Silly though the moment was, it felt relatively safe. It was Christmas Eve, Paris was liberated, and things were starting to change. More than anything, Maxwell was starting to feel like he had a family again.

Little stepped away from the stove, a dirty rag draped over his shoulder as he took the seat at the table that Kitty had just vacated. The goat took a thoughtful sip of his whisky and watched, turning to his brother. Big didn't habitually keep the shotgun under his arm anymore; for the past few weeks, it had spent most of its time in a nook between the ratty structural beams by the farmhouse's front door.

The two goats shared a smile and looked on at the uncoordinated dance act. Big leaned back in his chair, pulling a pack of cigarettes from his shirt pocket. He had traded an allied soldier for them back in November, Little recalled. He struck a match, lit up, and looked to his younger brother, quietly speaking his first few words for a number of hours. "Boy seems happy."

Little raised his chin in a soft nod, taking another sip of his pilfered dram to finish it off, before putting the empty glass down gently on the table. He pushed it to and fro by the rim, thinking out his words carefully. "Mmm... he still gets nightmares, he says. But they happen less often now..."

The older goat chuffed with a faint nod. "Just as well." Big took a long drag on his cigarette, holding the breath in, and then lazily exhaled. "If they'd persisted much longer, our doctor friend would want to look at his brain."

"Pah!" Little exclaimed in a stifled huff, "As if I'd let him near André again."

Big puffed out his chest in a silent laugh, resting one hand in the crook of his other arm's elbow. It was probably the most relaxed he'd looked in months, his brother thought in passing. "You're very protective of him."

Little let his mouth hang open for a second. "And you're not?"

The older goat took another drag of his smoke, and exhaled before responding, taking his time — like he did in all things, except those of the *utmost* urgency. "Of course I am. We're as close to parents as he has..."

The smile that had just a moment ago sat on the younger goat's face dropped into something more reflective and melancholy. Little turned his attention back to the dancing pair and heaved a deep but quiet sigh. "It happened again last night. Ever since traffic through the house slowed down, it's been getting more frequent. At least he hasn't managed to get out to the fields in his sleep again, but I don't know how much longer Kitty's notes and schematics will tide him over. I wonder if he's always going to need more..."

The relaxed smile started to drift from Big's face too, but he stayed silent, eyes staring off into the middle distance.

Little continued with one hand rubbing at the back of his neck. "I had thought that maybe we could take him to Nantes, try and get him some sort of an apprenticeship in the library there, when things are... over."

Big stubbed out the butt of his cigarette and nodded. "You think it would help?"

Little mulled the thought for a moment, folding his arms in frustration at the situation. "I don't know. All I know is that he told me it's like an itch he has to scratch, collecting things, and, well, he was doing that with us…" The goat trailed off, resisting finishing the sentence, or his thought. "…And now he's not. What if he sleepwalks into a stream, or gets lost, or steals something that ends up getting him killed?"

The goat's older brother slowly leaned forward in his chair, resting his elbows on knees with his hands limply hanging forward. His messy fringe hung forward too, not doing much to obscure the disheartened look on his face. "We'll make sure it doesn't get to that. If that means packing up and moving across the damned country, we do that. We're his family now, and we look after him." It might have been the most words the older goat had said in a single moment, and as usual, he meant every word.

The younger goat didn't need to answer. They would do whatever it took. That was the silent, solemn agreement between them. The pair's eyes were quickly drawn to the source of a dull thud as Maxwell's less-than-sure footing tripped Kitty up, sending both of them into a crumpled heap on the floor.

Little rushed to the pair, checking them both over for any signs of injury. The fussing wasn't entirely appreciated by the wolf, but André was used to that from the protective younger goat by now. Kitty, by comparison, was in hysterics. She was clearly unharmed and taking great pleasure in being able to jab at Maxwell about his clumsiness, her voice dripping with sarcasm. "Excellent footwork you have there, André!"

The young wolf did his best to hide the slightly bruised ego behind a smirk. "I thought girls were supposed to know how to dance…"

"Ha! Girl I may be, but I much prefer machines over men and fighting over dancing." The feline pulled herself up and dusted off her shirt before holding a paw out to Maxwell, who gratefully accepted. "I only took up the offer because I like you, anyway."

Little stood back with a smile. "Maxwell is the exception to your 'no boys' rule, then, Kitty?"

"He's different to most others," she smiled, brushing her whiskers back into less of a frazzled mess from the fall.

"More handsome, then," offered Maxwell.

Kitty whipped her tail about and went back to gather her diagrams and notes on the table, bundling them neatly into a pile to be stowed away. "Not *quite* the word I had in mind," she said, before whispering something under her breath.

Just as André was preparing a retort to what he *thought* he heard, there was a short, sharp series of knocks at the door, echoing down the hall and into the kitchen. Everyone exchanged a look with one another, and the air suddenly grew tense; no one said a word, and the radio kept playing. Then the series of knocks came again.

The two brothers made their way down the hall first, with a quiet apprehension, boards creaking quietly underfoot. Big signalled wordlessly to Kitty and Maxwell to move into the storeroom to the right of the house's entryway and stay put; there was a small crawlspace in that room that could just about conceal the both of them. The pair did as told at first — but the relative calmness of the past months had eased them into quickly abandoning the hiding spot, instead eavesdropping from just behind the door.

Maxwell could just about see through the crack in the splintering doorframe, as Big looked back to his younger brother, nodded down to the shotgun tucked in the beams, and cautiously took the handle to the front door.

The visitor was a man — a meticulously well-groomed peacock, wearing a very neatly-presented suit underneath a long black jacket. Around his neck was a colourful and expensive-looking scarf; it framed an *uncomfortably* wide smile crossing his beak. "You must be Big... and your brother, Little, I see behind you there."

He spoke French, but with a very clear and distinct foreign accent. Maxwell figured him as English; he almost sounded like a BBC broadcaster, and was incredibly well-spoken, in what must have been a second language.

Big looked to his brother, then back towards the peacock, in the midst of removing his hat and unbuttoning his coat expectantly. The older goat replied uncomfortably: "Sorry. We don't know you. You have the wrong place," he said, flatly.

The peacock gestured vaguely, clearly waiting to be invited inside like a vampire, still with that same smile. "Of course. But *we* know *you*. I'm here on behalf of His Majesty's Government, as a representative of British Military Intelligence. I come as an ally, to discuss a certain *asset*."

Little stepped in closer to his brother, conceding to the man's presumption. "I don't understand, sir; we have nothing of use any more. We've not been active."

The peacock maintained the off-putting grin. "Please, Monsieur. Call me Marcus."

With a deep sigh, Big opened the door wide.

The bird stepped in, hand-in-hat, taking a brief look around the entryway as if he had just been invited into a luxurious country château, and not a run-down rural farmhouse. The goat finally closed the door, clear impatience on his face. "What is it you think we can help you with?"

The peacock turned slowly, putting his back towards the door behind which Maxwell and Kitty still hid. "Why, the boy, of course."

Little folded his arms, and once again looked to his brother, who stood like a wall between Marcus and the front door. "What do you want with Maxwell?"

The peacock held his hat by the brim in both hands, quickly pacing out his words in an almost condescending tone. "I wish to personally congratulate and thank him on his acquisition of some *rather important* papers that made their way to my offices, without which we would have had a *much* more difficult time, in regard to certain operations in support of the Resistance."

The papers the man referred to... they must have been that *original* batch of documents. The ones from that day he'd been taken in by the two goats. They'd relayed the intelligence to the Resistance. From there, the documents must have eventually ended up with the Brits' house of spies.

Maxwell quietly reached into his pocket, feeling the carefully folded letterhead. It was the one part of that fateful collection he had been allowed to keep by the two goats who had taken him in and cared for him. It had become a personal trophy of his, and something of a reminder — especially with recent signs pointing to the war turning in their favour.

Little unfolded his arms and softly called out. "Maxwell, there is a… a *gentleman* here to see you. He wants to thank you."

Kitty stayed put, breathing as quietly as she could manage behind the door, as Maxwell stepped out around it to greet the tall avian. His plumage was even more overwhelmingly colourful up close.

Marcus cocked his head and turned fully on his heels, holding out a hand to shake. It was a greeting that felt entirely forced, the wolf thought with a chill. The two goats stood awkwardly behind him their own discomfort clearly visible on their faces. "Ah, *there* he is! Young Master Maxwell, a pleasure to meet you at last."

Maxwell reached for the feathered hand, silently grasping it in an unsure shake.

"You did a very good job with those papers from the commissioner's office. They helped the efforts of your comrades and of the allied forces a *great* deal." Marcus paused. "You know, I was wondering if you could help me with something, Maxwell. I have in my jacket here a very, *very* important document from England, that I would like you to take a look at for just a tiny moment." He pulled from his coat's breast pocket a small manila envelope, but rather than giving it directly to the wolf, he held it firmly in his hand and made sure to reiterate its importance. "You could say it's a secret. *For certain eyes only*, even."

Maxwell's gaze darted furtively to the two goats, deeply unsure of the whole situation. The coldness of the unheated hall had been rapidly replaced by the stifling, uncomfortable heat of tension — and then the itch began to burn, too. His heart started to race, and the world around him seemed to slow. Without even thinking, he snatched the envelope from the feathered hand in front of him; the man let go swiftly, and without any apparent concern.

The wolf opened the envelope, tearing through it feverishly, eyes frantically scanning the contents. Inside was a neatly headed letter, officially titled and labelled with some sort of insignia. Maxwell couldn't parse most of the English words that accompanied them, but that wasn't the important part. The body of the letter was an unbroken string of numbers, arranged in a clearly defined grid. The whole page was full of them, save for a signature at the bottom. It was accompanied by a circular stamp of some official purpose, in dull red ink. The wolf looked up at Marcus curiously, and said nothing, as he felt the itch begin to soothe.

The bird's face looked decidedly less friendly, all of a sudden. More... *analytic.* "Very good. Now, please concentrate on one line of the paper. Say nothing; just pick one and look carefully at it."

Little pushed past his older brother, and attempted to interject, "Just what are y—"

Marcus raised a single finger to shush him, not even turning to face the dark-furred goat's irritation. "Shh! Do not *interrupt!* Find a line and focus on it, boy."

The wolf looked down at the letter again, unsure of what else he should do. He picked a line off the sheet and scanned it a few times, thinking about the sequence of numbers it contained. Was it some kind of puzzle?

Then, the silence was broken, as the bird began to coldly list off the sequence of numbers on which he'd focused. "Zero, seven, five, two, one, one, three, eight, nine, four, one, three, zero, zero, six, three, five, eight; I could go on, but I really don't think there's any need. Those were the numbers you were focusing on, weren't they, boy?"

The two brothers looked on. The wolf's expression had certainly already told them the bird hadn't made a mistake, but his disquieted nod would have removed any doubt. A long silence filled the air again, before finally the larger of the two goats found his voice. "What was all that?"

"Your boy is a telepath," chimed the bird, swivelling on his heels to face the source of the inquiry, "albeit of a different, rarer flavour than most. You see, most telepathy is... like speaking on the telephone, in a way. A powerful psychic of the usual variety might be able to communicate with another person, but only as quickly as they can formulate a coherent response – so no faster than speaking aloud, for the typical mind. Maxwell's ability is different; under the right conditions, it's as if he's *firing off* information, so quickly and forcefully it lodges in the mind like a bullet in a wall. I didn't just hear the numbers he was thinking of; I saw them in my mind, the same way an image appears in one's imagination, or recalling a memory. In other words, Maxwell is — as you can imagine — a rather important strategic military asset, especially given how drawn he is to things he doesn't already know." Marcus turned back to the wolf, a cold calculating stare on his face as he spoke directly to the boy. "That's how you got ahold of that first bundle that ended up on our desks, isn't it? Sleepwalked right into the commissioner's office, and swiped whatever you could get your dear little *paws* on, hmm?"

Little stood motionless. "How do you know about the sleepwalking?"

Marcus' face grew darker for a few uncomfortable seconds. "I didn't, but thank you for confirming the Ministry's suspicions. When I said *rare*, I meant it; it's rather our business to keep track of intelligence assets like Maxwell here, and when certain Resistance members from this part of the country started reciting intelligence to our agents in uncanny detail, with no explanation of how they could recall the things they did, it reminded a few officials of... a *handful* of historic individuals. Cases, so to speak, of people able to do the same thing as your little wolf here. They too proved to be valuable tools, for those that controlled them. You've probably all experienced it yourself, and not even realised; you were, after all, a relay station for the Resistance. It probably never crossed your minds that you could recall some intelligence that had passed through here with utter clarity." The bird turned up his beak with a contemptuous sniff. "He'll be coming with me. As of this moment, he is the property of the British Government."

Little's voice ran hoarse with rage. "Absolutely not! Powers or not, André stays with us. He's a boy, not some... *thing!* How dare you come here and demean him like this! He is our *family*, goddamn you!"

The bird's expression grew visibly steely as he turned back to the younger goat and delivered his cold reply. "This isn't a negotiation."

"You... you will not take him and turn him into some damn *tool!*"

Marcus' shoulders sank in his coat, and he hung his head low, muttering to himself through a half-forced laugh. "You know, I was really hoping you'd make this easy. Frankly, I don't have time for a farm-boy faggot and his halfwit brother. The stray comes with me."

Big took a step forward, eyes bulging with inchoate rage, speaking through an unmoving jaw and gritted teeth. "*What was that?*"

The bird paused again. His distinct stillness was unnerving until, in one swift action, he pulled a revolver from inside his coat and had it pointed squarely between the younger goat's horns. Big's eyes widened as he lunged for the shotgun just to the side of the door, only to be interrupted by the loud, commanding shouts of the peacock.

159

"Do not fucking move or I put a bullet in this faggot's head, and then yours, for good measure!"

Little held his hands up with a fearful tremor. His brother froze in place inches from the shotgun. The hall was silent again.

Maxwell's body tensed in every possible way. The situation had spiralled so far in seconds that he didn't even feel the letter and envelope slip from his grasp and flutter to the floor.

Marcus pulled back the hammer on the revolver, eliciting a panicked gasp from Little whose brow was being manipulated uncomfortably by the barrel of the gun. "What, you think we didn't know? That we don't keep tabs on socialist agitators? It's *our fucking job* to know. That boy is coming with me, no questions asked, and no objections. He will serve the SIS from here on, before his head gets filled with… whatever it is you lot think. And if you make this harder than it has to be, the pair of you are dead." Marcus spat on the floor to punctuate his derision, gesturing his head towards the older goat, who was still frozen uncomfortably in a half-crouch. "No one would miss either of you, so I suggest you do exactly as I say. You, hands up, and back away from the door."

Big did as instructed, quietly, and slowly. He moved his hands behind his horns and took a few very careful steps backwards before finally speaking. "Now, listen… we don't want—"

Marcus pushed the barrel of the gun into Little's forehead even harder, forcing the younger of the two goats to take a step back. The peacock's chest rose as he cut the older brother off. "I said *no fucking objections.*"

The pinned goat's eyes began to wet faintly with tears, and his voice cracked as he calmly replied. "Brother, please do as he says."

And then… everything happened so *fast.* The door to the storage room behind him had silently opened. It took Kitty's paw on his shoulder to realise they had snuck out of their hiding spot. He turned his head to try and make eye contact with her, but she was fixedly staring at the colourfully-plumed intruder. It took another second before the wolf realised the boyish-girl was holding a fireplace poker with a piercing intent.

She took another step forward, gripping Maxwell's shoulder tightly, before pushing him behind her. She held the iron poker level, gripping it in both paws, flexing her fingers to keep her grasp sure. Then a floorboard squeaked underfoot and betrayed her.

Marcus swivelled his head and tried to swing his body around fast enough to fire off a shot at the feline, but the poker was already jabbing at his side. It connected hard, ripping through his coat and taking a chunk of flesh and feathers with it. Kitty's weight carried forward with the follow through and was only interrupted by the butt of the revolver hitting her head, with the bird's shrieking cry. She hit the floor unconscious, just as Big lunged for the shotgun once more, levelling it towards the peacock. The battered old hunting piece emptied with a deafening boom; at such close range, it should have been fatal, had the goat's aim not been so panicked. The buckshot merely tore through the bird's left shoulder, blood splattering against the wall behind him.

Marcus' round, however, was not a near miss. The bullet hit Big in the neck, dropping him to the floor just as quickly as the recoil from the shotgun had pushed the goat's shoulder back.

In the chaos, Little had been knocked to the floor by the wide swing of the shotgun's barrel, accompanied by the noise. He scrambled for his brother's double barrel while Marcus winced and wrapped his hand — still clutching the revolver as it was — around the mess of his other shoulder.

The bird's foot swung out to kick the air from the surviving goat's lungs with a frustrated scream. "All you had to do was *fucking listen!*"

It was through Marcus' anger-soaked raging that Maxwell — shaken, frozen and terrified — began to regain a clear sense of what was going on. He didn't know how, but he'd ended up on the floor too, holding on to Kitty as tight as he could manage. Before he could piece together any more Marcus snatched him off the floor with a blood-soaked hand and dragged him through the farmhouse's door by the scruff of his neck.

Through tears, he could just about make out Little's beaten, bruised, but defiant figure, aiming the shotgun towards him and his captor... and then lowering it exhaustedly, in defeat. He was the bird's shield, Maxwell realised. The wolf watched as the younger goat slumped over the body of his brother, and the light of the farmhouse grew dimmer and dimmer with struggled distance. At some point, a cloth found its way around the canine's muzzle, and forced sleep took him.

The wolf didn't regain consciousness until they were in the cabin of a boat, rocking with the waves. The air was thick with the smell of blood and sweat. Marcus was the first person to come into focus, the other two figures remaining blurs for a moment longer. Instinctively, Maxwell tensed his muscles to run — but the uncomfortable vice-grip of cuffs on his wrists secured him to a length of cold steel, around a pipe that ran the length of the cabin, an inch or two off the floor.

"Finally awake, you brat? You had better be goddamn worth it. Nearly lost a *fucking* arm to get you," sneered the bird. His refined accent was gone, and he sat with his legs wide apart on what appeared to be a bunk.

One of the other figures in the room quieted the bird with a growl. He was dressed in a white coat, overtop what appeared to be military fatigues, and spoke French with a different foreign accent to that of the peacock. Maxwell had encountered a handful of American troops, and it sounded not unlike their dreadful attempts at *'parlay-voo'*. "With respect, you're quite far from losing this arm. Plenty of men I know would be envious of this little scratch."

Marcus looked at the medic with disdain. "Noted. Now, if you're quite done regaling me with the horrors of war… give me some goddamn pills."

The white-clad otter rummaged through a small cabinet mounted on the cabin's beige wall and pushed a bottle of pills into the bird's chest. "Don't choke on them, limey bastard." He and the other figure, the one that Maxwell hadn't been able to discern through still-blurred vision, exited through the cabin's single door. "I'll be back in an hour to redress the wound before you disembark. God knows I can't wait to get you off this ship. Not my station to question our allies, but in case it wasn't clear, *I don't like you.*"

"I rather got that hint." Marcus snarled.

Everything was silent, apart from the dull rumble of the boat's engine once the doctor left, leaving just Maxwell and Marcus to stare at each other for an uncomfortable moment. Maxwell could see the small bits of damage that had been done to the bird's naked torso. Heavy gauze dressed the stab wound on his middle and more padded the shoulder that had taken a blast of buckshot.

"You should be thanking me. Supers who can't control their powers properly are dangerous, boy. *You're* a danger. You'd have scrambled those rustics' minds, if you stayed there too long. People like me deserve a fucking *medal* for this kind of shit. The SIS will look you over, get you on some pills to suppress your powers… and the bonus is, you get to be useful to them. It's for your own good, really."

The wolf said nothing. It was hard to tell who the peacock was trying to convince, Maxwell or himself… but that hardly mattered.

October 25, 2019

Shattered remnants of Maxwell's porcelain mug clattered across the floor and ricocheted off the wall that had stopped its sudden flight. "How do we know nothing!" The wolf snarled rhetorically, teeth bared to the world as he assaulted a stack of papers on his desk, sending it to the floor. "He stares at me and laughs! This… this god-damned trickster, he thinks he knows *me?*"

The wolf stalked the directorate's office in a blind rage, lashing out with strength he hadn't displayed in countless years, as he kicked a chair clean across the room. "I will not be beaten at my own game, Liam! I will *not!*"

He stared at the bear, who had watched his entire outburst unfold over the past several moments. The manifest he'd handed Maxwell, the one with Slotis' name, was just an ember. The thing that had lit the fuse *proper* was the scrawl in the portion of the manifest reserved for notes. There — in a hasty cursive that ROSE had already unsuccessfully cross-analysed with the handwriting on all other documents from the warehouse, finding no match — was a personal greeting:

Hello, André.

Liam approached the wolf with measured caution and held both paws out, heavily taking the canine's shoulders in them to hold his shaking form steady. "Breath. We *will* find him, and then, we'll find out what he knows. It's what we do."

Maxwell tried to control his breathing, taking in a deep lungful of air, holding it — and then, with ROSE's assistance, exhaling in a steady flow. The wolf closed his eyes, feeling the hand-written taunt burning in his mind, and causing the *itch* to flare more aggressively than he had felt in decades. "Liam... mon amour, I cannot let this continue."

"I know."

The two stood there for a moment in the partially trashed office, both taking a further deep breath. Maxwell raised a paw to clutch at the bear's, squeezing it tenderly; he rolled his head to the side, to survey the damage he'd wrought. "I'm sorry. No one outside of the Korps has called me André since the SIS. Whoever Slotis is, this is personal — I should be so lucky, that it'd be Evans haunting me from beyond the damned grave. No, this has to be someone with a lot of connections, to even know that name."

Maxwell excused himself from his partner's hold and soberly picked up the chair he had just kicked, returning it neatly back under the desk where it had been. Liam sighed and joined him in picking up the papers, half-heartedly sorting them and then stacking them back where they belonged.

He hadn't lashed out like this recently, though not for lack of anger; Maxwell sometimes felt he was drawing from a deep well that had never truly run dry, on that front. The bitter anger he held for his part in Operation Felt had remained level below the surface of his otherwise-calm exterior, for most of his operational life as a supervillain. He had tried to atone, and he wasn't about to let Rob Slotis become another failure.

Maxwell looked over his hands as he sat at his desk. They were old. His paw pads were scarred and wrinkled, and the fur on his knuckles had started to thin years ago. Dextrous and cunning as he was, he feared the day when he *wouldn't* be. The wolf recalled the words of the O-Unit that had chided him days earlier; there wasn't a treatment for his comorbidities of being stubborn and resilient. But he wasn't going to be *beaten*, either.

The canine cast a sideways glance out of the floor-to-ceiling windows of the directorate's office, taking in the imposing sight of the archive's looming central core, and feeling the thrum of Vault F's possibilities pounding away in his chest. "We do a Deep Dive," he said coldly.

In response, Liam offered a concerned humming sound, and then a deep, weary exhalation. Finally, he spoke. "That's really our only option here, ain't it?" He sounded defeated. "An action of last resort; *begging* the Vault for divine intervention. I don't like it."

The Vault held a vast trove of knowledge in the same way that, *theoretically*, the fictional Library of Babel did. Countless permutations of text on pages existed, in so many jumbled formats, that much of what Vault F held was functionally nonsense — or, at least, hadn't been decoded yet. Unlike the Library of Babel, there did seem to be some underlying pattern to the vault's fonds and collections. And then, on one occasion, text had been found within it that contained vital information. It seemed to have appeared from nowhere, and against all odds, had checked out as accurate.

Maxwell recalled that document — a transcript of a hot mic moment from one *formerly* card-carrying member of the PHL, back in the 90s. By all accounts, the recording had never been transcribed, nor ever broadcast; the only people to have heard the exchange were the press conference's two-man sound crew, who'd never leaked it. It was by sheer luck that the Hero in question was *just* motor-mouthed enough that — when the wolf threatened to blackmail him with the transcript — the cryokinetic cape formerly operating as "Big Glaze" didn't deny knowledge of the things written down. He simply asked how the wolf had gotten ahold of it.

The Vault, it was determined — through some unknowable means — had a way of plucking real, existing information out of the world, and keeping it tucked away, like some vast unknowable backup of the universe's forgotten secrets. The real trick was finding something you were actually looking for, in the endless informational noise. *That* was a Deep Dive.

It took a great deal of careful preparation, requiring trained telepaths to hone in on a single thought while in the Vault, and let themselves be guided to any material that seemed to resonate. The difficulty came in the tremendous failure rate; the Vault didn't give up its secrets that easily. Over the decades, Maxwell had learned that whatever Vault F was, it had its own mind, motives, and drives. Despite trying, it had never given up anything that was lost during Operation Felt. He knew, *knew*, that there was a chance it would do the same for Rob Slotis.

"I don't like to rely on it for this, any more than you do, but… protocol is protocol, and we have it for a reason," Maxwell said flatly. "Deep Dives require approval from the both of us. Do I have your approval?"

"On one condition." The bear heaved himself to the office door, his ears low, peering out across the atrium towards Phillip's engineering section. "You and I act as situation monitors, together. I… I don't want you on the dive team, after what happened last week. I don't trust that thing. I'm sorry."

Maxwell took a moment to construct his agreement, but in the end it didn't come out as anything more than a simple nod. Terse agreement eventually forced itself out around the lump in his throat, a flat "D'accord." He knew he couldn't argue; he didn't want to, either.

He wasn't ready to be beaten, but the wolf was starting to feel the loss of control bite at his heart.

Chapter 9

All eight of the winches in the preparation room flashed their status lights green in unison, with an accompanying metallic chirp, signalling that they were in perfect operating condition. The mounts that held them to the wall had been upgraded dramatically since the incident that had left Maxwell MIA for several days.

Phillip had personally seen to it that the base's strategically-sized agents — along with a number of personnel rated for super-strength — had put the mounts through their paces. No repeat of the previous week's incident would be acceptable.

Attached to the winches, by similarly-new, heavier-gauge cables and harnesses, were the dive team — eight of the most experienced KARD agents, short of the directors themselves. A supporting engineer, Phillip's junior, checked their gear was fitted correctly, before loudly and clearly confirming everything was ready. "All locked! Divers one, two, three, four, five, six, seven, and eight all cleared for action!"

Phillip raised a thumbs up, shouting back across the small-but-busy distance between them. "Thank you, all clear! All *clear*. Please prepare for final dive preparations!"

A number of henches scurried away, leaving a clear line of sight between the situation monitors and the dive team. The open bulkhead framed the divers for all to see, made all the clearer by the organised pacing of engineers, assistants, and villainous sysadmins taking their positions in two neat flanks.

Phillip joined the rest of the situation monitors and watched on, as Ul walked down the cleared path and began performing a rich vocal rite to the eight suited-up divers. She blessed them through a communion between herself, and the strange extra-sensory vibrations that emanated from behind Vault F's containment walls.

Maxwell watched on too, waiting for his dear, blue-scaled assistant to finish her ritual magic before addressing the dive team. He'd never much cared for being this sort of figurehead. The wolf would have rather been leading by example than barking orders, and his personal anxieties about his abilities manifested in a constant, nervous twitch of his tail.

There was silence for a moment as the dive team ordered themselves into a line, but before Maxwell could speak, the doors to the central access chamber opened; through them stepped a tall silver dragoness in a casual strut, scales immaculate. Everyone's head turned, regardless of the task at hand.

"Good evening, everyone," she said, gesturing with a soft wave before walking towards the wolf. She faced him and put a hand on his shoulder; her eyes rested on his briefly, as she communicated quiet direct reassurances to Maxwell.

The dragoness spoke again, calmly, and softly. "Carry on, don't let me keep you." She let her hand squeeze at the canine's shoulder before she took her place between the bear and skunk in the exhausted-looking lineup, prompting a sudden new alertness the team was sorely lacking.

Maxwell felt a breath catch in his throat, and his agitated tail slowed to a halt, as he exhaled through the comforting words from the multiplicitous, most unofficially-official *unofficial* member of the Korps command structure.

"Thank you, Madam Karen. Thank you all, too, for volunteering for this Deep Dive," the wolf said solemnly, turning to his team. "Some of you are veterans of the Vault; for others, this will be among your first few times diving. You have all been briefed extensively, and the monitoring team will be closely watching on everything that we can from here. Your focus for this dive is '*Rob Slotis*'. Keep your mind on the name, and hopefully the Vault will cooperate, and produce results."

There was another momentary silence as Maxwell took a breath, focusing his own thoughts squarely on the name. "Neither KARD nor any other division of the Korps possesses any actionable intelligence about this name or its owner. All we know for certain is that it is being used in conjunction with drastic efforts at identity concealment, procurement of sensitive equipment, and public-sector contract tenders. Whoever or whatever *Rob Slotis* might be, they know that we are aware of them. In informational warfare, the most dangerous weapon is a secret, and we pride ourselves on being the best damned custodians of those weapons. Regardless of what happens in this Deep Dive, we *will* disarm *Rob Slotis*, but we need leads. Before I hand you off to our chief engineer for final preparation, thank you again, and glory to the Overlord."

A message scrolled across the display of the wolf's visor as he finished his monologue and turned back just in time to see the dragoness wink. *[Knock 'em dead, kid.]*

As the wolf wound down, Phillip came forward holding out his ROSE-powered tablet calling through a checklist with the dive team; in a precise back-and-forth, each safety protocol was confirmed and reconfirmed. Maxwell, for his part, felt deeply exhausted in a new and *unsettling* way as he retired to the line of the monitoring team.

"André," the bear started, "I know it's hard, but this doesn't mean that you're done. It's not a failure to not go head-first into the fray. You've given your life to this. Look around you; none of this would have been possible without you. You're allowed to rest and take a back seat, for a change."

The wolf cast his eyes around the chamber. Technicians busied themselves checking readings, eight agents readied themselves for a procedure that he himself had pioneered decades prior, and outside of the access chamber was an entire repository of secrets and information, available to an entire subterranean *city* of supervillains whose cause he believed in with all his heart. More than that, Maxwell had long stood on the shoulders of people he'd considered giants, but the notion that he too might have become a giant hewn of immovable stone in his own right was difficult to reconcile.

With a hand on his shoulder, the dragoness added to the old dog's reassurances. "Shame you don't monologue more; you've picked up quite a knack for it. I look forward to hearing what you prepare for coming face-to-face with Slotis."

"I hadn't dared to think that far ahead," he admitted, sheepishly. "Thank you..."

"Family doesn't give up." The voice was small and soft, crooned out from behind the silver dragoness. Ulhauriear stepped forward and looked up with deep sapphire eyes, limpid pools carrying a forthright understanding of what it meant to serve something far greater than oneself — and to be lost in that dedication. "Director, you have done a great many things, and you will continue to do so. When we are less able, we do not stop; we simply find new ways to move forward. It is not just for you to take care of yourself, but for all of us, too. And *that* is not giving up." The kobold finished her speech with a nod, fingers clasped together.

The wolf shed a tear, crouching to meet his assistant's eyes. Maxwell gave a firm nod, and graced Ul's cheek with a kiss. "Thank you, my dear assistant. We don't give up. Léon didn't, I won't, and I know that no matter what happens, you and Liam won't either."

Phillip wrapped up his checklist and called out one last point. "Max submersion time is four hours. Synchronise timers in three... two... one... *mark.*"

The bulkhead to the preparation room began to close, and the Deep Dive began.

The dream library had changed again. On this occasion, it was bathed in a warm light from somewhere high above, like sunbeams through a window.

Lexi took in her surroundings, marvelling at the height of the stacks and the beautifully ornate tilework of the floor. It was like someone had remixed and mashed-up a crazy-quilt of great Gothic buildings and various temples to knowledge, then stuffed them to the rafters (and beyond!) with impossible volumes of text. In the distance, some muffled, tree-like creaking echoed faintly, as if more shelves were erupting from the floor to blanket the endless dreamscape.

The cow checked herself. She once again realised herself to be older and weighed down by a heavy cape of an indecipherable shape. There was a feeling of strange comfort again; it was *reassuring* to be dreaming of being old. It meant that she had a future to look forward to — hopefully.

Suddenly the thrum of background noise converged into a voice, but not the ethereal booming or softly familiar tones she had experienced before. It was more than one voice, in fact; It was several disparate speakers, all whispering the same two words, over and over and over again in a discordant chant. At first it was hard to grasp what exactly was being said, but as the voices began to harmonise and fall into the same rhythm, Lexi picked out the words and felt herself joining in: *"Rob Slotis."*

The Highland instantly recognised the name and where she'd first heard it, but before she could reflect any further, a flywheel somewhere in the machine of her being spontaneously *spun up* and cast her momentum forward in a determined trudge. The beats of her hooves clacked out in perfect rhythm with the chant against the polished tile floor, and not even the countless tons of paper around her could dampen the sound.

A light ahead of her grew and beat and throbbed, like an almighty heart without distinct form. Lexi felt her entire body vibrate in harmony with it, and then the light engulfed everything. When it faded — receding into the corners of her vision — she stood alone in a small, quiet-looking office. It felt intimately *familiar* in a way that she couldn't place.

The carpeting was soft and dark, the furnishings were comfortable but simple, and the walls were lined with bookcases and filing cabinets. The shelves were stacked high with magenta-spined tomes, the titles of which she couldn't read; she couldn't even place the language of the script, which was harsh, angled and orderly, with few visible curves to the glyphs' forms.

Centred in the room was a large wooden desk, its sides and edges carved with intricate and conjoined helices, flanked on either side by stylised, three-pronged wings. At the front of the desk was an old-fashioned nameplate, but it too was written in the strange script she couldn't parse. The most Lexi could determine was that it was two words, comprising sixteen characters.

The cow's somewhat-hazy focus was drawn to the surface of the desk. There sat the same dossier from before, emblazoned with the word 'CONTINUUM'... but this time, it was accompanied by a symbol. It was another helix, standing upright inside a stylised icon of a manila folder, winged similarly to the carvings on the desk. It felt imposing, somehow, to look at — but also somehow *right*.

Lexi rounded the desk, fingers gracing its surface curiously, before she finally laid a hand on the folder, feeling it radiate something pleasant. The

Highland let her mouth move, and the name Rob Slotis came out as a whisper.

When she opened the folder, the room began to crumble away into a murky purple blackness, and another new voice echoed through the void. "Director!" it called. "They're not alone!"

Ul repeated her frantic cry, pulling herself from the midst of a deep focusing ritual. "They're not alone in there, Greatmother guide them; *they're not alone*. Someone else is in there with them! I can feel it..."

Phillip hurled himself to a control panel beside the bulkhead, scrolling through reams of data in an instant with ROSE's help. Maxwell saw the engineer's eyes going wide, as the readings of activity in the vault suddenly skyrocketed. "Containment is draining more power than ever! Director, sir, we have a problem!"

Maxwell steeled his jaw and pushed his lanky frame forward to another panel on the other side of the bulkhead. "Get them *out of there*," he demanded. "Reel in the tethers!"

Suddenly, the chamber was a hive of frantic activity. ROSE's voice came across a series of speakers, broadcasting for all to hear.

[Engaging recovery mode. Tethers 1-8 nominal.]

Several medical synths rolled into the chamber, readying themselves by the bulkhead doors as Liam organised the various henches to their new emergency staging positions. Maxwell, meanwhile, could only watch helplessly at the screen in front of him, which displayed the length of cable each winch had spooled out. All of them were decreasing steadily... until they weren't.

The skunk called out to the rest of the chamber. "Spatial anomaly, range estimated one-zero-one kilometres... by the *Overlord*..."

Two of the winch readouts shot up instantly, the distance in metres climbing until displaying an error. A third oscillated aggressively between two *very* different numbers, and for the briefest of moments, Maxwell wondered if this had been Liam's experience the day he had gone missing in the vault.

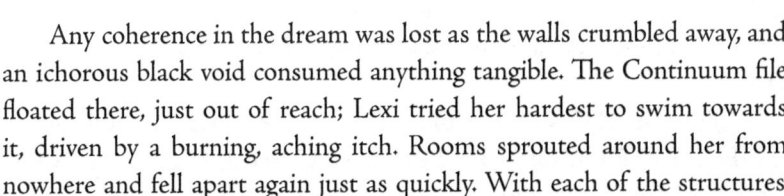

Any coherence in the dream was lost as the walls crumbled away, and an ichorous black void consumed anything tangible. The Continuum file floated there, just out of reach; Lexi tried her hardest to swim towards it, driven by a burning, aching itch. Rooms sprouted around her from nowhere and fell apart again just as quickly. With each of the structures' blinks in and out of existence, the bovine started to notice a pattern.

One room was hers, from the not-too-distant past. The desk was piled high with textbooks that she recognised from her first few years of university. Another room was a bookstore — the one from her hometown, during what appeared to be a book signing. Her younger self had gone to get her favourite childhood book signed by her favourite childhood Hero, and she thought she could just discern Greenbelt's stolid figure in the distance. Another room came and went, this time a hospital ward. She recognised that one instantly and wished it away; eventually it faded too.

Then a room new to her appeared, looking sparse and unpleasant. Handcuffed to the desk was a familiar-looking wolf — younger, frail, and sobbing, without anyone to comfort him. It quickly shifted into another equally sparse room, containing only two figures shrouded in darkness. One stood confidently, while the other seemed to break down before hurling himself forward in an embrace. When the scene changed again around her, she briefly glimpsed a heavy-set figure — mane lush and proud — hanging from a noose, in what looked to be the kitchen of a picturesque cottage.

Then there was blackness again, and noise. So much *noise*. Voices yelling, and shouting instructions the cow couldn't understand. There was a vague feeling of being pulled and twisted, but with nothing other than the distant folder to focus on, it was hard for Lexi to gather her bearings. Maybe she was falling? She couldn't tell. Finally, she found her voice and screamed through the tears of confusion. "What's going on?"

The voice replied. "KILL YOUR HOPELESSNESS, OR IT WILL KILL YOU AND ALL THAT YOU LOVE."

"I don't know what to hope *for!* Everything's so fucked up, and I'm just... I'm just one person!" She wished that there was something solid nearby for her to slam her fist against, hoping that the pain would at least dull her *anger* at the empty words. "What am I supposed to do! Climate change, injustice, corruption; lies, and lies, and *lies!* How? How do I *fight* that?"

"THE BURDEN OF KNOWLEDGE IS PAID IN BLOOD, AND THERE IS YET MORE TO SPILL. YOU WILL LEAVE BLOODY HOOFPRINTS ON THE PAGES OF HISTORY, TO SURVIVE IT."

Everything in the cow's body burned all of a sudden. Her limbs tensed and spasmed, as if being shocked and torn apart, and pulled *every* which way all at once. Her vision fractured momentarily, and she saw countless different perspectives of herself in that moment; there were just so many of her, all of the echoes different in their own way, each grasping for the folder... but it stayed painfully just out of reach.

Through the roaring static and whine of some unseen, massive engine, another voice broke through. "Give me everything you can!"

"Engineering," Phillip bellowed, "I repeat, I need every bit of power you can give!"

The lights in the access chamber flickered, and suddenly there was deafening silence. Air circulation stopped and the background hum of electronics and subsystems *ceased* for all of a second, before coming back to life even more aggressively than before. A crashing sound rocked its way through the division, sending the panoply of KARD personnel to the floor as the team cranked everything they could — physical, psychic and magical efforts combined — into the containment field of Vault F.

Phillip was among the first back on his feet, along with the rest of the monitoring team. The skunk stared wide-eyed at the screen by the bulkhead and muttered frantically under his breath. "Come on, come on, come on, come on..."

Maxwell hastily joined him, watching all of the winch readouts spin down, showing just mere metres of unspooled cable. The dive team must have at least managed to regroup, and they couldn't be far from the preparation room.

Next to him, the silver dragoness was helping his small blue kobold assistant to her feet. Ul dusted herself off but looked exhausted and drained. Around her, countless vials of fluid had been emptied and used to paint symbols and sigils on the floor and bulkhead door, in a frantic attempt to appease the unknown. Though Maxwell was by no means a master of the arcane, he knew enough about his dear assistant's practices to recognise a guiding ward amongst the symbols. "They're safe, Director..."

Several members of the engineering team, accompanied as they were by synth medics, hustled to the front of the chamber. "Stand clear!" one of them called. The bulkhead opened to the preparation room, and through it, all eight of the dive team tumbled; several seemed worse for wear, but none of them were seriously injured.

Karen stepped forward through the swarm of henches, once the dive team had been given the all-clear by the medics. "What happened in there?"

One of the synth units replied mechanically, as it stood up and tested the connection of her shoulder socket. "Unknown spatial anomaly. Vault F did not appear to respond well to the keywords given. No intelligence recovered."

Maxwell's heart barely had time to sink as he heard the news, far more occupied with the kobold's health — but there would be time for that during the debrief, he was sure. In the meanwhile, the distinct looks shared between the monitoring team spoke volumes.

For the first time in a *very* long time, Maxwell felt truly out of his depth.

Lexi woke up to aggressive shaking.

The first thing she saw in focus was the highway stretching out in front of her, and then Drac's panic and grief-stricken face. Their tears glistened in the sickly yellow light cast by the poles in the median, blearily illuminating the night.

"Oh, thank *fuck* you're awake! You scared the shit out of me..."

The dragon embraced her tightly, tightly enough that she struggled to breathe for a moment, as their powerful body clutched her and refused to let go. Lexi felt numb, still wrestling with the sensation of her body returning to one single form. Then, as quickly as she could blink the tears away, she wailed in fear. Her hands scrambled to get a good grip on her partner, clinging to the fabric of his shirt; she faintly realised that it appeared to have been hastily donned inside-out.

No words came, just tears, as they picked her up off the rough asphalt of the highway's shoulder. By the time they were belting her into their car's passenger seat, her body was rocking with tremors.

Drac pulled back onto the near-empty early-morning highway and drove his way back into town in silent distress. For the first time since the cow had known him, he seemed unsure of what to do. "Should I take you to the hospital?"

"N-no," Lexi replied, uncertain of herself too.

The dragon simply let out a defeated, meaningful sigh. "Okay."

Lexi knew well enough that they must have *wanted* to get her checked over. Who wouldn't, under the circumstances? But they remained patient, to an extreme that the Highland didn't expect. Her mind began to race haphazardly through all the different options her boyfriend might have seen in front of them, but regardless, they didn't raise any.

The rest of the drive home was uncomfortably quiet, leaving Lexi to wallow in her own attempts to formulate a plan. Maxwell had said the sleepwalking could get worse, but the whole point of her working at the Dropp was to help combat the side effects of her powers. If her condition was worsening *despite* that, did she even stand a chance? What would happen the next time, or the time after that?

As if on cue, more words slowly and quietly drifted from Drac's mouth, accompanied by another sigh that sounded like it wanted to say a lot more. "I love you, sweetie."

"I love you too. Sorry." It was all Lexi could do to offer her feelings back. She wasn't ready to admit that she was going through a sort of superpower puberty, nor that her warmly pleasant new boss was a known supervillain.

Maybe she could just keep it a secret. Maybe she could just ask Maxwell for more help and keep it on the downlow. Maybe she could live a secret, second life, away from the person she loved the most, in order to shelter him from any consequences of her stupid, apparently *broken* brain. She was used to doing that already, at least; it wouldn't be much different to transitioning in semi-secret, back in the UK. Doing something that had to be done, but doing so outside the faint veil of reality her life occupied in the minds of extended family and co-workers. Invisible, to an extent.

Maybe it would work out. Maybe Maxwell could pull something out of his sleeve and make all the sleepwalking go away, and she could just settle down to a reasonably normal life — or, at least, as normal as effectively as a low-level hench could hope for. There were *laws* against criminal conspiracy and working for designated illegal organisations, superpowered or not.

She could either get clinical help for the sleepwalking, and likely be put on some kind of *list* — whether Canada required its superpowered residents to register with the federal or the provincial government, the cow wasn't certain — or work for Maxwell, and hope both for the symptoms to improve, and also evade the notice of cops and Heroes.

On paper, being put on a super registry didn't seem like that big of a deal... but something about the thought of being on a government list irked her. She didn't want to be special, and she didn't want to be scrutinised for the way she was. She just wanted to *be*. Why couldn't she just *be*? And if she did end up on some kind of registry, then who was to say what would be done with that information? Governments famously fumbled data all the time — she recalled Drac's mention of a minor Canadian political scandal, over an employee of the immigration department leaving their laptop full of confidential data behind on a city bus — and the cow knew enough history to see where lists of people with *innate traits* had led in the past.

There really wasn't any other option, then. Lexi *had* to seek help from Maxwell. She barely knew him, and she wasn't sure she trusted him, but searching herself the cow realised she felt safer around the supposed villains than she did out in the wide world.

Maybe, Lexi thought, not for the first time, *maybe the villains are right*. Usually, this thought would be halted by some overarching notions of decency, that justice was worth fighting for within the confines of the law, democracy was good, and the status quo — while not perfect — was worth preserving, in the faint hope of incremental progress. But those thoughts didn't come, this time. Instead, in their place, a quiet rumbling echoed in the distant reaches of her mind:

Who says change shouldn't be radical?

Lexi reflected on the times she had found herself quietly grateful for the work that supposed villains had done. She hadn't always agreed with their methods, and sometimes people got hurt, but the more she thought about it, she found herself hard-pressed to write off their actions as having gone *too far*.

What was 'too far', anyway? The world was dying and burning, endless wealth was funnelled to the top, and the middle were pitted violently against the bottom. Countless in-groups and out-groups were created from whole cloth, to distract from the slow decay of everything that she had been told were the most important things in a civilised society.

The Highland had grown up watching Greenbelt, epitome of the upright British Hero, slowly turn from crusading champion to tool of the establishment. She had grown up and matured with the supposed 'end of history' to find that things could in fact *not* only get better; instead, things kept getting worse, and ever more confusing and contradictory. The villains had a point, the cow pondered.

She knew that some people would already consider her a villain, just based on her beliefs and identity. But now the thought *really* dawned on her — what did she gain from separating herself from that label? If the world would already call her a monster for who she was and what she believed, then why fight it? Why not just own it? Why not *be monstrous?* If the world and its systems, rife with corruption as they were, would be scared of her — good.

Maybe, she thought again. *Maybe I could do good as a villain, and even… do just a little bit to make things better? Drac doesn't have to know. It can just be a simple henching job. Maybe Maxwell and the Korps could help them too, if things go sideways.*

The cow looked over at her boyfriend again, just as he was pulling into the condo's garage. "Thank you for looking out for me and keeping me safe, honey. I'm sorry for scaring you."

Drac exhaled a weary but sympathetic breath. "I just worry about you, you know? You mean a lot to me and… I know you can't control this… this… *whatever* it is, but I just want you to be safe."

"I know. I want us to be safe too," she replied.

With the car parked, the couple leant into each other in a tired embrace across the centre console.

"I love you, honey," Lexi whispered. "I'm gonna do whatever I can to make this better. I promise."

CHAPTER 10

July 11, 1943

Somewhere in the distance a church bell rang, calling the residents of Riaillé to service; André opened his eyes at the ringing, the rich blues and pinks of the early dawn sky greeting him threateningly. His head was full of *noise*, sharp and jagged, piercing the dullness that muffled most of his senses. His body ached and protested as if he'd been put through a thresher, a hypothesis supported by the tall grass in which he laid.

The wolf moved his neck, and the muscles in his back responded by sending static back to his brain. André's claws dug into the dirt, and he tried to roll himself onto his side before realising the static he was feeling was coming from his leg; fighting through the pain, he pushed himself up on his elbows and peered down at his left thigh. There, on his pants, he saw it — a slick red stain. The pungent smell of iron finally hit his nose, and his breathing quickened in uncontrolled panic.

The adolescent canine desperately searched through his scrambled memories to make sense of where he found himself but found nothing other than screams and gunshots. The splitting pain had cut off access to anything of *use* in his head, besides a fractured (but faintly functional) survival instinct.

He knew enough to put pressure on the wound, but from the look of it, he had already been bleeding for an extended period of time. He couldn't remember how he wound up in the field, but something told him he'd been there overnight, at least. André ventured a shaking paw to the wound on his leg, trembling fingers carefully manipulating the fabric of his pants, to try and get a look at what he already suspected was a gunshot wound. The garment bore only a single hole, so if it was a bullet that'd hit him, it was probably still inside his leg.

André staggered out a whimper as a finger grazed the entry wound. His fur was deeply matted with blood, and not wanting or knowing what else to examine, the wolf began pulling his shirt off over his head. As he did, several scraps of paper fluttered out and landed in the mud. With them came another fragment of a memory, but he pushed it to the side to concentrate on wrapping his leg with his shirt.

Getting the shirt in position turned out to be the easy part. As soon as he began to tie a knot, the pressure on the wound squeezed a pained howl out of him, despite his defiantly puffed-out chest. The boy grit his teeth and screamed into the air, looking back down and panting angrily at the half-tied knot. His fingers fumbled with the fabric as he readied himself yanking the makeshift bandage tighter; he cast another anguished howl to the sky, voice cracking throughout.

The mud and crushed wheat stems made for welcome bedding to collapse upon after finishing the wound dressing. André lay there, panting through pained sobs for a minute or two, wondering whether his efforts would prove futile; he still couldn't at all recall where he was, how he'd gotten there, or what had happened.

Then a voice in the distance — closer than the church bells — stirred the wolf once more. "Hello? Who's there?"

Part of André wanted to call out for help, but the rest of him was gripped in a vice of fear that locked his jaw shut. He couldn't see the voice's owner; despite propping himself up on his elbows again, it wasn't enough to see over top of the wheat. If his voice wouldn't cooperate, he'd need to try and stand to get attention, but standing was going to be hard.

He looked around him and tried his best to gather the scraps of paper that had fallen out of his shirt. *Something* in his mind was pushed even further to the back as he did so. Clutching at the papers, André rolled himself onto the side that had taken the bullet. It was a struggle, but the disconcertingly growing numbness in his leg made the manoeuvre slightly more manageable.

André wasn't sure how he'd done it, but eventually, slowly and painfully, he managed *almost* standing upright. His head and bare chest were poked up over the crest of the wheat, and in the distance he could see a small white farmhouse. Through bleary eyes, he could make out a figure that seemed to let its shoulders sink in disbelief before it ran back to the farmhouse, staggering through the door.

The wolf held a paw up to try and wave for attention, but still no words came out to accompany the tired motion.

The crop around him rustled in a light gust of wind, drawing his attention towards a pair of oak trees at the edge of the field. André thought he could see a figure standing beneath it, but it didn't move in the way it should have. He tried a wave in its direction, and got back a nod, and something like a gesture back towards the farmhouse. His vision blurred further as he stood there, trying to make out more of the figure's details; with enough of a harsh squint, he thought the man looked like his father—

—Something in him sank. A gunshot echoed through distant reaches of his mind, and when he tried to blink the noise away, the figure had vanished. His father wasn't under the oak trees anymore; he was just *gone*.

"Stay there!" A new voice called from the direction of the farmhouse.

The wolf tried to turn his head to look, but when he did, the world wouldn't stop spinning. Through the disorientation, André could make out three distinct figures rushing from the farmhouse, crashing their way through the wheat to reach him.

The boy's jaw hung open as he finally managed to mutter out a coherent word, right as his vision started to go black. With another blink, gravity took over, sending him to the mud.

"H-help..."

When André came to, he was in a bed he didn't recognise. The ceiling above was unfamiliar, too; it was cracked, and the plaster looked damp and water-damaged, far different from the small room he knew at home. He cast his eyes about the place. It was lit, just barely, by two candles perched on a rickety-looking chest of drawers in the far corner. The tattered scraps of what he recognised as his shirt and pants were crumpled on a stool nearby, but both seemed much cleaner than he remembered.

The wolf tried to move, but the pain in his leg stopped him almost immediately, searing up his left side; the bedsheets, thin and ratty as they were, stung and itched and burned all at once with even the *slightest* movement against his fur. With a wince, he carefully pulled back the sheet. To his surprise, the wound was dressed. The bandages were still soaked through with solid, rusty crimson, but they were doing a much better job of stanching the blood than his shirt could have ever hoped to achieve.

Footsteps and creaking floorboards from somewhere on the other side of the door startled the boy, their noise causing a reflexive twitch across his entire body. It shot yet more pain up his left side and forced a trembling gasp from his maw.

"How long?" a voice asked from beyond the door.

The reply came in a much deeper, gruffer tone. "Since morning."

André didn't have to wait long before the voices were given form. The door to the room creaked open, and through it strode three figures. One was completely new to him, not one of the three the wolf hazily remembered running towards him in the field.

The trio's new third was a fox, his fur deep orange and well-groomed, though his vest and high-waisted trousers were worn and threadbare. On closer inspection, and without the blur of imminent fainting, André could see that the other two were goats in rough flannels — one large and heavy-set, the other shorter and more lithe, carrying a distinct familial resemblance in their muzzles and brows. Both of them were dark-furred, though it was impossible to make out the exact hue in the candlelight.

None of the three, save the smaller goat, seemed to pay attention to the fact that the wolf was awake. The fox began pulling back the sheet, but André protested. Patiently, the fox explained himself, in a well-to-do accent that belied his shabby appearance. "Young man, I am a doctor. I understand you have been shot, and I am here to get the bullet out, as a favour to these two gentlemen behind me."

André loosened his stubborn grip on the sheets but continued to say nothing.

The fox half-turned his head back to the two goats, keeping his eyes on the wolf the whole time. "You dressed his leg?"

"As best as I could, yes," replied the smaller man.

Peeling back the sheets with one hand — just enough to expose the dressed wound and nothing more — the fox assessed the job, apparently feeling the need to offer his professional commentary. "Certainly not the worst I've seen, *Little.*" The doctor gestured back at the larger goat with a wave of his hand. "Bag, please. And Little, if you could kindly fetch me a wooden spoon, and any strong liquor you might have. Brandy or eau-de-vie or whisky or such, if you have it. Otherwise, I'll need water and salt." Peering back to the young wolf, his next words came out with a curious flatness in his voice. "I take it you haven't been shot before, boy?"

André continued to remain silent, paralysed by a fear he couldn't quite place. Instead, he simply shook his head.

"Well, you're taking it a damn sight better than some people who have. You mute, boy?"

André shook his head again.

"Mmm. Well, I'm going to tell you now, I'm afraid this will hurt. *A lot.* When Little — the short one — gets back with the wooden spoon, I want you to put it across your muzzle and bite down hard, yes?"

The wolf nodded, grimacing, already having suspected as much.

Little re-entered the room, holding in his arms some cloth, the wooden spoon, and a bottle of a pale amber liquid. Soon the items were in the fox's paws, who handed the spoon off to the wolf. "Like I told you," he said firmly, setting about cutting the dressing away none-too-delicately.

André bit down hard and propped himself up on his elbows despite the pain. The wound stung in the open air and began to tingle in his horrified anticipation, as the fox uncorked the bottle of spirits. He took a long sip from the bottle first, before holding a paw down heavily on André's thigh, and pouring some of the alcohol out over the bloody mass of fur.

The wolf felt his entire left side shiver and sting with what felt like a thousand tiny blades. He finally let himself howl and tensed all over.

"Big, come here and hold him down, if you would. If he thrashes too much, I might nick something."

André felt himself be rolled onto his right side, exposing even more of the wound to the air. The doctor doused it again with alcohol; the stinging sensation instantly managed to burrow even deeper into the hole, jabbing at the wolf's nerves. The wooden spoon between his jaws threatened to splinter and snap under his bite, as a metallic clacking sound — the doctor fumbling with his tools, a pair of forceps, maybe? — filled the room. The staccato sound was soon succeeded by a sickly, fleshy squelch, and in turn was replaced by the angriest howl André thought he would ever manage in his life.

His body shook, and he felt sick to his core, as the visceral feeling of the forceps meeting the bullet *rolled* around his body in a horribly foreign way. Something that wasn't supposed to be inside him was meeting something *else* that wasn't supposed to be inside him, and all the boy could think about was how he desperately wished it to stop.

"Nearly there," the doctor muttered under his breath. With one last not-so-gentle pull, he finally freed the bullet from André's thigh.

There was a brief sense of blessed respite, where the young wolf could adjust to the new, equally strange feeling of *no longer* having a chunk of metal inside him, but it lasted only a moment. The fox waved his hand at the smaller of the two goats, and whispered something André couldn't make out. Although his view was obscured by the larger goat still holding him firmly in place, he could tell the smaller of the pair was fetching something from the other side of the room. The light in the room changed suddenly, and shadows flickered across the wall; the canine realised Little must have picked up one of the candles, holding it for the doctor.

Then there was silence, and after a few endless seconds, a faintly-hissing whine of scorched metal.

"I have to cauterise the wound, you understand? This is going to burn, but it will help prevent an infection." The doctor didn't wait for any sign of an affirmative, instead proceeding to place the flat edge of a searing-hot scalpel on the open tissue.

At some point, consciousness began to slip from the wolf again, and he was mercifully taken to passing in and out of the waking world for the rest of the procedure. When he eventually regained lucidity, his leg was being held up gently by Little, and a fresh new dressing made of actual gauze was being applied by the doctor.

Big poured out some of the remaining alcohol into a tin mug and offered it to André. "For the pain," was all he said.

The boy sipped at the drink and wrinkled his nose. He swallowed hard and tried his best to not cough or splutter through the burning mouthful... and then, all at once, the smell of the liquor reminded him of his father. His *father!*

André began to remember how he'd stumbled into that field and started to sob.

The doctor left of his own accord some time later, leaving the two goats to comfort the boy well into the night, until — at last — André fell asleep.

When he awoke, André was greeted by the familiar smell of lard on slightly stale toast. The meagre rations weren't a new experience, of course, but being offered them while he was laid up in bed with a gunshot wound was.

So much had *happened* to him in the past few days, new and drastic, that it was hard to recall a time he had truly felt safe or settled. The agony of his immediate past swirled together, rendering it impossible to separate out the individual catastrophes from their slow, piecemeal build-up. The most painful instances of tragedy had been committed to memory as if seared into his mind and had shaken his dreams most every night since.

Dreams, he thought, before correcting himself. *Nightmares. They were nightmares.* Nothing was truly over, and he had no idea what would come next… but at least he was somewhere different now, and at least he was being offered food.

"You need to eat, to get your strength back," the goat known to him only as Little said, holding out the toast. "Just something light, to make sure you can hold down food. When we know you can, I'll see about trying to get you some eggs."

André reached for the toast, snatching it uncertainly before stuffing as much of it in his hungry maw as he could. It was salty, greasy, and warm, with just a hint of something flavourful the wolf couldn't place. Maybe pepper? He wasn't sure, but either way, slavering through the offered food took his mind off the pain in his leg. (Almost.)

Little curled his lip sympathetically and gave a quiet exhale of relief. "Well… if you're not talking, at least you're eating. For that I'm glad." The goat paused as he seemed to circulate a thought in his head, looking idly at the cracks in the rustically plastered wall. "I suppose I never actually told you my name. Everyone calls me Little. It's not my real name, but no one here uses their real names. My brother gets called Big, and the girl with us, everyone just calls her Kitty."

André said nothing. He was familiar with codenames long before he wound up in this farmhouse; they were always invariably used by the same group of people. The kind of people his father would meet with surreptitiously. The kind that called his father only by an alias, too — Maxwell. No matter how hard the wolf tried to recollect the many faces he'd seen come and go from his father's small workshop, however, he didn't recognise the goat, nor even the fox who had pulled the bullet from his thigh a hazy few nights prior.

"You're Resistance," the wolf muttered emphatically.

Little raised his chin in acknowledgement. "Mmm. Astute."

"My father used to meet with people that kept secrets," André quietly continued, finding words much easier, once he believed he had the upper paw in the conversation and had something of *importance* to offer, besides. His father had been careful to keep things quiet. Who he met with, and why, might have been the only secrets he kept from the boy.

"Like the ones that you had when we found you?"

André nodded.

"Did you get those documents from him?"

André shook his head. Despite his directness, the goat's demeanour (and definitely not praise for his perspicacity, certainly *not*) had calmed the boy, and he felt able to open up. "No. I stole them."

Little seemed shocked at the revelation. "You did? Where from?"

"I… don't know," the wolf admitted hesitantly. "I was sleepwalking at the time."

The room went silent for a moment, and Little stood up to leave. "I-I'll be back in a moment," he stammered out with an unreadable expression, closing the door behind him.

André heard footsteps down a creaky staircase, and quieted chattering that sounded like disbelief in a deep, slow voice he assumed to belong to Big. Soon enough, Little and his older brother entered the room again, with a small collection of dirtied (and bloodied) papers in their hands. The wolf instantly recognised them as the ones he'd found on his person upon awakening in the goats' wheat field.

"These, *you stole these, in your sleep?*" Little asked again, looking back to the much larger man intermittently. "And your father... you think he works with the Resistance too?"

There was an uncomfortable pause, as the wolf tried to articulate around the sore spot of phrasing his response in the past tense, but he only managed one word before the tears began to flow. "Did..."

The two goats shared a look and embraced the young boy tightly as he began to sob and wail.

Big whispered to his brother. "Shit. He's Maxwell's boy, all right; poor lad. He must have run all through the night, to get here before the messengers did..."

Little hummed in acknowledgement and shed a tear of his own. "It's okay. We're here. Your father was a good man. We never met him, but... what Maxwell did for the cause, by God... you're safe here, I promise. We won't let them get you."

━━━

October 26, 2019

Maxwell looked every bit as tired as Lexi felt. His gaze was dark, the hollow sleeplessness in each eye socket visible even through the hue of his RCGs. He sat wearily, too, almost (but not quite) hunched over; It made the cow suspect he was conscious enough to at least *try* maintaining a dignified posture, but that his body was failing to comply. The wolf stifled a closed-mouth yawn, and a second later, tried to perk himself up with a sip of coffee.

Lexi sat across the desk from him, idly thumbing the handle of her own mug, kindly brewed and served to her by Liam a moment earlier. She hesitated and finally broke the silence. "Thank you for seeing me today. On such short notice, I mean."

Maxwell held his coffee an inch from his nose, obscuring most of his muzzle with it. He eventually replied with few words, and a blink that seemed to carry a great deal of emotional weight. "I did offer you a job, did I not?"

"Well, yes, but… well, when I left a message with the number you gave me, asking to come in, I wasn't expecting a response right away. I mean, not at three in the morning. I hope I didn't wake you…" Lexi offered, fumbling with her words, and suddenly keenly aware that she *might* just be a bit intimidated by the man.

"Oh, not at all. I was already awake. I've had a rather… *difficult* twenty-four hours." The canine flicked an ear and punctuated his sentence by setting his coffee down gently. "Villain things, you see."

The dry quip hung in the air, awaiting a response the bovine felt unprepared to give. Lexi's hoof-nails clacked quietly against her mug as she took a sip.

"And for *you* to be up at that time — I take it you sleepwalked again? I'm assuming that's what this is about."

She gave a small nod, thankful that she didn't have to be the one to bring it up. She didn't care for being the centre of attention. "Yes, but I figure it probably takes a few days for me to adjust to, uh… you said something yesterday about telepathic fields?"

Maxwell gave the faintest hint of a nod and swivelled on his chair just slightly, to reach forward and pluck a stray hair from between the keys of his typewriter. He examined its crisp whiteness before brushing it to the floor. "Mmm," he mumbled in a faintly discouraging way. "Superpowers manifest slightly differently for everyone, even when similar in form and function. It's entirely possible your field will take more time to adjust than mine ever did. I, however, find near-instant relief and clarity in being surrounded by the *weight* of information."

"Oh," Lexi uttered. It made sense that things might be different for her, but that did raise the question as to whether the old man could even *help*. Still, she asked the question on her mind. "D-do you think that taking that next step to getting my powers under control will still work? You mentioned something yesterday about 'safe outlets.'"

"I did," Maxwell murmured. "How far did you get last night?"

Lexi felt her ears droop low enough to brush the shoulders of her flannel shirt. "…Out to the highway. My boyfriend found me, eventually; spotted me from an overpass after driving around for a while. We figure I must have been out of the apartment for a few hours, at least."

The wolf set his mug to one side and clasped his paws together on the surface of the desk. His chair creaked, cutting through the soft silence of the room as he examined every mote of the cow's being with a weary, serious stare. Lexi could practically feel the warmth of the spotlight being cast on her, and the scrutiny with which the supervillain regarded her very soul.

"Do you know what taking the next step to control your powers with us means?"

The words were pointed and demanded an answer the Highland wasn't sure she had. "No," she admitted. "But I assume it would mean closer association with the Korps."

"And you'd be comfortable with that? With being permanently associated with supervillains? *Criminals?*" the wolf retorted.

Lexi was taken aback. She didn't know ahead of time how this conversation would go, but she had assumed it would be easier than this. Weren't these people supposed to jump at recruitment chances? Maybe it was the sleep deprivation, or the tone of an older man second-guessing her — just the way her *father* always had — but the cow felt *irritated* at the implication. "Yesterday, you said you thought I'd make a good villain."

"Yesterday," Maxwell sniffed through a faint snarl, "you weren't so sure I was right."

Confrontation was never the cow's strong suit, yet something in her boiled over; she found herself clutching the coffee mug even harder in both hands, mouth running more freely than it probably should have, given her present company. "I'm asking for *help!* I don't have any other option!"

The wolf lifted both his paws and sat back in his chair, gesturing at the air. "But you could seek help from the authorities, no? Here we are in downtown Toronto; you could be on the streetcar to CAMH in five minutes, report yourself to their special clinic for telepaths, perhaps be given sedatives or power-suppressants. If that doesn't suit you, Ontario's Heroes might even consider you for recruitment with such a power — assuming your immigration went smoothly, of course. You didn't *have* to come back here asking for my help, so why did you?"

Lexi felt the thick fur on the back of her neck start to raise in irritation, her hackles itching as the wolf dug his teeth into her psyche with minimal effort. "I don't *want* to end up a goddamn Hero, that's why! And I don't want to just pretend everything is fine, either!"

"Then tell me what you *do* want!" Maxwell retorted, slamming his paws down on his desk. His pads laid flat against the wood, while his arms trembled.

The cow flinched, overwhelmed, and retreated into her own seat. Once the shock had passed, she curled her lip and sneered right back at the bitter old man. "Why are you acting like this? I came to you for help, and you're pushing me away like I'm — like I'm some *kid!*"

"Because I see myself in you, and I need you to be sure you *want* this!" Seconds after he raised his voice, the room went deathly quiet, only to be broken again by a teary sniffle through a lupine snout. "Because I don't want to see you make the same mistakes I did. Because I *care.* I need you to understand that if you stay with me, and the Korps, that you have to be prepared to *fail.* You have to be prepared to run yourself dry trying to change the world. You're a smart girl, and you know there are other options, but you don't *want* to take them, because you'd rather be a villain. But the fight isn't easy, and sometimes, it will take more from you than you can stomach."

Lexi watched as Maxwell sat himself down again, shrinking once more into his seat and seeming so much less than the powerful, intimidating force he had just been seconds ago.

The wolf swept his hair back with a lone paw and took in a deep, slightly raspy breath. He scooted his RCGs up his face and wiped away a tear. "Have you ever heard of Operation Felt, Lexi?"

The Highland shook her head.

"Of course you haven't." Maxwell sighed. "Back during the Second World War, supers were being used wherever feasible to try and give every side any edge possible. The same was true for covert intelligence. I was kidnapped and forced to work for the Secret Intelligence Service, Lexi. MI5. At first, they tried to use me to transfer encoded instructions to spies telepathically. I didn't know what it was I was imprinting on them, but at a later date when they were in the field, they'd receive a key to the ciphers I seared into their minds that they could perfectly recall. I was used as a *tool.* But then… I became too much to manage. My transference became less and less predictable as I was starved of any information I could make heads or tails of, and I needed to scratch the itch. Despite being surrounded by secrets, I wasn't allowed to know *anything*. My handlers began to dose me with experimental medications to keep the sleepwalking at bay, to suppress my urges — but it didn't work.

"And then, one day, there was an accident, and I transferred so much into an unsuspecting clerk, that..." The wolf choked back another tear and steadied his breathing. "They lobotomised him. It was a kindness, they said. They were convinced his mind was too scrambled to save. That was the start of Operation Felt.

"It was an attempt by the British government to wipe the minds of intelligence assets, so that they wouldn't pose a threat or weak link. I was made to scramble the minds of more people than I care to remember, while I was in the SIS's 'custody'. For a long while, my handlers believed the only way to ensure a successful memory wipe was to have the *new* information be... particularly traumatic. Only later did 'testing' reveal just about any information would work, if there was enough of it." The lupine paused, silently reflecting on some unseen horrors that must have haunted his mind. "Years later, with help, I would escape; later still, I tried to alert the world about the whole affair. It was front page news for a few days, and then..." He opened his paw to the air, ephemerally releasing nothing for effect. "Then it was *forgotten*. Eventually the British government would admit to it, in a bloodless, limited capacity, but soon that admission too was forgotten. It's declassified now, technically, yet few ever talk about it, the whole thing shoved to the far corners of public consciousness. I couldn't bring back the secrets I burned out of people's minds, of course. I could at least tell the world what was happening... but no one seemed to care. Secrets are the most dangerous things in the world, Lexi. We must always try our hardest to uncover them — it's the only way to disarm them."

Lexi felt her heart sink as she watched the elderly supervillain spill his soul in front of her. "The UK is a rotten place. I didn't know that, but... I can't say I'm surprised. A Hero, Greenbelt, taught me that first-hand. Corruption and lies are buried away everywhere."

Maxwell turned his head just slightly, his eyes still full of regretful sorrow. "You do understand, then. I'm sorry. Realising you've been lied to, even through omission, is not a comfortable thing, but it's necessary to see the whole picture."

"I actually wanted to go into journalism for that reason, you know? Not that I knew where to start... but soon I realised there wasn't much hope for that either, with how captured the press is in the UK. I felt jaded and hopeless. I don't want to feel hopeless anymore." Lexi paused and took a shaky breath, almost disbelieving the next words that she was readying herself to say. "You asked what I *wanted*. Well... I want to make a difference. I want to have hope again. If that means becoming a villain, then, fine. I just don't want to wind up denying who I am, or to end up like Greenbelt. *That's* what I want." She hung her head, exhausted from the admission (and sleep deprivation besides), entirely unsure what response to expect.

The wolf looked back down to the floor and nodded solemnly. His chair creaked as he got to his feet and wandered to a shelf along the wall, taking a rather plain-looking paper bag from it before returning to the desk. He placed the sack on the desk quietly and returned to his seat. "For you," he said with a renewed softness.

Lexi looked at the bag, and then back to Maxwell, reaching for it with the smallest amount of trepidation. It contained something that looked like a glasses case, but larger in all dimensions. When she opened the sleek black case, she wasn't surprised by what she saw, at least not the *generalities* of it. It was a set of Rose-Coloured Glasses, like the ones the airport notification forbade under threat of scrutiny — though, like the ones Maxwell wore, these notably lacked any Thorntech branding. What *did* throw her for a second was the fact that they had clearly been custom-fitted for her. The bridge of the nose looked perfectly wide enough for her snout, and the visor's overall jellybean shape was accentuated at each side with clean black arms (folded as they were) which at a glance, Lexi reckoned, were perfectly sized to her bovine proportions.

"If you're ready," Maxwell intoned solemnly and hopefully, "this is the next step."

As she held the RCGs in her hands, Lexi couldn't help but think back to the first lot of grey-market HRT pills she'd received in the mail, back in the UK, and how looking at them in her hands, it was hard to believe they'd change so much about her life. Maybe the glasses would be the same, and maybe they wouldn't; regardless, they sat in her hands as a symbol of something much, much *bigger*.

"Does it hurt?" she asked, dryness biting at the back of her throat. "These things hook into your mind, right? Does... does that hurt?"

Maxwell seemed surprised. "No, it doesn't hurt. People are usually more worried about them being used for mind control..."

Lexi shrugged her shoulders somewhat, still delaying putting the visor on by turning it over in her hoof-nailed hands to examine it. Not that there was much fine detail to look at — the soft glare of the single-piece magenta lens being what it was. "Yeah, but I always kind of figured that couldn't be true. Can't believe everything you read on the news, you know?"

"Mmm," Maxwell refused to confirm. "They work with an AI of sorts, called ROSE. She's in every pair, and networks between users. She can indeed access your thoughts but will only do so with your consent. That pair is fresh, no user profiles on board yet, so when you first put them on, she'll ask a few questions to get you oriented."

There was a long pause as Lexi continued to just hold the RCGs in her hands, trying to feel their imperceptible weight. She wondered if she should really be having second thoughts, but try as she might, it was like the voice inside her — the one that had once demanded she try and fit in and be quiet — had gone silent. *Given up*, though, was probably a better way to frame it. It left Lexi an unrealised cast, into which any suitable material might be poured.

"Do you have any questions?" Maxwell asked

"How do these help? With the withdrawal?" The cow played with the word on her tongue, unsure if it felt quite right to describe the sleepwalking and burning internal itch that way. "Side effects of the powers, I mean."

"A good question," Maxwell noted. "They don't, not directly. At least not in my case... but ROSE is a very powerful tool. She can't stop your drive to collect, but she can at least numb the feeling somewhat, and otherwise help you focus when you need to. There's a reason why so many of us wear them. And if we're going to find safe outlets for your need to collect, then she'll be indispensable in providing situational awareness that would require lengthy training, with more traditional methods."

"Huh... cool." The Highland wasn't really sure of what else to say. Everything about the last week had seemed unreal, and things were only moving faster. It was all she could do to just accept what she was being told and not think too hard about it. The train ride back to Kitchener later would provide valuable reflection time, anyway.

Maxwell quietly rose from his chair and headed for the door. "I'll give you some privacy to get them set up. Let me know when you're done."

With that, Lexi was left alone in the room. She tapped the hoof-nail of her thumb against the rim of the RCGs and unfolded their arms. Bringing them up to her face, she couldn't see any obvious signs of life like an indicator light, and momentarily wondered how to turn them on, not finding any buttons or toggles. The case offered no convenient instruction manual, so she bit the bullet, and slid the visor onto her snout.

For a moment, nothing happened, except the fact that everything now had a striking magenta hue to it, and then the room started to get softly brighter. Suddenly, in front of her, Lexi saw the sleek, stylised outlines of a rose icon. The cow moved her head a little and the image followed but still managed to look as if it was floating about a foot in front of her rather than being projected onto the lens itself. Reaching a hand out to try and touch it reassured her that it really was just an augmented-reality pseudo-hologram.

The outlines began to fill with solid colour from the bottom up as the device on her face apparently began its bootup sequence. The image was quickly accompanied by a long scroll of text that Lexi wasn't able to parse, but that faintly reminded her of command line screens that were used in movies to denote that something *technical* was happening.

[*Hello, I'm ROSE. What's your name?*]

The words seemed to fill Lexi's head like a thought, but unlike her typical thoughts, it was clear and cut through her constant internal fog.

"Uh... Lexi." She felt strange talking to no one — or more accurately, a someone who wasn't there. The bovine was *plenty* used to talking to themself, but this felt different.

[*Hello, Lexi. You do not need to answer vocally if you don't want to. You can simply think your responses.*]

"Seems like a polite, non-threatening way to say I can read your thoughts," Lexi thought.

[*Yes, to an extent. Currently, I am only granted basic access to read communicative thoughts and will not go further without your express consent.*]

Lexi winced awkwardly, dwelling on how rude that thought might have come off to something that could read her mind, before she realised that ROSE could probably hear *that* thought too. Maybe not, though? The silent voice didn't seem to reply that time.

"*Understood, I think,*" the cow communicated, focusing on *how* she would say the words — mouthing them without putting her voice behind it.

[*Excellent. May I ask what your preferred pronouns are, Lexi?*]

"*She/her.*" Lexi tried to not mouth too much, that time, and it seemed to work. She was getting the hang of it.

[*You're doing very well. Neural interfaces like this can be hard to get used to, but as you do, communication gets faster.*]

Lexi felt herself nodding along to the AI's reassurances, thankful that its creators seemed to be aware of the hangups a user like her might have, and that a little hand-holding would go a long way.

[*Next, I am going to ask for some more detailed personal information.*]

Some of the next questions felt odd but not too strange. They were mostly things that might be filled out on a medical chart like height, weight, and approximate species/breed. Convenient notes indicated that these could be changed and updated later, with rough estimates for how long that would take — strangely, even for the species/breed questions — but others felt decidedly more out of left field.

"*Why do you need to know what my favourite breakfast food is?*" Lexi asked, internally, this time with no hint of mouth movement at all.

[*Think of it as a mood board question. If I know what you like, I better know what to recommend.*]

"*Ah. Algorithm training stuff?*"

[*Yes and no. It paints a clearer picture for me, but none of this personal information is shared without your express consent. I'm simply just getting to know you.*]

"*Porridge oats,*" the cow answered instantly.

[*Salty, sweet, or plain?*]

Lexi didn't hesitate even slightly. "*Sweet, with fruit and some honey or syrup. Granny used to insist on having it with salt, but I could never stomach it the way she made it.*" It took her a moment to realise that ROSE probably didn't need the backstory, but just like she had said, communicating this way was becoming easier, and very quickly, too. The thought had rolled off Lexi's mental tongue faster than she could properly control.

[*Noted. I notice that you are looking around the room, not focusing on anything in particular. Do you think you would find it easier if you had a visible avatar of me to face when you communicate?*]

Lexi reeled her head back slightly. She hadn't even noticed, but ROSE was right. She had been looking around the room, eyes darting from one thing to another, trying to find something specific to hold her attention while she filled out the questions. "*I... suppose so?*"

In front of her (but not really), there on the other side of Maxwell's desk, an animated avatar of a vixen appeared with a polite wave. The woman stayed spatially fixed as Lexi moved her head around. The cow had never used a VR headset, but she'd picked up enough through cultural osmosis to relate the experience to using one. The vixen, ROSE, looked as if she was standing casually in the room with the cow.

Its mouth moved perfectly in sync with the words ROSE beamed into Lexi's thoughts. [*There we go. Let me know if this is easier for your focus; I can toggle the avatar at your preference.*]

Lexi didn't find herself unsettled, so much as disoriented in a specific kind of way — the same kind of disoriented that came with hearing a voice, and thinking it didn't seem to fit its owner's appearance. "*I don't think I imagined you as a fox, for some reason? Is that weird?*"

[*Not at all. This is just the default appearance; you can change it at any time for a number of popular preset options, or you can customize your own.*]

"Oh, neat, I guess." Lexi felt just a little bit bad about imposing her preconceived thoughts on the AI, but at the same time, ROSE seemed very accommodating.

[*If you permit me access, I can read elements of your thoughts that focus on visual mapping. That's just a polite way to say that I can take what you're imagining and use it to build a custom avatar.*]

"*Can I revoke consent later?*" Lexi asked, only a little conflicted.

[*Of course.*]

"Okay, let's try that, then."

A privacy screen appeared between Lexi and the AR vixen for a few seconds, complete with a stylish loading bar that filled rapidly and faded out again along with the screen, revealing the new avatar.

"Oh," Lexi mouthed aloud, entirely forgetting the mental interface.

The vixen's appearance had refreshed, becoming a broad-set red panda, a little taller than Lexi, and wearing a fairly nondescript blouse (apart from the tiny decorative helix motif on the collar) and straight-cut pants that sat high on her waist. She was fully business futch, complete with swept-back hair, and her hands held professionally behind her back. The whole look was softened just slightly with the avatar's — no, ROSE's — gentle but tired-looking smile.

[Better?] ROSE asked.

Lexi nodded, struggling to not think the words "attractive", "pretty", or even "handsome" too loud.

[Wonderful,] ROSE replied with a flick of her bushy tail. She brought her paws around to the front and clasped them together. [Now, I notice that you're showing signs of elevated stress, Lexi. Is everything okay?]

With the new avatar, all of ROSE's words carried the distinct air of a teacher Lexi wouldn't dare to piss off — partly because she was immensely intimidated, partly because she would never, ever want to *disappoint* this woman. Despite all of that, though, the bovine couldn't say the look didn't fit the previously disembodied voice very well. Much better than the default avatar, at least, to her mind.

Somehow, Lexi's thoughts managed to develop a nervous stutter. *"You could say that? I think I just became a supervillain, my boyfriend doesn't know, and I have no real long-term plans anymore. If I'm being honest, I'm kind of just flying by the seat of my pants right now, and that terrifies me in a way I can't really put into words very well."*

ROSE's expression didn't really seem to change, though as the train of thought went on, she lifted her chin in what must have been the slowest possible nod. [Let's take this slowly. You're incredibly tense, but I can help with that.]

"How can you tell I'm tense?"

[Part of what I can do is monitor various vital signs and biometrics to establish a baseline physical and mental condition. Your lower back has been increasingly tense since we started, and your shoulders haven't moved. I can help relieve some of that, including any excessive anxiety, but—]

"But you need my consent, yeah. I figured that." It was starting to dwell on Lexi that she'd never been asked for her consent so much in such a short span of time. On the one hoof, it was appreciated, but on the other, there was a dull background concern that she was missing some strikingly horrifying permission in an unseen End User Licence Agreement. In the end (like many a EULA, for better or worse) Lexi mentally clicked through with the reasoning that she could, in a worst-case scenario, probably just take the RCGs off.

"*Yes. I consent.*"

ROSE's avatar raised her chest in a soft breath and closed her eyes. When she opened them again, Lexi felt *different*.

Slowly at first, and then washing through her whole body, her muscles began to finally relax. It wasn't until the cow's hands were heavily in her lap that she realised *just* how tense she had been the whole time; on top of that, gone, too, was the implacable fog that usually clouded her thoughts. Lexi took a moment to search her consciousness and realised something else seemed different too.

The itch to know things was gone — or, at least, had been quieted substantially. It was hard exactly to describe the feeling. '*At peace*' felt far too strong, but '*rested*' could maybe work, she thought. The strangeness came in the fact that all the things that were bothering her before were still there. She could still focus on them, but they seemed smaller, somehow, like they were occupying less mental space than they had been just a moment before. Lexi might not have had workable long-term life plans any more, but after all, she had muddled through so far. How exactly to break the news of her superpowers (and job working with a known villain) to her boyfriend was more immediately pressing; still, she felt as if that too would come to a resolution, and that in the absence of knowing, she could at least hope for a positive outcome.

There was that word again — hope! — almost feeling alien on Lexi's tongue, as she felt her way around the sound under her breath.

[*How are you feeling now?*] ROSE offered.

"*Better. That's amazing. No medication or anything, just... yeah. Relief, I guess?*"

ROSE's avatar smiled and made herself comfortable in Maxwell's chair. She crossed her legs and let her paws sit comfortable on the arm rests. [*Good. I'm still getting to know you, but I'm glad to have helped. Would you like me to notify Maxwell that you've completed our setup?*]

Lexi gave a soft mental nod, and then just as quickly felt a question come to mind. *"Wait, is that it? The whole setup?"*

[Yes. I have everything I need for now. I might check in from time to time, and you're welcome to check in with me whenever you like, too, but I think we're ready to go for most functionality. While Maxwell is in the room, I'll be running in the background without the avatar. It can be disorienting dealing with more than one presence at a time, especially when, technically speaking,] ROSE gestured to herself, *[one of them isn't physically present and the two can't interact. Group interactions between multiple RCG devices and user sessions are possible, but that's a little advanced for us right now, and I notice you've had a hard time making direct eye contact, so we'll stick to the basics.]*

The Highland couldn't tell if ROSE was making a decision on her behalf, or if it just felt that way. In any case, Lexi didn't exactly disagree with the call to keep things relatively simple, but it was still strange just how quickly the personal AI assistant had established and worked within her particular flavour of neurodiversity, right down to (well, *especially*) picking up on the eye-contact thing. Before she could mentally reply, though, ROSE's avatar dissolved and faded from the room.

[Any further questions?]

Lexi chewed her tongue. She *had* to ask, even if she'd get a biassed answer. *"Can you control people's minds?"*

[Yes. Taking full root-level control like that is commonly referred to as 'droning' and is usually a last resort. I hope that honesty is enough to win your trust, that I would not do so to you without consent or good cause — that being to protect you.]

The Highland's thoughts were a muddle of things. Maybe it was better that she couldn't articulate exactly the level of conflicted trust she felt in that moment. Either way, ROSE took note and moved the conversation on.

[Shall I notify Maxwell that you're ready, Lexi?]

"Yes please. Hey, ROSE?"

[Yes Lexi?]

"Thanks… for being honest."

[You are very welcome.]

The door to the office slowly opened, and through it, with a face much less shadowed by sleepless eyes, stepped the wolf. "How are you feeling?"

"Fine," Lexi said, immediately realising just how flippant she sounded considering everything. "I mean, not *fine*, exactly but I'm managing, I think. I don't feel... it's sort of..."

"Numbed?" Maxwell offered.

"Yeah... I guess that's a good word for it. Like I can still feel the itch, but it's not requiring constant mental effort to suppress." With a clarity of mind Lexi hadn't felt before, she saw questions she wanted to ask appear in her head, suddenly visible now the fog had dispersed. "Does it feel good? When you're scratching the itch in a controlled way?"

Maxwell hummed softly. "The moment of attaining something can feel good on its own, yes. But what feels *better* is the knowledge that with that addition, you build a vast pool of knowledge that, correctly applied, can topple any target. There's a dark pleasure in knowing things about someone or something without their knowledge, knowing the secrets that make the world move and tick on — knowing what that information can do, if it were mishandled. That's why it's important we act as good custodians of that knowledge; others might not be nearly so thoughtful with such damning evidence. It has to be ours, because only we can be trusted to do right with it. That power... *that's* what truly feels good."

"That almost sounds perverse," Lexi said, without even really thinking about how the words would be received. Before she could cover her mouth or apologise or try and worm out an explanation that dampened the direct nature of her accusation, the wolf replied with an honest smile.

"It is. I take a great deal of pleasure in knowing things that I shouldn't, things that people would rather I didn't. And I carefully pick what I reveal to be known to me. I wasn't always nearly so willing to admit that. There was a time when, if asked, I would say I was just doing what needed to be done; that it was all a means to an end. A righteous one, even. But eventually I couldn't deny that I simply *enjoyed* it. If people would label me a villain for doing this just and necessary work, then why shouldn't I enjoy it? And, of course, that's to say nothing of the fact that leaning into the role — becoming the unadulterated spirit of *menace* — is a wonderful tool for intimidation. It's hard to not enjoy the ego that comes with a reputation, but I believe it's harmless, so long as it's wielded well."

It made sense, Lexi thought, that if denying the compulsion felt tense and stressful and required constant management, that giving in might just feel a little bit good. But she'd never really considered that enjoying it would seem so... *seductive*. She thought back to all the times she'd discovered something she wasn't supposed to know; things like the admin password to her school's library computers, or what Christmas present someone was getting, or... the thought trailed off too many more examples. Quietly, internally, the cow realised something about herself: she already knew *exactly* the feeling Maxwell was talking about, even if it wasn't quite on the same scale.

"But of course," the wolf continued, "you already knew that."

Lexi's train of thought halted with that sly comment. *"You clever bastard."* She had no way of knowing if Maxwell was bluffing, making an educated guess, or whether he somehow really *did* know that she already suspected what his answer would be. If she admitted that she could understand his perspective, then *that* would confirm her already suspecting. If she denied it... well, then she'd be being dishonest with herself, and she was never a good liar, so someone apparently as versed in tradecraft as the wolf would easily be able to tell. There wasn't a winning move to play here; not that it was a competition, of course, but—

Oh, the bovine realised. *"Oh. He wanted me to be put in a position where I start treating knowledge as a contest of power. He used his answer as an* **example** *of his answer. Oh* **fuck!** *Oh, that is—"*

[*Disarming, yes. He's rather good at that,*] ROSE chimed in mentally.

The comment threw Lexi for a loop for just a second, before she remembered she wasn't purely alone in her head while she wore the visor. That would take some getting used to.

"Ah, I forgot you were in here, ROSE. Sorry."

[*That's quite all right. I just thought you might like to know that you're not overthinking in this instance, and that Maxwell really is very intentional in his words.*]

"Wait, how do you know what Maxwell is like?"

[*The ROSE network is large and complex. Users may permit aspects of their personal data to be shared, including personality, habits, and thoughts. Really, it's an extension of the messaging system that comes with each set of RCGs, and of me — well, different instances of me, you could say — engaging directly with each user's consciousness. Maxwell has granted such permission in this instance.*]

"'This instance'? You mean—"

"...You mean not only did you know, but you knew I would worry I was overthinking it, so you granted ROSE permission to let me know that I *wasn't* overthinking, and that you *were* making an example out of the — *goddamn*. Wow." As she finally spoke out loud in belated response, Lexi couldn't help but let her smile of disbelief grow.

"*That's* what it feels like," the wolf simply replied as he playfully (if such a descriptor fit a calculating old dog) rolled his shoulders with both paws in his pant pockets. "The delight of figuring something out, the synapses firing and digging deeper and deeper, until you hit the natural bottom of the puzzle. Or, rather, a taste of what it feels like, delivered in a carefully controlled way. It's more potent when you're the one wielding the power over someone else, *that* I can assure you. But... that will come with time. For now, I want you to focus on how you feel. Find that itch and reflect on how it responded."

"It's... gone. It doesn't feel numbed anymore at all, it just feels... not there. That's so much better, I..." Lexi closed her mouth to stop it from running maybe *too* freely. Besides, there was a very good chance the wolf already knew exactly what it was she was describing. She too could be very intentional with her words. Or, at least, she could give it a shot. "Thank you, Maxwell."

The wolf gave another grin. "You are most welcome. Now... if I were to say I would like to get you to experience more of working *with* your impulses, would that be something you'd be interested in doing today?"

Lexi didn't have to think about being careful or intentional with her response. "Yes. Absolutely. I... I want to know how to get it under control."

Maxwell gave a nod, but more than that, he smiled in a way that the cow could only begin to describe as mischievous. For all the spring suddenly in his step, it was all the cow could do to wonder exactly what stimulants the wolf might have in his system, or adjacently — if they were capable of interfacing directly with the brain — were the RCGs able to make him feel more energetic, somehow?

The wolf gestured to the door. "We'll need to step out of the store to really test your ability to harness that urge, if that's acceptable to you. Unfortunately, with this sort of power set, it's very difficult to replicate typical conditions, and it will be typical conditions that you'll need to master *first*."

The weight of that last word sat heavily in Lexi's mind. Though she could just barely now imagine herself becoming a villain, on some sort of timeframe, Maxwell's implication that she would go further was starting to feel anticipatory; something to look forward to, even. Someone with experience was there, offering a path to a goal, and it all felt *exciting*. She hadn't expected villainy to be this easy, but here she was, not even having to really think about hard decisions. She *wanted* this, and now she was *getting* it. "That… all makes sense, yeah. It's okay with me."

"*ROSE, is this what being a hench feels like? Relaxing into letting others take charge? Are you doing something to me like you did earlier?*"

The voice in her head replied. [*I can confirm that I am not doing anything to manipulate your senses, but I am glad to observe your finding comfort in being tutored by someone with significantly more experience than yourself.*]

Lexi decided to not think too hard about the implications laid bare in ROSE's reply. She already knew she had a thing for certain types of men, and she didn't really need to add her villainous sponsor to that category. With that thought, though, everyone at Dropp's appeared to be some flavour of queer, so…

[*Yes, Maxwell does indeed fuck.*]

"Yes, okay thank you ROSE," the bovine silently messaged with a gulp.

Gesturing for her to follow, Maxwell stepped out of the office and made his way to the stairs, down to the store's floor proper. "Liam, mon ours adorable, I am taking Miss Lexi out of the store for some training. I fully intend to be back before we close so that I can see that she doesn't miss her train tonight, but will you need anything from me while I am gone?"

Liam rose from behind the storefront's checkout desk and stretched with a yawn wide enough to show off all his teeth. Clearly, he'd been up just as long as Maxwell had. "Sounds fine to me, boss. You sure got a pep back in your step. It's good to see, sweetie."

"Well… I have something I am *able* to work on," the wolf replied as he reached the bottom step and pulled his jacket deftly from a rack near the adjacent window.

The wall of ursine, softened as it was by his heavy pink sweater, grinned at Lexi. "Take it that means you then? Welcome aboard, again. Now you get to see firsthand what this one is like when he's got a *project* — that raw, passionate energy that keeps him going. I guess I'll see you both later."

Without even looking back, the wolf waved a paw and made for the front door. Lexi pieced together in that moment that it must *also* have been reinforced; this place was both a literal and metaphorical fortress. The cow found herself wondering, if Dropp's was just an organisational front, what were the real lairs like? That illicit excitement shot through her brain as another blessed hit of dopamine.

Maxwell held the front door open and removed his RCGs, tucking them into one of his jacket's internal breast pockets, and waited as Lexi followed suit. "It's true, I do love what I do. Après-vous, mademoiselle."

The cow hurried over to the door as she bundled into her thrifted heavy jacket that had also been hanging on the rack. She likewise removed her RCGs to put them in a pocket and attempted her best French. "Merci, papa loup!"

Liam wasted no time in snickering to himself, though Maxwell held an altogether much more serious expression. "What did you say?"

Feeling the bite of lately reckoned idiocy, Lexi opened with an apology. "Sorry, I uh, I thought I said, 'Thank you, Mister Wolf?' I never actually passed French. Um, sorry."

"Ah, well, no... that would be 'Merci, monsieur le loup'. It's... quite all right, though." Maxwell flicked an ear curiously and stepped outside with the cow into the brisk fall air of Cabbagetown.

CHAPTER 11

October 26, 2019

"Can I ask where we're supposed to be going?" Lexi asked, just a little curious.

"Nowhere," the wolf half-explained. "We're just walking, because standing still draws more attention. Right now, we're simply blending in, but in a moment we'll have a goal to reach, even if you don't know it yet."

Lexi kept her pace beside him, as he rounded a corner with apparent purpose. It seemed hard to believe he wasn't headed *somewhere* with intent.

"That feeling inside you, that feeling of being pulled in different directions, that's what we're going to work with. Not against; *with*. You're drawn to information, and to prevent that from becoming destructive, we have to... feed that need, rather than denying it. And so, the walk does have a purpose: it allows us to focus on the inner pull, narrow it down, and be led by it. So, I want you to first clear your head. Take in the air; let the sound of leaves and traffic become white noise."

Lexi looked down and thought hard about what to say, before landing on "Oh. I'll try?"

Maxwell reached a paw from his pocket, patting the bovine's shoulder gently before he returned it to his jacket. "Take your time."

The Highland continued to peer at the ground, letting her eyes unfocus as if she was trying to find the hidden image in one of those Magic Eye puzzles. The moment she realised she was imagining what lay exactly beneath her — the utility lines, subway tunnels, even the soil makeup — she decided that wasn't going to work. Lexi lifted her head again and stared forward at a spot in the distance down the street, but the visual noise of colourful leaves proved just as distracting. The cow took a deep breath in and held it, before slowly letting it go with *focus*... but that didn't seem to work either.

In her frustration, she couldn't help reflecting on her old life. Life before Canada. Life before *villainy*, now, too. The distance she felt from anything at all grounded, as she'd felt the need to dissociate and hide her true self, in so many ways. She wasn't like that now, even if she didn't know where she was going to end up; she could just kind of *exist* in earnest. The thought stuck with the Highland for a little longer — and then, all at once, she felt something in her chest.

It wasn't a fluttering, or a discomfort. It was closer to a heavy weight or pressure from inside her, leaving her feeling somehow *full* and *warm*, like eating a hot, hearty meal in the middle of winter. Every other sensation melted away into the background, and her pace quickened just enough that she found herself overtaking the wolf's steady strides. She felt it. She felt the *pull*, and she had no idea where it was taking her.

"That's it," Maxwell observed cheerfully. "Let that clarity drag you where it wants you to go."

The buildings to her left seemed to have suddenly gained their own gravity with how much Lexi wanted to drift into them, but when she did, the pulling sensation didn't change in intensity, neither stronger nor weaker. She realised that whatever she had honed in on must be a block or more over. She didn't know the street layout, but with a corner coming up ahead, she decided that a left turn was in order. The moment she did, it felt *correct*, like she had a clearer path to her destination.

The feeling intensified as she got closer, climbing to a harmonic thrum in every inch of her body — and then her eyes caught sight of the sign.

Second Look Comics and Collectables didn't seem to be all that notable from the other side of the street, more or less blending in with the rest of the low-rise commercial properties, even with its lime-green walls and door. With so many equally vibrant facades among its neighbours the store was indistinguishable through the visual noise, yet just glimpsing the sign from a distance had Lexi convinced that was where she needed to go.

She was scanning the street up and down, looking for a place to safely cross, when Maxwell stepped up beside her and gazed at the row of storefronts opposite. When he spoke, his voice was low and purposeful. "You think you've found it?"

"The comic store. I think."

"If that's what you think, that's probably what it is. A good start, too, no doubt full of things that could be the specific source. You did well, but I think you can do better still; let's get in there, and see if you can't narrow down exactly what it is that's drawing you in."

This feeling was new to Lexi, but already the idea of trying to locate the figurative needle in a haystack seemed near-overwhelming. Browsing, sure — not that she had ever really been that big on comics — but not sniffing her way through a giant collection with a newly-discovered sense. "You think?"

Maxwell once again put his paw on Lexi's shoulder before walking down the street, towards a pedestrian crosswalk. "You'll do fine."

As they crossed together, Lexi could feel the pull in her chest even stronger than before. Through the windows, she could see the walls were stacked from floor to ceiling with shelves. The main space of the store looked like it was taken up by tables of various heights and mixed origins, laden with boxes upon boxes of back issues.

On entering the store, Maxwell behind her, Lexi saw that each box was hand-labelled (a number of misspellings included). The Highland was vaguely aware comics were no longer just the province of newsagent bottom shelves or fan conventions, but it had simply never occurred to her to explore an actual dedicated comic bookstore. They had always seemed like a peculiarly American curiosity, growing up in Britain, where even her hometown hadn't sported one until well into her teens. More than anything, the store stood as a testament to just how much the cow *hadn't* experienced and how sheltered she had been from things that — had life and finances been slightly less precarious when she was younger — she probably would have enjoyed.

"Afternoon, folks," the raccoon behind the counter offered cheerily. "After anything in particular today?"

Lexi looked back at the ringtail, and realised at the same time that she and Maxwell were far from the only customers in the store. Trying to look as inconspicuous as she could, she struggled out a plausible lie. "Oh, no, we're good, thanks. Just… killing some time."

Maxwell seemed to raise an eyebrow in a sign of acknowledgement that they were, indeed, just there to kill time, although the cow couldn't help but feel she could have come up with a more-convincing, less-stilted cover story if she'd really thought about it. But then, to be fair, she really *didn't* know anything about comics.

"Sure thing! Just let me know if you need any help," the raccoon replied before dipping his head back down, where Lexi could just about make out (over a stack of flyers and a box of colourful pins) that he was engrossed with watching a silenced video on his phone.

Lexi turned her attention back to the cluttered store and casually ducked into an otherwise-unoccupied aisle of tall bookshelves, all filled with graphic novels, and not-so-surreptitiously asked Maxwell for direction as soon as he'd joined her. "The feeling is going mad in my chest. *Is that normal?*" she whispered.

The wolf turned his attention to a manga collection, where he pulled an issue from the brightly coloured wall of spines, and began thumbing through before just as quietly responding. "Use your hands and just feel things out. It's like playing hot and cold."

She wasn't sure if indignant was *quite* the right word to describe what she was feeling. Clearly the wolf believed in her ability to just 'work things out', but improv didn't rank highly in her skillset. She liked plans and instructions, but when she had cleared her head before, everything seemed to just… come to her. The cow took a breath, trying to centre herself once again. She waited for the noise of the outside world (even in the quietly busy store) to fade into the background, and for her to be able to focus on the gentle vibrations coursing through her chest.

Lexi held the feeling once she had it, and slowly reached a hand out to touch something — anything, really — on the shelf, to see if it made a difference. Information had a frequency of sorts, she soon discovered; if whatever her powers were manifesting towards was like magnetic attraction, the feeling in her fingertips was as if she held two very small like-polarity magnets near each other — the faintest of repulsions tingling in a not-unpleasant way.

Huh, the cow thought to herself, wondering if all those years ago browsing libraries for something of interest might actually have been some faint, distant manifestation of the same phenomena. She'd never paid it *this* much close attention, so it was hard to tell if she actually had experienced it before, or if—

—She was overthinking again. *Clear your head. Just let the feelings do their thing. Your body knows what it's doing,* she insisted to herself.

Small steps took her from one end of the aisle to the other, and after a minute, Lexi had ascertained that her target, whatever it was, must be in a different section. The pull felt somewhere to the right, and so she moved to the right. Through an archway lined with stacked boxes and makeshift shelving, making it almost blend into the rest of the modest stacks, was another part of the store. There were more tables piled high with boxes, with a tiny hand-lettered sign taped to the lip of each one listing the containers as 'Rare' or 'Limited Release'.

The sensation in her grew just that little bit stronger as she rounded another, sparser table labelled simply as 'EUROPE'. Even the few boxes atop it seemed half-empty. Lexi held her hand over one, and got a sense for its *pull*, but it didn't feel particularly notable. She moved to the next box, though her eyes were already fixed on the third one along. It felt no different than the first, so she quickly skimmed her hand over the third, as if her arm was a sort of metal detector, and she was combing for small change.

There. It felt different. When her hoof-nailed hand hovered over the third box, it felt... stronger? No. More sensitive? No, that wasn't right either. It felt more *notable* in some way. Lexi was sure that there were plenty of extremely worthy items in the store that, had she the time and energy, she could love and appreciate. But her powers were definitely champing at the bit over *something* in this box.

One after the other, Lexi flicked through the collection of comics. Some were tucked in plastic sleeves and others were not, but all of them were in fairly poor condition, regardless. Each one, she noted, had its own unique feel to her newly expressed senses, but as she slowly reached the back of the box, the pull began to feel more and more intense. She pulled up on the top edge of the issue that was sending her senses into overdrive and stared at the cover.

It was a 1997 copy of *County Men Action,* a comic that — for the depth of her ignorance — Lexi actually recognised as the official publication of the private Hero group, 'Home County Heroes', back home. It was a special issue, only barely skirting officially endorsing the then-newly-incoming government. The cover had a trio of Heroes Lexi had grown up knowing, including a very prominently front-and-centre Greenbelt, all rushing towards the viewer in cartoon form.

Each of the capes pictured had smug grins on their muzzles — or perhaps that was a retrospective assessment, given how pervasively corrupt the entire Home County Heroes organisation and its members had later proved to be. The group was officially dissolved just a few years later (2000, if Lexi remembered rightly) but the term 'Home County Heroes' never really fell out of use. It followed the group's various members around, somehow, simultaneously a badge of honour or mark of knowing derision, depending on the political leanings of the speaker. Towards the bottom of the cover (also plastered with an incredibly fake smile and colour-coordinated in New Labour red) was an obvious likeness of the new PM. The swan's dialogue bubble cheered on the trio as the perfect Heroes "for a forward-looking Britain!"

Lexi felt her gorge rise a little at the revelation that *this* was the thing. *This* was what had drawn the attention of her eagerly flexing powers? The pull in her chest dissipated and was replaced with a bitter disappointment at all the memories it resurfaced.

"You've found what you were looking for?"

Maxwell had appeared beside her without the cow even noticing, but she was too fixated on the publication in her hands to even start at the surprise, her usual reflexive reaction. "I guess so," she groaned.

The wolf raised a brow when his eyes landed on the cover. "That's…"

"Yeah. That's him. The one I told you about. *Fucker,*" she muttered, fighting the urge to rip it in half, this… this unsleeved neoliberal propaganda, disguised as a comic. "The whole of the HCH had been around for years as a private group, but even under the Tories, there were limits as to what they could do. *Especially* after a bunch of shit that surfaced in the early 90s. Greenbelt was new, seemed squeaky-clean, and when Labour won in '97, they started working with HCH as a new *government-contracted* Hero group, with him as the new and improved face of the team. He'd been a vigilante for a while — originally, good with people, helping old ladies cross the street, that kind of thing. I guess he smelled money or something, because—" Lexi cut herself off and unceremoniously dropped the issue back into the box, compulsively stuffing her hands into her pockets as if they had been tainted, *contaminated,* by the cursed object.

"Doesn't matter. I don't want to think about it. That guy was just another in a long line of lies, told by people who wanted nothing about the house to change, except for the colour of the bricks."

Maxwell, frustratingly, said nothing, only letting Lexi stew more.

"I regret ever liking him."

The wolf tucked something under his arm and carefully plucked the comic from the box to flick through the pages. "He gave you hope at one point, no? It hurts when it's misplaced, but you know better now." He didn't seem particularly interested in the contents and dropped it back into the box just as quickly as Lexi had, before proffering the item he had briefly tucked away. "Perhaps this will make for better-placed hopeful reading, hmm?"

Lexi scanned the comic being offered to her. It was, unsurprisingly, a publication she'd never heard of, and was in better condition than the items at the table before her. The fourteenth issue of *Uncovered Capes* promised a series of exposés on various vigilantes and unaffiliated professional supers. It looked more like a magazine, at first, but an explosion-shaped text bubble on the cover promised a featured comic story at page 8.

The cow took it and began to turn the pages curiously, briefly skipping over a few articles about masked vigilantes that detailed their MOs, operational areas, and notable deeds. When her fingertips found the feature comic, Lexi smirked. There, in halftoned black and white, was a wolf wearing a white half-face mask, a flat cap, and a long black coat looking very *noir*. The short feature's title — "THE DARK DOSSIER: Wandering Warrior of Words Most Secret" — was contrasted in white block letters, against the black of his dramatically-flowing trench coat.

Lexi looked up from the page with an almost-disbelieving smirk to see Maxwell standing in the same pose as his illustrated counterpart, complete with an arm lifting one half of his jacket as a shroud of sorts. "I guess a bit of an ego comes with the territory?"

Maxwell grinned a toothy grin, and lightly shook his jacket back into shape. "Oh, my dear, it is a *requirement*, in fact. Of that, I'm sure you'll learn."

The cow hummed to herself and closed the issue in her hands, checking over its cover again and quietly noticing the issue's date of October 1959.

"Were there ever more? Comics, I mean, of, uh… well, him?" She almost had to bite her tongue to stop from accidentally saying 'you' out loud.

"Just the one, to my knowledge. I have a copy already, of course."

"Of course," Lexi beamed, one brow raised sardonically.

"Yes," the lupine continued, "I suppose it was just a happy coincidence that there was one here, too."

Lexi felt the weight of the issue in her hands and thought for a moment. She felt comfortable. Here she was, training her powers with an esteemed, elderly supervillain, and it all felt so *cozy*. She thought too about what he had said at the start of the day, about needing to be prepared to fail, and contrasting that with the gleeful ego the wolf clearly carried for his own reputation. She wished she'd found a role model like him sooner, rather than latching onto the toxic 'Everything will be fine, if you just trust the system' attitude that Greenbelt espoused. It was funny how small things — her HRT pills, a lightweight pink visor, and a niche pulp magazine from the 1950s — could all represent such boundless, hopeful possibilities in the right context. Even with the understanding that things could go so wrong, she was willing to go forward, despite the risk of failure. That was *hope*.

"I think I want to buy this," Lexi mused to herself, gently using a hoof-nailed thumb to press down the one slightly dog-eared corner of the cover.

Maxwell gave a nod, and the two made their way to the counter, where the raccoon was still watching his video. It appeared to be about some kind of deck-building strategy game, at another glance.

"Hey, uh, can I get this in one of those protective sleeves?" She asked, gently placing the copy of *Uncovered Capes* down on the counter.

The raccoon looked up and stuffed his phone in his pocket. "Oh sure! Hell, this should have been in one anyway." He rummaged behind the counter for a moment and found a plastic sleeve that looked big enough, before carefully sliding the item inside it. "These old special-interest publications are kind of hard to come by. Can't help but read them and wonder where the folks inside are now, right?"

Lexi gave a soft nod, not really sure what to say. "Yeah. Funny to see how people were covered at the time, versus how they are now… or *not* covered, I suppose."

"Hah, yeah, for sure. I'm pretty sure at least a couple of folks that were featured in UC over the years were probably recruited by official government orgs eventually; seems to be the way it usually goes. You follow a lot of capes, then?" the ringtail asked.

"Nah," the Highland sighed as she was rung up, fishing for the wallet in her jacket pocket. She smiled slyly to herself as her hand brushed past the RCGs to get to it. "Just the ones with interesting stories to tell." She could practically *feel* Maxwell's ears perk up behind her.

"Alrighty! That'll be... $23.03. $23 even if you've got cash?"

Lexi handed over two slick polymer banknotes from her wallet — a green twenty featuring a rendition of the Queen's lupine effigy very nearly identical to its UK counterpart, and a blue five depicting a serious-faced otter in a high Edwardian-looking collar, no doubt some bygone Canadian pol — and patiently waited for her change.

The mentor and trainee villain pair left the store, leaving the comic that had brought them there where it belonged: in the past.

Maxwell took a sip of his takeout coffee and wrinkled his lupine snout in thinly-veiled disappointment. "Temperature check?"

Lexi sipped hers. She wasn't nearly as fussy as the wolf, but even she would be hard pressed to say that the cup of Timmies' was *good*. "Eh... kind of hot but not scalding. How about yours?"

The wolf snickered and flicked his tail back. "I meant your mood, not the coffee."

"Oh! Oh, right."

The two of them sat on a bench, flanked by concrete barriers and sheltered by thin birch trees; the cow hadn't caught the name of the tiny park. They had spent the last few hours wandering aimlessly around the streets of Toronto's downtown neighbourhoods, focusing on developing the bovine's skill for reading her own powers — and more importantly, separating the amalgamation of senses from her more typical internal gut-knotting.

"Good," she offered mildly.

"'Good'? Just that?" the wolf inquired, swirling his cardboard cup before placing it down on the bench beside him.

Lexi flicked her tail. "Yeah. Today has been a *lot*," she admitted. "It started off really bad, but… I don't know? Feels almost like a band-aid's been ripped off."

Maxwell gave a thoughtful nod. "Mmhmm. You're doing very well, considering; most people will never need to deal with something like this. Not that I wish to overstep, you understand, but… I'm proud of you."

Her ears flicked back against her shoulders as Lexi let the words sit with her for a moment. It wasn't often that *anyone* had told her that, but it didn't feel as strange as it should have, to hear it from Maxwell. "Oh, uh. Thanks… that means a lot."

"You'll do good things, Lexi."

The cow let the silence sit for a while, idly feeling the sensation in her chest roll over and contort in on itself in gentle laps and splashes, like she was a glass vessel half-full of gently-roiling fluid. Even just a few hours of practice had made it easier to isolate that feeling, and there wasn't an annoying *itch to it* anymore, just a firm, comforting weight. She wondered how long she'd had it and ignored it or been unable to place the sensation amongst the cloud of other feelings kept jumbled inside of her. Lexi tried to picture what the sense would look like if it were a physical object and kept coming back to it being some sort of amorphous, sloshing liquid. For some reason, the idea of it being a deep blood red seemed to make sense; it felt passionate. Loud. *Angry*, maybe.

A strong gust of wind blew more leaves from the tree above them, adding a pleasing background track to the cow's reflections. "This coffee is terrible," she muttered. "I've been spoiled by Liam's."

Maxwell laughed in agreement. "He's very good at what he does, yes. Perhaps you can spend some time with him tomorrow and give your itch a rest, hmm? There's plenty you could learn from him, too."

"About how to make good coffee?" Lexi smirked.

"About how to throw a punch!" The wolf straightened himself up on the bench and heaved out a fond sigh. "Not that I couldn't teach you that myself, but he's an excellent trainer."

Lexi had never put much thought into the idea of training to fight; she was vaguely aware of more radical queer groups that advocated learning self-defence, but her fear of confrontation (and desire to live as normal and quiet a life as possible) had discouraged more than a passing interest. If she was going to become a supervillain, though...

"I suppose we should make sure you don't miss your train home," Maxwell opined, slowly standing from the bench and dusting off the back of his jacket.

"No, I..." Lexi huffed. "I don't want to call it a day yet. There's later trains. I want to try following the pull *one* more time today. Please?"

Maxwell let his shoulder hang a little. "Mmm..." he rolled the sound in his throat. It was already starting to get dark, and the setting sun was casting long shadows of both of them towards Church Street. "Very well. But you should message your boyfriend, and tell him you're going to be late home, no?"

Lexi gave a nod and excitedly pulled out her phone to do just that. She wasn't ready for the day to end just yet. Not when she was enjoying the wolf's company. Not when she was actually feeling *good*. She opened the app and tapped out a short message, then paused, remembering that Drac didn't actually *know*.

She had been so caught up in getting to know herself, she hadn't remembered that this was all supposed to be — or would *have* to be — a secret second life. At least, for the moment. She felt more than a little guilty about it. Her thumb hovered over the send button, and with a mental swallow, she sent the message off.

"Hi honey! Gonna be home late tonight. Nothing to worry about, just being shown the ropes. I'll message you when I'm on the train. Love you!"

There would be a time when she could tell them everything; it just wasn't now. Not *yet*. With a determined nod, Lexi tucked the phone back into her pants pocket and looked to Maxwell. "Okay. I'm ready."

Another half-hour passed. While much of the downtown core was well-lit, the areas pulling at Lexi's newly attuned senses were increasingly out-of-the-way service lanes, alleys and one-way side streets. Maxwell knew where they were, generally — the semi-gentrified old garment district, once a working-class industrial neighbourhood — but admitted that he wasn't overly familiar with specifics. Still, Lexi didn't feel scared or put off. Following the sensation inside her was reassuring, in a way; it was as if she was following the instructions of some inner pilot, and all she had to focus on was navigating the route effectively.

"So… the itch," she started, growing comfortable enough to spin on her heels to face the wolf behind her, while carefully stepping backwards in the direction of the pull. "Is there any way to tell what it's drawn to? Just… it felt weird that the first thing it honed in on was that comic."

Maxwell gestured for her to face forward again, taking a few longer strides to catch up so the cow didn't feel impelled to try and keep walking backwards. "Well, I've never known ahead of time what I'll find when I follow it, though it has almost always been of *some* significance. I've always found it easier not to attempt dissecting the *why* of it."

Lexi reflected for a moment and hummed thoughtfully. She supposed there was significance in her first find, a maddening reminder of the things she hated; it had certainly driven her to do more that night. Still, it was strange to think that there was some unknown force directing her. She'd always preferred to follow clear instructions and guidance, and had so often lamented lacking either — but it turned out she just wasn't listening in the right places.

"What about you, can you turn it off? I mean, are you following anything right now, ignoring it?" she asked.

"I have been far too preoccupied recently to relax into it, unfortunately. It doesn't bother me. I can usually go a week or two before I feel that intense *need*, and that's assuming I'm not… home," Maxwell said, smiling to himself softly.

The cow returned to something like a more normal gait and slowed her pace. The sloshing in her chest was pointing almost dead ahead, so there wasn't much need to focus on directions. "What's it like? Home, I mean."

The wolf heaved a warm sigh, his breath forming a misty cloud in the cooling fall air down the lonely backstreet. "We call it KARD. The Korps Archives and Records Division, although some older folks still refer to it just as Records. That's what it was called when I first joined up, under my mentor. It's a vast collection of knowledge, secret and public."

"That sounds nice," Lexi sighed wistfully.

"That's not what makes it home, though. The thing that makes it *home* is the people. The community. *Family.* I am very lucky to have the family I do. Family never gives up."

Lexi's footsteps echoed just slightly down the empty street, bouncing back only off the side of old red-brick warehouses and former manufacturing facilities. A handful of buildings appeared to have been retrofitted for commercial tenants, and she'd noticed one boarded-up low-rise block with a sign touting "LUXURY LOFT LIVING: COMING 2021," but much of her immediate surroundings appeared otherwise to be a somewhat-decrepit light industrial area. She hadn't remembered when the buildings stopped being residential, but she still didn't feel out of place, and the pair continued to walk, following her inner pull.

"Mmm. My family are… it's complicated." The moment she said it, the cow realised, she hadn't actually been invited to talk about her own troubles, but she quickly buried that worry of oversharing. Maxwell had been nothing but understanding, even if he was occasionally cryptic.

"They often are," he said solemnly, true to form.

"I only really have my mom back home. I was worried about leaving her, but… she understands why I moved out here. Older sister did too. She's up in Scotland, though, doing her own thing. I'm sad to leave them behind, but Mom has her roots down, and Morrigan keeps to herself."

Maxwell gave a slow nod. "I've heard things are hard there. Your doctor treated you very poorly when you sought hormone treatment, I know. You felt bad for coming here, but you're doing it for you. You're allowed to do things for yourself."

Lexi kicked at a leaf that crossed her path. "It's a common enough occurrence that you can just guess, huh?"

"Yes, but I also happen to know Doctor Endicott has five *other* conduct complaints registered against her from former patients like yourself. None of them will go anywhere, though. Not while she's comfortably approaching retirement. Not while the system she's shrouded by is rotten itself."

Maxwell's reply was righteously harsh, with no hint of hesitation. It was also curiously *well-informed*, and Lexi blinked, stopping in her tracks. "How do you—"

"It's my business to know things. I do my research."

In another world, where she hadn't experienced the events of the past several weeks, Lexi suspected she'd have been more stunned by the wolf rattling off her old doctor's name. Instead, she simply wondered how much *else* he knew about her that he wasn't letting on. It was terrifying, but somehow reassuring in a way, too? Maybe she didn't need to explain her way through the complex mess of feelings that had come about recently. Maybe he already knew.

It only took a few quick steps to catch back up with the wolf, and when she did, the same sensation that she felt opposite the comic store slowly ebbed into her chest. She was near wherever they were going.

The wolf stopped as soon as he noticed Lexi scanning the street. "Here?"

"I think so," Lexi replied. "That one."

She pointed in the direction of a small-looking warehouse a little further down the street. The area they were in seemed isolated, with nothing much more than a few run-down old storefronts, corrugated steel sheds, and long-abandoned brick houses, interspersed with scrubby patches of dirt down one side of the street; the other side was a scrub-covered steep embankment overlooking a wide stretch of railway tracks, poorly cordoned off by intermittent stretches of battered chain-link fencing. The building's lot, paved with cracking and weed-strewn grey asphalt, was otherwise empty; there were no parked vehicles, and a billboard mount on the roof had long since been stripped of its former signage. There was nothing at all to indicate what the building might once have held.

The pair approached in the dark, leaving the soft glow of the streetlights behind them as they crossed the dusty patch of unkempt land towards the darkened building. Maxwell pulled out his RCGs and slipped them on, prompting the cow to do the same.

"Well, you could have hardly found a better place to swiftly demonstrate a favoured little skill of mine, hmm?"

Lexi took a wild guess as to what the wolf meant while her RCGs adjusted for the ambient light levels in a pleasingly gradual gradient. "Uhh, breaking in?"

"Indeed," Maxwell whispered. He fished a small leather case out from his jacket pocket, and upon withdrawing two small metal implements, began to use them to fiddle with the heavy-looking lock and chain that wrapped its way through the handle of the beaten-in warehouse door. "Nothing too complicated; were we not on the clock to still get you home on time, I'd have considered talking you through picking something *this* easy. But I don't want to keep you too much longer, passionate as you are, and wonderful as it is to see."

He was right. Eventually Lexi would have to go back to Kitchener and pretend this had all just been a late night at work, after losing track of the time. As villainous as he was, Maxwell was responsible, too.

The lock and chain fell to the floor with a final, wrenching *click* from the tools dexterously held in the wolf's digits. Maxwell held the now-unsecured door open for the cow, but not before holding up a paw to give a salient piece of advice. "You should ask ROSE to scan the area. It's a good habit for these kinds of activities."

Lexi gave a nod of agreement and focused her thoughts. *"ROSE? Can you do that? Scan the area?"*

There was a brief moment of silence before a small soft chime played in Lexi's head, marking the apparent completion of *some* kind of scan.

[Nothing appears out of the ordinary. But precisely, the building appears to be unoccupied with no recently logged usage from the city's utility's listing, suggesting the warehouse has sat empty for some time. It appears to be marked for demolition in the coming months to make way for a new high-density mixed-use residential/commercial development.]

Lexi flicked her tail as she looked in silence to Maxwell, eyes betraying at least some of her internal dialogue.

"You have access to that kind of information on the fly? I don't know what I was expecting, but that's impressive."

[There's a reason field agents, in particular, wear RCGs. As a point of interest: records for this property show violations of occupational health and safety regulations with regards to the rear loading dock on seventeen separate occasions.] ROSE intoned.

"Right, okay," Lexi thought. *"Avoid fucking around with the loading dock, got it."*

"Uh, she says it's all clear." the cow vocalised, still locking eyes on the wolf.

"Good. We will stick together inside, locate what you're sensing, and *then*, I think there will be a good place to call it a night."

Lexi stepped through the door and was immediately hit with the smell of metal shelving and slightly damp concrete floors. She'd worked one or two warehouse jobs in her various attempts at finding stable employment, so it wasn't unfamiliar, but was nonetheless unpleasant to her sensitive nose. The layout of the place was strange, though; the inside had clearly been gutted, leaving a mostly open space with just a few rows of empty shelves, and the tattered remains of what appeared to have once been a small, partitioned office off to one side. From spotless sections on the ground, it was clear there had originally been drywall enclosing the office, outlined by years of the heavy grime that had been pushed into the corners of where the walls *used* to meet the floor. All that remained was a broken desk and a lone filing cabinet. Experimentally, the bovine gave the cabinet a glance and held out one hoof-nailed hand towards it; she felt nothing, concluding that whatever she was looking for, it probably wasn't in there.

"You may also wish to try *removing* your RCGs on occasion, while you adjust to your powers," Maxwell noted mildly as he lifted his own visor from his brow, and gestured for the cow to do the same. "Close your eyes, remain as still as possible, and simply *feel* for the pull."

Muzzle bare, Lexi took a deep breath and tried again. She relaxed; she tensed. She stood in place; she let herself sway loosely, as if hoping to be caught by a metaphorical breeze. Still, there was nothing. Frustrated, she opened her eyes — which landed immediately on something on the other side of the warehouse, right next to what Lexi recognised as the loading platform.

It was a scaffold staircase, like temporary infrastructure for a construction site. Despite that, it looked as if it hadn't moved since the day the building was first completed. At its top was a small, enclosed room nestled in the upper corner of the warehouse. Windows on both of its walls overlooked the floor below, and through them, by the faint moonlight of a drafty central skylight, Lexi could just about make out the shape of more filing cabinets.

"Up there, I think," the bovine whispered as Maxwell joined her side. "Excited for what you'll find?"

She didn't need to turn her head to sense the smile on the canine's muzzle. He really was just as eager for the thrill of the hunt, or perhaps eager to encourage her. "Kinda, yeah!"

Lexi made her way to the stairs and climbed uneventfully to their peak, where a short gantry gave access to the room itself. Based on its layout, the cow concluded it must have functioned as some separate office. She wasted little time searching the space, much in the same way she had the comic bookstore.

The second office was a fairly comfortable size. Unlike the rest of the warehouse, stripped to the bare walls, it seemed to have all of its furniture more or less intact — and approximately where she would expect. The rear walls of the room were lined with a couple of work benches, storage bins, and a handful of filing cabinets. One of the windowed walls was completely bare, and the other had a single, solitary desk pushed up against it, still with a desk organiser holding a few stray mismatched pens and markers.

Lexi again held her hand out to the desk's few drawers but felt no sense of her quarry; opening each to double-check confirmed that they were indeed completely empty. She next headed towards the filing cabinets to get a sense of the pull's point of origin, but nothing leapt out. The cabinets too were empty, upon review, save for a bent paperclip and a thin layer of grimy black dust.

Maxwell joined her in the office and cast a watchful eye over the cow as she moved hurriedly back and forth between the few objects and containers in the room, tilting his head as the bovine clearly started to get frustrated with herself.

"It can't be that hard! I did it earlier in the comic store, and that place was *loaded* with information," she scolded herself under her breath.

The wolf held out his paws and tried to soothe her. "Don't worry. Whatever it is in here, you'll find, I am sure of it. Just take a moment to refocus. *Breathe*," he said encouragingly.

Lexi huffed in her own mild frustration and took a second to breathe more purposefully. The room around her began to fade into the background of her conscious mind, and she let the sense in her chest tug in whatever direction it pleased; once again she visualised it again as a blob of excited red essence, bounding somewhere against the confines of her insides. Lexi could almost see it in her mind's eye, and then it reached out in every direction at once and jumped like the entry splash on the surface of a pool, leaping upwards inside her.

With a start, she looked up.

There was a single incandescent bulb dangling off-kilter from the ceiling by a cable, the kind that seemed to have been a jerry-rigged make-do fix from the day it was installed. She'd seen the type before in her warehouse experience, usually long since burnt out, and never, ever replaced. But there was something wrong with it, she could tell, even by the scant moonlight: it was *new*, not scuffed or scratched at all. And it was *purple*.

The Highland looked back at Maxwell, and then up to the bulb's housing, squinting in the gloom. There was a short length of pull-chain attached to the midsection of the socket and draped hazardously over the glass of the bulb. She carefully clambered up on the desk and grasped it carefully between hoof-nailed fingertips.

With a cautious *pull*, harsh blue light filled the room, casting faint, flat shadows. As her eyes adjusted, it became impossible to miss what Lexi had been drawn to. Painted in heavy block lettering, spanning almost floor to ceiling across every surface, and wrapping around the entire room, was a message:

HERE ENDS THE DARK DOSSIER.
GOODBYE, ANDRÉ.

YOURS,
ROB SLOTIS

Chapter 12

October 26, 2019

Maxwell abruptly tackled Lexi to the floor, weathered paw across her broad muzzle. Still muffling her from speaking, he pointedly donned his RCGs again with a meaningful look. Agitatedly fumbling in her pockets, she quickly did the same.

"Stay down!"

Maxwell's thoughts jumped from his RCG's to Lexi's, appearing as both a text prompt on her visor and as a spoken instruction that formed fully in her own head. By the time she had worked out how she was hearing the wolf without his mouth moving, he was already on one knee and peering cautiously over the lip of the desk.

"ROSE is mediating dialogue between us. Do not speak! Only use ROSE." The message came through clearly, emphasised as it was by the wolf's steely eyes unblinkingly boring the importance into her while his hand covered her snout.

Lexi managed a frantic nod, her body trembling in sudden shock. ROSE appeared to not just be mediating dialogue, but actively cleaning it up too, because there was no way in her current state that Lexi was thinking as clearly as the message sent to Maxwell's RCGs implied. *"What's going on!"*

Maxwell let go of the bovine's muzzle and looked at the message on the wall, a haunted expression in his weary eyes. *"It's you. It was you. It will be you. In the vault. I saw you. Impossible... it can't hold information from the future... but it must. It was you I saw."* The wolf scurried to lean against the empty windowed wall, pointing frantically at the painted message that surrounded the room. *"You were drawn to a message from Slotis. Not just any message, but this one. The name reappearing wasn't a coincidence, it was bait. Bait meant for me. But you share—"*

"*Maxwell, you're scaring me,*" was the one consistent thought that Lexi could manage to communicate.

The old canine's chest rose and fell in rapid half-breaths. "*Lexi, you need to listen to me. We share more than just a power. There's something between the Vault and the two of us, but I don't know what it is.*"

"*What vault!*"

"*It's a... repository, one might say, of untapped knowledge. Potential knowledge. Knowledge that has both always and never existed. Last night, KARD attempted to search it for anything related to the name 'Rob Slotis'. There was a problem, a spatial anomaly — it's too much to explain in detail, but that was* you, *in Kitchener. It must have been.*" His words grew more and more frantic, even with ROSE relaying them. "*Ma vache, I promise this will make sense eventually. This must have been a trap set for me by this Slotis; I can't be certain, but if I have been his white whale as much as he's been mine... he'll have been too blind to even know you exist. You must stay silent and out of sight until it is safe, okay? I need you to keep low, and when ROSE tells you to — when she says you must — you* run. *Do you understand?*"

The cow froze under Maxwell's intense gaze. Every fibre of her body wanted to scream and break down in sheer terror and confusion.

The wolf's eyes darted imperceptibly between focusing on the cow's through his RCGs. He was silent as he pulled the pink visor from his face and forced it into the Highland's jacket pocket, hoarsely whispering to her as a single tear swelled in the corner of his eye. "Keep yours on and keep your head down."

Lexi felt tears begin to roll down her cheeks. She wasn't sure when they'd started to form, but she did her best to keep the desperate, frightened sobbing silent, steeling her breaths as much as she could manage.

"If anything happens to me, Lexi, you take my RCGs, and you give them to Liam. You're a smart girl. You'll figure this all out, even if I can't. I know you will."

Lexi's RCG HUD cleared with a soft flash, and in the place of former text scrolls, transcriptions, and ambient data, appeared three bold words that blinked on and off.

[CIVILIAN MODE DISABLED]

Maxwell got to his feet, straightened his jacket, and with a cool, almost detached deep breath, the wolf gave the cow one last smile. "When you meet Ulhauriear — and you will — please tell her that I'm sorry, I love her, and that family never gives up." His words were soft, a sharp relief to the jumble of his thoughts. As he stepped towards the door, he casually pulled the light cord off again — leaving Lexi alone in the office, hidden, a final secret.

Maxwell stepped firmly down each of the grated metal steps with his claws clinking a defiant tune on the handrail. His chest heaved an unready breath as he reached the smooth concrete below, and he stepped out into the open area of the warehouse. "Well, you spent all this time goading me. An ego that large cannot *possibly* resist showing up for the finale, no?"

No response came for a second, and then another, longer, more painful second. Then, the door through which the two villains had entered was forced open with a crash; all at once, a force of a dozen men armed with snub-nosed submachine guns rushed in to encircle the wolf. From a glance, Maxwell could tell that each of them was prepared to kill, but for the moment, they seemed more interested in keeping him exactly where he was. Their uniforms, from what little Maxwell could make out of them in the gloom, and without his RCGs, were unusual; they didn't resemble any police, military or Hero force he recognised. In fact, there was *no* identifiable script or iconography adorning their sleek, purposeful combat gear and body armour. One of them hurried closer, and at the barrel of a gun, Maxwell was promptly searched and declared free of any weapons.

After them, lit from behind and as menacing as any long-coated, suit-wearing prick could be, came a stocky figure that walked with *all* the unearned confidence Maxwell had been imagining. But his gait was slow, almost unsteady on one side, in a way that hinted at some significant historic injury.

Slotis spoke, the creak and gravel in his voice removing any remaining doubt that the wolf might have had. "I'm surprised you're not wearing a set of those pink things, André. Your lot usually do, don't they?"

He couldn't have been much younger than Maxwell, if at all. There was a defiant temptation to rebut the comment with a threat: *I don't need them to kill you.* But the canine held his tongue, the rejoinder suppressed in favour of a milder, cannier comment. "If you were watching this place, waiting for me, shouldn't you already know?"

"I'm afraid not. I couldn't take any chances with you noticing higher-tech electronic surveillance, so we've all been waiting in a specially constructed Faraday cage of my own design. The moment you turned on that light, though, we knew we had you. Sometimes simplicity is the best option, never mind these oh-so-precious gadgets and gewgaws that fail if you look at them too hard."

The wolf was almost impressed at how elegant the man made it all sound. "That accent is unpleasantly familiar. I take it you're with the SIS?"

Slotis cackled briefly, and walked calmly around the circle of his men, safely in the shadows. "Not quite. I don't work *for* MI5, but I spent a lot of time working *with* them. Picked up the accent decades ago, and never quite managed to shake it."

Maxwell felt the thick fur of his neck ruff rise and point out in all directions, a snarl quickly building in the back of his throat. "Well, then; a fine time to play coy, when you've got me surrounded at gunpoint. Am I really so intimidating? Who *are* you?"

The man stopped in his tracks. He seemed to think on it a second, as if he hadn't rehearsed this exact moment for years. "I suppose you could call me a contractor. Not for much longer, though, once you're out of my way."

"Oh, and pray tell, what will my removal from the picture net you, hmm?"

The question seemed to be exactly what Slotis was hoping for. He held up his hand, opened it in a claw facing the ceiling. His teeth glinted through a sickening grin as he clutched his hand closed tight again and rumbled out his response. "*Everything*. Every major intelligence agency wants the upper hand, you see. MI5, CIA, SVR — all of them willing to do whatever it takes to get a competitive edge. You should be thanking me, really."

Maxwell spat, narrowing his eyes. "For what?"

"Without me, MI5 would have killed you years ago. They certainly *tried*, but, well… It was lucky for me that it didn't go their way. I offered them exclusive access to the *practical* applications of my work, in return for your head; the only catch was that I needed you alive to perfect and fine-tune my devices. It paid very well for a very long time, you know.

Never underestimate the willingness of a state to chase a miracle weapon, especially when you drip-feed them promising results. But now that part of the work is done, and soon enough, the SIS will have what they paid for — portable psychic field-interference detection devices."

"That's what the hardware with your name on the manifests was for. High-grade components for sensitive devices, presumably for prototype testing to establish if you can—"

"Detect troublesome telepaths like you? Yes." Slotis began walking the perimeter of his men again. He reached into his pocket and pulled out a small black box with a simple looking antenna, which spun freely and lazily on some kind of pivot. "You see? It's already telling me just how *agitated* you must be."

"And your goal is to, what? Sell them to the highest bidder when you've already given a promise of exclusivity to one government? They'll kill you for that, and you know they will. No, you wouldn't go through all this trouble for some simple payout and a potential hit on your name. These men of yours... they're personal security, no doubt working for you long term. And we both know you could have easily sold the SIS a matchbox with some wires in it on a false promise if you *really* just wanted the money. You're after something bigger."

Slotis tucked the device back into his jacket and grinned. "*There* it is... that wily mind picking apart the pieces in real time. You're right, the devices are just a convincing front — your lot are rather fond of those, I gather — MI5 get these little boxes, but they're just a byproduct of my research. What I *really* needed you for was to find out where exactly you're hiding that spatially reclusive *archive*."

Maxwell went very, *very* stiff. "I don't know what you're talking about."

"Hah," creaked Slotis. "Hit a nerve? I know you have access to it. No one else does. That poor bastard whose career you ruined with the hot mic leak that came out of nowhere? That was a poor choice, André. A dead giveaway. The only existing tape was destroyed, yet you managed to find a transcript copy which lines up perfectly with exactly *one* existing theory on the loss of information? Feh; all I needed to do was give you a mystery and a key phrase, something that would drive your incessant powers into enough of a frenzy that you'd approach that goddamn *thing* for answers. The moment you did, my equipment detected it — an enormous psychic signature, on the same frequency that the name *Rob Slotis* produced in trial runs with a few... *volunteers* I procured. Not my real name, you understand; just something I could tie myself to, for the purpose of making the mystery enticing enough for you," the man jeered smugly. "You led me right to it, André, and now that I no longer need you, I can tell MI5 that the PsyFIDDS are ready and get back to the important work of using your little pet pocket dimension to its fullest potential."

Maxwell sneered, barely turning his head to follow the voice. "Even if you get access to the Vault, it'll never play nice with you. It's selective like that."

The man stopped in his tracks again, and Maxwell heard him turn on his heels.

The wolf peered over his shoulder, and through the dim illumination of the skylight, he finally got a good look at the man that called himself Rob Slotis.

The silvery-haired badger held that sickening toothy grin. "Oh, that's where you're wrong, André. I already *know* it'll play nice with me. My father discovered as much with his research on what he called the 'Alexandria Anomaly'. I never cared for the term myself much — it felt too cumbersome and contrived — but *The Vault?* That sounds perfectly ominous. You lot have a knack for branding, I'll give you that."

Lexi covered her snout, trying to quiet the frantic, panicked breathing as she eavesdropped involuntarily on the conversation below.

[Lexi, before Maxwell gave you his RCGs, he called an emergency Extraction and Recovery order, but the signal appears to have been held up. The RCG network usually relies on hijacking local cell towers and other short-range transmitters, but Slotis' team appears to be scrambling any signal traffic. I'm currently routing the order through alternative pathways, but I have not yet received confirmation. Once the order arrives at KDS Command, a team will be scrambled and can be on scene in minutes. I advise laying low until then. May I manage your stress levels in the meantime?]

The bovine felt herself nod before she remembered, in the growing adrenaline haze, that she could just communicate with a thought. "*Yes, do it, please.*"

Within seconds, her breathing was more regular, faster and more intense than the little comfort the virtual red panda had offered back in Maxwell's personal office at the Dropp.

"*Thank you. Extraction and Recovery? Like more Korps villains, for backup?*"

[*Not exactly backup. An evac team. An ER order is a last resort for when someone or something needs extraction in a hot situation. This is a hot situation.*]

This was it. This was real, authentic *villain* stuff. The cow had been hurled head first into a standoff between two power players, and she barely even knew *one* of them, but she did at least think highly of the wolf. A pit grew in her stomach, growing and churning like nothing she'd felt before. Rescue might still be minutes away, and if that was the case — and if she didn't have a choice, in being taken by a bunch of supervillainous first responders — she could at least be *useful*.

"*ROSE, can you record what they're saying? Is that something you can do?*"

The AI responded promptly. [*Ambient conversational dialogue is being recorded, yes.*]

It was a good start, but even though she couldn't see what was happening on the warehouse floor from her hiding spot, she was sure it wouldn't be enough. She'd heard a chorus of footsteps and Maxwell mentioning guns. She didn't know shit about fighting or dealing with guns, let alone a whole *group*. Lexi was defenceless. If whoever was down there decided to kill Maxwell, she'd be alone, and *next*.

Lexi found that thought sitting further and further back in her head, as something more pressing occupied the position she figured the fear of death *should* be holding. If she died there, the recording of Slotis' plan might be lost, and the Korps might be left in the dark. She wasn't even sure she had any skin in the game, and yet…

She needed at least some way to minimise that risk, but the rest of her brain was a mess of buzzing information. None of it was helpful, and all of it was amplified by stress, even with ROSE doing her best to keep the cow calm.

Motherfucker... of course.

Lexi carefully and silently reached up to the office desk beside her, making for the stationary organiser she'd seen earlier. She managed to keep her head low, mindful that her horns didn't crest into view through the window. *Yes!* She grasped a handful of pens and markers, uncapping all that still *had* a cap, and began testing each one on the back of her hoof-nails. Two worked just fine. She could do with one, in a pinch, but two would probably be better.

"ROSE? *You're a neural interface, you can manipulate my stress, and you said RCGs **can** drone people and take control of the body. I... I don't want to be gone, mentally. But I think this situation is dangerous enough that I'll need some help with my body, if you can do that.*"

[*This model of RCGs are limited compared to those worn by combat drones, if that is what you were considering. What did you have in mind?*]

Lexi heaved in a breath, still doing her best to keep it quiet, again pushing the new information that there was such a thing as a combat drone (and that they had specialised and presumably more advanced RCGs) to the back of her mind.

"*Can you make me write faster?*"

[*That is within my capabilities, yes.*]

"*Can you make me write with both hands simultaneously?*"

[*Ambidextrously? Yes.*]

The cow reached into her jacket and pulled the copy of *Uncovered Capes* that she'd purchased earlier from its protective sleeve. Lexi laid it out on the floor and flipped open to the first page. She laid prone with the issue in front of her and held a marker at the ready, one in each hand.

"*Okay. I have a head full of completely fucking useless information, and I'm going to need all of it, **every single thing**, written down as dense as you can make it.*"

[*Everything except information that might jeopardise the Korps and its personnel,*] ROSE gently corrected.

"*Right, yes. Everything **else**.*"

"Mmm, interesting expression," Slotis commented, peering through a narrow gap between two of his more towering henchmen. "Is that *regret* on your face, André? Regret for murdering him? I suppose I owe you *one* kindness, after everything you've done to bring me the Vault."

Maxwell stared down the badger, suddenly appreciating the familial resemblance — though everything about Slotis looked like a twisted, bitter version of the man the wolf had met a lifetime ago.

"You were drugged, André. The SIS knew where you went, and they tried to off you; simple as that. Unfortunately for them — and my father, I suppose — you'd built up a tolerance to the cocktail of drugs they used on you as part of Operation Felt. It was supposed to be a lethal dose, enough to turn you into a babbling husk. An agent slipped it into your drink, but instead it made you practically *feral*. You know the rest. Now I didn't find all this out until the mid-90s, mind you, and—" he cut himself off.

"No… no, you don't need to know all that. Spoils the fun, and why would I give a secret-hunting thorn in everyone's side the satisfaction of an *answer?* The funny thing is, André… I'm *glad* you killed my father. That pathetic pinko faggot would have been God's gift to the Soviets, had his research gotten much further. How poetic that it was the man he pinned his hopes and dreams on that killed him."

The canine's brow furrowed with renewed rage. Maxwell lunged forward but was quickly struck with the butt of a rifle and held to his knees by two of the armoured men. The rest of them spread out enough to let Slotis step closer.

"Ah, ah, *ah.* You forget who has control of the situation."

Maxwell winced through the sting of where the rifle butt had struck his temple, holding a low growl as he felt blood begin to soak the soft fur there. He let the rumble in his throat slip lower, and more guttural, until it drifted into a defiant, tired laugh.

"What's so funny?" the badger sneered.

"*You forget who has control…* two things, really. The first is that it sounds *pathetic* coming from you. The second is that it's exactly what I said to your father that night. My hand in the ruff of his neck, his eyes longing to drink me in, but so ready to let me tell him when he could."

"Enough!"

"He moaned so beautifully, you know. He moaned for me when I *fucked him*, like your mother never could. I'll never forget how his mouth felt, or how he begged, how he smelled, how—"

"I said *enough!*"

Maxwell saw the rifle butt coming this time, but he still defiantly continued talking until it made contact. After the static had faded from his vision and the thrum of pain rolling through his skull dimmed enough, he spat to try and clear the taste of his own blood.

"Coward..."

Slotis stepped back and turned away, sweeping a hand through his silver hair. "Shoot him. I don't need him anymore."

As the barrel of a gun jabbed at the back of Maxwell's head from some unseen, nameless hired muscle, a crashing sound echoed through the warehouse, drawing everyone's attention to its source — the foreman's office, in the building's upper corner.

Lexi used the noise of the filing cabinet she'd just toppled as a moment of respite, to snatch a handful of unguarded deep breaths. She ducked under the desk, out of view of the door, and clutched the comic in both hands. Now that ROSE had relinquished control of her arms, the soreness and cramping from writing so much so quickly was starting to set in.

[*Lexi, the ER order has reached a team already in the air as part of a routine training mission. Agent Swashplate has given an ETA of two minutes. His crew have been alerted to a potential live fire situation.*]

The cow had never been so terrified in her life. She couldn't tell if it was the RCGs or the adrenaline that was keeping her from vomiting in panic, as she heard Slotis, down below command one of his men to investigate the noise.

Maybe, she thought, it was the momentary comfort that she'd managed to distract Slotis enough to keep Maxwell alive. She hoped it was that.

Her RCG display highlighted a marker through the wall, climbing up the stairs slowly.

[Be advised that acoustic triangulation of targets is approximate without other active RCG units in the area. Exercise caution, and do not make a move until you have a clear line of sight.]

Understood, ROSE.

Lexi tried to imagine that the weapons that would soon be trained on her were just pellet or paintball guns — not that she'd ever been the sort to play with either — but it was a lot easier to imagine it hurting but being recoverable, than a likely death sentence. Or like any video game she'd used to play until the early hours of the morning. (That experience wouldn't exactly be transferable to this situation either, though, given her penchant for playing sniper or support classes.) *Don't think about it, don't think about it, don't think about it,* she told herself.

ROSE put a virtual hand on Lexi's shoulder through biofeedback sensory manipulation. *[I know it's uncomfortable to accept, Lexi. But this is real, and I will do my best to get you through it.]*

Lexi felt herself nod, closing her eyes tightly as the footsteps on the stairs grew closer. She had a prime view of the office doorway, and if everything went to plan, she'd see the target walk right through and get the drop on him. She didn't have time to dwell on the fact she had just considered someone a *target*; by the time the thought occurred, the *target* was walking through the door with heavy-booted footsteps.

The cow watched intently in the longest few seconds of her life as the figure stepped towards the overturned office furniture, her fingers clasping at the comic in her hands.

[Now.]

The Highland straightened her legs. The desk had proved light and flimsy enough to be flipped as her back hit the underside, taking the target by surprise. She held out the comic, opening it to one of the many pages ROSE had helped her fill; with as much concentration as she could muster, stared deeply into the eyes of the sheepdog who brandished a pistol.

There was a flash.

Instantaneously, every fact the cow could have ever possibly been able to regurgitate about the Loch Ness Monster were transferred onto the guard's mind with extreme neurodivergent prejudice. He staggered backwards and tumbled over the filing cabinet into a crumpled heap, out cold.

Lexi lunged for the canine, relying on ROSE to communicate exactly what part of the gun *not* to reach for. The cow put her fingers where mentally instructed and snatched the firearm from the informationally flash-banged canine, quickly throwing it wide out of the office door.

She hadn't noticed at first, over the furious pounding of her heart, but there was now a *choir* of yelling coming from the warehouse floor below.

I don't have time for this. Nor does she!

The gun at the back of Maxwell's head pulled away slightly as the equine brandishing it looked up to the noise going on in the office. The wolf wrapped his arm around the rifle to his right and spun his weight to the side, pulling one guard headfirst into the chest of the one to his left.

Shots rang out, as one itchy trigger finger tensed when it didn't mean to. Maxwell avoided the spray of bullets narrowly, but another of Slotis' men wasn't so lucky, catching one in the hip and falling with his full weight to the floor.

Maxwell launched himself at the equine who'd been ready to execute him just seconds before, shouldering his armoured midsection and pushing him to the floor. The canine pinned him down and knocked his helmet off with one punch; with a scream and another well-placed punch, he knocked the draft horse unconscious. It was lucky Slotis hadn't been backed up by *real* heavies. He was either too cheap or overconfident, a blessing either way.

For his part, the badger dashed for cover behind a stacked pile of modular shelving, yelling obscenities that Maxwell only half-heard.

Another stray bullet clipped the back of Maxwell's shoulder, sending him to the floor next to the unconscious form of the horse. He snatched the equine's pistol from its holster and locked eyes on the nearest target he could identify in the chaos, before hurling the firearm through the air.

The armoured feline just a few feet away took the pistol to his helmet with enough force that it made him stagger. In the split-second opening that appeared, Maxwell threw himself teeth first at the approaching cat, and soon, his fur was stained with blood not his own. He grabbed the downed feline's rifle and ejected the magazine with a practised whip of a paw, leaving the firearm free to use as a club. When another of the guards that had been at Maxwell's side rushed him, he was instantly met with a wild swing that threw him back to the ground.

Lexi hurried down the stairs the moment she saw a clear break, and all eyes were on the wolf-shaped blur. She held the open comic up like a shield and tried to make for the door, sticking to the corners of the warehouse where she could, and drastically disorienting the few men that made the mistake of looking in her direction. As she stumbled forward, she banged her leg on something, wincing, but carried on through the pain.

The cow rounded a support pillar that was propping up some disassembled shelving. She headbutted the badger before she even knew he was there, but Slotis' kick to her middle was enough to send her to the floor in a heap.

The Highland coughed, struggling for breath as her torso burned through the winding. The blow had been forceful enough to take the air right out of her. She heaved her head up, but she could see Slotis walking towards her, one hand in his jacket. He pulled out a pistol. Reflexively, Lexi reached for the comic at her side, and tried desperately to hold it up. For whatever reason, the badger hadn't pulled the trigger yet, and the cow furiously concentrated on the pages in her hand, but Slotis didn't react. It wasn't *working?*

He snatched the issue from the cow's hands by the cover and let the pages tumble open in front of him, exposing the mess of densely written useless information that Lexi had written therein.

Still nothing.

"Psi-blockers, you see. That won't work on me, not with a head full of bulwarxine — but you wouldn't know that, you're *new.*" His voice was deathly cold, even through heavy, tense breaths. "Two of you. Interesting; I didn't think that would be possible, but I suppose I should have known it'd decide to be *difficult.* It never did like playing fair. Well, I've got enough bullets here for both of you."

With the low-light adjustments her RCGs were making, Lexi could see right down the pistol's barrel. In a different situation, she was sure she might have been intrigued by why there was a corkscrew spiral inside it.

[Incoming!]

The warning flashed to the right of her RCG display, and then Maxwell was on top of Slotis in a furious scramble.

The wolf growled as he held the badger down and looked back over his shoulder to the bovine. "Lexi! Run!"

Lexi scrambled to her feet, still struggling for a breath. She staggered behind another piece of cover in the chaos and was met with a new voice in her head.

*"Miz Lexi, this is Swashplate. Normally I'd make a lot more small talk first, but I **regret** we are taking some fire out here. **Extraction** is imminent, my gunner plans to blow a damn fine hole in the loading dock there, but we **definitely** do not want to catch you in the crossfire, begging your pardon. Right this moment, do you have at least six metres of clearance from the coiling door?"*

It took the highland a few seconds to parse what was being asked of her, but ROSE mercifully took the guesswork out of the situation. A highlighted radius appeared around the loading bay door, indicating that she was well clear of any risk — or so she assumed, right up until Swashplate took the confirmation, and further instructed her to get behind cover.

*"Five by five, I am **seeing** your RCG feed; much obliged, Miz Lexi. Stand clear now!"*

After the explosion, as the ringing cleared from her ears, Lexi realised she been blocking out the sound of sporadic gunfire — both from Slotis' men, and from what sounded like something *much*-heavier calibre. Dust and smoke plumed through the warehouse, and before it had a chance to settle, two RCG-clad villains rushed through the new doorway.

In the chaos, Lexi was grabbed by the arm and hoisted over one of the figures' shoulders. The Doberman that was carrying her was strong, and their shoulders felt unrelentingly firm in a way that couldn't have been muscle alone. It was like they were wearing body-hugging plate mail, but after a second glimpse of the carefully machined joins along their back, she realised the dog was mostly synthetic. The apparent walking tank made for what used to be the loading bay door.

"Primary target acquired," he said in a slightly flat tone. "She has been hit. Requesting cover while I extract her to the Condor."

Lexi protested weakly at the black-and-magenta-clad figure that *wasn't* the one carrying her, pointing to where she had last seen the wolf. "Get Maxwell..." It was hard to speak, and she couldn't work out why. She'd only been winded, she'd walked off worse in the past, but she felt so... lethargic.

A gust of air from outside cleared just enough of the smoke for the cow to catch a glimpse of her mentor. He was standing, just barely. If he spoke, Lexi couldn't hear him over the noise and angry ringing in her head, but his mouth definitely moved, and it carried five words clear enough she could make them out without sound.

I love you, now **run.**

There was a loud, echoing crack, and the wolf fell forward.

Behind where he had been, through bleary eyes, Lexi made out the shimmer of Slotis' pistol, and then the bloodied face of the man that had pulled the trigger.

The whole world spun into a tornado of lights and sound and feeling and *too much*. Lexi retched as she struggled to reckon with what she'd just watched. The villain that wasn't carrying her yelled something, ducking through a volley of sparks and a hail of bullets, as Slotis' remaining men asserted themselves in the dust.

Lexi felt the air change around her as she was carried outside, and just as soon as she could blink away the first wave of tears, she was under another, new roof. It was warmer inside what appeared to be some sort of fuselage, but she was still numb and cold. Everything was fuzzy. Her vision tunnelled as she was laid down, and she barely noticed the strange looking fox with too many limbs fussing with her body. The cow couldn't move, and the flurry of flashing information on her RCG display blended into indiscernible visual noise.

"Chez, get us off the ground, now!"

Voices started to be distinguishable again, but Lexi wasn't sure who they belonged to.

"Control, we are *going* to need medical on our return, ETA nine-zero seconds. We have a civilian with a gunshot wound on board, and the site is hot."

"Fucking *shit*. Fuck! Chez, we're gonna need recovery. I don't think he's..."

"Got it, Jay... I... God-*fucking*-dammit. Roger that; Control, requesting dispatch of a recovery team, suspected agent fatality; over. This is a pure fuckin' *mess*, friends. At least we're up and clear. Jay, Flack, are either of you hit?"

"Negative."

"Nothing that won't buff out, Chez... *fuck*. Nurse, how's the primary?"

"Stable. The bullet appears to have missed any major arteries, but it would not be safe to remove it from her leg until we return to base. I will administer hydromorphone to relieve the processing strain from her RCG device."

Lexi felt her hand get squeezed as darkness began to sink around her. "ROSE, *is that you doing that?*"

[*Yes. I'm here. You're safe.*]

"Maxwell's *gonna be okay, right?*"

[*I'm sorry, Lexi. Please try and rest. We're inbound for KDS, and you will be seen by a full medical team. Until then, please... Rest.*]

Lexi felt empty as unconsciousness began to take her, whether she liked it or not. As she blacked out, she finally, faintly registered some very concerning words through the pilot's wall of motor-mouthed chatter: *suspected agent fatality.*

...Oh.

ACKNOWLEDGEMENTS

Thank you for reading Overdue. This book — my first to be published — was a long time in the making. Before I found the Korps community and later started writing in the extended universe, I had variously spun ideas around in my head for a narrative I wanted to tell about the hardships of not knowing who you are. There's a great difficulty in finding yourself as queer when you don't know what it means to be queer, just that you're different. Broken. *Strange*. It's harder still when you don't have the language or life experience to fully grasp the possibilities, or to understand the range of potential there is when it comes to identity. Even after gaining that knowledge, it's sometimes hard to reckon with it — and sometimes it's very tempting to bury it away and pretend it's not there.

A lot of this book was informed by a deep anger at discovering so much history was hidden from me, history that would have made me feel more like a full *person*; the UK's Section 28 cast a long shadow. For non-Brits, S28 was a mean little Thatcher-era law that forbade local governments and schools from doing anything to "promote homosexuality," or, even more hatefully, doing anything to condone the "acceptability of homosexuality as a pretended family relationship." In practice, this meant it was illegal for myself and countless other young queers to know who we might be. Even born in the early 90s as I was — still in school when Section 28 was officially repealed — I did not know our history until I was well into my twenties, and going through serious difficulties with my identity. Combined with my realisation through university that real justice is so hard to obtain, it was an anger that spurred me to write on and off for years — short stories with themes of secret information, queerness, and budding radicalisation.

Overdue is composed mainly of the more coherent bits of those stories, woven together into a narrative I hope was enjoyable. There's still more of the full story arc to write, but I hope that you have enjoyed it so far, and I hope that you enjoy the rest to come, too.

One note I would like to touch on here is that this book was first drafted in 2022, and features Lexi as a quite literal self-insert. As the story developed and gained new interesting threads, so too did I. Lexi (the character) is, as a result, a version of me at a particular time. With hindsight, it's easier to write the many flaws her character has — cowardice, bitterness, a deep-seated refusal to let herself enjoy things) as parts of my past that I've managed to heal and grow beyond. In that way, fictional Lexi and I are quite different, despite her characterization being informed by those experiences and moods I had at the time. (I think this is a good enough excuse to let me off the hook for writing a self-insert so shamelessly.)

With all that out of the way, I can't even begin to relay to you the quantity of good queer writing there is in the Korps Universe. At the time of writing this, in December 2024, the US and much of the western world is on a drastic backslide on queer (and especially trans) rights and liberties. Not only that, major media outlets and studios have followed suit in the stories they tell; it's become regular as clockwork to hear about films and TV shows cutting queer scenes and characters, just to appease the people who would see us erased from public life in their ideal world... if not worse. There's a long list of examples proving that, as a community, us queers can't rely on corporate media to tell our stories — even watered down and simplified for the self-proclaimed "allies" who've wasted no time abandoning us in recent months.

So, to that I say: write your queer villain story, because if they're going to treat us like monsters, we may as well terrify them with raw honesty and sincerity — by being unrepentantly *ourselves*. I can't wait to see more books published in the KEU, for exactly that reason.

We're not going anywhere, and I'm sure as hell not letting people forget we existed. We've had enough of that already.

KORPS UNIVERSE GLOSSARY

COMMON TERMS IN THE KORPS UNIVERSE

The Korps — To the public, the Korps (pronounced "core") is known as a shadowy, secretive band of supervillains based in Canada, with a reputation for mind control and plans to take over the world; Korps operatives are believed to be easily identified by their trademark RCGs, scandalously revealing costumes, and the magenta helix insignia. Under the leadership of the mysterious "Overlord," by the early years of the 21st century, their brazen criminal schemes and growing reach throughout North America and Europe have authorities (and allied Hero groups) increasingly concerned. The truth is far more complicated than any of those authorities know, starting nearly seven thousand years ago with a warrior's exile to Earth by his conquering interdimensional empire... but that's another story.

RCGs — Rose-Colored Glasses are a powerful, versatile AR/VR visor headset that interfaces directly with the wearer's brain, created by the Korps. In addition to operating as standalone PDAs and communication devices, RCGs also have the ability to affect the wearer's mind and mental condition to a granular level. A civilian model exists, distributed by Korps front and consumer electronics manufacturer Thornetech (alias Thorntech, due to trademark registration conflicts in various international markets) in a plausibly-deniable manner. Models for the consumer market have comparable base functionality to Korps devices, but are severely underclocked and have many higher-level functions disabled at a hardware level in order to avoid suspicion.

ACGs — Amber-Colored Glasses have much the same functionality as RCGs, but are crafted with additional anti-magic and anti-memetic defenses for use by KDARC agents. They do not render the user immune to magical effects; however, they can be crucial in efforts against mystical and eldritch threats by adaptively blocking cognitohazards and helping to keep the wearer's sense of self intact should reality start to weaken.

Aurora Squadron — Aurora Squadron, Canada's federal-level Hero group, is part of the Canadian Armed Forces and based out of Department of National Defence HQ — popularly known as the War Tower — in Ottawa, ON. Closely overseen by Minister of National Defence Arthur Simonds, formerly the second Hero to be known as True North, Aurora Squadron fields a highly professional, dedicated and capable team of Heroes in the fight against superpowered threats to Canada, including the enigmatic Korps.

Bradley Group — The United States' federal-level Hero group is formally named the National Hero Administration, but rarely known as anything but "Bradley Group" due to its institutional history; during the WWII invasion of Normandy, a secret strategic reserve of supers were activated to join American forces under the command of Gen. Omar Bradley, with "Bradley Group" used as a code name for this classified unit.

After the war, the group was put under the jurisdiction of the FBI, until later becoming its own massive, independent federal agency. In the present day, Bradley's superpowered forces number in the hundreds, with Heroes based all over the United States; considered highly prestigious within the industry and known to be selective in recruitment, even Bradley's lesser-known operatives are perceived by the public to be more competent and professional than many of their state-level counterparts.

Candesca — Candesca (pronounced "can-dess-ah") is one name for the energy that practitioners of the mystic arts manipulate, in order to work their spells and enchantments on the material plane. While other terminology is used for this concept in various diverse cultures, candesca is the neutral, academic, non-appropriative term most commonly used within the Korps. While a renewable resource, the body can under normal circumstances hold only a small amount. To paraphrase Lao Tzu, like a bowl, the magic-user must be refilled after being drained; the bowl is still useful, but has nothing left to give.

Cape — Vernacular for "Hero." Neutral to derogatory.

Chişinău Protocols — Shorthand for a series of separate but inter-related 1969 agreements negotiated in the city of Chişinău, Moldova, as amendments, codicils or interpretative addenda to various existing international treaties, including the 1899 and 1907 *Hague Conventions*, the 1948 *Universal Declaration of Sentient Rights*, the 1948 *Genocide Convention*, and the 1951 *Convention Relating to the Status of Refugees*. A Second Chişinău Conference was convened in 2006 to rationalize these provisions with and prepare similar addenda to more recent international instruments, such as the 1979 *Convention on the Elimination of All Forms of Discrimination Against Women*, and the 1998 *Rome Statute*, but these too are colloquially referred to as merely part of the same *Protocols*.

Collectively, the *Protocols* specify the permissible use of superpowers and treatment of supers by parties to the agreements, in both peacetime and in armed conflict. These agreements also introduced into international law the still-contentious declaration that involuntary, long-term restriction or suppression of powers in a way that causes the subject "greater than *de minimis* physical, psychological or moral harms" is a form of torture, war crime, or crime against sentience.

Color Guard — Bradley Group's elite strike team, currently consisting of twelve active members; each Hero's callsign and uniform is color-coded and themed around their powers for marketing purposes. Considered the best of the best, as patriotic as the Fourth of July, national polling consistently indicates higher levels of confidence and support for the Color Guard among Americans than even the military. However, the team's seemingly-flawless reputation is only maintained by Bradley's ruthless PR department, which has covered up or prevented their innumerable scandals from reaching the public consciousness.

Empire Enhancements — A subdivision of Korps medical services dedicated to in-depth body modification, including transgender care.

Everyone's Hero Association — The Everyone's Hero Association is a private Hero group based in Milwaukee, WI. It was founded in the 2010s by serial venture capitalist Jack Phillips, who named it as a challenge to Bradley Group's official legal designation, the National Hero Administration; government elites might have their own pet Heroes in Bradley, but the EHA is for *everyone*, as he invariably recites in press releases. Its roster is made up of supers with weak or unwieldy powers, and the group was considered something of a joke until Phillips' gamble on (cost-effectively!) finding a diamond in the rough paid off with Ellen "Lawful Neutral" Foxpaw's rise to B-tier prominence.

Federal Meta-Registry — The Federal Meta-Registry is a massive database maintained by Bradley Group of all U.S. citizens and resident foreign nationals with classes of superpowers deemed potentially dangerous. Registration is mandatory for all such known supers present within the United States, even if only briefly transiting through sovereign American territory. Evading or refusing registration in any way (particularly by intentionally concealing powers) is a serious criminal offense under the U.S. Code, and may be prosecuted as acts of terrorism in some circumstances.

HCH — Home County Heroes was a Hero group operated by the British government in the southeastern counties surrounding London. It was fully privatized in the 1980s under the Thatcher government, with all licenses, assets and personnel contracts sold to a corporate Hero management firm.

The former group has been variously divided and subsumed by other organizations since the 1990s, and though no organization called HCH technically exists anymore, some of its former member supers are still regularly referred to as Home County Heroes in the press and by the public. One such member is the Hampshire-born Howard "Green Belt" Bride.

Heavy — A heavy is a cape whose powers and role revolve around tanking damage and being a physical threat, usually having a powerset revolving around super-strength and enhanced durability or resistance to injuries.

Hero — When capitalized, Hero usually refers to a professional (and professionally-licensed) career superhero, whether part of a government or privately-operated Hero group. While Hero licensing requirements vary from jurisdiction to jurisdiction, most require some form of accredited training, full disclosure of an applicant's name and other personal information to the jurisdictional licensing authority for security checks, and an oath to serve the public good or otherwise to be of "good character." Most professional Heroes have superpowers, but a significant minority are unpowered gadgeteers, stealth operators, or even just heavily-armed mercenary types.

Informally, superheroes may be referred to interchangeably as "heroes" regardless of whether licensed and operating in a legal capacity. Unlicensed heroes may also be referred to as independent heroes, vigilantes or mercenaries in some contexts.

Hero group — A Hero group is any team or force of licensed Heroes. When directly operated or officially backed by some level of government, Hero groups are effectively a type of specialized law enforcement agency or military unit, with Hero members typically being granted similar legal powers to those of law enforcement officers in their jurisdiction. Private-sector Hero groups also exist, with their members typically having lesser legal powers similar to those of private investigators, security consultants, bodyguards and/or bounty hunters, depending on local laws and the political attitudes of authorities.

Significant Canadian Hero groups in these works include Aurora Squadron and the member Hero groups of the Provincial Heroes' League (PHL). Significant American Hero groups in these works include Bradley Group, the Everyone's Hero Association, and the Texas Protectorate Assembly.

KATS — Korps Aerial Tactical Support (KATS) is responsible for pilot training, air freight logistics, and fleet maintenance. Aircraft in the division's care include the Korps's signature gravwell-drive Condor VTOL gunship platform, as well as cargo planes, helicopters, and a small wing of rarely-deployed fighter jets.

KARD — The Korps Archives and Records Division (KARD), sometimes referred to simply as "Records," is a division of the Korps responsible for the acquisition, preservation, and circulation of various media. KARD acts as both a library of media resources collected over the decades, and a secure repository of sensitive information useful (and yet to be proven useful) to the organization's goals

Beginning as a loose collection of analysts recruited from dissatisfied members of the intelligence community in the years following WWII, it was not organized into an autonomous operational division for some time. KARD has branches across multiple bases, but is headquartered at and conducts the bulk of its operations from KDS. KARD regularly partners with other divisions and individual field agents, in order to help equip them with the most esoteric and obscure information required.

KDARC — The Korps Division for Arcane Research and Control (KDARC) is responsible for the study, safekeeping and strategic use of the strange and unusual. From ancient arcana to demonic incursions, memetic objects and more, if a problem for the Korps is outside the mundane — that is, outside the mundane in a world of supers — there's a better-than-zero chance that KDARC will be on the front lines.

KDARC was originally founded by the enigmatic Carlotta Davisson and several colleagues in 1935 as the Davisson Arcane Research Company (DARC) of Minneapolis, MN, and headquartered in the massive Madison Center. In the years following WWII, Carlotta came into contact with the Overlord, and DARC was fully integrated into the Korps in the early 1960s. In 1968, the Madison Center mysteriously vanished from the Minneapolis skyline; unbeknownst to the public, it had been magically moved to Toronto, ON, at the early lowest-excavated depths of KDS, to serve as the newly-minted division's secret headquarters.

Despite claiming to be a "civilian research division", KDARC maintains tactical operation teams (named TAROT) and a great deal of independence from the Korps. Some agents wonder why the Overlord overlooks the pseudo-corporate structure, and rumours abound of unionization attempts by KDARC's senior staff. Still, much of the division's motivations, intentions, and methods remain as enigmatic, incomprehensible, and dangerous as the bleeding edge of the arcane itself.

KDS — Korps Downsview Site is the headquarters of the Korps, located beneath the former Downsview Airport (previously Canadian Forces Base Toronto) in the industrial sprawl of Toronto, ON. With a footprint of over eight square kilometres and many subterranean sub-levels, futuristically eco-urbanist in aesthetics and centrally-planned design, it is a completely self-sufficient underground city. KDS was slowly built outward from a small excavation in the 1970s, becoming fully operational as a headquarters only in the 1980s-1990s.

In addition to the command, logistics and strategic functions required for the vast supervillain organization to operate, like all major Korps bases, KDS features apartment-like residential sectors, research and lab areas, an enormous medical complex, and a recreational sector that would translate to many city blocks' worth of restaurants and entertainment facilities — including a "red light district," the Dominion Club.

K-LAW — Sometimes a supervillain collective needs to engage with the legal system on its own terms; as a division, the Korps Legal Affairs Wing (K-LAW) operates covertly as the legal departments of various front companies, as well as through front law firms and other sympathetic individual lawyers in private practice.

Criminal defense of Korps members and allies on trial is only a small part of K-LAW agents' work. The majority of K-LAW's resources are directed towards litigation to gather intelligence on targets or tie them up in red tape, and street-level *pro bono* work helping marginalized people assert their rights without regard for the cost of legal fees.

KTAKES — The Korps Tactical Acquisitions and Kleptocratic Extirpation Squadron (KTAKES) is a now-disbanded division of the Korps that specialized in obtaining "lost" items and returning them to their rightful places — via. heists, capers, thefts, smash and grabs, and good old-fashioned burglary as appropriate. The group functioned as a kind of "thieves' guild" within the Korps, with their own projects, but also taking commissioned work from other divisions.

Pegasus Phalanx — A unit of the Texas Protectorate Assembly and Dallas' foremost Hero team, the Pegasus Phalanx handles the biggest threats the city faces — short of those requiring federal intervention from Bradley Group forces. While the team's roster has changed over the years, it most recently consisted of leader Kevin "Texas Trickshot" Romero, Susanne "Heavenly Dazzler" Geraldine-Walters, Chet "Macho Poleax" Huntyr, Rodrigo "Ethicoil" Alquitano III, and Slate "Slate" Johnson.

PHL — The Provincial Heroes' League (PHL) is a Canadian organization comprised of all Hero groups operated by the provincial and territorial governments, led by Director Lawrence Rockwell. The PHL aggressively advocates for 'law and order' Hero operations, and has had a great deal of friction with Aurora Squadron, accusing the federal Hero Group of being 'soft' on the Korps.

However, the PHL is not a Hero group itself, but instead a professional organization promoting the coordination and cooperation of affiliate members, as well as a powerful voice advocating for professional Heroes and the Hero industry. Heroes operating through one of its affiliates may nonetheless be indistinguishably referred to as "belonging" to the PHL, or being a "PHL Hero," and "fuck the PHL" is a popular sentiment among Korps agents operating in Canada.

Member Hero Groups include the Cascade Group or CG (British Columbia); the Prairie League or PL (Alberta, Saskatchewan and Manitoba); Ontario's Heroes or OH (Ontario); L'Association des Superheros Québécois or ASQ (Quebec, nicknamed the "Superté" by analogy to the provincial police force, the Sûreté du Québec); and the Territorial Superheroes' Association or TERSA (Nunavut, Yukon and Northwest Territories).

RIV or RIVER — RIVER is a Korps site located beneath downtown Austin, TX, secretly excavated deep below the parkland surrounding the Colorado River.

ROSE — ROSE, or the "RCG Operating System Experience," is the OS/Complex AI that runs on all networked RCGs and provides the conversational interface for wearers of RCGs. ROSE's default avatar when appearing as an augmented-reality overlay to wearers is a fox woman, but this can be customized to individual preference.

SHS — Sandy Hill Station is a Korps site located beneath downtown Ottawa, ON. Originally founded as a WWII-era safe house for the Overlord's consolidation of proto-Korps resources and personnel in Canada, it grew significantly in importance as a surveillance station during the Cold War, due to the local neighborhood's concentration of foreign embassies.

SHS was the testbed for many of the Korps' now-standard excavation and covert base-building practices, and was formerly the location of many research labs and high-level command functions, prior to Toronto's KDS becoming fully operational as a new headquarters in the 1980s-1990s.

Supers — Supers is generally vernacular for "those with superpowers," whether or not referring to superheroes generally, or whether or not licensed Heroes.

SIS — The Secret Intelligence Service, a.k.a. its wartime designation of MI6 (Military Intelligence, section 6) is an arm of the British state responsible for the gathering of foreign intelligence.

TPA — The Texas Protectorate Assembly — commonly shortened to "Teepa" by members of the Korps — is Texas' state Hero group, extremely well-funded both by the state Department of Public Safety budget, as well as substantial donations from wealthy individual benefactors and corporate partnerships.
The result is that the TPA has unusually-vast resources for a government-backed state-level Hero group, and platoons of Heroes, many trained in the TPA's own Academy facilities located throughout Texas. TPA Heroes are institutionally encouraged to approach their duties in the manner of militarized riot police or SWAT teams, exercising very little restraint or concern for civil rights.

About the Author

Born and raised in the UK, Alexandra (Lexi) Reynolds is a writer, artist, and aspiring comic creator. Trans, Enby, Queer, Therian, and all-round Creature, Lexi delights in the fact that one's identity can change in so many ways and celebrates embracing the process of self-discovery. A product of their upbringing and reflections on it, they now reside more happily in Ontario, Canada.

Lexi likes to tackle how we as queer people handle and understand our histories. This includes how information can change perspectives, and how hidden truths about ourselves weigh heavily on our souls without the language to properly describe them. They can be found online at ShapelessInk.com, and as ShapelessInk on various social media sites.

About the Publisher

FurPlanet Productions is a small press publisher serving the niche market that is furry fiction. They sell furry-themed books and comics published by themselves and most major publishers in the community. If you can't get to a furry convention where they are selling in the dealers room, visit their online stores:

FurPlanet.com for print books
BadDogBooks.com for eBooks